P9-CER-044

CHUCK WENDIG

BLIGHTBORN

THE HEARTLAND
TRILOGY
BOOK II

SKYSCAPE

SKYSCAPE

Published by Skyscape, New York

www.apub.com

Amazon, the Amazon logo, and Skyscape are trademarks of Amazon.com, Inc., or its affiliates.

ISBN-13: 9781477847701 (hardcover)
ISBN-10: 1477847707 (hardcover)
ISBN-13: 9781477847886 (paperback)
ISBN-10: 147784788X (paperback)

Book design by Sammy Yuen and Susan Gerber
Editor: Marilyn Brigham
Jacket art by Shane Rebenscheid
Jacket design by Katrina Damkoehler

Printed in the United States of America

For my father, long gone from the Heartland.
And for my mother, who remains

CONTENTS

PROLOGUE

THE POSSE

IT'S BEEN DAYS, and she hasn't heard a damn thing. Proctor Simone Agrasanto sits at Mayor Barnes's old desk, running her hands along the cold wood. She picks up a frame showing a digital photo of his wife and son—the wife a fat dumpling and the son a dull clod. As she lifts it, another, smaller photo—this one on curled paper—drops out of the bottom. Filomena McAvoy. Long, cascading hair. A pretty, if pale, face. A long, strong nose—elegant, graceful. *An Empyrean nose,* Simone thinks.

Or, at least, that's what she sees with her one good eye.

The other eye is . . .

Well, she dares not think about it. The doctors aren't sure they can do anything for her. She's heard mumbles about an *experimental* fix, but for now, the ruined eye sits in the puckered socket behind a black patch.

She opens the bottom desk drawer and finds a bottle of Jack Kenny whiskey. She takes a pull.

Events have escaped her control. But she's reclaiming power. Slowly. The first order of business was to storm the McAvoy farm and take the father. The proctor should have figured that would be a no-go. He and his wife were nowhere to be found. The house and barn were burned to the ground. The only items left unburned were the corpses remaining in the driveway: the faceless Grey Franklin, the trachea-collapsed Pally Varrin, and—this one, quite a surprise—a bullet-in-the-head Mayor Barnes.

That meant Arthur McAvoy was armed.

McAvoy is one mean sonofabitch. Though he *had* left that note staked to the ground. It read: "See that these three get a proper burial up Cemetery Road."

Seems even terrorists have some semblance of honor in their black hearts.

She takes another sip of whiskey. Warm, smooth, a drink too good for a Heartlander.

There's a knock at the door.

"Enter."

Devon Miles, her awful attaché, sneaks in through the doorway. He holds the door open with his one good arm. His other sits in a fabric sling, broken. She knows it's broken because she's the one who broke it. When she'd found him, after he'd ran and abandoned her, she pressed him against the wall of Busser's Tavern—face-first—and bent his arm behind his back until she heard a not-so-gentle *snap*. A snap heard above his cries.

"Your guests," he says, waving in three visitors.

"I'm glad you came when I called," she says, looking upon the three miscreants. The mayor's son. The fat boy's drunken father. And Cael McAvoy's spurned bride. Boyland, Jorge, and Wanda. A motley crew, no doubt, but still, she thinks, it just might work.

"Hell do you want?" Jorge asks.

"I've got my people looking for the McAvoy family and a few of their friends. Lane Moreau. Rodrigo Cozido. And Burt and Bessie Greene. But my people don't know the Heartland very well, and, for them, this isn't personal. But for you three, this is *real* personal."

"I hate you," Boyland says. He looks drunk. No surprise. He is perhaps already becoming his father, assuming the mantle of lugubrious, inebriated blowhard. "You stole my girl."

Simone shrugs. "Oh, quit your mewling. I'll tell you what: if you do what I want, I will get you your girl back. Is that acceptable?"

He searches her face. "You . . . you mean it?"

"I mean it."

She doesn't mean it. It's a lie. The girl is beyond her reach. Beyond anybody's reach now.

"Okay," the mayor's son says. "I'm in."

"I want my Obligated back, too," Wanda says. Her head, Simone notes, looks too big for her body. It bobbles like a buzzard skull on a broomstick.

"Can you get me my son?" Jorge says. "He belongs to *me*."

"*You'll* get your son back yourself," the proctor says. "I'm forming a posse, and you three are in it. Plus anybody else you feel will help you in this endeavor. You'll be paid. You'll have a boat. Any resources I can offer you, you'll have. But there'd better be results."

"You'll have your results," Boyland Jr. says. "I'm not king of the scavengers for nothing."

PART ONE

BLOOD
AND CORN

CORN-CATCHER

CAEL MCAVOY DREAMS OF FLYING.

His arms are wings. Stretched out. Palms flat to the earth. Air sliding beneath them. His mouth dry. His eyes wet with wind-stung tears.

Blue sky above. Green stalks and yellow corn below.

A pair of toothy motorvators churns through the field. Carving a set of parallel lines. White smoke drifts in lazy coils above them.

Cael flies for the horizon line.

Again and ever more he thinks, *I can go higher,* and there above he sees one of the flotillas drifting. The sun behind it frames the floating city with lines of searing white, gleaming off fluted towers and scalloped edges. White brick and black tile. Starbursts and zigzags. A city of many levels strung together: platforms and chains and billowing pocket-bladders of air. The hum of hover-panels. The growl of engines. The *whiff whiff whiff* of tower-topper propellers chopping the air.

He lifts his head. Tilts his arms back. Cael moves higher.

Toward the flotilla. Toward the sky.

Then he sees something. No—some*one*. Standing on a gang-plank extending outward like an unfurling tongue, a woman on the edge of it, a girl with strawberry hair done up in an Empyrean braid that forms a collar around her neck and—

It's Gwennie.

He calls out to her, tells her he loves her, but the wind swallows his words in a great, gusting gulp, and he sees her pointing something at him. A rifle. Light pooling in the blue-steel receiver.

But then—a white flash behind her. It consumes everything. She's gone in a searing hot burst, and so is the flotilla, and the concussion hits him at the same time as a thunderclap booms in his ears and his throat and his chest, and suddenly he's tumbling ass over teakettle, falling down out of the sky—blue, then green, then blue, then green—

He hears someone calling for him. Gwennie?

No. Wanda.

The ground rushes up. The corn reaches for him. Stalks stretch. Leaves like tentacles curl and coil. They meet him as he falls, catching him, stopping his descent. He thinks, *I'm alive. I'm alive!* The corn begins to lower him back toward the earth, and he scans the sky above for the flotilla or for Gwennie—but it's all gone, just an empty space.

A leaf of corn crawls its way under his shirt—

A pain cuts through him as it slices into the flesh above his heart.

He feels it slide under the skin, seeking entry. Over the breastbone. Around a rib. It burns like a saw cut. Feels like paper sliding under flesh. It finds his heart. It cradles it. It bores into it like a finger pushing its way into a pie. Cael screams. A voice whispers in his ear—

RAIL RIDERS

COME TO ME, CAEL.

Cael lurches upright with a gasp, patting at his chest, the sharp pain fading to a dull murmur before revealing itself as the remnant of a dream that flees like a shadow in sunlight. The voice in his head (*Come to me, come to me, come to me. . . .*) falls apart, too, a chip of dirt in a closing fist.

The rail-raft slides over the tracks, the magna-cruxes buoying them above the rails. A frictionless ride that calls to mind flying. A sudden pang of loss strikes him then: he misses his boat. *Betty*, the cat-maran.

On all sides, a familiar sight: corn. Endless tall stalks of it whoosh past, each pregnant and bent with the burden of many ears. Above their heads, a distant flotilla, big as a dirty thumbprint on a set of clean bedsheets. That flotilla, or one of them, is where they need to go.

Rigo sits cross-legged, carving slices of parsnip. He hands

one to Cael, who takes it and pops it into his mouth. Sweet and bitter. *Crunch crunch crunch.* Lane lies back next to Rigo, his long, lean body taking up the whole back end of the raft. His legs dangle over the side. Just out of reach of the hungry, searching corn.

"Parsnip gives me the runs," Lane says, smoking.

"You say the sweetest things," Cael mumbles, rubbing his eyes and yawning. The skin above his heart itches. The dream, lingering?

"Got any rat jerky left?" Lane asks.

Rigo shakes his head. "You know we don't."

"Meh. I'm tired of eating root vegetables."

"I'm just tired," Cael says. "Amazing how doin' nothing feels like doin' everything."

They've been sitting on the raft for a week now, stopping whenever one of the Empyrean trains comes barreling down the track—each a charging beast of black iron and eye-blistering chrome. When that happens, they pull the raft off the rails and use it as an opportunity to stretch their legs and perform nature's other unpleasant necessities.

"Guys," Rigo says, "look around you. We're free. We've got food. Got a rifle. Haven't seen a piss-blizzard or a tornado. Beautiful day. No Agrasanto chasing our butts. Life could be worse."

Rigo. Ever the optimist. Cael neglects to grouse about how they're now officially hobos—probably worse. They're likely enemies of the whole Empyrean, their faces on every proctor visidex in the Heartland. Cael's got no idea where Pop and Mom are, or if they're even alive. Gwennie's gone. Wanda probably hates him. His sister, Merelda, is . . . well, that's who they're supposed to fetch if they ever get to where they're going.

Cael may not say all that aloud, but Lane isn't afraid to complain.

"I thought it'd be more exciting," he says, finally sitting up and popping his knuckles, his elbows, his knees. "I mean, Jeezum Crow, it's corn, corn, more corn. Big sky. Barely a cloud in it. At least if there were a couple clouds I could say, 'Hey, that one looks like a fell-deer, that one like a caviling grackle, that one like Boyland Barnes Jr. licking dirt off the end of my boot.' We've seen—what?—a few off-load way stations. One kill-sprayer. No towns. No people. How close are we? We gotta be close."

Cael looks at the number of hash marks carved into the top board of the rail-raft. "Seven marks, so seven days. Pop said it'd take us little over a week."

"Slow and steady wins the race," Rigo says, echoing the proverb from the old story of the Haiphong Hog and the Ryukyu Rabbit.

"Blech," Lane says. "Slow and steady puts my ass to sleep. I always liked the rabbit more, honestly." He suddenly gets a look on his face. His eyes narrow. His mouth twists into a mischievous smile.

Cael knows the question that's coming, and frankly, he's surprised it took any of them this long to ask.

Lane asks it: "How fast do you think this thing can go?"

"Oh no," Rigo says.

"Oh yes," Lane answers.

Cael holds up a hand. "Wait a minute, now. Lane might be right. Dang, I'm bored, too. Maybe we can get a move on and make it to the Provisional Depot by nightfall—wouldn't that be a peach?"

"Guys," Rigo says, "I dunno about this. . . ."

Lane waves him off. "Let's do it."

"Hell yeah." Cael grins. "Let's see how fast this baby can fly."

THE PEGASUS GIRL

IN A ROOM FULL OF MUTANTS, Gwennie still feels like a freak.

Her shovel scrapes the bottom of the stall, scooping up bedding made from dried corn husks and corn leaves—bedding that is also soaked through with the waste of the stall's inhabitant. An inhabitant that now stands in the next stall over, probably soiling *that one* while she cleans *this one*.

The horse—or rather the "horse"—shoves its head over the stall wall. It whinnies and snorts, nostrils flaring and expelling a fine mist of snot.

Gwennie scowls, wipes her cheek with the back of her hand.

She looks at the animal—this one pinker than the skin of a baby's bottom, as pink as the frosting atop a cake made by an Empyrean baker—and shoots out her tongue, blowing a raspberry that gives the creature a taste of its own medicine. Her own spit flecks the animal's nose.

The "horse" blinks, irritated.

She calls this one Pinky.

She props up the shovel, her muscles aching. The sour smell of the soiled stalls has crawled up inside her nose like a cobsnake coiled around a cornstalk, and it just won't leave.

"What are you looking at?" she asks Pinky.

The horse's gums peel back, showing off yellow teeth.

Whenever the horse moves, she hears a clicking, a scraping—and though the lights here in the stable are dim, she can see the shadows rising and falling on the animal's back. Shadows like black fingers. Shadows that are in fact long, long bones—jointed and bent like parts of a busted umbrella, bones that rise off the shoulders and curl to the ground.

They were supposed to be wings.

But they didn't "come out right," according to Balastair Harrington, her keeper and their designer—they came out featherless. Skinless, too. Just bones. Bones that jut out of the horse's flesh, painful at the source. That's another of Gwennie's many jobs: apply a salve to the juncture of bone and body. A job that Pinky finds none too pleasing, and just yesterday he stomped down on Gwennie's foot with a heavy, cracked hoof. Nothing broken, but she still feels it.

Pinky is not the only inhabitant of this stable of freaks.

Across the way is Blackjack, a black horse with black wings—wings that are neither swan-like nor elegant but rather bat-like and diseased. They twitch and tighten, even in the creature's sleep. Blackie's a real unpleasant animal. He bites. Thrashes. Has milky eyes that look right through her.

In a farther stall is Goosedown (a horse with no wings and

no fur at all but rather an entire body covered in dirty white feathers) and then Stubby (four too-short legs and a set of stubby nodules protruding over the animal's shoulders as if the creature once had wings but someone clipped them off).

None of these are their official names.

They're just the names Gwennie's given them. Better than calling them Subject #312 or Subject #409.

These animals are the lucky ones.

Many others were born with deformities far too severe. Horses without skin. Without legs. Blind, deaf, hearts outside their bodies. One of them was finally born with a beautiful chestnut coat and wings like feathers from the softest pillow—and then when they asked it to fly, they shoved it over the edge (for it's not a horse's inclination to leap into the void), and the wings unfurled and tried to catch air. . . .

The horse pitched forward, heavy in the front, and dropped like a brick through the air.

Sure to die a terrible death upon striking the ground somewhere far below their feet. *Probably*, she thinks just now, *crushing some poor Heartlander's house.*

Flying horses. *A Pegasus.* The Empyrean wants a Pegasus. Like the one on their official sigil. Something to represent them. Some iconic ideal of—what was it that Harrington had said? "The iconic ideal of man's dominance over nature and proof that he deserves to sit at the manor table with the Lord and Lady themselves."

He didn't seem convinced by that line of nonsense, and neither was she. Not that she had much room to argue anyway, what with her being the stall-mucker of mutant Pegasuses.

The life of a Lottery winner laid bare.

She scoops another load of soggy corn piss-mush into the small wagon, and the horse apples (or as she likes to call them, "Pegasus pears") thud-bump against the metal bottom. Then she pulls the wagon to the far end of the room past the other stalls—Blackjack stomps his hooves and gives her a demonic look—and grabs the handle to the hatch and lifts.

The wind fills the room and rustles her hair, and the volume of the flotilla's engines and hover-panels becomes more than just a droning thrum—it fills the space, an ear-ringing roar that upsets all the horses.

She stops for a moment. Gazing down, down, down—there, below, the endless corn of the Heartland carved into squares and lined by the various motorvators (tillers, threshers, seeders, sprayers), all of which look like Scooter's toys from way up here.

Scooter. The Heartland. Cael. Boyland.

Her heart hurts. She blinks back tears. Gwennie bites the inside of her cheek, tastes blood, and feels that little jolt of pain that spins the thread of her grief into a tattered rag of rage—*I hate this place; I hate these people; I want to go home.*

Eyes winced, she upends the wagon.

Corn husks and Pegasus waste go out through the hole.

And fall. Breaking apart in midair. Bits turning to specks turning to nothing. She thinks, *We always used to wonder exactly why shit was falling on our heads.* And not necessarily metaphorically, either.

Just then the door to the stable flings open.

Young Balastair Harrington, the man behind the genetic half of the Pegasus Project, hurries into the room, leading as he always does with his head and shoulders. Gwennie thinks he looks as if he's in a perpetual state of almost falling forward, his legs the eager and only saviors that stop him from landing on his face.

He's a few years older than she is. Different from the Heartlanders she knows. They're rugged, dirty, broad shouldered. He's thin and bony, like an articulated wooden doll. Handsome, though. In his own peculiar way.

He is not dressed in his usual white coat. His hair is not in its typical disarray: the blond wisps atop his head have been tamed and forced to lie down, and his white coat has been replaced with a pinstriped mandarin collar suit, the stripes themselves a liquid gold that bubbles and climbs from hem to shoulders. An effect that is, in its way, quite hypnotizing.

A caviling grackle with a small jeweled collar hops about on his shoulder. Wings fluttering. The bird is Erasmus. Forever on Balastair's shoulder—though Gwennie's never seen the jeweled collar on the bird before.

Or the pinstriped suit coat.

"Why are you—" she starts to ask, but he interrupts her.

"We're late!" he barks—a sentiment of panic, not anger.

"Late!" Erasmus chirps. The small, bruise-colored bird shakes its wings and dances side to side.

"Late for what?" she asks.

"Late," he hisses through clenched teeth, *"for the party."*

THE RIVER SLURRY

THE RAIL-RAFT ROCKETS FORTH.

Lane hoots and cackles while Rigo winces, eyes mostly shut.

For Cael's part, he just likes the reminder of how it feels to captain his own boat and to stand at its helm. As if he's the knife that cuts the sky in half—wind sliced in twain, rushing on all sides.

They got the raft moving pretty fast by jamming a pair of dry, broken cornstalks against the earth—stalks they'd taken on the first morning of travel to use as makeshift oar-poles. The brace roots were thick; the stalks were stiff. Rigo asked Cael if he could use the butt end of Pop's lever-action rifle, but Cael shot him a look that contained the singular message of *Have you lost your cotton-headed mind?*

Only took a minute or two to really get the raft zipping along.

The tracks ahead of them are a steely blur. Individual railroad ties smear together in a single dark streak. The corn, too, is just a blend of green, like so much spilled paint.

Ahead, a shuck rat squeaks in terror and hurries across the tracks.

Lane fishes in the food bag, plucks a carrot, sticks it into his mouth like a cigar, and fake-puffs on it as the air tousles his dark hair.

Then Cael sees—ahead, the corn disappears. Drops off the map. The earth sinks. The Heartland isn't much for topography—a few hills here, a shallow valley there—but for the most part everything is as flat as a sheet of hammered tin. The train tracks continue over the gulf.

He knows what it is even before they get close.

It's a slurry river.

Corn-processing plants dot the Heartland. Pop's explained the process a few times, but mostly Cael just tuned out—he didn't like hearing about breaking down protein bonds or microbial fuel cells or whatever else Pop tried to tell him. Talking about corn was about as much fun as talking about dirt, and Cael used that time to let his mind wander and think about Gwennie and her sweet-smelling soap and the smooth roundness of her freckled skin on the rare occasions that they managed to find time together and get each other out of their clothes—

But one thing he knows for sure is that the processing plants make one helluva lot of waste. Silage and starchy soups and chemical syrups—anything that can't be used from the corn is pumped out of the plants in rivers of gray-brown slurry that end up in massive, concrete holding tanks, which are eventually filled up, capped, and buried.

He's seen them up close before when he was out scavenging with his crew. Bubbling muck crawling. A stink that's both sweet and sickly, *wrong* in a way that the mind knows but can't properly put together.

They're going to pass over just such a river in . . . about thirty seconds, he figures. He points, calls it out: "Slurry river ahead!" Lane gives him a shrug, and Rigo peeks between the fingers of his hands.

Lane says, "Should be all right. Tracks go over it on a trestle."

"Maybe we should slow down anyway," Rigo says.

"I said we'll be all right, so we'll be all right," Lane yells.

"I'm kinda scared."

Lane waves him off. "That's life in the Heartland. Besides, being scared usually means you're experiencing a life worth living, so shut your jabber-jaw and enjoy the—"

"Oh shit," Cael says.

He doesn't need to explain.

They all see it.

The chrome reflects the sun; the black steel just eats it. Ahead it's a small thing, a dark square in the distance. If it were only a stationary object, Cael wouldn't feel as if he was about to piss his britches. But it's an auto-train, one of the motorvator locomotives. Which means it's coming *fast*.

Which means it's going to meet them on the bridge.

Rigo yells one word: *"Traaaaaain!"*

Cael and Lane move fast, grabbing the cornstalk oar-poles and jamming them against the hard earth—the stalks are tough but brittle, and they begin to disintegrate as soon as they meet the dirt. Cael tosses his and grabs his rifle—he thrusts it into Lane's hand.

"We gotta bail," he says to Lane.

Lane's eyes go as wide as moons.

"Tuck and roll," Cael says, and gives Lane a hard shove off the raft.

His friend disappears into the corn—the stalks shudder and shake; he sees a glimpse of Lane's heels, and then he's gone.

Rigo babbles a steady stream of entreaties: "Lord-and-Lady-Lord-and-Lady-*Lord-and-Lady.*" Spit so fast the words start to lose meaning.

"We gotta jump!" Cael yells.

"I don't want to jump."

"On three! One . . ."

"I don't want to jump!"

". . . two . . ."

"The food! We need the food!"

Rigo reaches for the bag.

". . . three!"

Cael leaps backward off the raft.

Rigo jumps, too, getting hold of the bag's strap as he does so—

But the strap catches on the front corner of the raft.

The raft launches out onto the trestle over the slurry river. Cael catches sight of Rigo still clutching the bag-strap, dangling over open air as the raft hurtles forward—

And then Cael's world goes dizzy, spinning end over end as his shoulder hits the ground, and he rolls forward, crashing through cornstalks that reach for him and slice him with quick cuts of thin leaves. The ground beneath him starts to slope, and he begins to roll. Cael reaches for stalks, but his hands fail to find a grip. In the back of his mind he realizes why the ground slopes suddenly downward. *I'm heading for the slurry.*

But then his hand finally catches a stalk, fingers hooking into the brace roots and halting his fall—

His legs dangle over the edge of a crumbling earthen lip, a crusty berm of dry ground bulging with broken stalks and tentacular roots—

Cael looks up at the trestle extending out over the river, one hundred feet up from the churn of chemical molasses—

He sees the train coming.

He sees the rail-raft flying toward it.

He sees Rigo dangling from the raft by the strap.

Let go let go let go—

Cael's fingers slip—he loses his grip, starts to fall, catches himself again—and by the time he looks up once more, the train's toothy cattle-catcher smashes into the raft, turning it into a shower of splinters.

THE PAINTED LADY

"WHAT PARTY?" GWENNIE ASKS.

Balastair freezes in place. She knows he's thinking because he does this thing—his pupils flit and twitch, back and forth, back and forth, as if he's surveying data in the dark of his mind. His eyes—as green as leaves—suddenly lock on to hers again, and he says quietly, "I didn't tell you about the party?"

"No!" she barks, suddenly confused, panicked, and more than a little angry. "I don't want to go to some party."

"It's the Architect's Party," he says. "It happens once a year on every flotilla—it's held by the architect of that flotilla. Or the architect's family if the architect has, ah, passed on." He suddenly looks uncomfortable. Pink cheeks gone white. "I can't believe I didn't tell you. It's today. On the Halcyon Balcony. In an hour. *In an hour.* And you're not even dressed!"

He runs his hands through his hair—and the once-tamed wisps of blond lift and rise again.

"I'm dressed," she says.

"Not for a party. Certainly not for the Architect's Party. You're barely dressed for a carousal of vagrants. I . . . I never sent a dress down?"

"No!"

"It must still be upstairs then. Come on. *Come on.*"

"Come on!" Erasmus the grackle cackles.

"I'm not going to the party," she says as she hurries after Balastair, his long strides carrying them around the filthy, trash-swept hallway toward the elevator. There, the elevator sits behind a metal accordion gate. It's a gate she's tried to open many times on her own, a gate kept shut by—

"*Hello, Balastair Harrington,*" chirps the auto-mate from the tinny round speaker that serves as its "mouth." The mechanical half man stands on a pillar, two pairs of long, disjointed arms hanging from the bell-shaped torso. The creature blinks copper lids over stained glass eyes, *click click click.* "*Are we going up today?*"

"Yes, Elevator Man," Balastair says. "And she's coming with me."

"*Hello*—" Here the auto-mate pauses, and she hears a sound inside the bell of its body like cards being shuffled. "*Heartlander Gwendolyn Shawcatch.*" Except it mispronounces her name: *gwen-DO-LINN shewkitch.*

"Shut up, tinbody," she hisses.

Balastair shoots her a look. "You're terribly angry; has anybody told you that? It's very off-putting."

The mechanical mimes the act of pulling back the accordion

gate, though it's just an automated illusion—the gate pulls back as part of its own chain-driven mechanism.

Inside, the elevator is gleaming: diamonds of dark wood alternating with tiled squares of copper discolored with a green patina. It is the opposite of everything that exists down here in the Undermost. Everything at this strata is dirty and falling apart—the lights flickering from dim to bright, a strobe effect that leaves streaks across her vision.

Balastair is already in the elevator, and he's pinching the fabric at her elbow and pulling her in. "Hurry, we don't have much time to transform . . ."—he waggles his fingers at her—"*this* into . . . something else."

"Something else!" the grackle mimics.

The gate slams shut—*click-click-click-BOOM.*

A brass plate next to the door pops open on a spring, revealing a screen not unlike a visidex; it shimmers and distorts, and suddenly a face appears on it, the face of the Elevator Man with his bulging speaker mouth and his stained glass eyes.

"*Where to, Balastair Harrington?*"

"Home," he says.

"*Home it shall be.*"

Behind the walls, something whirrs and rattles. Suddenly the elevator shudders and moves—Gwennie's feet feel unmoored, and dizziness threatens to pull her to the ground. She gets the sense of flying through the air, the way her stomach seems disconnected from her body.

"Home," she says, the word bitter on her lips.

"I'm sorry?" he asks, distracted.

"I want to see my family."

"I'm afraid that's not possible."

"*Make* it possible."

He laughs—not a happy laugh but a laugh of truth, of irony—the kind of laugh that comes out because if it doesn't, something worse will struggle free. "I don't have that power."

"You're . . . the Grand . . . whatever you are."

"I'm one of many Grand Geneticists." He grumbles under his breath: "It's not as wonderful as it sounds."

"You're making flying horses for them." *And I'm cleaning up after them. If only Heartlanders knew that's what winning the Lottery got you.*

"We all have to do things we don't want to do."

She scowls. "Wait, you're saying you don't *want* to . . . cook up these flying horses? You're young. I thought it was some kind of privilege."

"It is. Of course it is." Those words come out through stiffened lips. In fact, all parts of him stiffen and bristle—his back gets straighter; his arms lie flat by his side. "It is a great privilege."

"Whenever we're Obligated to people we don't want down in the Heartland, we're supposed to act grateful, too. Sounds like a bucket of corn slurry to me." Her jaw pops as she chews on her own frustration. "I want to see my family."

Balastair sighs, then says, "Elevator Man, stop the elevator."

"*Yes, Balastair Harrington.*"

The elevator grinds to a halt—*chung chung chunnnng.*

He flips the brass panel closed and turns to face Gwennie. Nose to nose. She smells his breath: a whiff of strong mint. His eyes sparkle.

"I don't know where your family is," he says softly. "If I did,

I'd tell you. Not that either of us could do anything about it anyway. I am . . . sympathetic to your plight. I know . . . you Heartlanders have it hard, and I know this isn't what you envisioned would happen when you won the Lottery." He pauses, then speaks more frankly: "I'll try. Okay? I'll try to find out some information. But I need you to be . . . patient."

She seethes. "I don't want to be patient. They're my family. As soon as we set foot on this damned flying city, they ripped us apart!" All the Shawcatches, taken their separate ways. Screaming. Crying. Scooter was the worst—all the muscle tension gone out of him, sagging like a scarecrow off its pole, wailing in a way she hadn't heard since he was knee-high. "It was horrible. You don't understand."

"My mother and I—" he starts to say, then tightens his mouth. "We all have difficulty."

"I hate you. I hate all of you."

"You don't mean that."

"Damn right I do."

He pulls back. His hands clasp in front of him defensively.

"We're good people," he says. "Some of us. Most of us."

"You're all monsters to me," she says. "Monsters who never knew a day of real work in your lives."

"Work is beneath us," he says, but it sounds rote, like something an auto-mate might be programmed to say. As if he doesn't quite believe it.

"I know. I *lived* beneath you and still do."

He flips open the brass plate and tells the Elevator Man to continue.

• • •

The elevators do not merely go up and down. The ascent slows, then after more banging and clicking, the elevator begins to slide right. Then up again. Then both up and to the right.

Eventually the Elevator Man chirps: *"Home of Balastair Harrington."*

The accordion gate opens.

Outside, an identical mechanical man pivots on its pillar and uses one of its spindly arms to point the way.

Not that any other option exists.

The elevator opens onto a long skybridge—wide enough for two people to walk side by side but no more. The skybridge extends out for a hundred feet and ends at a doorway framed by a pair of Pegasus statues, the beasts rearing back, huge front hooves high in the air as if to stomp flat some unseen predator.

She's been here before. Harrington's home.

He hurries onto the skybridge, pulling her along. Out here, her dizziness does not abate—in fact, it swells into total vertigo. Her life was one of tall corn and hard dirt, a life of plasto-sheen roads and wooden floors. But up here—it's all *air*. Out there beyond this skybridge are a hundred others just like it, connecting buildings that rise up like spears, whose tips scrape the very ceiling of the sky. Massive chains, each as big as a fat-man's thigh and some much bigger than that, drape between buildings, holding them together—and beyond them, above them, below them, the ships of the Empyrean. Skiffs and ketches, skipjacks and djong-boats, and far more opulent vessels, too: ferry-cruisers and motoryachts the likes of which the Heartland has never seen. Some of the ships fly past; others dock at buildings or at the fringes of the city.

This, the flotilla of the Ormond Stirling Saranyu. A city of disparate parts strung together and turned into a massive moving island.

A *flying* island. An airborne city.

She feels the flight of the entire flotilla beneath her. The wind in her hair. The gentle but present sway of everything. She turns, clasps the cold railing of the skybridge. *Don't puke, don't puke, don't puke.*

Then she looks. A mile down she sees the bottom of the flotilla, a massive base shot through with channels and pits through which she glimpses the Heartland below—she wonders without warning what it would be like to plunge through open air toward the corn, toward home. *Didn't Cael have a dream like that—?*

She throws up.

"C'mon," Harrington says, softening his sharp tone. He pats her back. "Let's get you cleaned up."

Gwennie sits at a mirror rimmed in crystal.

She dips her pinkie into the pink powder and rubs a little on her cheek. A carnation bloom rises to the skin, lending a small burst of color to her face. A clean face, too, no longer streaked with mud (or worse). She reaches for a small, silver tube and puzzles over it for a moment before giving it a twist—a cone of pink lipstick pushes through.

Behind her, Balastair watches. She spies him in the mirror. She tries to figure out what he's thinking. Is that lust? Or fascination? Or is it just the look of a man perplexed by a woman? That's a look she knows well, because she knows Cael McAvoy.

"This can't be exciting for you," she says, her mouth forming a grim line as she applies the lipstick. She hears her father's voice inside her head: *Ain't you a real painted lady.*

"You don't know that," he says. "Are you sure you don't need help?"

"Why? Does it look bad?"

"No. Of course not. A little plain, perhaps. You're ignoring all the prettiest colors. Peacock powder, the blue blazes, viridian, chameleon—"

"Plain is how we Heartlanders like to be. We're not simple, but we're straightforward. Most of us anyway. No need to be ostentatious, not even on your Obligation Day." She thinks back to that day. Her hair in its simple braid wound in a circle. How handsome Cael looked. But Boyland, too . . .

Balastair dips into a little burlap bag and pulls out a sun-flower seed. Erasmus the grackle darts in and snatches it in his beak. The bird bites the seed, cracks it, eats the inside, then flicks the shell over Harrington's shoulder. It lands on the marble tile with a *tic.*

"You just don't want to look like us," he says plainly.

"We can't afford to even if we wanted to."

"You can today."

"I want to be me."

"Sure. Of course. You look nice." He coughs. "It looks nice. The makeup, I mean."

"Thank you." She puckers her lips. Lips blushing pink, almost peach. "I figured you'd have some kind of . . . mechanical makeup man to handle this."

"We do. Well, I don't. But I can get one if you need it."

"No. They creep me out."

He harrumphs. "You and me both."

She turns in her chair to face him. "You don't like them? The auto-mates?"

"I'm fine with them as long as they remain a novelty but . . . that's a long story and an old complaint, and it carries little value for you; plus it's taking up our time. We are already late. And people are waiting to see you. Come on; let's stand up. Get you in the dress."

She stands, but as he reaches for her wrist, she pulls it away.

"One more question," she says.

"We have to go."

"One more question or I'll kick and scream and fling myself over the edge before anybody can ever lay eyes on me."

"That sounds bad for you."

She narrows her eyes. "And probably not too great for you, either. I was left in your care, after all."

Harrington rolls his eyes. "Fine. What?"

"The makeup. Where did it come from?"

"What? Why?"

"You're a man. Men don't wear makeup."

He laughs an oh-you-silly-girl laugh. "We do here."

"Fine, but *you* don't. Not any other day. Not today. So where'd it come from? You married?"

He leans back against the wall. "Yes. No! I was engaged. But . . . we're very . . . open with our relationships, and we're on a break. . . ."

He tries to hide how sad it makes him feel, but it's there in the way his eyes pinch a little, the way he nervously gnaws a lip, as if maybe he's trying to bite back words.

"Who was she?"

"What?"

"The woman. The one who left her makeup behind. Your Obligated."

"Her name was Cleo, and we aren't Obligated in the way that you Heartlanders—" He draws a deep breath. "We really don't have time to talk about her."

Erasmus blurts, "Cleo!"

Balastair pivots then and pulls a dress off a rack nestled between a series of suit coats and lab coats. He holds it out and drapes it over his forearm—silver fabric like a waterfall of pearls and diamonds pours over and almost touches the floor. It's not just a dress. It's a dress plus . . . feathers and fringe and other brazen accoutrements.

"It's too much," she says.

"It's nothing." He smirks, eyebrows lifting—as if he's proud of himself, somehow. Head up and chest out, same as the little grackle on his shoulder.

"No, I mean it's way too . . . crazy. Here." Gwennie yanks the dress out of his hands, holds it up. "What are these on the shoulder straps?" They look like the tail feathers of some exotic mechanical bird. She rips them off, and Balastair gasps and makes a sound in the back of his throat not unlike a shuck rat squealing after being whacked with a broom handle. He makes a horrified face as Gwennie begins performing other surgical alterations: a few tassles gone, another set of silver feathers ripped from the spot that would sit just above the base of her spine (she says, "What am I, a turkey?").

She holds up the dress. It's still shiny. And the back is way too skimpy (she has little interest in showing off her too-sharp shoulder blades to anybody, thank you very much). But at least she won't look like a human-peacock hybrid. Balastair folds his fingers under his chin and *hmm*s.

She begins to undo the robe and then pauses to give him a cross look. "Well. Turn around."

"Oh. Yes. Sorry." He does an awkward half spin. "You don't need to be modest here."

"It's good manners." She slides the dress over her head. The material is cold against her skin, drawing goose bumps to the surface. "Why, do you want to look?"

"No! What? No."

"So I'm not worth looking at."

"You're just trying to get me into trouble."

"Turn around."

"Are you—"

"It's on. Turn around."

He pivots his head before his body. His eyes narrow, then go wide. "Oh. Well."

"This is the dress," she says.

"It's plain. But it works."

"Are you saying I look nice?"

His pale cheeks go pink. "Yes. I suppose I am saying that."

"Good. Because I'm wearing it no matter what you think. Now, let's go to this damn party you say is so important."

THE REMITTANCE MAN

A BURNING ITCH lives on the flesh above Cael's heart, below his shirt, but he can't think about that now, no sir, because when he looked up and saw that rail-raft explode into splinters, he didn't see Rigo at all—didn't see him fall, didn't see him tumble through the air like a poppet doll, didn't see hide nor hair of him.

Cael tries to get hard earth under his feet, but clumps of dirt crumble away, leaving his heels to skid on the slope. He grabs the cornstalk with his other hand, pulling himself up and hollering himself hoarse for Rigo—but just as he starts to holler, the auto-train goes past only ten feet to his right, and the roar of the metal beast drowns his voice like a farmer killing kittens in a washtub.

Cael grits his teeth and struggles to stand on wobbly legs. The auto-train is a long, dark blur, a tar snake of great length

and terrifying speed; by the time it's gone Cael sees Lane on the other side of him, one hand cupped around his mouth and yelling for Rigo, the rifle held gingerly in his other hand.

"I saw him hanging on," Lane says, panicked.

"He wouldn't let go of the damn raft!" Cael bellows for his friend again.

Together the two of them hurry onto the trestle, careful not to lose their balance, because there stands only a foot of construct separating them from a far drop into the murky river of corn slurry.

"We shouldn't have gone so fast," Cael says. "Godsdamnit!"

Lane shakes his head. "It's my fault. My stupid idea. Shit!"

The two of them call together.

Rigo's name, echoing out over the slurry canyon.

Cael's got the eye. Everyone knows it. He can spot things nobody else can—that's why he made a fine scavenger back in the town of Boxelder, and he and his crew would've been top of the pops if it wasn't for Boyland Barnes Jr. always playing havoc with their advantage.

So when Cael looks down and scans the river and sees nothing, he gets worried. Rigo is gone. As if he never existed. As insubstantial and unreal as a soap bubble popped by a child's finger.

But then—

A round shape bobbing in the slow-moving slurry. Heading south. The round shape turns like a log rolling over.

Rigo's face emerges.

A pair of chubby hands waves before he's lost again beneath the sliding muck.

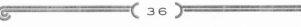

Cael barks, "He's in the river!"

"Cael!" Lane says, pointing to a narrow opening leading down to the river—a precarious path awaits: a short shelf of dry dirt supported by clusters of corn roots. Dangerous, but it'll do.

Cael bolts off the trestle and runs into the corn. He hears Lane crashing through the stalks behind him. The corn leaves twitch and swipe at him, leaving little, stinging paper cuts across his forearms and collarbone.

That voice from the dream—

Come to me, Cael.

It crawls into his head like a fat earthworm.

He pushes it out of his head as Lane hurries up next to him.

Cael spots Rigo again. Arms flailing. Slurry falling off his hands in gloppy blobs. The two of them charge down the narrow path—the decline is steep, and Lane's arms pinwheel as he struggles not to pitch forward.

He's got his eyes on Rigo, so he doesn't see what's at his feet. The toe of Cael's boot clips on a bundle of corn roots popping out of the ground—"witch's hair" is what they call such bundles, for they look like the dry and brittle hay-hair the Maize Witch is said to have on her old, haggard head—then he's falling forward again, catching himself this time with his palms. Lane grabs him by the scruff of his neck as Cael's legs pump beneath him to keep him moving—

And, just like that, they're only feet from the river's edge.

The bubbling gray-brown sludge doesn't churn forth so much as it sluggishly crawls forward. The smell at this level is truly overpowering: a sugary fist to the nose with a sour stink-slap after.

But that's not what matters now.

What matters is they see Rigo.

He's not alone.

A man stands on the far side of the river, opposite them. He's got the look of a hobo. Older. Hunched over in a pair of dirty denim overalls with nothing underneath except the worn and leathered skin of a well-traveled vagrant. The man looks up at the two of them with dark eyes under a single knitted brow, his face so scruffy with black stubble it looks like coal silt.

Cael and Lane scream at him, but the man ignores them.

The hobo reaches back and pulls up a long pole—really two poles bracketed together, by the looks of it—that dead-ends in a copper wire loop. They see Rigo, suddenly, bobbing back up to the surface.

And heading right toward the man.

The man dips the looped end of the pole into the river.

"He's going for Rigo," Cael says, panicked.

"Maybe he's trying to help."

But Cael doesn't want to hear that. Even after everything with Pop and the garden and Martha's Bend, he still doesn't know if he trusts vagrants—he hears tell of all kinds of stories about what the rail-riders and other wanderers are like. Thieves and madmen, exiled from their towns. Some of them killers, or kiddie-catchers, or even cannibals.

Cael screams for the man to stop, but he doesn't pay attention. Cael snatches the rifle out of Lane's grip and points it just as the loop of the pole catches around Rigo's head and arm, cinching tight.

Like the man's going fishing or something.

Cael whoops a wordless threat and cocks the rifle's lever action.

Ch-chak.

It's loud enough to get the vagrant's attention.

He looks up. Rigo thrashes and splashes. The man doesn't say anything. He just stares. Cael feels those dark eyes like two black seeds tucked into the dirt of the man's face.

The hobo grunts, looks back down toward the river. He begins hauling Rigo up to the cracked, dust-blown bank of the slurry river.

"I'll shoot!" Cael yells. Finger curling around the trigger.

The rifle's not loaded.

But no way for the vagabond to know that.

All the hobo hollers is "So shoot."

The rifle wavers, the iron sights like horns of Old Scratch framing the man. Cael wonders if he could do it. Shoot a fella the way Pop shot Mayor Barnes. Wasn't in cold blood. No matter the temperature of the blood, it ended the same way, with a dead man lying there.

Of course, Cael has his own dead man, doesn't he? Pally Varrin. Empyrean Babysitter for the town of Boxelder. Throat closed and crushed by a single ball bearing from Cael's slingshot.

It haunts him, suddenly: the image of Pally on the ground, gasping and gurgling. Legs shaking. Feet juddering as everything went to hell outside Cael's once-safe homestead.

He shudders.

Meanwhile, Rigo flops onto the bank with a splatter— looking like a shuck rat pulled out of an oil barrel.

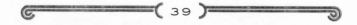

But, whoa-dang, he's still holding the bag! The bag that contains their food, their ammo, a host of other minor necessities.

Cael bares his teeth but lowers the gun.

"Rigo!" he yells. "You all right?"

Rigo looks up from his place on the ground. He wipes sludge from his eyes and finally sees that the person who rescued him is neither Cael nor Lane. He screams.

The hobo just frowns and shakes his head.

He looks across the murky river span.

Then he points to the trestle.

"Meet me up there. I'll bring your friend."

The man smiles suddenly. Cael can't help but think it's meant to be friendly—but damnit if that smile doesn't look *feral*.

The hobo hauls Rigo to his feet, then begins to climb back up the hill.

"What the hell?" Lane whispers to Cael.

"I don't know, but we better go make sure Rigo's all right."

They climb back up to the trestle, and as they walk, they talk about the possibility that the hobo and Rigo will be gone, vanished into thin air. Or maybe Rigo will be dead, and the bag of food and ammo will be what goes missing. They imagine any number of doom scenarios together: the man with a knife to Rigo's throat, or a gun, or a whole gang of hobos looking for a taste of food, or violence, or the pleasures given by young boys.

But they get to the trestle and see the vagabond standing at the far end with Rigo sitting next to him. Rigo offers them a lazy, tired wave.

They cross. One after the other. The river oozing far below.

As they approach, the vagrant just stares at them, offering only a curt nod as they get close.

"Mister," Lane finally says.

"Boys," the vagrant says, his voice surprisingly soft for such a gruff-looking fella. Even that one word rises and falls with a curious lilt. "Here's your friend."

Rigo takes Cael's hand in a sloppy, greasy grip, and Cael pulls him to his feet.

"Thanks for saving him," Cael says, hesitant.

"I was fishing for junk. Saw him bobbing along."

"Fishing for junk?" Lane asks.

"Mm-hmm. Sometimes the folks at the processing factories throw away trash. Floats downriver. I take it."

"You're a hobo," Cael says, a statement as obvious as the man's crooked nose.

"I am. And who are you, little mice?"

"I'm Rigo. Those are my friends, Lane and—"

Cael shushes him with a hiss, but it's too late.

"—Cael."

"Pleasure." There again: that smile. Cael thinks it's the smile of a fox sliding up on a pair of sleeping hens. But his friends don't seem too worried. And, he reminds himself, he thought the same thing about all the vagrants under Pop's command. *Maybe you're laying down judgment where you ought not to be judging*, he thinks. Because isn't he a vagrant, too? The hobo continues: "You little mice seem a bit lost. Saw that raft of yours get hit." He grunts as Cael's reminded that their ride is now gone—and with it the magna-cruxes. "Raft on the rails. Pretty smart."

"We're scavengers," Cael says. Not a lie, not really.

"What town?"

Cael thinks to say Boxelder, but—that's too far away for it to make sense. He's trying to think of what's near, but he can't conjure any names, and his mouth is working like the lips of a parched and thirsty man—

"Wheatley," Lane blurts.

"Wheatley, huh." The man looks them up and down. "Nice town. People there are good folk. Put an old dirt-paw like me to work without condemnation. That tree of yours in the center of town sure took a licking."

"It did," Cael says, lying through his teeth. *What tree?*

"Lightning's a helluva thing," the hobo says. "My name's Eben, by the way. You heading back toward Wheatley?"

"We, ah, we are," Cael says.

"Night'll be here long before you get back, what with your raft blasted to toothpicks. I got a little place carved out for me and my boy not far down the tracks if you want it. Besides, you'll be crossing back over the Rovers' territory on foot."

"The . . . Rovers?" Rigo asks.

The hobo gives them a look. "I know you got a problem with Rovers in Wheatley. Those dogs are mean and hungry. Travel in big packs, too."

"The *Rovers*," Lane says. "We, eh, call them something different."

"Oh yeah?"

Cael steps over the answer and blurts out, "We'd love to come with you, and thanks for the offer." He tightens the hinges of his jaw at saying this, but it makes good sense. Especially if

these . . . Rovers are truly dangerous. "Plus, I figure we owe you some for saving our man here."

"Let's scurry, little mice," Eben says. He doesn't stop to wait for them, just turns tail and starts walking down the track, shoulders slumped forward, loop-pole in his hand.

HATING LIFE ON THE HALCYON BALCONY

IT STEALS THE BREATH from her chest. Vertigo robs her of balance. Her palms feel instantly sweaty. Her mouth feels immediately dry.

This is not natural, Gwennie thinks.

The Halycon Balcony is, to her mind, no mere balcony. The entire thing is textured glass, and it extends out toward the sunset and horizon on every side. Beneath her is the Heartland, miles below her feet, the retreating sun smearing the land in liquid fire and pooling shadow. And all around her is the other thing that's not natural: the *people*.

Gwennie's used to the Harvest Home Festival—a hundred people on the street of Boxelder, getting more ornery as the night tumbles forward. Folks laughing and singing. Drinking bottles of fixy or bowls of chicha beer. Some folks fight. Newly Obligated fondle and explore each other. By the end of the night, with the Obligations and all, somebody ends up crying. But the

people of Boxelder, well, Gwennie *knows* them. She knows them not just intellectually but emotionally, because she *is* them.

And these people are all strangers to her. Strangers in so many ways.

This single event is already bigger than Harvest Home by a magnitude of ten. People as far as the eye can see. That word she used earlier, *ostentatious*? Saying these people looked "ostentatious" is like calling a piss-blizzard a "little dust storm." At a quick glimpse she sees men walking around in suits made from ribbons of reflective metal, tuxedos of raven feathers, hats that somehow hover just above their heads. Women wear suits and dresses that to her seem utterly absurd: feathers and flashing lights, translucent panels that swirl with blooms of color, see-through dresses of metallic lace or plastic beads or fabric made to look like a series of delicate hands covering inappropriate spots. Some ladies waltz around in not much more than underclothing—clothing far skimpier than Gwennie's own bra and bloomers. Heat rises to her cheeks.

Seeing all these people makes Gwennie even dizzier. In fact she suddenly wishes the whole balcony would crack like an old barn board and drop her through. Anything to get away.

Balastair spins her around and looks her in the eye. He raises his voice so he can be heard above the dull roar of the crowd. "We will now begin the social circuit. You and I will walk the party, and we will stop and see those you need to see, and the circuit will culminate in a visit with the Grand Architect of the flotilla, Stirling Ormond. Do you understand?"

"I want to go home," she says.

He's about to say something else—not a rebuke, it seems, by

the soft, even sympathetic, look on his face (that says to Gwennie he doesn't want to be here, either)—but he doesn't get the chance to speak.

Hands grab Gwennie's shoulders and whirl her around.

"Let me look at you!"

There, a beautiful woman—elegant, almost as if sculpted out of stone, skin like milk, hair like spun gold, and a dress of such grave immodesty that Gwennie feels her eyes bug out of her head. The dress is entirely see-through—a plastic dress whose only obfuscating feature appears to be that water is running down over every inch of it. And yet it doesn't spill and pool beneath her. It reveals everything: the roundness of the breasts, the dark shadows of her nipples, and the triangle between her legs, all of it blurred *just slightly* by the cascading water. Gwennie knows she's gawking.

"The dress!" the woman says. "Yes, yes, do you believe it? I went off-flotilla for this one. You know the designer? Arnaud Spark? You know he has a yacht, right? He never moors at a dock! Such independence."

"Ahhhh" is all Gwennie can say.

Suddenly Harrington darts in—and the woman gives him a dire stare. Gwennie sees Balastair almost shrink in deference. Not physically, but . . . something about him crumples inward.

"Gwendolyn, this is the praetor's wife, Annalise Garriott."

The praetor. The administrator of the entire flotilla. Ashland—wasn't that the name she's heard time and again? The woman confirms this quickly: "Ashland is with the Grand Architect. We'll go to them." She loops her arm in Gwennie's. "Dearest Balastair, I'll take it from here. I'll return her to you at the end of the night." Way she says *dearest* sounds as if she means anything but. Gwennie wonders if that's how the Empyrean people are: always saying things they don't really mean.

Balastair smiles, nods. "Of course, Annalise."

And then the woman whisks Gwennie into the throng.

Balastair feels for the girl. He really does.

To him she emblemizes the Heartland. She *is* a hard worker. She's tough. Plain in the best way. (*Pretty, too*, says a small but persistent voice inside him.) Uncompromising. (*And did I mention pretty?*)

Which is why it's so frustrating that he can do nothing for her.

He tells himself, as a salve, *It's better up here for her. This party. The drinks. The food. Better than rolling around in the dirt. Killing rats and growing corn you can't even eat.*

But then—

There. Across the room.

Eldon Planck.

Those rugged good looks. The salt-and-pepper stubble. That aggressive jawline. Almost robotic in his handsomeness— improbable, artificial, smooth skin, bright eyes.

Eldon sees him. Of course he does.

He gives a slight lift of his chin.

Eldon, that cocky prick. Always was. Always will be.

Balastair fake-smiles back.

He needs a drink, he decides, before he deals with Eldon Planck. It will be a bitter quaff of medicine since Planck designed all the auto-mates including the Bartender-Bots, but medicine it shall be.

Gwennie feels like a drop of soap in a puddle of oil—she and Annalise Garriott together seem to *repel* the crowd. The people do not seem to retreat out of disgust or concern but rather out of respect and perhaps even fear, almost the way a crowd parts when one walks past carrying something delicate. Yet their interest in Gwennie is keenly felt: they hover and gawk, mouths forming curious Os and eyes looking her up and down and up again.

Annalise appears to give them permission—subtly, unspo-ken, something with her eyes or her mannerisms, Gwennie's not sure, but as they move through the crowd, they occasionally stop, and, one by one, partygoers dart in, given the privilege (how absurd is that?) to talk to her.

An old man with skinny arms and matchstick legs but a fat, pig's belly straining against the buttons on his gossamer shirt reaches in and grabs Gwennie's hand—she tries to pull it away, but he locks the fingers of his left hand around her wrist and turns her hand palm up with his right.

"Such calluses!" he says. He touches the tips of her fingers with his own, light, moth-wing touches that show her how soft his hands are—and how hard hers are in contrast. "These hands speak of work. I practically smell the dust, the blood, the grind-ing donkeywork. How delightful."

Gwennie finally wrenches her hand away from his.

All he does is laugh. "Such spirit! Sharp as a biting wind, this one."

BLIGHTBORN

His eyes then drift over her. As if his lust is suddenly awakened by the rebellion of Gwennie pulling her wrist free.

"Yes, yes," Annalise says, drawing Gwennie away. She hears the man calling after her, but Annalise mutters: "That was Harl Purgin, a second cousin of Ashland's—a necessary if unpleasant stop. Onward!"

Thus begins the parade of people and questions:

A woman with a dainty pillbox hat and a sharp-angled pink suit studded with dangling black pearls asks: "Have you ever met a real hobo?"

A dark and dapper gent with a feathered fedora and the ends of his mustache twisted into ornate spirals: "How bad was it down there in the dust and the pollen? I bet being up here in the sky is a dream far greater than any you could've imagined, isn't that right?"

A round, plump woman with eyes that call to mind the winking asterisk under a cat's tail: "Have you ever"—and here she cannot contain her excitement, the fingers of her lacy gloves tickling the air—"killed someone? For food? For love?"

To all the questions, Gwennie stammers and stumbles, feeling pinned beneath an avalanche: "Ahhh, uhhh, well." She buries real answers in all her fumbling before Annalise whisks her to the next group.

Another woman, this one not much older than Gwennie, saunters up, a sway in her matronly hips. She's wearing an ivory dress that Gwennie first thinks is embroidered with flowers, but soon she realizes the flowers are moving, shifting, blooming, and dying right there on the fabric—a strange illusion she finds both beautiful and creepy.

CHUCK WENDIG

The woman asks, "Do you have a boy down below? A young
stallion champing at the bit to see you again? Or two young
bucks? Or *three*?" The woman giggles and winks. Gwennie says,
"I . . . had a boy but then I was Obligated to another."

The woman gasps and clutches Gwennie's hands in her own
as the flowers along the dress sleeves bloom in simultaneity and
die back to shriveled nubs. Gwennie wonders suddenly if they're
tied to the woman's mood—would such a thing even be possible?

"Awwww," the woman says. "Obligation! Unrequited love!
Torn between two lovers. A heart in twain. The simple stuff of
Heartland poetry."

Roses bloom along the women's heaving, fabric-clad bosom.

Then the woman kisses her on the cheek and is gone again
in the crowd.

"Ah!" Annalise says. "Drinks."

Gwennie whirls to meet another body—

This one entirely mechanical.

A tin man in a pinstriped vest and a bowler cap rolls up on
a base of treaded, threaded wheels. An extensor arm makes a
clumsy, mechanical flourish, and a steel jaw below the auto-
mate's black Bakelite mustache wobbles as it speaks: *"Would you
two like a concoction?"*

Annalise looks to Gwennie. "Guest's choice first."

"I . . ." Gwennie wants a drink. But what? What can she
even order? She thinks back to the bottles Boyland's father, the
mayor, had. "I'll take a Jack Kenny whiskey?"

The auto-mate reaches into his own chest and withdraws a
highball glass. The claw-hand at the end of the mechanic's other

arm pops open on a hinge, and from it sprays amber liquid. Two perfectly spherical ice marbles rattle into the glass afterward. Gwennie takes the glass gingerly.

"No-no-no." Annalise clucks and tuts, taking the glass back *out* of her hand and handing it off to a passing guest. "You're not the whiskey type."

"I'm not?"

Annalise turns to the auto-mate.

"I will have a Pegasus Neck. The young girl here will have a Tuxedo Tassel." The auto-mate gets to making each drink in turn: sprays of bubbly tonic, pink liquid, red liquid, gold liquid. The mechanical even goes so far as to hum as it—he?—makes the concoctions. Annalise once more turns her gaze to Gwennie. "How are you enjoying the party?"

"It's . . ." Something catches Gwennie's eye. Over Annalise's shoulder. A shock of dark hair, a set of familiar features. She feels Annalise's gaze burning a pair of holes through her, so she lets the word trickle out of her mouth: ". . . fine."

Annalise looks behind her, following Gwennie's gaze.

She turns back around to study Gwennie's face. "Do you see something, dear?"

"No, I—"

There. *There.* The crowd parts as a woman in an odd outfit of corn husks and leaves (headdress and all) steps away with a tall man in some kind of rubber suit held together with countless loops and buttons. A face emerges. Staring right at Gwennie.

Merelda McAvoy gives a tiny nod. Barely perceptible.

Cael's sister. Is here. *On this flotilla.*

Gwennie's mouth slackens. She feels it go but can't seem to snap it shut.

Merelda merges with the crowd once more.

The auto-mate hands out both drinks.

Annalise reaches for hers. And while she's distracted, Gwennie darts past her and hurries into the crowd after Merelda.

THREE BLIND MICE

THE HOBO, EBEN, walks ahead of them, humming—
or rather, mumbling—some song, some hymn. The sun is
scalped, the top of it chopped off and left to lie atop the corn,
the whole thing slowly sinking beneath the horizon as eventide
creeps forth.

The three boys lag about twenty feet behind on the tracks.

"I don't know if I like this," Cael says, his voice low.

"You aren't the judge and jury, you know," Lane whispers.

"What?"

"You judge people, Cael. Just because this fella's a hobo
doesn't mean anything except that *something* he did pissed in
the Empyrean's faces and they kicked him into the corn because
of it."

"It's not *just* that he's a hobo. He, he . . . he seems strange."

Lane chuffs a mirthless laugh. "Strange that he rescued our
friend, you mean, after the little dum-dum fell into the slurry?"

"Hey!" Rigo protests. "I'm right here."

Lane offers a shrug.

"No, I mean—" Cael tries again but then gives up before he gets anywhere. He's got no reason to worry . . . probably. "It's fine. You're right. I'm just being an asshole."

"What else is new?" Lane says, and Cael's about to start in again until he sees Lane's mouth twist into a mischievous smile, and instead, he dead-arms his lanky friend with a couple of piston punches. "Ow! Dang."

"Where'd you get Wheatley from anyway?" Cael asks.

"Heard the name before, knew it had to be a town around here somewhere—always heard it was about a week off from us by boat. I figure the hobo won't think twice about it."

"I think we can ask Eben for help," Rigo says.

"Help with what?"

"Finding the Provisional Depot."

"We already know where that is," Cael says. "Follow the tracks in the direction we're going, and we'll be there."

"But maybe there's a better way. Or maybe he's seen it and can tell us more about it. How many guards and what kind of fence and all that."

"Yeah. Maybe." Cael chews on the inside of his cheek. He doesn't want to give up too much, but help is help, and the hobo *did* save Rigo.

Just then the corn shudders somewhere off to their right. They all startle—three gasps in unison. Cael reaches instinctively for the slingshot in his back pocket despite having a rifle in his hand.

"Just a shuck rat, most likely," the vagrant calls from ahead. He's stopped and is standing there in the tracks, staring at them. Tapping his thumb against the loop-pole. "They make a lot of noise for such little creatures, don't you think?"

They laugh it off. Awkwardly.

"We thought it might've been a Rover," Rigo says, letting out a relieved breath.

"Rovers tend to travel in packs," the vagrant says. "And they're silent as a soft breeze, the Rovers. Creep up on you while you're sleeping. Three of them at a time. The lead dog, he'll come up around your head or your neck while the other two come at your sides. Then, like *that*"—he claps his hands loud—"they take you. The two monsters at your side bite deep, tearing holes in you so your guts spill out. The lead dog, well, all you'll get to feel is his long, lean jaws crushing your skull like a boot grinding a cigarette into the plasto-sheen." He sniffs. "Any of you want a smoke?"

Lane clears his throat, offers a hand and a waggle of fingers. "I'll take one if you got it, mister."

Eben pulls out a crooked little hand-rolled cigarette, hands it to Lane—then pulls a shiny silver pop-top lighter. He flicks it open, and on it Cael sees the sigil of the Pegasus: the Empyrean.

A hissing blue flame whispers from the lighter, and Eben waves it under the ditchweed cigarette. Lane draws in a breath and lets out two thin jets of smoke from his nose.

"That's an Empyrean lighter," Cael says.

The hobo turns and looks it up and down. "I suppose it is."

"Where'd you get it?"

"Must've fallen from the sky. C'mon, little mice, the road's up ahead. Almost dark now, almost dark."

The road is a crumbling, crooked thing beneath a pitted and pocked sheet of plasto-sheen. It comes off the tracks and cuts through the corn. By the time they get to it and begin heading down the strip of broken asphalt, night already has its claws in the Heartland, dragging it into the dark.

They pass a moldy, tilting wooden sign. The town name is rotted out, long gone from sight. A ghost town, then. Not like Martha's Bend—not preserved and kept in a bubble. But rather abandoned. And left to fester like a carcass in the corn.

Ahead, the town sits, hollow, gutted, a series of half-collapsed shadows. Buildings with blown-out windows. Corners roughly rounded as if by the swipe of some mighty hammer.

"Welcome home," Eben says.

In the street is a shape, a cylinder almost as tall as Rigo. The vagabond walks to it, picking up a piece of blowing trash as he does. He flicks the lighter open with a *tink*, conjuring the little blue flame. He tips it to the trash, and it ignites, a flare-up of ghostly fire.

Eben tosses the burning trash into the object.

It's a barrel—a rusty drum that suddenly burns with fingers of fire, orange light through corroded holes. Heat pushes off it, aggressive, blistering; Cael has to take a step back. Rigo blinks. Lane basks.

Somewhere, not far away, the sound of a child crying rises up—a sad, hitching cry, plaintive at first but then more insistent,

more intense. It echoes over the empty street, and the boys give one another looks.

Cael can barely suppress a shudder.

The hobo harrumphs. "Sounds like Little Arthur's awake."

"Arthur," Cael says. He thinks of Pop then. How could he not? "That's a . . . good name."

Rigo jumps in. "That's Cael's pop's name. Arthur."

The hobo rubs the back of his hand against his stubble—*scritch scratch scritch*. "Is it now? Huh. I gotta go feed him. Got a bottle of dog's milk in my bag." He turns, starts to head off.

"You need help?" Lane asks.

"No. You stay. Warm yourselves."

"The . . . Rovers . . . ," Rigo says.

"They won't come near the fire."

And then Eben stalks off toward one of the nearby buildings. Head slung low, shoulders slumped.

Soon he merges with the darkness and is gone.

"Lord and Lady," Rigo says. "He's got a little baby out here."

"That's messed up," Lane says.

"That's life in the Heartland," Cael says. "Little Baby Arthur. Huh. I wonder what Pop's up to." Worry and fear chew at him. He hopes like anything that Pop is okay. Keeping Mom safe. Keeping himself safe, too.

"I'm sure he's okay," Rigo says.

Lane says, "It's well-established by this point that your father is a bona fide secret badass, McAvoy. He'll hold his own."

"But he's with my mom. She . . . she won't travel well. All the stuff that happened that day is going to be on his head, not mine. Grey Franklin. Pally Varrin. The damn proctor's eye."

"Don't forget the mayor," Lane says. "Your daddy shot him dead."

Cael rubs his eyes. He feels tired all of a sudden. Not just the tired that comes when the sun and the moon switch places but the kind of tired that he feels in his bones—like the rot and ruin all around him. And his skin itches, too—a hard itch, hot from the heat, dry from traveling through dust and pollen. His cheeks puff out as he exhales. "Is what it is, I guess. I just hope Pop and Mom—"

The child's crying stops suddenly.

Rigo nods. "Somebody's enjoying the bottle."

"I think I want to enjoy the bottle, if you know what I mean," Lane says. A scuff of shoe on cracked asphalt announces Eben's return, and Lane calls over to him: "Hey, hobo, you got a bottle of anything around here?"

Eben sniffs. "I got my own brand of lullaby right here." He holds up a brown jug. Something splashes around inside of it. "Bottle of rotgut fixy." He pats the jug and hands it off to Lane, who takes a long pull and comes away wincing and clearing his throat.

"That's like drinking"—Lane hacks into his fist—"like drinking motorvator fuel."

He passes the bottle to Rigo, who takes a swig and spits it out—right into the burn barrel. The fire flares up, vengeful, and Rigo yelps like a startled puppy. Cael can't help it; he starts cracking up, and soon Lane follows. Even Eben chuckles, a shoulder-shaking *huh huh huh.*

"That's the worst thing ever," Rigo says, looking stung. "You guys, seriously, it was really gross."

Cael reaches for the jug, takes a turn. It's like swallowing piss-soaked razors. The jagged glass slides all the way down his throat and into his belly, but once there a wave of heat radiates outward, filling him with a pleasant warmth. "That's a real horse kick," he says, voice raw.

He hands off the jug to Eben, who takes a swig.

"I make it myself," he says. "It does the trick." His eyes rove over them, flashing in the firelight. "I'm hungry. What's in the bag?"

Seems pushy, Cael thinks, *but that's all right.* They told him they'd share, so they'll share. Rigo starts pulling the last of their vegetables: a bulbous sweet potato, another grub-white parsnip, a few stubby, fat-bellied carrots. Eben whistles.

"Don't see vittles like that much," he says.

They all pause, a collective hesitation. Cael fumbles around for an explanation. "We, ah, we have a little garden on the side."

"Root veggies grow well in hard soil," Lane says, lying.

Rigo just buttons up and stares, visibly nervous.

Eben shrugs. "I don't care where you got 'em. Food is food. Like the saying goes, You don't pick fleas off a shuck rat."

He wanders away, and Lane looks to Cael and mutters, "Actually, I'd pick fleas off a shuck rat." Cael shrugs and says, "Shoot, me too."

Isn't long before Eben comes back with a couple pieces of wire that they use to spear the vegetables and hold them over the barrel, slowly turning them so that the vegetables grow dark from the fire's kiss. He pulls out a couple strips of rat jerky, too— it's hard and salty and tastes like it's just this side of gone south, but it goes okay with the sweet char of the vegetables, and once they all start getting enough fixy in their bellies, nothing tastes like much anymore.

Soon they're telling stories—Lane talks about the time he stole what he thought was chicha beer from Busser's but it ended up being mop water ("I drank the whole damn thing, too, wondering why I wasn't getting drunk!") and how he threw up for hours after. Rigo talks about that time he got chased around by one of Bende Cartwright's goats, but that story ends on a down note when Rigo mentions what his father did to him after. ("He locked me in the shed for the night because he said no son of his was scared of no goat.") Cael talks about the first time he and Gwennie were fooling around, how they found a space in the attic of her house and how her little brother, Scooter, caught them with their shirts off, pawing at each other like clumsy bears. ("That poor kid cried for a week!") And that gets everybody laughing again, and they're all drunk, and Cael can't see straight—he can feel his teeth but not his lips; his hands are like numb mitts; his toes are soft clay-blobs in his ragged boots.

He takes note that whenever they pass the jug to the hobo he doesn't take too big a swig, and when Cael finally asks, Eben shrugs and says, "Got to be clear for my boy."

That's when Cael asks him, "The mother's not around anymore?"

"She died" is all he says, and for a moment his face sags with sadness as he looks into the fire.

But just then the baby starts crying again, making that hitching, stitching cry that ramps up fast to hunger or irritation or whatever it is that upsets a baby in this dead and empty place.

Eben starts to get up but then looks at Rigo and says, "You—Little Brown Mouse. Go check on the boy."

"Me?" Rigo asks, flummoxed. He hasn't been drinking like the other two, not as much anyway, so Cael gives Rigo a shove.

"Go help the man out. He *did* fish your butt out of the slurry." Speaking of slurry, he can hear his own words running together, mushy like mashed peas. "Least you can do is go . . . do whatever that baby needs."

"Probably needs a burping," Eben says. "Pick him up, pat his back."

Rigo stands, laughing, saying, "Okay, okay," but then a horrified look crosses his face. "What if he's got . . ." Rigo points to the back of his pants.

"Shit in his britches?" Eben says, and that makes Cael and Lane whoop with laughter. "For the sake of Old Scratch, what do you think? If his wrapping's fouled, Little Mouse, change it."

"Sure, sure," Rigo says, and then scurries off like, well . . . just like a little mouse.

Cael and Lane both keep laughing until their guffaws kind of . . . lose steam, like a motorvator slowly powering down. Eben comes up behind them, taking the jug and then circling back around to the far side of the barrel. He looks over both of them, his black eyes catching the dancing firelight, and he says with a flinty smile, "You know the Rovers aren't real, don't you?"

LOST AT SEA

GWENNIE HEARS ANNALISE calling for her. But she's already marching forward, ducking into the crowd and around it, peering over it, crawling through it, and it's then that the party reminds her of being out in the Heartland on the boat, over the corn. Lost with no sense of bearings. The horizon a meaningless guide.

Here it's a sea of strange faces. Weird clothing. Some hands reach for her; others step away, giving her curious, even frightened looks. As if she's a savage hobo plucked from the hardscrabble.

Merelda. I need to find Merelda.

But all around her, a dizzying array of sights and sounds that only serves to distract and confuse—

That woman in a corn maiden costume. A headdress of corn husks. A bra of pointed cob-tips. Showing off for a small crowd.

Beyond her: a giant clock face, except it's made mostly of *people*. Humans in black bodysuits. Forming hands and numbers each. Are they slaves? Artists? Both? She doesn't know and can't care.

Gwennie nearly staggers into a trio of androgynes in flamboyant costumes that call to mind living firework displays, who all stand over a single musical instrument: a giant brass thing with a bell at the one end and a series of levers and plungers and bladders at the other, the whole thing bleating a discordant warble-and-honk. They give her a look, and she pirouettes past, feeling like a tin can spinning—

Her shoulder catches a tray of drinks carried by a Bartender-Bot, and it flips end over end. Fluted glasses topple and shatter. Foam hisses beneath her feet; the Bartender-Bot makes a disappointed noise from its speaker ("*Ohhhhhhhh*"); and a hatch opens at the base of the auto-mate, and many-hinged spider arms begin scooping the mess into his body.

But there—*there!*

Merelda again. A flash of ravensblack hair.

Annalise sees her. "Gwendolyn Shawcatch! You're jumping the line!"

Damnit. Gwennie presses her hands together and uses it as a wedge to separate a couple lapping at each other's mouths like thirsty dogs and winds after Merelda—

Cael's sister looks over her shoulder, sees Gwennie following. She makes a panicked face and darts right through a gauntlet of partiers holding visidexes—they all look at their screens and not at one another, tapping and swiping and laughing. As Gwennie shoots through them, they erupt in some triumph she doesn't understand, arms raised: "Wooooo!"

Merelda. Only ten feet ahead.

But someone steps suddenly in front of Gwennie.

It's another Heartlander.

That's her first thought. Because of the clothes. A simple flowered dress with a crocheted collar. Wooden shoes with raised heels. Hair in a simple braided ring—white baby's breath flowers throughout.

But something's off. The lipstick—the color of pulped cherries. Or the eyeliner, so thick and dark it might as well have been slapped on with a paintbrush. The woman beams and grabs Gwennie by the shoulders even as Gwennie tries to get past her—

"How do I look?" the woman asks.

"Wh . . . what? You look fine."

"No, no, I mean, how *authentic* do I look?" The woman lets go and does a twirl. "Humble-drab will be all the rage; just you watch—I really tried to express the plain-folk ennui, but I worry the flowers in the hair go against that and the style—"

Gwennie smiles the biggest fake smile. "You look perfect!"

Not far behind: Annalise. Cutting through the crowd like a knife.

As the fake-Heartlander is beaming, Gwennie shoves past her.

"Hey!" the woman calls after her. "Ow."

Again Merelda's gone. Melded with the crowd—

Except, no. She's above the crowd now. Gwennie sees a set of steps—glass like the rest of the balcony, and again she's reminded that the whole world now sits below her, a world slowly drenched in the darkness of the coming night. Those steps ascend to a balcony (where, of course, more people stand packed shoulder to shoulder like squealers in a pig chute).

On the steps. No one else is there. Perfect place to catch her.

Gwennie throws caution and propriety to the wind and darts through the crowd, shoes clicking on the glass balcony.

Merelda looks over the crowd, pausing halfway up the steps. She's searching the wrong places, because already Gwennie is charging up behind her. Merelda sees, tries to hurry away—

But Gwennie catches her arm.

"You," Gwennie says.

The two of them share a moment of silence. Looking each other over. In Merelda's face Gwennie sees the absurdity of the situation reflected back: two Heartlander girls from the same town and connected to the same boy standing face-to-face on an Empyrean flotilla. It's like something out of a dream.

Or maybe, Gwennie thinks, *a really weird nightmare.*

Merelda's about to say something—

When another hand grabs Merelda's arm.

The arm belongs to a pale man. High cheekbones. Hair so blond it might as well be white. Everything about him is sharp angles: the shoulders and elbows of his silver-skin suit, the long dagger nose, the tips of his pointed fingernails. Even his lips look as if they're cut out of pink paper with a few spare clips from a pair of scissors.

"My love," he says. Then he kisses Merelda on the cheek. He stares at Gwennie, and she feels as if his gaze is dissecting her, cutting her apart for purposes of examination. "You are the Shawcatch girl."

"I . . ."

Behind her: footsteps clicking up the glass steps.

Annalise locks her in an incredulous stare.

"Girl! So impudent. *So impatient.* You can't just . . . bypass all these people! It's an art, *an art*, like a . . . a butterfly flitting from flower to flower. Collecting a dusting of pollen before—"

The man with the white-blond hair interrupts: "I think it will be fine, Miss Annalise. Let the throngs think her a wild girl plucked from the corn. It'll be gossip fodder for weeks."

"Well. Yes. I suppose—"

"Certainly we are the ones who set the rules, are we not?"

She smiles. And laughs. "Of course. *Of course!*"

"Then come, Miss Shawcatch. Time to join the *real* party."

THE JAW TRAP

RIGO CREEPS INTO the dark of the building, his ears filled with the sound of a yowling infant. It's not a house but a storefront. Or it was. It's hard to see anything, but through the torn-up roof, shafts of moonlight lean like spears thrown from far away. Rigo can make out shelves bracketed to the wall and also freestanding shelves in the middle of the room, suggesting this was a provisional store: just a few goods here and there, some for sale, most earned by Heartlanders as payment for work. The goods that stocked these shelves would've come from the Provisional Depot nearby—the very place where they're hoping to catch a ride up into the sky.

The baby cries, an insistent wail that sets Rigo's teeth on edge. It sounds wrong somehow—maybe the baby is sick. Babies get sick and die all the time out here. Sometimes they're born too early like the Blaymire's little girl—she lived, but now, three

years later, she's still a frail thing with matchstick legs and bulging eyes. But Eben didn't say anything about his baby being sick, and that's something he would've mentioned, right?

Rigo winds his way around one shelf and sees what he thinks is the crib in the middle of the floor, but the room is dark, and he's afraid to be fumbling around a tiny baby without seeing what he's doing. On the other side of the room he sees a faint glow: a light source of some kind. Rigo takes a few quick steps, and there on the counter is a visidex lying flat, screen up toward the ceiling. It's the screen that's giving off the light.

A visidex, he thinks. *Heartlanders aren't allowed to have those.* Another image suddenly flashes in his mind: the lighter with the Pegasus sigil emblazoned on it. A fear tickles at the base of his mind.

Rigo reaches for the visidex.

As he picks it up, the light from the device washes over the back wall behind the counter, and Rigo sees the sign: WHEATLEY PROVISIONAL STORE.

Wheatley. Lord and Lady, that's where Lane told the hobo they were from. Is *this* town Wheatley? Rigo tilts the visidex toward him.

His heart leaps into his throat and lodges itself there like a frog caught in a cat's mouth.

On the visidex is his face. And Cael's. And Lane's.

It's a Most Wanted alert. Words pop out at him from the screen: *terrorists* and *sedition* and *dangerous*. Then the image flips and becomes a different alert, this time for Arthur "Pop" McAvoy and Filomena McAvoy. Same words. Same alert. This time with an added text in big bold letters at the bottom: **DEAD OR ALIVE**.

"Wait, what?" Cael asks, trying to cut through the gauze of his own drunkenness to understand what the hobo is getting at. "Rovers?"

Eben leans in, face framed from beneath by the fire. "The dogs. The packs of dogs I was telling you about. They're not real. Not around here anyway. Haven't been Rovers seen around here. Not ever."

"Oh," Lane says, laughing it off, drunk and obviously bewildered. "Yeah, right. So?"

"And that tree, in the center of Wheatley?" the hobo asks.

"The . . . lightning tree," Cael says.

"You see a tree around here?"

Cael joins Lane in laughing, but now it's just the sound of his nerves jangling, because something's gone off-kilter here, dipping and swaying in a way he can't quite get his hands around yet.

"I don't . . . I don't see a tree," Cael says, and he's about to ask what the vagrant is getting at, but he catches the cold look on Eben's face—a look of ill-contained rage, of hate trying to push its way out, stretching his mouth into a grim, flat line—and he realizes what's going on. "This is Wheatley."

Lane keeps laughing. He doesn't get it, not at all. "This isn't Wheatley; this is—" He suddenly goes silent. "Wait, what town is this?"

"Wheatley's a dead town," Eben mutters. "And you're sitting in it."

"I . . . ," Lane stammers. "I don't understand."

"He's been playing with us," Cael says. *Like we're little mice.*

Then Eben drops a real firecracker, saying, "I knew your father, Cael. I knew Arthur McAvoy."

Everything feels hot and tense, and Rigo breaks out in a fast sweat on his hands, under his pits, and it feels as if someone crammed his heart and all his innards into a tin pail and threw it down a bumpy hill.

If this is Wheatley and if Eben knows who they are . . . he's an Empyrean agent. A *secret* agent. He must be. Or he's planning on selling them out to the Empyrean. One way or another, they're in deep.

Rigo tries to call out but finds his throat dry and the crying of the baby growing louder and louder, and he thinks, *I need to hush that baby,* and the stranger thought that comes after is *This isn't a place for a baby. I need to take it away from here and keep it safe*—so he grabs the visidex and tilts it forward to give him some light, and he hurries toward the crib.

The crib is a ramshackle thing, something someone made out of old chair legs and a few wooden pallets. Inside it is a bundle of ratty brown blankets, the edges fraying and tattered. The sound of the crying baby is harsh to his ears, reedy, and Rigo, he reaches down and pulls back the blanket, and he thinks, *It sounds almost metallic*—

Oh, Lord and Lady.

It's no baby.

A dead dog stares up from the crib, its dry, puckered-grape eyeballs staring out from their sockets, lips peeled back over gums that look like jerky, teeth yellow and crooked.

Around its neck hangs a little box with a speaker on it. A small wire antenna winds from the box and up the side of the crib.

Rigo rips the box from the wires. The crying dies down, the sound slowing in a way that suggests melting.

Oh no oh no oh no.

He turns to run out of here, this time ducking between two shelves right for the doorway—

His foot lands on something—

He feels something give. Pressure. Followed by a *click.*

A rusty jaw trap snaps shut on his ankle.

Hot fire lances up from his foot. Blood runs into his shoe as he tumbles forward, the teeth of the trap scraping flesh from bone.

Rigo screams.

Eben reaches into his dirty overalls and pulls a long, makeshift knife—the steel blade showing the clumsy scratches of an amateur's forging and whetting, the handle swaddled in strips of raggedy leather. The hobo shows his teeth—teeth so clean, so white, they gleam and glow in the light of the licking flames.

Cael reaches for his slingshot—

But the vagrant holds it up. "Looking for this?"

He tosses it over his shoulder into the darkness.

And the rifle—

It's over by the man, too. Along with the bag.

Eben circles toward them.

Cael and Lane go the other way—but as soon as they get near the rifle and the bag, Eben moves back in the other direction. Swiping the blade through the air, cutting it with brutal hisses.

"Who are you?" Cael asks.

"Name's true as I've told it. Eben Henry is my name." He snarls, again slicing the blade across the fire. "Your father and I go way back."

"What do you want?"

"Justice."

"I can't give you that."

"You can't give it. But I can *take* it." Madness dances in his eyes. "I can *cut it from your pretty skin*, boy."

Lane says, "I don't know what you think you know—"

"I know I need to take what's owed to me. Like the chronicles of Jeezum Crow say, 'I have found that the justice must match the injury, bone for bone, tooth for tooth, blood for blood.'" The man's knuckles begin to go white around the hilt of the knife. "I want your blood. The blood of Cael McAvoy to pay for the blood of my boy, Arthur Henry. I want your blood, your teeth, your eyes. I'm gonna take what was taken; I'm gonna—"

From inside the darkened building nearby they hear the child's cry cut suddenly short. Eben chuckles, and only moments later do they hear Rigo's spit-curdling scream—an animal sound of grave pain.

"Rigo!" Lane calls, and he makes a break away from the barrel.

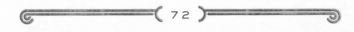

Eben lunges with the knife, a long stride into a mean leap, and Cael gets asphalt under his feet and crashes into him. His head swims; his body feels slow like it's stuck in a puddle of molasses—the impact of his body into Eben's and the *sensation* of that impact are disconnected, as if he's feeling everything a half second too late.

And it costs him. As the two of them tumble to the ground, Eben gets the advantage. He pushes Cael aside and holds him down, his filthy denim knees pinning Cael's shoulders to the shattered street.

"This is for my son," Eben growls.

He raises the knife and slams the blade down.

Rigo lays facedown on the dusty wooden floor of the old provisional store. He reaches out with both hands and gets his fingertips around the break in the floorboards and tries to pull himself up, but even the slightest movement sends lightning bolts of pain blasting to and from his trapped ankle.

He winces; one of his fingernails snaps. He cries out again, reeling in his arm and tucking it under his armpit. *Don't cry,* he thinks, *damnit, don't cry,* but already he feels the hot tears pushing at the corners of his eyes, and it's like a dam starts to break. Everything hits him at once: the loss of his town, his family, his home; the scene of carnage back at the McAvoy farm only a week ago—all of it culminating in the grim revelation that *It's all over; I'll never be the same; I'm going to die out here.*

Footsteps heavy on the floor—Rigo looks up, expects to see the leering vagrant or whoever the hell he really is, but instead

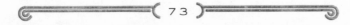

he sees Lane's face, a face forge-struck in horror. Lane bends down and scoops his hands around Rigo's midsection and starts to lift him—

"No no no!" Rigo cries out. "My ankle, my damn ankle!"

"Holy shit," Lane says. He hurries to Rigo's feet, gets his fingers between the rusty, monster teeth of the jaw trap. Lane struggles and grunts, the cords in his lean neck standing taut as he wrenches open the trap. He mutters, "Not yet . . . not yet . . . move your foot *now*."

Rigo grabs his own thigh and yanks his leg—a leg already starting to feel numb and cold—and his foot and ankle pull free from the trap.

Blood drips on the wood.

"Is Cael . . . ?"

"I don't know," Lane says, breathless. "You okay?"

Rigo tries not to whimper. He nods.

"Good."

And then Lane bolts back outside.

The knife slams down just as Cael wrenches his head to the left—the blade *chink*s against the broken blacktop, sending up sparks. Eben roars in rage and raises the knife once more—

Cael has a move planned out in his head: he'll fling his hips upward and swing both legs with them, hoping to hook his ankles around the vagrant's neck in order to pull the bastard off him. Instead, Cael's limbs flail upward, and the tip of his boot connects clumsily with the side of Eben's skull—not the maneuver

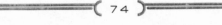

he'd hoped, but the hobo falls to the side, giving Cael the chance to wriggle free.

Both Cael and Eben hurry to their feet.

Eben quotes again from the books of Jeezum Crow, snarling each word through clenched teeth: "'The Lord and Lady, gracious patron and glorious matron, slow to anger, quick to love, know yet that the hearts of sinners must be fixed with pins'"—here he stabs the open air with the knife—"'and if a father escapes his toll, the children must pay the pennies.'"

The hobo lunges again—

Cael sidesteps, swings a fist—

It's a worthless, desperate punch. Eben doesn't duck but rather slaps it aside like it's an irritating fly. The vagrant flicks the knife upward, and Cael feels a burning slash across his chin.

He stumbles backward. Something wet splashes down his neck. He touches his hand to his chin—it comes away smeared with red.

The vagabond flips the knife so it's pointing downward, blade tucked back against his forearm, and again he lunges—

It's Lane's turn to intercept. He races behind Cael and slams up and under Eben. The hobo lurches with the hit but doesn't fall—Eben plunges the knife, but Lane is lithe, almost liquid, and he twists his body out of the way—

The vagrant isn't fast, but he is strong.

He picks up Lane and throws him aside.

Lane's head slams into the burn barrel. A whorl of embers rise, a demonic fireworks display. He doubles over, pressing his head into his knees. Eben moves toward him, knife out—

Cael has to move fast. The rifle lies on the ground nearby; it's not loaded, but it'll have to do. He rushes, scoops up the rifle, and holds it by the barrel. The vagrant descends upon Lane with the blade—

He sees Cael coming.

But it's too late.

Cael wallops him in the cheek with the butt end of the rifle. The wood cracks and splits as Eben drops to the ground by the barrel, knife still clutched in his bloodless grip.

Move fast before he gets up.

Cael shoves the burn barrel.

Away from Lane.

And toward the vagrant.

The rusty drum vomits burning trash onto Eben Henry. Hot orange ash forms a mask on the man's face—he shrieks, a ghastly sound that rises up and out of him like the howling of a rabid wolf, and he thrashes around on the ground, clawing at his face, kicking at the broken street.

Cael helps Lane up. "We have to *go*. Where's Rigo?"

"Here," croaks Rigo, hobbling out. Blood trails him. His face is the color of spoiled goat's milk. Cael scoops up the bag and slings the rifle over his shoulder as Lane runs to Rigo. Cael follows soon after, and as he hurries over—the sound of the screaming vagrant filling the air behind him—his boot nudges something.

His slingshot.

He grabs it, tucks it into his back pocket.

And together the three of them hurry-hobble into the hungry corn.

THE PRAETOR
AND THE PEREGRINE

MERELDA'S STARE GIVES Gwennie all the information she needs to know: the look is equal parts panicked and paranoid, with a tinge of rebuke. It says:

We don't know each other.

Gwennie learned long ago that if you can't suss out the situation, you should listen first, talk second. Cael was always the opposite: jabbering and giving up the ghost at the earliest opportunity. It's why he was a terrible card player (which got him naked pretty fast, she remembers). The boy could talk his way into a tightening noose without even realizing it. And Boyland was no better: brash and cocky, thinking he knew everything so there was no reason to hold anything back.

Boys, it turned out, are sometimes dumb as dirt.

But Gwennie pays heed to Merelda's look and stays quiet.

Before she realizes what's happening she's whisked up to the top of a balcony, its edge underlit with flickering firefly lights.

The only thing preventing anybody from tumbling off into the crowd on one side or off the edge of the flotilla on the other is a delicate banister made to look like a flock of birds taking flight. Again Gwennie feels the fear of falling—vertigo strikes, and her pulse starts to kick like a rabbit scratching its belly. *For the love of the Lord and the laurels of the Lady, do not throw up.*

Suddenly she's thrust forward by Annalise—a gentle but urgent shove.

There stands a trio of people wreathed in velvet smoke.

On the one side, a masculine-looking woman with short, dark hair and skin the color of creamed coffee. She looks at Gwennie with an unwavering glare. This woman's stare is a smashing hammer, and Gwennie feels her pieces broken and examined with swift, merciless dismissal. The woman's jaw tightens, and her brow furrows until she sees Annalise—then her face softens like warm butter in a hot pan. The two of them come together, and the praetor pulls Annalise's face toward her own and plants a hard kiss on the woman's cheek.

The man in the silver-skin suit says, "This is the praetor, Ashland Garriott. She oversees all the day-to-day functions of the Ormond Stirling Saranyu." *The praetor is a woman*, Gwennie thinks. *Did not see that coming.* "And this—"

He gestures deferentially toward the older man in the middle, a man smoking a long, thin, porcelain pipe.

"This is Stirling Ormond, Grand Architect of our flotilla."

The man mumbles an acknowledgment and uses the finger and thumb of his one hand to smooth the wiry white hairs of his mustache and chin-beard. He cocks his head toward the third and final person of the trio, a woman far younger than he but still showing age in the way her blond hair is going ashy and how the lines around her mouth and eyes deepen as she smiles. "This is my wife. Karya."

Karya beams at Gwennie, grabbing her hand and shaking it furiously. As she does so, a set of breasts far too large and round shimmy and quake behind the woman's apple-red dress.

"It is an honor to meet one of our Heartland brethren," Karya says, her voice breathy—an almost squeaky whisper.

"Quiet, Karya," the architect mutters. "You're embarrassing yourself."

The man with the snow-blond hair turns and puts a cold hand on Gwennie's bare shoulder. "I'm the peregrine, Percy Lemaire-Laurent."

"The peregrine . . . ," Gwennie says. She has no idea what that is.

"I'm the right-hand man to the praetor."

The praetor speaks up. "Pish. Not at all true. I have assistants for that. Percy is the law around here. Every flotilla has a peregrine. Though perhaps none as effective as ours."

The peregrine laughs and casts his gaze downward: an expression of humility, though Gwennie can't tell if it's genuine. "You honor me with such kind words, Praetor."

Gwennie turns suddenly toward Merelda. "And you are . . ."

Merelda freezes as if caught in a beam of harsh light.

"Of course," the peregrine says. "This is my house-mistress. La Mer."

"It means 'the sea,'" Merelda says. She extends a trembling hand. Afraid that Gwennie will ruin it all for her? "It is a pleasure to meet you, Heartlander."

"And you," Gwennie says, hearing the coldness in her own voice. "Skylander." It's not a word they use, clearly, because they all chuckle a little, but she doesn't care and can barely hear their dismissive chortles, because all she's thinking is:

Traitor. She's a traitor to her own people. A traitor to the land. Godsdamn you, Merelda McAvoy. Godsdamn you into the arms of Old Scratch.

Three glasses of bubbly in quick succession and already Balastair is feeling it. His stomach flutters. His head drifts. He turns to flag down another Bartender-Bot, and just as he's trying to suppress a little burp, he runs face-first into Eldon Planck.

"Hello, Balastair."

Balastair holds a fist against his lips and ill suppresses the burp. "Eldon. I was going to come and say hello."

"Of course you were."

Eldon smiles that cruel, handsome smile.

Erasmus whistles and says, "Uh-oh!"

The smoke rising from the architect's pipe is acrid and skunky; it stings Gwennie's nose and brings water to her eyes. Whatever it is, it's softening the man's eyelids and making his mouth droop more than a little. He keeps making this wet, plying sound with his mouth: *smack smack smack.* Occasionally he jolts back to awareness.

For her part, Gwennie can't escape the attentions of the architect's wife, Karya. That woman keeps drinking and pushing

closer and closer against her—Gwennie first thinks it's not out of lust but rather some mad, sodden fascination, as if she's a strange object or an odd animal. The woman's hand falls to Gwennie's knee, and she keeps leaning in, boozy breath washing over them both in waves. And suddenly Gwennie isn't so sure.

"What are you drinking?" Karya asks, and before Gwennie can answer, the woman says, "I'm drinking a Gee-Whiz," and shakes a tall, slim glass of something unnaturally blue. It splashes on the woman's own knee.

Gwennie's about to say that she's not drinking anything, but then Annalise flits along (butterfly pollinating flowers) and places a drink in her hand. "A Tuxedo Tassel," Annalise says. "As ordered before you . . . hurried off." And then she's gone again, once more joining the praetor and a crowd of other hoity-toity types whom Gwennie can't possibly relate to or understand on even the barest human level.

She takes a sip of the Tuxedo Tassel and finds it awful. As if she's drinking an old tree. A piece of something—skin from some kind of fruit maybe—collects on her teeth, and she suddenly feels very awkward trying to pull it off.

"Let me," Karya says, reaching in with too-long, bloodred fingernails to pluck it free from Gwennie's teeth. Like a bird picking seed. Then her hand falls to Gwennie's knee again and gives it a squeeze, the fingers doing a drunken waltz up toward her thigh—

Gwennie coughs, clears her throat, and stands up suddenly.

"I need some air," she says, and quickly shoulders her way through the small balcony crowd toward the banister.

Wind sweeps over her.

She feels loose, unmoored, as if she might fly away at any moment. A fluffy seed from a ruptured pod cast skyward.

Out beyond the balcony is the Heartland. A black blanket with a few pinpricks of light—towns maybe, or processing plants. Motorvators performing their tireless chores through the corn. The land below is black. The sky above is lit by a panoply of stars.

Someone comes up behind her. A hand at the small of her back. A jab of fear sticks her along with, she has to admit, a weird worm-turn of excitement in the deep of her belly as she thinks it might be Balastair—

But it's the peregrine who speaks.

"Karya's a flighty one," Percy says. "Is she bothering you?"

"No. Ah. It's— No, she's fine."

"You Heartlanders are modest people. Simple folk."

She's not sure if he's being plainspoken or if he's insulting her, but she nods anyway. "That sounds about right."

"Are you enjoying your time here?"

"It's fine," she says, hearing the strain in her own voice.

His hand remains at the small of her back. She can feel the cold of his palm through the dress.

"You're under Balastair Harrington's care."

"I am."

"A smart man. How goes the Pegasus Project?"

I'm cleaning up lots of Pegasus shit, if that's what you want to know. "Great. I guess. I wouldn't know; I'm just simple folk."

"You seem a tad hostile."

"I'm not good at small talk."

"Of course. Heartlanders like to be direct."

"We're not all one person who likes one thing," she snaps.

"Yet I'll do you the favor of assuming *you* like things to be direct. As a further favor, I'll be clear: I know that you know her."

Her. "Merelda."

"La Mer, if you please. It means 'the sea.'"

"Yes, she said that. And I *do* know her."

His hand leaves her back, and he comes up next to her, and she realizes then how tall he really is—his elbow almost touches her shoulder. He leans forward and begins talking, never once looking at her, always keeping his gaze fixed on the darkness of the Heartland below.

"Correction: you don't know her," he says. "You think you do, but you don't. She isn't a Heartlander. She's from another flotilla. A flotilla far away, toward the coast." *The coast?* she thinks. "Stay away from her, and all will be well. In fact, if you—"

Gwennie narrows her eyes. "You're the law, right? Might complicate your job if I told them who she really was. Might mess with this nice thing you got going."

"See, I was about to offer you a taste of honey, and you have to go and pour vinegar all over it." He sighs. "Let me revise my sentiment. You tell them what you know, they'll give me a slap on the wrist. I'm too entrenched in my work. The praetor likes what I do and will forgive my dalliance as just that: the sins of the flesh taken hold. But what will happen then is they'll take your friend Merelda, and they'll march her to the end of a gangplank, and they'll push her off it. Maybe with a noose around her neck so she dangles, or maybe just so she plummets all the way down to the dry and dusty fundament you call the Heartland."

"You sonofab—"

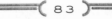

"—I'm not finished. What will come *next* is, I will be very distraught and blinded by anger, and I will go and find your mother, your father, and your little brother. I'll hurt them very badly. I'll hurt them personally if I can manage the privilege, claiming I caught them in . . . some act of sedition, some madness deserving the mercy of my pistol. Do you understand? Then I'll make you identify the bodies just so you see how they suffered."

"You're a monster."

"I'm merely protective, as I'm sure you are of the things you hold dear. Which is why I know you'll do the smart thing and keep quiet. I have a wife and two beautiful sons, and they all know that I am deeply in love with La Mer and that I take my job very seriously, and I'll not have some scrubby callus-hand from the corn-blasted below threaten that."

The wind grows suddenly cold.

Gwennie cannot suppress the shiver.

"Are we clear?" he asks.

"We are," she says, barely finding her voice.

"Excellent. I'm going to tell them you're not feeling well. Go find Balastair and have him take you home."

He reaches up and touches her arm.

"You look very pretty," he says. "You clean up nice."

Then he's gone, and she dry heaves over the side of the balcony.

Flustered, feeling as if she can't catch her breath, Gwennie finds Balastair standing face-to-face with some other Empyrean, an older man whose looks hover somewhere between dapper and

rugged. Next to that man stands a young woman—pretty, a streak of silver shot through ruddy-red hair. Gwennie comes up and tugs on his arm, and she's about to tell him it's time to go, but they seem in the middle of a conversation—

"You're really quite bitter," the older man says to Balastair. "A few glasses of bubbly and you fall to pieces. Unlike my automates, of course. You've heard of the Initiative, have you? Down there in the Heartland?"

"The who now? The what?" Balastair looks flummoxed. Erasmus chirps and burbles on his shoulder.

"Ah. Well. I daren't split my lips to spill news that isn't mine to spill. But this Pegasus thing is really just a drop in the bucket. We'll be airborne by the end of the week and . . . you can go back to your lab. Isn't that where you want to be? Back doing *real* work? If they'll let you, of course." He takes another sip. "After failing to create a true Pegasus to embody the Empyrean ideals, a living sigil to demonstrate the pride of the heavens. Failure is like honey, Balastair—it's really quite sticky."

"*You're* sticky," Balastair hisses, what Gwennie assumes is a nonsense insult that comes plopping out of his fool's mouth.

"Sticky!" Erasmus echoes.

The other man just laughs.

Then he turns his gaze toward Gwennie.

"This is your . . . charge," he says, swishing his drink around the bell of his glass. "Your *ward* of the flotilla. How interesting. Heartland girl, is she?"

"I'm right here," Gwennie says. "I can *hear* you."

"Gwennie," Balastair says, and she hears the droopy slur in his voice as he gesticulates with a sloshing glass of something

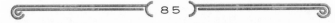

pink and bubbly. "This is Eldon Planck, the men behind the mechanical man—er, the *man* behind the mechanical *men*, and that there, the woman *right there*, is his lovely wife. His new wife. *Cleo* Planck."

"Great," Gwennie says. "We seriously need to get the hell—" She pauses and looks at the woman. "Cleo?"

"That's right," the woman says.

Gwennie takes Balastair's glass from him and splashes the drink in her face.

All around her are gasps and mumbles followed by a swift silence.

She feels a hundred pairs of eyes on her.

Damnit.

Gwennie can see the raised balcony and the persecuting glares of those truly elite members of the flotilla: the praetor, the peregrine, the architect, and yes, Merelda McAvoy. *La Mer.*

Eldon Planck grabs her wrist and twists.

"You little bitch," he says. "Throwing a drink in the face of my wife—just because you get on your knees for this fool—" He lifts his chin to indicate Balastair, but before he can say anything else, Balastair throws a wonky punch into his chops. Eldon staggers back, looking shocked more than anything else. Erasmus cackles.

"Be nice to her!" Balastair roars, and by now they've *truly* drawn the attention of everyone. Even the trumpeting *oompah*s of the strange brass instrument have stopped short.

"Your end comes soon," Eldon hisses, leaning in and waggling a finger. "I've almost completed my Pegasus. And the Initiative will begin soon, and with it you'll be marginalized into a corner where you can drink and sob and stick it to your earth girl all the livelong day."

Balastair grabs Gwennie's arm and begins pulling her away, hurrying toward the exit. As they flee, she hears Eldon calling after them: "Your end is soon, Balastair Harrington! *Soon!*"

THIRSTY STALKS

THE THREE BOYS hunker down toward the bracer roots of the tall stalks, Rigo lying flat on his belly, the other two hunched over and shoulder to shoulder. Down this far it's hard for the corn to seek out their injuries, though the stalks creak and strain, leaves licking the air, looking for a taste of their blood.

They've been hiding here in the corn for the better part of the night.

And now the sun's coming up. Fingers of light push away the night's stubborn darkness. As the light finds them, they can finally see the extent of their injures.

The side of Lane's head is scraped up—red and raw with flecks of rust from the barrel stuck in the skin. Cael apologizes in advance and starts picking metal out. Lane winces, sucking in air.

Cael's own chin-cut has crusted over; every time he talks or frowns, it tugs at the scab, and he feels it run fresh and wet.

But it's Rigo they're worried about.

The jaw trap did a number on his ankle.

"Maybe it looks worse than it is," Cael says. "Like with Lane." But they all know that can't be true. The ankle is bloody—the skin and what little meat the ankle has to offer is torn up. His socks are soaked through. Blood has pooled sticky in his boot.

Sometimes when Rigo moves, Cael thinks he spies bone.

"I can't really feel it," Rigo says. "That's a good thing, right?" Cael and Lane look at each other. Together they lie.

"A real good thing," Lane says.

"That's how you know you're healing," Cael adds.

"That guy was crazy," Rigo says, his face still a pot of ash. "I thought he was Empyrean, you know?"

"Shitfire," Cael says, "I don't think he was Empyrean. I think he was a . . . crazy coot hobo who had some made-up ideas in his head."

"He seemed to know Pop," Lane says.

"Maybe he did. Maybe he worked for Pop at Martha's Bend with the other tramps."

"That doesn't explain why he was so cranked up about it."

"Damn, he sure was. Something about his son—he said his son was named Arthur but then . . . Rigo, you said in the crib . . ."

"That wasn't a baby in there. That was a dead dog."

"Godsdamn," Lane says.

"Gods*damn* is right." Cael shakes his head. "I hope that fire did a number on him, and he's not out here hunting us. Because we gotta get back on those tracks and keep moving."

Lane begins rolling a cigarette, tucking a little bindle of ditchweed into the paper and licking the edge to seal it. "Those tracks are gonna be the first place he comes looking, Cael. If he finds us—"

"He finds us, I put a dang bullet in his heart and in his head, and we move on. We owe him that much anyway since he tried to, oh, you know, *kill us* and all." Cael can hear the angry bravado coming out of his mouth. The others are nodding along as if they believe it. But right now he doesn't want to think about killing anybody. The hobo's scream as his face caught fire is still echoing around in the dark of his mind. Goose pimples rise up on his arms along with the hairs on his neck. Not the good kind, the kind where Gwennie is running her fingers along his arm or back, but the kind where you get a sense of how death dogs your every step out here.

"You think I can walk?" Rigo asks.

"We'll help you along," Cael says.

Lane cocks an eyebrow. "Though if I'd have known we'd be helping to carry you, I woulda said to lose some weight before we went on this little vacation. Even after a week of being hungry all the time, you're still shaped like an overstuffed tamale."

"Hey, shut up! I've got big bones."

"Sure, and I'm not tall—there's just two of me stacked one on top of the other." Lane strikes a match, lights the cigarette, and as Cael gives him a look, he shrugs and whispers, "Just trying to make everything feel like usual." Then he says to Rigo, "C'mon, tamale."

They both help Rigo stand.

Rigo cries out, and they hush him.

Then, underneath Rigo's belly, they see something:

It's a visidex.

"What the—" Lane asks. "That what I think it is?"

Rigo looks down. "Oh, Jeezum, yeah. Eben had it, and I took it. When we ran, I stuffed it down my pants, and with my leg and all I kinda stopped thinking about it."

"We have a visidex," Cael says, laughing. "A real one, a working one. We can use this. I'm sure of it."

"How do you think he got it?" Rigo asks. "The hobo."

"Same way he got the lighter," Lane says, blowing smoke. "He killed someone. Took it from them. You see that knife? He's a killer; that's what he does."

Cael takes the visidex, sees the screen light up as soon as he brushes it, almost as if he woke it up. On the screen is Pop's face. And Mom's. And an issued warrant for their arrest or assassination. A few seconds later the image flips, and he sees *his* face. And his friends'. Nobody's calling for their assassination. Not yet anyway.

Pop, Mom, please be okay.

He sighs. "We better hit the tracks." He puts the visidex in his bag for now. "C'mon. Tracks gotta be just north of here."

They begin moving through the stalks.

The corn leaves swipe at them. Thirsty, desperate, mindless.

Cael bats them away as they continue forward, but he can't help feeling as if there are eyes, watching. Eyes in the corn. The eyes *of* the corn, maybe, though that's about as absurd a thought as a fellow can have out here.

His chest itches, and he reaches up and scratches it.

Probably just a rash, he thinks.

THE MANY WORDS
FOR DRUNK

THEY GOT BACK TO Harrington's house hours ago, Gwennie helping him across the skybridge and desperately praying that her vertigo wouldn't kick in and send them both over the railing to their deaths—but somehow they'd made it inside. And it hadn't been a half minute after he'd gone to put Erasmus back in the bird's cage that he returned and unlocked a little cabinet, its doors marked by the phases of the moon. He'd withdrawn a fat-bellied, lean-necked bottle.

He'd uncorked it with his teeth. *Ploonk.*

On the label, a flower made see-through—like a blue specter against a black background. "Ghost Orchid," Balastair had said at the time, adding, "the finest orchid brandy," and then he'd begun to gulp and guzzle and laugh and mumble and even cry a little as the night deepened and morning crept closer. He'd tried to get her to drink some, but she'd still been feeling as if her guts were tied up in nervous, too-tight knots. For a long time he just rambled: about Cleo, about how once he was doing good work. Even as a young man, he'd said. A teenager under the tutelage of his mother. Doing good work with a girl he loved and now . . .

Sometimes he made sense, other times, not so much.

A little while ago, someone had come pounding at the door, and he'd screamed at them to *go away, go away*, almost pitching the half-empty brandy bottle at the wall before Gwennie caught his wrist and took the bottle.

And now the two of them sit. She on the floor against the red chaise on which he is sprawled.

"This must all be quite interesting for you," he slurs. "What you must think of me. Of *us*. There we are, these enormous city-ships above your tiny little heads. You Heartlanders thinking we've got it all together. But we don't—*we don't*! Incestuous, backbiting, treacherous people, we Empyrean, we wind-dancers, we *keepers of the seventh heaven*, blessed are we, the true children of the Lord and Lady—"

"Wait, is that true? You think you're their children?" she asks. *Huh.* She didn't know that. The story as she knows it from the catechism is that the Lord and Lady had a child who ran away from their manse in the sky, and that child went to the earth to hide from his parents. Once there he was tempted by an old devil—often depicted as a rag-swaddled hobo—who arose from the land beneath the land, a plane called King Hell, and that temptation lured the son into wooing one of the children of the earth: a woman named Mary Mags. Having his own child of the earth forced the son of the Lord and the Lady to remain— and he took the name Jeezum Crow, a name the earthers gave him. The name of a fool. A jester.

But if the Empyrean think they're the direct descendants of the Lord and Lady, well . . . "That's pretty cocky," she says.

Balastair laughs. "It is! *It really is*. We think we're as good as them. Better, even. We have the power of machines and genes; we command the wind and fly high above the earth and the sea. We feel that puts us on the same plane as the gods. Or above them."

"Sounds pretty stupid to me."

His face twists up like a wrung-out rag. "We've screwed you, you know. The whole Heartland. And we just keep screwing you deeper into the dirt. We never saw you as equals, not really, but we had a partnership of sorts. We taught you. We let you grow what you wanted. We gave you resources to learn and ways for you to study here on our flotillas, and then one day . . . the Praetorial Council up and decided, Hell with you dogs and cats down below. All we needed from you was corn. Corn for our fuel. Corn for our bio-plastics. *Pssh*, once upon a time we used your corn for food—syrups and cornmeal and blah blah blah, but then it became too poisonous for us, and the corn became aware. Not long after that came the Blight, and now all the Heartland is Hiram's Golden Prolific. Our gift to ourselves. Our curse upon you." He thumps his head back on the chaise once, twice, a third time, moaning and rolling his shoulders and neck.

"You're drunk," she says. And smiles.

"I am not merely *drunk*," he proclaims, and reaches out to hold her hand. "I am toggled, zozzled, canned, corked, tanked, owled, ossified, *pleasantly embalmed*." He slaps his cheeks hard, too hard, eyes bugging as he laughs. "I'm dancing with Old

Scratch, I'm out on the roof, I'm seeing two moons, I'm three sails to the wind, I'm falling through air, I'm a flock of falling stars, I'm . . ."

He sighs. His head leans back one more time and stays that way.

Ten seconds later he's snoring.

"Oooookay," Gwennie says.

She drums her hands on her knees.

What to do, what to do? She has a bed, and it's somewhere else. And the elevator probably won't take her anyway. Which means she's here for what little is left of the night—she can already see the fireglow of sunrise creeping in through the teardrop-shaped windows of Harrington's home.

First things first: time to get this awful dress off.

As soon as the dress is off, she misses having it on. It's not that she likes it. Oh no, not at all—at least, that's what she tells herself. But then she has to step back into her old clothing—clothes she brought with her, clothes that now smell of hay and horse and horse piss.

She thinks of the dress, and all those pretty people, and how ugly she found them. And then she thinks of her fellow Heartlander—

Merelda.

Merelda.

"La Mer," *she says.* "It means 'the sea.'" *Bleh. It means, "my foot in your boot-hole,"* you dumb, twaddling girl.

The peregrine called her his "house-mistress." She hopes that just means she's there to wash dishes and change nappies and occasionally hang on his arm like a piece of pretty jewelry.

But Gwennie suspects it means something . . . more.

What that must be like for her.

How much Merelda must've hated the Heartland.

As her mind wanders, Gwennie's body wanders, too. Out of the room. Down a hallway with lights—frosted glass chevrons—that glow only as she approaches and dim as she passes. Past bronze swans with wings that look like knife blades, past lamps that resemble the skyscraper buildings here on the flotilla, past a small marble side table piled high with ornate books (*The Catechism of Manners*, *The Epistles of the Lord to His Lady*, *The Illuminated Artisan*).

First she stops by Erasmus's room—and there it's hard not to hate the Empyrean extravagance, for here a little bird gets his own room. Most Heartland children end up stuffed together in a single room, two to a bed.

She goes to the gilded cage, lifts the sheet.

"Hello!" Erasmus says.

"Hi, bird," she answers.

She waggles a digit, and the grackle hops beneath it, letting her fingertip pet the top of his wine-dark head.

"Gwennie!" Erasmus says.

She laughs and shushes the bird, then withdraws her finger and re-covers the cage.

Then she leaves, goes up steps that curve and swoop like a corn sickle. Her toes plunge into carpets so plush she feels as if she'd sink deep and be gone if she were to pause for but a moment. She traipses down a hallway, the walls of which are papered with designs reminiscent of bird feathers—the dark purple of spilled wine fringed with gold leaf. Gwennie lets her fingertips drift along the walls, and she finds that the wallpaper is textured: bumps and ridges, the eyes of the feathers each a slight depression.

For just a moment she understands the allure; she sees what Merelda sees. A laughable vision plays out where she seduces Balastair Harrington, and he takes her in and makes her his own, and this becomes as much her place as his. There is something about him, isn't there?

Truth is, Gwennie couldn't seduce the leaves off a tree in autumn (not that she's ever seen the leaves fall off a tree for any reason other than it was dying). It's not her way. She takes what she wants. Like she took Cael. She wanted him. He wanted her. That kind of relationship is easy because there you both are, reaching for each other with selfish hands and hungry mouths. It's as if you fall *into* each other.

Boyland Barnes Jr., well, he's a whole other wasp's nest. Thuggish brute. What was it Cael always called him? Buckethead. And yet Boyland really liked her; no two ways about that. He stood up for her. Tried to protect some semblance of her honor. He was different to her when they were alone those times on his yacht. Cael was like jumping fire, like hungry lightning—all hands and knees and wicked grins, and she was the same. But while Boyland had all the grace and aplomb of a bludgeoning club, when they lay together, he was slow and gentle and—if she had to guess, she'd say he was nervous.

Bah! Why think about any of this? What does it matter?

I'm never going to see either one of them again.

She has more pressing concerns.

Like finding her family and making sure they're all right.

At the end of the hall, a red door. Open just slightly—an invitation. She nudges it open. Finds a bedroom inside: a bed with a dark-wood footboard and headboard carved with reliefs of moths and butterflies in symmetry. The room is a mess. Clothes on the floor. An empty bottle of something by the nightstand. The rest of the house is immaculate, but this room is dim and messy.

The bedroom is as big as the whole downstairs of her house back in the Heartland. Larger even.

Beyond, she sees a small antechamber. She ducks inside. A dangling bulb with a pull chain graces her hand—she pulls. *Click-click.*

A desk against the wall. Corkboards to the left and right. Pinned there are charts of spiraling helixes and symbols she doesn't understand. Against the far wall is a map—a map she thinks at first must be something out of some dream or fantasy but a map, she soon realizes, that is of the world beneath them.

A world that goes well beyond the Heartland.

She feels herself leaning in. Staring. Gaping.

The Heartland. A massive stretch of space in the heart of a singular landmass, the domain marked with symbols of corn and auto-trains and little icons of men in straw hats tilling soil.

But beyond it . . .

To the west, a line of mountains with many names: the Workman's Spine, the Crowsblood Mountains, the Black Peaks.

Beyond that, a broken and disparate coastline called, aptly, the Shattered Coast, and beyond it the Sea of Angels. To the east, a thin margin of land before the sea: the Moon Coast, the Atlas Ocean. To the south, a morass of dark rivers and lakes with another series of names: Bleakmarsh, the Braided Glades, and along a jutting peninsula are the River Glades. And finally, to the north, a big, arching phrase in bold, ornate text: *The Frozen Nowhere*.

"Oh gods," she says, gawking at the map.

It's as if the world has just grown beneath her feet—a dizzying sensation, as if the world is too big, too strange. She knew something had to be beyond the Heartland, but everything she heard was just stories: "Oh, that's where the Maize Witch keeps her monsters," or "Beyond the Heartland is a wall, and past the wall is a wasteland of barren rock," or "a sea so salted you can walk across it."

Something on the desk goes *bleep*.

A visidex, behind a cover of gold silk and surrounded by scattered papers and book pages.

She flips it.

The screen brightens in her hand.

She doesn't understand what she's looking at. A series of boxes connected with lines—boxes with little images and symbols inside them. She touches one, and it drags beneath her finger; the other boxes turn to circles and jostle out of the way. When she withdraws her finger, they snap back like elastic bands.

It bleeps again.

A message appears at the top:

Peregrine: *You made quite the show.*

A window pops up beneath it. A blinking, swirling whirlpool beckoning her to—what? Respond?

She doesn't know how. And is afraid to.

Another message appears with a chime:

Peregrine: *I hope the girl isn't rubbing off on you.*

A few seconds later another message:

Peregrine: *Though, rub her all you like; I won't judge. Just keep her controlled, Harrington, or the hell that heaps upon your head will be a thousand times as heavy as what it is now.*

The message winks out of existence.

She lets out a breath she didn't realize she was holding.

Then her eyes track something else on the desk.

A single name on a piece of paper buried beneath other papers:

Shawcatch.

She sets the visidex down, reaches for the paper.

The paper is marked WARD ORDER.

It seems to be some kind of legal document that outlines the parameters of Balastair's relationship with her. It's as if she's some kind of . . . burden. Property, of sorts.

Then she reads at the bottom:

The mother shall clean homes on Helicon Hill; the father shall work in the Engine Layer; the son will be found suitable placement in a home seeking an adoptive child.

The fire in her belly is stoked with an iron poker.

They're talking about her family.

Balastair knows where they are, and he didn't tell me.

And to think, she was growing fond of him, wondering if maybe . . .

No use thinking about it. These people are all the same. They're not gods. They're monsters.

She snatches up the visidex.

It's time to find her family.

NOURISHMENT OF ANGELS

THE PAIN IN RIGO'S LEG comes and goes—it rises up out of numbness like a monster out of dark, still water. When it breaks the surface it bites hard, sending a twisting braid of misery through his whole body before once more settling back down in the shadows. Then comes the pins and needles. Then comes nothing.

That's been going on since last night.

They'd helped him hobble along before Cael had the idea to use Lane's little knife to cut another stalk free for him to use as a crutch. The corn had thrashed and shuddered as it was cut, like an animal in pain. They'd got it up under Rigo's armpit and it worked—for maybe ten minutes. But then the stalk bowed and eventually splintered.

So they'd gotten another two stalks and robbed themselves of their bootlaces, bounding together all three stalks.

They'd swaddled the top in rags cut from the hems of their shirts and pants, and that's what they shoved up under his arm.

It's been working for him.

Now Rigo feels as if he's going to melt, as if he belongs with the slurry back at that river. He's dirty. And hot. Not hot from the outside but hot from the inside. His mouth is as dry as a sun-baked hardtack biscuit: all crumbs and flour. Worse, they're out of water. No rain's come this way for a long time, so there's no chance to milk the corn roots of their stored-up moisture.

Lane and Cael are lagging behind him, not because he's somehow faster than they are but because they're still fiddling with that visidex, trying to figure out how to use it. He hears *bing*s and *boop*s and other chimes and alarms, and sometimes Cael curses or Lane hoots in what might be triumph, but Rigo doesn't much care right now.

Really, he just wants to lie down.

Ahead, the corn shudders.

As if something's moving through the stalks. Toward the tracks.

Rigo mutters, "Fellas."

He hears his own voice, and it's quiet and dry like a little lizard fart, and he tries to say something again, but they're back there, all consumed by the glowing screen passed from hand to hand.

Whatever is in the corn, it's coming fast.

Rigo stops limping along.

He sees what's coming.

Warm piss goes down his leg.

It's the hobo.

Eben Henry steps onto the tracks. Mouth screwed up into a mean grin. That knife of his, the makeshift blade Cael was talking about, glints in the noon-peak sun, and he spins it in his hand.

"Cael," Rigo says. "Lane. *Guys, please—*"

But they're too busy; they don't hear him.

Eben presses a dirty finger to his chapped lips. "Shhh."

Rigo conjures a yell from deep within his middle, and Cael and Lane come running and see who waits for them only fifty feet ahead on the tracks—

"What is it?" Cael asks.

"Him," Rigo says, pointing, a low whine rising in the back of his throat. But it's then he realizes:

Nobody's there.

"He, he, he was just there," Rigo says.

"Who?" Lane asks, pitching his cigarette into the corn.

"The hobo. Eben."

Cael looks forward, panicked. He looks back at Rigo and then at Lane. They share some silent understanding, and Lane presses the back of his hand to Rigo's head. He pulls it away as if he touched a hot stove.

"You're on fire," Lane says, voice quiet.

"I . . . think I pissed myself," Rigo says. He pats his thighs, but his hands come away dry. He shrugs. "Oh, maybe not."

"You all right, Rigo?" Cael asks.

Lane stares and adds, "You look like King Hell, kid."

"I just need to lie down for a while," Rigo says, and as they start to protest and say something about being almost there,

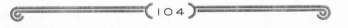

Rigo feels the warm chair underneath him and lets his jerry-rig crutch fall away so he can fall into the chair's embrace, but then there's no chair at all, and the others are reaching for him, but it's too late because his butt bone is slamming onto the hard wood of a railroad tie. More pain for the boiling-over pot of pain soup that his body is becoming. He leans back. Shoulders and head against the gravel between ties. "Ow."

The other two quickly hunker down next to him, one of them putting the bag under his head, the other checking him for further injury. A wave of chills sweeps across him as if he just dunked his head in an ice-cold bath.

Cael says to Lane, "He doesn't look good."

"Doesn't look good? He looks like a fell-deer who ran head-first into a corn thresher."

Rigo startles as the image of a Blighted Earl Poltroon falling into the thresher jaws replays in his head—the sound of his bones banging against the inside of the motorvator's bin like so many corncobs.

Cael shushes Lane, and they both look at Rigo.

"I can hear you," Rigo murmurs.

The two of them step away from Rigo and begin to argue over what they're going to do about him. He can't distinguish who's saying what. Someone says, "He needs medicine, man. He needs cillin-pills fast." One of them answers, "Where the hell we gonna get those?" "The depot." "We don't know where the depot is. Or if there even *is* a depot out this way. Not like we have a map. Or a clue. Just moving in a straight line hasn't gotten us anywhere yet no matter what Pop said." "I trust Pop, and after everything, so should you, and—"

Meanwhile, Rigo lies there.

He has to push his breath out and suck it back in. Each time as if it's running over a wood rasp. A dry whistle in the back of his throat.

His forehead feels like a hot plate.

He hears his father's voice in his ear: "Rodrigo, Rodrigo. You're a shit kid. *Nobody wants you.* And now you're going to die."

Rigo winces, pauses for the strike of his father's hand.

It never comes.

He opens his eyes instead and sees a black shape drifting across the sky above. Not a flotilla. Lower than that. And flying lower still.

A ship.

To take them all away.

Suddenly he's getting up, and his leg is okay, and he's walking toward the ship as it lands in the corn, smashing stalks. Cael and Lane haven't caught up yet, and Rigo thinks this is good; this is him doing something before them; this is him escaping this world before they can.

They always get to do everything first.

He laughs, but then that laugh dries up like the last drops of water falling out of one of their water bladders, and he finally says, "Oh."

Rigo must've said it pretty loud because Cael and Lane look over.

"What?" Lane asks.

"I just realized."

"Realized what?" Cael says.

"That it's a hallucination. The ship."

"What ship?"

He lifts a shaky finger and points.

They follow his finger.

The two of them start laughing.

"A ship!" Cael hoots. He slams into Lane, and they hug. Together they clap him on the shoulder. "Rigo, that's no hallucination. That's a real ship!"

That's it, Cael thinks as he watches the ship descend out of the sky and fly over the corn and away from them. *That's our ride.*

He knows that ship isn't just a ship—it's a scowbarge—and those are meant to carry heavy loads. A scowbarge means the depot is near.

It means they're close.

He laughs as he and Lane help Rigo stand once more.

Cael positions the crutch under Rigo's arm, and he starts saying, "Rigo, the depot ain't far now, and if anybody's going to have cillin-pills or some other Empyrean medicine, it'll be them." And he's telling Rigo about how it won't be long now, they just need him to power through and hobble just a little farther, and hey, Heartlanders are made of mean stuff, tough as the corn, hard as the earth, and just as they get Rigo settled, Cael feels it.

That itch again on his chest. This time it comes with a hot twinge of pain almost like someone's trying to twist a screw into his breastbone.

He winces and reaches under his shirt.

Everything stops. His blood goes cold.

No no no this isn't possible it's not what you think it is.

The back of his wrist tents his shirt as his fingers find the soft margins of the thing growing out of his chest. Cold and smooth, with a faint indentation on one side that manifests as a ridge on the other.

A leaf.

It feels like a leaf. With a little stubby stem.

He blinks back tears and tugs on it.

Pain, electric and sharp, shoots from his skin. Same kind of pain that comes from pulling a scab. The stem won't give, though. The leaf stays.

And by the balls of Old Scratch, it sure does itch.

He tries not to make any sound. Tries not to show the fear that is crawling through him like a colony of termites.

Lane catches his eye. "Hey, you all right? Looks like you just saw the Maize Witch."

I have the Blight.

"I'm fine," Cael lies. *I have the Blight.* He forces a smile. "Just worried about Rigo."

And then a thought that isn't his own enters his mind like corn shoots prying apart floorboards or pushing up asphalt—

Come to me, Cael.

"You're not gonna die," Lane says, mussing Rigo's hair. "We won't let you, because life just wouldn't be as much fun without you to kick around. Ain't that right, Cael?"

Come to me, Cael.

He swallows hard.

"Totally right."

"Then let's go hitch a ride," Lane says, and whoops with glee.

Cael nods and tries to smile, helps Rigo along.

But that one thought keeps turning and flipping in his head, jumping around like a bird with a broken wing trying to fly: *I have the Blight.*

PART TWO

BLACK MIRRORS, BROKEN KEYS

THE MAN FROM WHEATLEY

THE MIRROR ISN'T MUCH. A shard of reflective glass sitting between two corners of old frame, held there as if by divine providence. The bottom of the glass is blackened from smoke and soot—this whole house is burned up, and the mirror is one of the few things left.

He'd laugh, but it hurts too much. Every twitch of his lips sends sparks of pain jumping as the skin breaks and blisters pop.

His face looks like a shuck rat turned inside out.

Cael McAvoy.

That name. That boy. At first he thought *that* was the divine providence—he'd been looking for Arthur McAvoy for a good long while, waiting for that snake to pop his head up so that Eben could cut it off. And then what should happen? An alert on the visidex he stole from that Empyrean guard—before he broke the fool's neck—that said Arthur McAvoy was some kind of "terrorist." And that his son was wrapped up in it, too. Well, gosh-and-golly.

At the time Eben had been far west, toward the squealer town of Baird's Furnace, pretending then to be just another hobo looking for work but doing his *own* work in the meantime, the work of the Lord and the Lady. The first thing he did was pack up everything and start heading east. McAvoy was in a town called Boxelder, so that's where Eben figured he'd go.

And then there, across the trestle, he'd spotted them.

The fat one with the raft—*sploosh*. Into the slurry.

An easy introduction.

He thought he had them.

Eben lashes out, kicks a burned-up chair into char-dust. The rage rises inside of him, and he growls and then whimpers in pain as the burned mask that is his face stretches and pulses and just plain *hurts*.

Back to the mirror. His forehead is still smooth except for a lone blister. His eyes were blessedly untouched, though the brow-hair burned. But the lower half of his face is pitted and pocked with red, raw flesh. The ash stuck to him like tar. Burning and burning. He has some lesser burns on his forearms where he tried to wipe away the ash, but those aren't too bad. His face, though, his face . . . will never be the same. Not without some of the voodoo they got on those Empyrean flotillas, and he doesn't see himself going back to one of those anytime soon.

Another spike of rage pounds heavy into his heart. The Empyrean.

The Empyrean people want to be like the gods. And the Heartlanders want to be like dogs. Both disgust him, and they

114

disgust the Lord and Lady, too. He knows, because they tell him things. Sometimes Jeezum Crow comes to him in visions. Or Old Scratch even, who's evil as anything but a part of the plan just like he is. Sometimes he's visited by the Saintangels, like Agnes or Bethesda or Hypatia or Lyria, and they tell him things, too, whispering the sweet songs of the two gods in his ear.

And right now he needs a message bad.

Eben moves to the floor, and it groans beneath him as he clasps his hands together and makes a silent entreaty to the Lord and Lady in their manse above, begging them to come to him and guide him, to bless him with a message once more.

He doesn't know how long he sits like that, but soon his knees begin to ache, and the shadows in the room shift with the passage of the sun. His face pulses with a heartbeat that feels like the heavy hooves of spooked cattle stampeding across the dead and blasted earth, and each beat brings a widening, thickening aura of pain. It moves beyond the margins of his skin, feeling as if his head is growing, swelling, twice as big, then twice that again, then as big as the face of the fallen Wheatley clock tower, then bigger than this house, then the moon, then the sun, then—

Outside. Voices.

He scrambles to stand.

Eben goes to the second-floor window and peers out over the street as a fancy, fat-bottomed boat slides into town, the quartet of sails bulging with the wind the way a child's cheeks puff out as he tries to blow spit-bubbles. The boat slows, and a drag-anchor drops.

First one off the hovering yacht is a spindly, gawky thing—a young girl whose copper-wire hair is all akimbo, and when she hits the ground, he sees the wobble in her knees. She doesn't have her sail-legs.

Next onto the ground is a little towheaded urchin who crawls from the mast like a monkey and lands like a spring—one hop, then a second.

Third off is a man almost as old as Eben himself—a man both lean and paunchy, with mussy hair tucked under a crumpled blue hat. The man moves slowly, peering out from under the brim of that hat with a dark, muddy gaze. *Looks like he's been run through a corn-press*, Eben thinks. He recognizes the signs of sin. The wages of a wasted life.

Last off: another boy. Teen. This one built like a bull, with broad shoulders, thick neck, and a head to match.

The bull whoops and turns his finger like a carousel.

"All right," he says. "Take a few. Poke through the buildings. They might be here or might've stayed here."

That one's the captain then.

The gawky girl puts her hand over her brow like a visor.

"You think Cael and the boys would've stopped here?" she asks.

The other boy scowls. "Don't ask me stupid questions, Wanda. Just close that flytrap you call a mouth and do as I say, okay?"

Eben smiles.

He just found a new path toward vengeance. He utters a small prayer of thanks to the Lord and Lady and quickly gets to swaddling his face with some dirty rags he found in the kitchen downstairs.

Then the Remittance Man hurries to meet some new friends.

• • •

Wanda doesn't like being hated. And Boyland Barnes Jr. hates her. She's used to being dismissed, sure. Pushed aside or looked over or downright forgotten, but nobody's ever seemed to *hate* her before, and the look in his eyes tells her that Boyland is the first. His gaze wills her to wither, and she does, though she imagines a day when she does not.

Wanda wonders why he hates her so bad.

Cael, she figures. It's irrational that he'd hate her as much as or more than Cael, but Momma always told her that you can't count on people to make as much sense as you want them to.

Still, it wounds her that Boyland despises her for something she didn't even do. Hate by association.

Damn that Cael.

And damn her for the butterfly flutter in her chest and belly any time she thinks of him. Even that name: *Cael.*

She wants him back. She *needs* him back.

Because Cael is her Obligated.

That has to mean something out here. *That* is a bond that counts. It's not just love. It's a promise.

And Wanda is real about her promises.

Still. Boyland may hate her, but Rigo's father, Jorge, doesn't seem to care one whit about her. She doesn't think he's looked at her once in the couple-few days they've been out here. And as for Mole . . .

The kid hurries up to her. Eyes all a-goggle. He thrusts something out toward her. Rope waggles, twisted into a curious shape of four loops bound by a central bundle. "What is this?" she asks.

"It's a flower," he says, and he winks. "Er, a flower knot."

"Oh. It's very nice."

"Yeah." He adopts a cocky pose. "I know *all* the hard knots. The Treasure Knot. The Star Knot. I know . . ."—his tongue presses the inside of his cheek, making a bulge—". . . the Cob-Twister, the Anchor Bend, the Clove Hitch, the Braided Glade, the—" A big hand falls on the boy's shoulder and pulls him back.

Boyland scowls. "This doesn't look like either of you jabber-jaws is going through the houses. Now, see that damn burn barrel fallen over there in the middle of the street? That tells me somebody's been here."

Mole thrusts out his chin. "That don't mean poop-squat, Cap. That barrel mighta been here for years—"

"The ash is still *warm*." Boyland growls.

"Oh." Mole shrinks.

Wanda rolls her eyes. "We'll get looking, okay? Jeez."

"Don't roll your eyes at me, you little twit." Boyland sticks a finger and pokes her hard in the chest once, twice, then—

Jorge Cozido grabs the finger with his one good hand (the other is bundled up in rags and tape) and shoves Boyland—who's larger than he is by a good bit—backward.

"Leave the girl alone," Jorge mumbles.

Wanda can't believe it. Neither can Boyland, apparently, because he breaks into braying laughter like a tickled mule. "Sorry, what? You're . . . you're protecting the girl now?"

"I'm not protecting; I'm just saying maybe you ought not to go pushing around a girl who can't push you back."

"I can push him back," Wanda says in a small voice that nobody seems to hear.

More laughter. "This is . . ." Boyland wipes his eyes. "This is priceless, priceless like a day of rain. Mr. Cozido, I think we all know you like to whup up on your wife and boy."

"If I had a daughter, I'd do different."

"That why you beat on the other two? Your wife gave you that squealer of a son instead of a pretty little daughter?"

Jorge sniffs, pulls a small tin flask with a cork. "My son might as well be my daughter. Just the same, you touch this girl again, I'll bust you up like an old dry cow pie. Make you swallow a couple teeth." He takes a swig of whatever's in the flask. Wanda can smell it. Makes her eyes water.

Boyland takes a step closer.

"That a threat, old man?"

"Less a threat, more a promise."

The mayor's son puts up two fists and storms forward.

Just then a loud, shrill whistle cuts the air.

They all turn. There, coming up out of an old, half-burned farmhouse, is someone Wanda doesn't recognize. A hobo, by the looks of him. Dirty denim overalls and falling-apart shoes. But what's striking is that half of his face is wrapped up. Whatever's beneath those rags is some kind of injury, and it's fresh: pink fluids stain the mask.

"The hell are you?" Boyland asks.

"You little mice looking for a trio of boys?" the hobo asks.

"Little mice?" Boyland asks. "Who you calling—"

"Yes!" Wanda says. "We're looking for three boys."

Boyland throws her a treacherous look as the hobo speaks. "Three boys scurried through here last night. They took what little I had. They burned me . . . burned my face." As the man speaks, Wanda sees the pink fluids spreading, now joined with yellow. His words sound pained, every utterance a croaked agony. "I know where they're going."

"So tell us," Boyland says, puffing out his chest.

"I can do better than that. I'll *show* you."

RATS IN THE CORN

IT TAKES MORE THAN an hour to get there, and by the time they do, the scowbarge is already loaded up and hovering out over the corn, higher and higher, the green light from the hover-panels underneath glowing brighter and brighter. It drifts upward, a gravitationally irrational brick—

This, then, is the Provisional Depot.

Their goal sits right in front of them. And all Cael can think about is the burning itch under his shirt. The leaf. The stem. *The Blight.*

He can't let them see his hands shaking. He keeps pulling his shirt down as if it might suddenly fly up, give them a show.

Don't think about what's underneath that shirt. Eyes forward, McAvoy. The goal is right in front of you. You mess this up, you won't ever see Merelda again. Or Gwennie. Or Pop or Mom or anybody.

But the itch beneath his shirt is maddening. What's worse is the itch in his mind. Like a rash from blister-ivy in the back of

his brain. An itch that's impossible to scratch except by acknowl-
edging it, and that's the last—*the very last*—thing he wants to do.

Come to me, Cael. . . .

For now the three of them lie on their bellies atop a clay
berm right where the corn starts to die out—killed by a radius of
chemicals, no doubt, or maybe by a buried layer of plasto-sheen.

Down in a shallow valley sits a spare, cement building. A
warehouse of sorts. Gray concrete with a black-shingle roof lined
with solar panels. All around the building are crates and boxes,
pallets and drums. Every bit of it exposed. No fence. No guards.
Just a series of tall silver poles every ten feet or so. Cael shakes
his head.

"Like a dang pie on a windowsill," he says, his voice low. *Itch
itch itch.* "Like they *want* us to stick our thumb in."

Rigo rolls over onto his back. Wheezing. Still, he manages to
say, "Gotta be . . . protected somehow."

"Rigo's right," Lane says. "Doesn't add up. That building's
probably thick with provisions. Provisions Heartlanders want.
Food and fuel and drink. It can't just be . . . out in the open like
that."

"Sure looks like it is."

"Go get a rat."

Cael cocks an eyebrow. "We don't need to be messing around
with rats right now, with Rigo—" He doesn't finish his sentence.
Though Rigo doesn't even seem to hear.

"No, seriously, I want to test something out."

"It's okay," Rigo murmurs. "I like just lying here. Go. Rat.
Yeah."

Cael grumbles, and slinks off into the slashing corn to find a rat.

Pressure pushes in at Cael's temples. Rigo's hurt. Some hobo is out there hunting them. And he's got what may very well be the Blight.

Don't think about it. Just think about the rat.

His hands shake as he takes a small knife at his belt. Cuts an ear of corn off the stalk—the stalk tries to pull away, shuddering and shaking like the train trestle when the auto-train passed over—but eventually he cuts through it and is able to unwrap the rough husk.

With the knife he cuts into a few kernels. Lets some of that corn juice come out. Milky white beads. Sweet smelling.

He chucks the ear onto the dirt.

It's then he thinks: *I can take a look.*

He draws a deep breath. Makes sure nobody is behind him—no Lane, no Rigo, no Eben, nobody. He rolls up his shirt gingerly, and reflexively he closes his eyes as if he doesn't want to see even though he knows he *has* to look. He feels the fabric snag on something—the leaf, the stem, the Blight.

He pulls the shirt higher.

Then he tucks his chin to his chest so he can see it.

The leaf is as green as algae atop the water in an old drainage pond. Bright. Alive. Greener than corn leaves.

He looks at the corn—

It can't be.

The corn is leaning away from him. Nothing dramatic, just a gentle tilt in the other direction—as if it sees what's under his chest and doesn't want to be anywhere near it.

Hiram's Golden Prolific is scared of the Blight.

Scared of *him*.

He swallows a hard knot. Takes a few deep breaths. Wonders what Gwennie would think of him. He knows Pop would be okay, and Pop might even be able to help him. But though Gwennie's as sweet as pie, he knows she'd recoil because, hell, who wouldn't?

A pinprick of guilt comes with the thought: *Wanda wouldn't. Wanda would hold your hand and kiss your cheek and say something awkward but sweet because that's what she is. Awkward but sweet.*

"I'm such a dirt ball," he says with a sigh.

Again he looks back at the leaf and stem.

It has to go.

He takes the knife, and he brings the blade against the stem and presses his thumb against the green, as if he's about to cut into a parsnip. The stem is cool. Smooth. Just touching it, he can feel it throbbing with a kind of energy. Vibrating a kind of . . . rhythm. A life signal.

He winces and jerks the blade upward.

It slices through the stem.

Hot pain like a string of firecrackers goes off in his heart, down every limb, lighting up his brain like Eben Henry's burn barrel.

Lips trembling, teeth chattering, he looks down. Sees the leaf and stem there in the dirt. Bright red blood trickling from the stem. And down his chest in a zigzagging line.

He quickly folds his shirt back over it. A little blood bleeds through.

There. That's done. *Blight's gone.*

That's what he tells himself.

Then Cael lies down in the dirt and waits. Slingshot in hand.

"Do you wanna talk about it?"

Lane arches an eyebrow. "Talk about what?"

"That thing you told me."

"What thing?"

"About the . . . not-liking-girls thing."

Lane sniffs. "I like girls fine."

Rigo groans, moans, rolls his eyes. "I'm dying over here, and you're playing games. Never mind."

"Fine, fine. Yes, I like boys. No, we don't need to talk about it."

"I just thought—"

"Well, you thought wrong."

"You didn't tell Cael."

"No, I did not. Any other facts of life you feel like reiterating? Sky's blue. Dirt's dry. Life's hard."

"Why didn't you tell him?"

Lane sighs. He thinks about giving some aloof and evasive answer—stick and move, duck and dodge—but Rigo's like a little kid. He'll just keep asking. *Why, why, why, why.* He's a nattering grackle.

Instead, Lane tells the truth, or most of the truth anyway: "Cael wouldn't get it. He's . . . simple. Not stupid—don't gimme that look—just simple. For him things are the way things are, and that's mostly okay until it pisses in his eyes. If all this hadn't gone down he'd have been half content to settle down with Wanda—or Gwennie, if we're talking fantasyland here—and pop out a litter of squall-babies and put the Empyrean leash around his own neck every day as he tottered off to work at the processing plant. Cael doesn't see things beyond his own two eyes. Like I said, he's simple."

"The hell's that mean?"

Lane turns around and finds Cael standing there in the corn, a shuck rat hanging limp in his hand, the rodent's collar wet with red. Some of the beast's blood stains his shirt, too. He scowls and repeats, "The hell's that mean, I'm simple? I heard you talking about me. What's your problem, Moreau? You got something you wanna say?"

Damnit! Just cover your tracks, Lane.

"Lord and Lady all a-mercy," Lane says, trying not to splutter or stutter. "I'm just talking about how you feel about the Sleeping Dogs—"

"You're gonna keep ringing that bell, huh?" Cael comes and kneels down next to them. "You still got stars in your eyes for those raiders?"

"They're not raiders. They're freedom fighters and—"

"Save it for another day, Lane. You had me go fetch a rat, so I went and fetched a rat. Can we get on with it?"

Lane's shoulders slump, losing a little bit of tension. Cael didn't hear most of that conversation. *Good.* Lane feels his cheeks starting to go red.

He tells Cael, "Fling the rat down there. Make sure it goes between two of those posts."

"Mind telling me what that's supposed to do?"

"Jeezum Crow, Cael, let a guy have his surprises. Throw it."

Cael shakes his head, then grabs the rat by the tail and pauses. He chuckles as if he just thought of something else. Then suddenly he's pulling out the slingshot and stuffing the rat's wadded-up body into the pocket.

"You're a sick boy," Lane says.

Cael shrugs, winks, and draws back the rat-shot—

Thwap.

The rat-ball flies high in an arc—

Tumbling through the air—

It lands dead center between two of those metal poles.

The two poles spark. A sonic pulse flashes between them, a warbling sound that leaves their ears ringing. The rat carcass lies there on the other side, stretched out and kinked up. Even from here they can see how the pulse deformed it. Probably broke all its bones.

"Twisted that rat up good," Lane says. "If you hadn't killed it, that sure as King Hell would have."

"Shit!" Cael says. "Sonic fence."

"Sonic fence," Lane repeats, happy to be back to the mission at hand. "Any idea how we get past it?"

Rigo lifts a sweat-shellacked brow. "I do. I think we have a key."

They both give him a quizzical look.

He holds up the visidex and offers a weak smile.

SCRATCHING AT THE DOOR

THE WIND FILTERS through her hair as the boat zooms over the stalk-tops, the fringe tickling the underside of the yacht, but Wanda isn't present in the moment. She's thinking instead of that night out in the pollen drift with Cael and his crew. That was the night, she thinks, that she fell in love with him. Even though he wasn't nice to her and even though he lied to her to get her family's boat, he was so *in command* of everything. He knew what he wanted, and he was high-bound to get it.

Of course, what he wanted then was their strange little garden. That ties into all this somehow—him being on the run, the McAvoy farm being burned up, the proctor sitting at the mayor's house like a goose on a nest of eggs. Folks haven't seen the mayor, but some say they saw the proctor and her guards pulling a body out of the McAvoy house, and it was the elder Barnes.

Killed, they say, by Arthur McAvoy. And they say Cael killed Pally Varrin and Grey Franklin with naught but his slingshot.

Wanda doesn't know all the details. She just wants Cael back. She hopes that bringing him back means they'll pardon him of whatever crimes they think he committed.

She knows he didn't commit them.

Cael's not a killer. Nor is he the type to burn another man like this . . . vagrant is claiming. A contrary voice inside her asks, *Or is he?*

As if he can sense her thinking about him, Eben the vagrant sidles up next to her.

"You don't have your sail-legs yet," he says.

"No, I suppose I do not."

"This ain't your crew."

"Well. No. There was another girl, but . . ." She doesn't know the whole story so she doesn't bother telling it. All she knows is that Felicity tried to get on this boat, but Boyland denied her. She cried. Jeez, the girl didn't just cry; she fell to the ground and wept like a mother who lost her child. Wanda knew the look in Felicity's eyes. Felt its familiarity. The girl was in love with Boyland, and he didn't love her back.

Well, they weren't Obligated, so she can just shove off, Wanda thought at the time. The coldness of that notion surprises her as she remembers it now. Just the same: Obligation has to mean something.

Eben adjusts his damp swaddling. "I'm going to need to change this. Do you have a first-aid kit?"

"You're gonna have to talk to the captain about that." She

gestures toward Boyland, who stands at the front of the boat, looking out over the corn. Jorge Cozido is at the other end, lying down, shielding his eyes from the sun above, sipping at his flask.

"Boyland is his name," the hobo says.

"Boyland Junior. His father was Boyland. He was mayor."

"Was?"

"As in, he's not anymore." She doesn't say any more than that. But already she wonders if it's too much.

Dangit. This hobo's like her dog, Hazelnut, scratching at the bedroom door to be let in—old Haze would scratch real quiet, almost so you couldn't hear it. But eventually the scratches would grow louder and louder, all the more insistent, and . . . well.

He'd end up in the room. Snoring and farting and scratching.

But she doesn't want to let this mongrel in.

"Why you hunting these boys?" he asks. "You seem a strange crew for that. Figured this sort of thing was up to the Empyrean."

"We've been deputized!" says Mole, suddenly hanging above their heads from the mast-pole. Dangling there like a possum.

"Deputized, huh."

Wanda shrugs. "I guess you'd say that."

"But it's different for you," the hobo says.

"It's different for all of us."

"How's that?"

"I'd rather not say."

He laughs. "It's okay, Little Mouse. I'm just making talk. Killing time. We don't have much if we don't have each other. People, I mean. Heartlanders." She feels his eyes cutting holes in her.

"Cael was my Obligated," she says, blurting it out.

"Sorry to hear that."

She wheels. "Don't be. He's a good boy. Still a boy, though, which means he makes mistakes, and that's okay because I'm still a girl, and *I* still make mistakes, too. But don't misunderstand me. I know he didn't burn up your face like that. Not how you said it. He's not that way."

"He's a mean whip is what he is."

"Shut up." She feels tears building behind her eyes, which surprises her, but she stiffens her lip and folds her arms over her chest as if tightening her body will stop them. It works. For now.

The hobo continues: "Apple doesn't fall far from the tree. Vipers are born of other vipers. Bet the whole family is a nest of troublesome types."

Suddenly, Jorge Cozido is there.

"This piss-soaked guttersnipe botherin' you?" he asks Wanda, giving Eben a long look over.

She shakes her head. "No. No, Mr. Cozido, it's fine. Thank you."

Eben holds up his hands: a sign of surrender.

"Gonna go see about that first-aid kit," he says. "If you'll excuse me."

AN UNSCHEDULED VISIT

BALASTAIR'S DREAMS RUN together like spilled paint on a white-tile floor, colors crawling between grout-lines, drips of red against rivulets of purple, or blue, or black. He dreams of being stomped by horses without skin, horses who are all bone and who have wings made of book bindings and black leather. He dreams of kissing Gwennie, and bedding Cleo, and punching Eldon Planck in his handsome-yet-unobtrusive nose. He dreams of falling, of flying, of dancing, of drinking—and it's this last one that lingers with him, the taste of the Ghost Orchid floral brandy leaving with him the taste and scent of elderflower, hibiscus, and rose petal. His stomach clenches like a fist and then—

Next thing he knows, he's vomiting in the drawer of his bedside table.

His head pounds.

Boom boom boom.

"Uh-oh!" Erasmus says, hopping about on the back of the

lounge. (The little bird, free from his cage. Not that it's ever locked. Erasmus has the freedom to fly where he chooses. He is less a pet and more a friend.)

The hangover throbs louder: *Boom boom BOOM.*

"At the door! At the door!" Erasmus chirrups.

Balastair groans, sits up, tries to stand.

His head is pounding, yes.

But so is the front door.

He staggers forward, thinking, *You really fell into your cups last night, didn't you?* Feels as if he almost drowned in them.

Balastair opens the door.

"Peregrine," he says. Trying to hide his shock and failing utterly.

The grackle flits through the air and lands on Balastair's shoulder.

The peregrine's mouth tightens into a small, stiff smile.

"Harrington," Percy Lemaire-Laurent says. "You look well."

"You're being sarcastic."

"Of course I am. You look like a half-digested cat. May I come in?"

Can I stop you?

"Absolutely. Yes. Please."

"Please!" Erasmus squawks.

They sit across from each other at a mirror-topped nook table. Above their heads, a small chandelier hangs, and the pink water-drop crystals *tink* together with the flotilla's gentle, undetected movement.

Balastair pours boiling water slowly over a carafe and filter of ground coffee. Steam rises. The scent of coffee parts the brandy fog.

"Would you like a cup?" Balastair says. "They're, ah, my own beans. I mixed two strains: Corwin's Winedark and Allborn Redjack's Robustness."

"You'd rather be doing that, wouldn't you?"

"What's that? Drinking coffee?" He tries to take a sip and burns his lips. *Like Vikare, flying too close to the sun with wings of wax.*

"No, growing your beans. Or any plants at all."

"It was my mission in life, yes."

"Your mother's mission, you mean."

"And her father's before her. And it was mine, too. But I have been . . . retasked."

"The Pegasus Project."

"Yes. Of course. Not toward the *Initiative*," he says, dropping that word, the same word that Eldon Planck dropped just last night. He hopes that it will elicit some reaction—anything at all!—from the peregrine, but Percy's face remains as undisturbed as a blue sky.

"Well, to the point of my visit, then," Percy says. "You made something of a mess at last night's party—"

"I did, and I'm truly sorry, a grave social error on my part. Won't happen again. All better now."

"You didn't answer any of my messages last night."

"Messages?"

"I came to check on you and the girl."

Balastair's guts turn to slush.

Oh, by the seventh heaven. Gwennie. He goes through it in his mind as quick as a lashing vibro-whip: *We were here. I was drinking. I was babbling. What was I babbling about? Doesn't matter, doesn't matter, I rested my head, then . . . then she left. Or she stayed. Or was she . . . did she . . .*

Did we?

"Balastair?" the peregrine asks, snapping his fingers around the margins of Balastair's face. "You in there?"

"Ah. Yes. As noted, I really lost my rudder last night, and I'm trying to get it back." He clears his throat into his fist. "We're fine. Gwendolyn and I. Just fine."

"The girl. I want to see her."

"See her? The girl?"

"Yes, Balastair, the girl."

"She's . . . gone to work," he says. "Mucking stables."

"How would she have operated the elevator?"

He's on to you.

"She . . . didn't, of course. I did. Me. I took her down and then came back up here for a little, you know. A little winky-eye."

"Winky-eye!" the grackle grackles.

His headache is bright and cruel. A living, laughing thing.

"So you will not mind if I go and see her?"

"See her."

"In the stables, yes."

Balastair forces a cock-eyed smile. "It wouldn't be my place to stop you. You're the peregrine. No door is locked to you."

"I like to ask. Manners are important to men such as we."

"Then please, let me acquiesce to your manners and say, of course you may"—*What if she's not there oh no oh no oh no no no*— "go to the stables and see her. You have my permission."

"You should come, too."

"Should I?"

"You should."

"Then let me find a more presentable outfit than the one from last night. I shall don professional garb."

"Please," the peregrine says. "But make it snappy."

"Of course."

He goes upstairs.

Into his bedroom.

He stands at the foot of his bed for a little while. Trying to remember. Reaching back through the ache and the fog to see if he can conjure any memory of what Gwennie did. Or where she went. Or—

Something's off.

The door. To his desk-room. It's wide-open.

The light is on.

She didn't—

She couldn't have—

He steps through the door, and instantly he sees what's missing.

"My visidex," he says.

His headache leaps and grows, a fire fed by a thousand fears.

THE KEY

IT'S LANE WHO figures it out. The three of them lie on their bellies behind the clay berm, playing with this device far fancier than anything Heartlanders are used to. The screen glows bright and is projected a quarter inch off a hard glass backing, which is itself backed by a scalloped titanium shell.

On the flip side is the Empyrean logo. Beneath that, another bit of text, not embossed but on its own backlit screen: **Archaway Noribishi Collective v4.2**.

"Check this out," Lane says, tapping the screen. He's good with this thing already. Opening up all kinds of screens: a camera, some documents, schematics. Said he was good at it because his father used to let him help set the programs on the motorvators, which used screens like these.

When Lane taps the device, a small map opens—Cael figured the *map* icon would've loaded that, but that's why Lane's holding the visidex and not him, because by now he would've

winged the thing into the corn and been done with it; the map on the screen is explicitly local.

They can see the clay berm—a topographical lump. Beyond it, the Provisional Depot. On the map it's just a big rectangular block surrounded by a lot of smaller rectangles and circles (crates and barrels, Cael realizes). But inside the depot, within that larger rectangle, is another, smaller icon: an antenna with little lightning symbols radiating away from it.

"Someone in there has a visidex, just like us," Lane says.

It takes a second for Cael to understand what that means. He suddenly yanks the visidex out of Lane's hand and starts feeling around for a rock—"We need to break this thing, shatter it so they can't see us."

Lane snatches it back and scowls: "They're not *looking* for us. *We're* looking for *them*. I can use this visidex to talk to someone in there."

"I don't understand why we'd want to do that, announce our presence—why not just stand up now like a whistle-pig at the hole and start yelling that we're out here, and, golly, we'd sure like to be let in."

"I'll show you," Lane says, and taps the icon indicating the other visidex. Again the screen is sucked back down into a hole and is replaced by one word in big, bold text:

Connecting.

Lane looks smug and excited. Cael just wants to slap that visidex out of his hand—but Lane seems to sense that and holds up a patient finger, mouthing for Cael to *just calm down*.

That word—*Connecting*—suddenly twirls off into nothing.

It's replaced by a face.

The face belongs to a jowly man with a thin, chinstrap beard and a nose that looks less like a nose and more like a cluster of mushrooms growing together. He's got a crumpled flat cap pressed over his head, and he peers forward and says, "This is Peterson. Who's that out there?"

Lane gasps and quickly covers the camera with his thumb.

He spits on his other thumb and then smears it across the pinhole.

"Who is that out there?" the man says again. Voice like he's talking through mushy grits. "Identify yourself."

Lane clears his throat. "This is, uhhh, ahh, this is the provisionist for—" His eyes light up, and suddenly he affects a familiar voice, a voice Cael can't place until Lane says it. "This is the provisionist for Boxelder. This is Bhuja Pepke. Here to, uhh, pick up the provisions."

The man squints down at something offscreen.

"You're not scheduled to pick up from here."

"I was, uuuuhhh, I was told I was."

The man leans into his own screen. "I can't see you very well."

"Visidex took a fall. Dropped it. On a rock."

The man pries his cap back, shaking his head and scratching a balding scalp. "Pieces of junk, these things. We got the cheap Ganymede Electronics models. I'd kill somebody for a Noribishi. Am I right?"

"Totally right," Lane says, giving Cael a shrug. "Hey, can we—" Cael punches him. "Can *I* come inside? I'd like to check your records and see where this all went south—"

"Sure, sure, hold on one sec. I'll disable six and seven by the loading dock around front. See you in a minute, Mr. Pepke."

The screen goes dark.

They look at each other. Stunned silence.

"I think we did it," Lane says.

"I think *you* did it," Cael replies.

They slam into each other in a big hug.

"Not to interrupt this love-fest, but *I* think we're gonna need a plan," Rigo says with a wheeze. "And fast."

LEAPS OF FAITH

IT TAKES HER A WHILE to figure it out. Long enough that she assumes she'll get caught standing at the elevator with a stolen visidex in her hand, yelling at the mechanical Elevator Man, who denies her entry once every thirty seconds. *You are not authorized for this portal, Miss gwen-DO-LINN shewkitch.*

But eventually tapping and swiping and clicking things on the visidex shows her what she needs.

Images. Pictures. A whole spread of them.

Erasmus the grackle. Horses—er, Pegasuses—like Blackjack, Pinky, Goosedown. Pictures of Balastair, too. Many of them with that woman from last night. Cleo. The one who's now with Eldon Planck, the man Gwennie believes is working on the Pegasus Project from the other side, the *mechanical* side. First up, a picture of Balastair and Cleo on the Halcyon Balcony with bright smiles and windswept hair. Then the two of them on a small skiff out in the open sky. Next a picture of the two of them standing on a sandy beach, the ocean lapping at their bare feet.

Beaches and oceans. Things she once thought belonged only in stories. *The world is large*, she thinks. Large and strange, and she resolves at that moment to visit other places—the sheer possibility of a greater world than she knows overwhelms her with a kind of fluttery, bubbly giddiness. The very thought that she might possess the ability to just say "to King Hell with it" and flee to places unknown, sights unseen, makes her dizzy.

But this is no time to dream.

Unfurl those sails, girl, she thinks. *You aren't going anywhere if you can't get on this damn elevator.*

The pictures give her an idea.

She uses the visidex to find a picture of Balastair and Cleo at some hoity-toity Empyrean party—she in a red dress, he topped by a black top hat (itself topped by Erasmus the grackle).

In the corner she spies a little magnifying glass icon. She presses her finger against it—and the image suddenly swells on the screen.

It zooms in on his face.

She holds the visidex up so that the screen faces outward. Then she holds it in front of her face so that his replaces hers.

"Down," she says. "To the Engine Layer."

The Elevator Man replies, *Vocal print not recognized.*

She clears her throat, tries again, this time lowering her voice just enough, mimicking Balastair.

It's enough for the stupid machine.

"Hello, Balastair Harrington. I regret to inform you that you are not currently authorized for the Engine Layer. Please obtain

authorization from the Carriage Conveyance Authority or from the Office of the Peregrine."

Damnit! She takes a deep breath. Where could she go?

A thought strikes her. A silly, stupid thought. Impossible. Perilous. An idea so bad it should've never crossed her mind.

But it did, and this seed grows quickly.

She tries again: "To the stables."

The Elevator Man responds: *Of course, Mister Harrington.*

Ding! The elevator gate opens.

It takes her all the way down to the Undermost.

Now it's time to find her family. She'll start with her father, she figures. Because he'll know what to do.

But first—

She hurries by each of the stalls, petting the horses as she passes—Blackjack snorts and blows a sneeze at her, and suddenly she's left wiping off her forearm and face, but he gets a nose scratch just the same. She's already got a bag full of stuff she stole from Balastair's pantry: a handful of fresh fruits the likes of which the Heartland has never seen, a half-dozen individually wrapped Flix-Brand Protein Bars, plus a bottle of something fizzy called Klee-Ko Club Soda.

The visidex turned out to be a pretty vital instrument—no wonder these people walk around with them all the time.

There, at the end of the stalls, is what she's looking for.

A board with peg-hooks on it.

Hanging on those peg-hooks: tack gear for horses. Reins. A saddle. A harness. Every last bit of it unused—wishful thinking on the part of Balastair and the Pegasus Project since these horses don't fly.

She grabs a harness, tugs it taut. The smell of oiled leather crawls up her nose.

The gear is meant for a horse.

But today it's going on her.

She cinches the girth belt around her middle, tightening it as far as it'll go—which is still loose, but that's okay, because she's going to need it that way. Gwennie's never put tack on a horse before—horses in the Heartland are rare and frequently ill creatures—so she's not really sure if she's doing it right or if that even matters. Long as it's on her she guesses it's fine.

Deep breath. In, out, in, out.

She steps over to the hatch, dragging the bag with her.

Okay. You're going to do this.

You got this.

It's just being in a boat, flying over the corn.

Except, okay, fine, much higher up.

She grabs the hatch, throws it open.

Cold wind hits her.

Fear nests in her heart. She tells herself, *The wind is a sign, a sign to turn around, that this is stupid, too dangerous; this is something Cael would do, not you; you were always the sensible one in that crew!*

But then she imagines the faces of her family.

They need you.

Father. Mother. Scooter, especially.

Gwennie grits her teeth, suppresses a scream, and climbs down out of the hatch.

• • •

The peregrine eventually tires of the game.

He goes upstairs, finds the window open, the curtains fluttering.

Outside, he sees Balastair at the far end of the skybridge, his daft little bird hopping from shoulder to shoulder with a nervous flutter as he waits for the Elevator Man to crank back the accordion gate.

Percy feels at his hip and finds the sonic needler there—a Rossmoyne Vitiator 505, a brilliant gun with a long, silver barrel and a snug, leather-swaddled grip around a mold fitted specifically to his palm. He takes aim as the doors open. Eyes down over the sights—

He lets the pistol drop with a sniff and sigh.

This is not the weapon for this shot. A rifle would serve him well, but he can't traipse about the flotilla with a sonic rifle strapped to his back. The medium-to-long range capabilities of his needler are woefully imperfect. Damaging the Elevator Man or the elevator itself would not be ideal.

And so Harrington ducks into the elevator. Alone. The girl is nowhere to be found.

That's fine. The peregrine has other ways to find people. That's why he's the peregrine, after all.

THE OUTLAWS
MCAVOY & MOREAU

KSSSH.

A rock picked up from the ground flies straight and true from Cael's slingshot—and whacks into the camera hanging above the bay door.

The camera hangs limp now, like a dog's wounded paw.

The two sonic fence posts glow suddenly, thrumming loudly before powering down—the glow doesn't fade so much as it cuts short. The sound is like a motorvator running out of fuel before dying in a field.

"We good?" Cael asks.

"Only one way to find out," Lane says.

The two of them step between the fence posts at the same time, elbow to elbow, and Cael holds his breath without realizing it, waiting for the horse kick of a sonic blast to break his back and wad him up like a snotted handkerchief—

But their feet crunch in the stones on the other side.

Lane laughs.

Cael lets out a breath and flicks a bead of sweat from the end of his nose. He tosses the slingshot over to Lane, then shrugs off the shoulder strap and drops the lever-action rifle—now with a cracked stock, thanks to that vicious hobo—into his hands.

Just in time, too, because a half second later the bay door ahead—a door big enough to accommodate a scowbarge—starts to rattle. A mechanized whine sounds behind the metal curtain, and the gate begins to open.

The man from inside, Peterson, trudges over with visidex in hand.

"Something's wrong with our cameras—" Peterson is starting to say, but then he looks up and gets a gander of what's waiting for him.

Cael jacks the lever action on the rifle—*ch-chak!*—and raises the barrel, lining up the sights at the same time Lane pulls back the pocket of the slingshot.

"Whuh . . ." is all Peterson can say.

The rifle feels tight against Cael's shoulder. And heavy in his hands. It's loaded up with ammo this time, not like before. It strikes him that this is an item of some consequence. A real weapon. A slingshot is bad news in Cael's hands, but a rifle—

The image flashes in his head of the bloody rose blooming on Mayor Barnes's chest. Pop standing there. Gun in hand. Smoke drifting and stinging Cael's eyes. The rifle's a hell-bringer. A death-dealer.

Some consequence, indeed.

"Knock knock," Lane says, breaking Cael's line of thought like a stick over the knee. "We're home."

"Outlaws," Peterson says with a hiss.

"Back up," Cael says. Then when Peterson doesn't budge, "I said, back up! We're coming in, mister, and you make one funny move, I'm gonna put a lead slug somewhere above that big nose of yours."

Peterson reflexively touches his nose, as if stung by the comment.

Cael, on the other hand, wonders: *Would I really? Kill him just because he did what came natural to him? Just because I've killed doesn't mean I'm a killer. Does it?*

"That thing isn't real," Peterson says. "Just some prop. They don't make rifles anymore. Certainly don't make ammo." He suddenly puffs out his chest as if this revelation proves that he's the smartest rooster in the chicken yard.

He smiles.

Lane gives Cael a nod. They talked about this.

Cael lifts the rifle and fires.

Bang!

The shot is louder than he remembers. Loud enough that he almost drops the rifle out of surprise. The gun kicks, too, bucking like a bull who doesn't want his bits cut off. It jars Cael so bad he barely hears Lane calling to him and pointing—

Peterson drops to his knees, head down, cowering, shaking.

But behind him, back toward stacks of crates and drums, come two more figures—each armed with a blue face shield and sonic shooter.

Lane grabs Cael's elbow and pulls him forward.

He can't hear Lane tell him to "Come on!" but he sees Lane's lips form the words. And before he even tells his feet to comply, Cael's running through the gunsmoke haze into the Provisional Depot.

Rigo's torn.

He's lying there, not thinking of much. He's back to feeling numb—his leg seems like it isn't much more than a string of cured sausage dangling from his hip by a ratty old string, which of course is why the others didn't want him tagging along. He's torn because on the one hand he'd prefer to recline on the hard berm and maybe, just maybe, take a nap.

On the other hand, that visidex sure is cool.

He picks it up. The screen brightens.

He uses it to block out the sun, holding it above his head like a shield while tapping icons to see what happens. Not much here he understands: documents with numbers and measurements, charts with symbols he doesn't comprehend—all technical stuff that does nothing for him.

Nearby he hears the sound of what must be the sonic fence powering down: *VOOOOoooooooooo* . . .

Dang, their plan is really working.

Rigo thinks about flipping through more virtual documents, but what's the point? He doesn't know what in King Hell he's looking at. Instead, he goes back to the map screen where they found that man Peterson's visidex—maybe he can keep a distant eye on what's going on.

But something curious shows up. Something new.

Two arrows pointing to the margins.

He sees a magnifying glass button labeled ZOOM OUT, so he taps it.

The map gets a little smaller as his view gets a little bigger.

And sure enough, two more visidex icons appear on the screen.

One west of the depot. One coming in from the east, the way they came. At first Rigo thinks nothing of it because right now his mind is slow to connect things, like two red ants swimming through molasses, but then it hits him: *That isn't good, is it?* The only folks who might have a visidex are Empyrean. Which means—

Oh dang, oh dang, oh dang.

Just then: a gunshot splits the air.

Rigo's heart leaps.

He's got to tell Cael and Lane they're gonna have company.

Inside the depot, a sonic blast splits the air with a high-pitched *trill* and clips the side of a pinewood crate, shouldering the box back and sending up a little cough of splinters. Lane darts right, diving behind a pallet of blue plastic barrels, and Cael pulls left, grabbing Peterson by his scruff and dragging him behind the crate that just got clipped.

By now Cael's hearing is starting to come back, though his ears are still ringing something fierce. He trains the rifle on Peterson, who sits there, a wet stain spreading across the lap of his dungarees.

"Don't kill me," he says, lips pinched and sucking inward as

if he's trying to eat his own mouth. "Please. I got an Obligated. She's pregnant, too, and, and, and we've been trying for a good long while now but finally—"

He's a Heartlander? Shoot, of course he is. Empyrean wouldn't leave their own here, same as they hire Babysitters from Heartland stock.

"Shush," Cael says. Peterson keeps blabbing, so Cael hisses through his teeth, a sound he used to make at Nancy the goat to get her to stop chewing on his pant legs. When Peterson's quiet, Cael yells over the crate: "I got a rifle trained on Peterson here. And presuming the both of you have ears, you heard that it's a real damn rifle loaded with real damn bullets."

All's quiet out there. Like they're not sure what to do. Or, Cael suddenly worries, *like they have some other plan in mind.*

He asks Peterson, voice low, "Who's out there with the guns?"

"Wh—what?"

"Their names."

"The one's, ah, Horace Eggbaum and the other is Melinda Swiggins. You'd think that Horace would be the one who's good with the shooter, but nope, it's Melinda, and just because she's a she—"

Cael scowls. "Her being a girl doesn't matter. My girl back home could've kicked my ass three ways from a dog's day."

Peterson's eyes brighten. "You got a girl?"

"Jeezum Crow, shut up, we're not talking about this right now." Cael shakes the gun a little to remind the man of what's pointed at his heart. Then he yells over the crate: "Horace. Melinda. You're Heartlanders, we're Heartlanders, so I tell you

what: we don't want to hurt nobody, so go ahead and put down those pistols you got trained on us. We're just looking for a ride off this dirt-clod. My sister was through here a couple months back—"

"Young girl," Peterson says. "Name like Melinda's but not Melinda."

"Merelda."

"That's the one. She did come through here, ayup."

"Where'd she go?"

"Like you said. Hopped a ride. Took off to . . . if I remember it right, the Ormond Stirling Saranyu. Flotilla that hangs high in the sky about fifty klicks south of here. You might could see it out there in the clouds—"

Suddenly, another high-pitched warble slams into the crate—

More splinters. A second sonic blast on the other side of the room. Cael hears Lane yelp and curse.

"Godsdamnit!" Cael shouts. "I'm sitting here having a nice conversation with Peterson and, and"—he looks to Peterson—"you their boss?"

"I am."

"Then for the Lord and Lady's sake, tell them to drop their weapons!"

"Oh, sure, right." Peterson clears his throat. "Eggbaum. Swiggins. Drop those pistols now—we're gonna pop our heads up, and it's okay, it's okay; these boys are just looking to get out of our hair." He says to Cael, "We got a barge coming here in about three minutes. I can get you on there."

"That seems too easy. Why?"

Peterson gives him a look like, *Well, duh.* "You have a gun."

"Oh. Yeah."

"And your sister was nice."

"*How* nice? You didn't mess with her, did you?"

"I told you; I got an Obligated! I'm honest in the eyes of the Lord and Lady looking down from their manse. I'd never—"

"All right, all right, I believe you. Stand up."

Peterson groans and staggers to his feet.

Nobody shoots off his head.

Cael stands up behind him, rifle trained on his back just in case.

Sure enough, across the small depot warehouse stand two others in face shields: a pooch-bellied, saggy-limbed fellow with dark skin and bright eyes, and a tough-looking tree stump of a woman. Eggbaum and Swiggins. Eggbaum's gun lies by his feet.

But Swiggins is still pointing hers.

"Melinda," Peterson says, holding out his hands. "Drop the gun, girl."

"I ain't your girl, Ronnie."

"These boys don't mean to do us no harm."

"Then tell that one behind you to drop his shooter."

Cael sees Lane pop up from behind the barrel. The slingshot is in his hand, pocket pulled back. He's nowhere near the shot Cael is, but he's lined up nice and got the time to aim. As long as his arm doesn't tire.

"Miss," Cael says—

"I'm a missus, dumbass. I'm Obligated like the rest of us."

"Fine, *missus*, we're just looking for a—"

At the far end of the depot, behind Eggbaum and Swiggins, a red flashing light starts strobing. Cael startles a little, and

Eggbaum sees his chance and scoops his pistol back up off the floor.

"Aw, godsdamnit," Cael mutters.

"Eggbaum!" Peterson yells. "Swiggins! Drop 'em! Lord and Lady!"

"Hell no," Swiggins says, showing her teeth like a feral pig. "We get audited or the Empyrean catch these hayseeds on the barge, we're the ones who will hang from a gangplank, Peterson."

The back bay door starts to open.

"Scowbarge is here," Peterson says just as a siren starts to wail in time with the strobing red light.

Rigo pokes the visidex furiously, *tap tap tap tap*, trying to figure out how to get a message to Lane and Cael. He tries to call Peterson's visidex, but it just . . . sits there, saying **Connecting** over and over again.

Then—

A sound through the air, the vibro-hum of hover-panels, and he rolls onto his belly and crawls forward, peering out.

A big, boxy moo-cow of a scowbarge is flying in low over the corn. Aiming for the far side of the depot, opposite to the side where Cael and Lane entered. He looks down at the visidex screen and thinks, *Okay, that's one of the visidex signals, probably*—

But it doesn't seem to line up right, and then there's the pesky *other* signal that suddenly blips and judders and leaps forward, showing on the screen as surprisingly close—

So close it should be just about on top of him.

A hard knee suddenly presses into his back, and the heel of someone's hand shoves his face into the crusty clay. He tries to cry out, but fingers snake around his face and clamp his mouth shut.

As the gears turn and the door starts to lift, as Eggbaum and Swiggins both point and wave their guns, as Cael's chest starts to itch once more, and as Lane's arm starts to waver, Cael sees how this is going to fall apart: the scowbarge will start to come in for a landing. The pilot will see that they've got some kind of showdown going on, with a couple of outlaws trying to pilfer provisions or sow general discord, and the scowbarge will crank up the hover-panels and lift back up into the sky. They'll call Empyrean agents, who will swoop down on them like a sky full of rat-hawks. Then it'll all be over, a week's journey for nothing, all of it for naught.

He looks at Lane, and Lane looks back.

Cael offers a little nod.

The slingshot lets fly.

Cael fires the rifle.

The rock from the slingshot pocket smacks into the woman's hand—she reels it back, howling, the sonic shooter spinning up in the air at the same time that Cael's shot finds the light fixture above their heads. A spray of sparks and glass rains down on them—Eggbaum hollers as if he's got a face full of honey-wasps and flails about, doing a panicked dance.

As the door starts to open, they see the scowbarge.

Cael waves Lane on, and they each leap their respective barriers and charge toward the back, toward the barge, knowing they need to get on board that ship and keep it on the ground long enough to fetch Rigo.

Movement from their right—

Melinda leaps up, arms out, and tackles Lane.

The slingshot spins away.

Cael makes a snap decision—his friend can handle himself. The barge is the goal. The barge is *everything*.

He keeps running.

The scowbarge isn't much to look at—just a large, chunky box, the spectacled pilot barely seen behind a tinted wind-visor. The ship starts to land, docking pistons telescoping, ready to engage—

Twenty feet. Ten. Cael makes a run for the front nose cone of the boat, which is more *nose* and less *cone*—a hard-angled grille with rusty metal ribs. But then he catches sight of the pilot, who sees him charging, whose gaze flits to the fumbling fracas in the depot. The pilot's mouth forms a panicked O shape—

Cael leaps—

The scowbarge jerks backward, hover-panels glowing bright.

Cael's fingers grace the rusty grille of the scowbarge even as it starts to lift back up—he feels it carry him up, up, up, his fingers burning at the knuckles, rust biting into his skin—

He loses his grip.

The ten-foot drop isn't a killer, but his legs fold up underneath him, and his back smashes flat against the dirt yard outside the depot gate. His own rifle smacks him on the head, and for a moment his eyes go wonky—vision drifting into two halves,

BLIGHTBORN

each distinct from the other and bouncing from blurry to clear and back to blurry again.

The scowbarge drifts backward as it lifts upward.

A slow escape, but an escape just the same.

The blurry shape begins to ease away—and with it Cael's hope of hijacking a ride to the flotilla.

He reaches up a hand, as if that'll do anything.

Then—

A black shape streaks fast from the east.

It strikes the scowbarge—

Fire geysers from the opposite side.

The scowbarge explodes.

THE WIDE-OPEN NOWHERE

GWENNIE DANGLES.

She feels like a ladybug on the underside of a cat-maran, clinging there with the whole world far beneath her.

Green corn and blue sky and dry, dark earth. Little cold wisps of clouds sliding underneath her feet. The air feels thin. Panic is thick. She thinks again about Cael's dream. About falling through the sky, toward the corn below . . .

Don't think about falling right now.

Doesn't help that she almost lost it climbing out here. The wind hit her in the face, a cold and uncaring *smack*, and though she reached out and grabbed hold of a loose pipe as if it were the rung of an upside-down ladder, it jarred her just enough that she didn't ease outside so much as her body slipped through the hatch, and suddenly she was hanging there by one arm—an arm that already felt as if it were coming out of its socket, burning like a fistful of matches right at the joint.

She was able to get her other hand around a bundle of cables and pull herself up, using the crook of her left arm to brace herself. After that she took the harness straps and loose reins and strapped herself to the underside of the flotilla, allowing her arms some freedom.

Time for a break. She's already tired. *And I haven't done anything yet.* Then, *No,* she tells herself, *don't do that. You just climbed out of a hatch and nearly fell to your death, but instead you saved yourself.*

It's early still. Time for breakfast.

She wrestles the bag to her front and dips her hand in, comes back out with the only fruit in the bunch she recognizes: an apple.

A round, luscious apple. Big, too—so big it barely nestles in the curve of her palm. To be safe, she uses two hands to eat it.

The *pop* of the skin beneath her teeth. The sweet tang of the apple's flesh on her tongue. Juices run sloppy in a pair of lines down her chin.

That's a good apple.

No, that's the *best* damn apple she's ever had.

The orchards at home are all dead, blackened things now— but even when some of the trees were still healthy, back when she was a kid, the apples never tasted like this. Those apples were small and knotty, more sour than sweet. But this, *this* is like eating honey. She can't help but smile.

But her bliss is flagging. She has to remember the purpose here.

As she eats, she gazes all around her—the underside of the flotilla is nothing like the topside of the city. Down here it's dirty, rusty, some parts dripping dark water, other parts pissing little jets of water. To her it almost looks like someone dumped a crate of old tools and pipes and wires; arranged them on a big board; and fixed them there with screws, wire, and nails before flipping it upside down.

And the farther you look, the more you can see that the flotilla is not just one single entity but rather a fractured one, like a dinner plate broken in ten places—each fragment, each shard, distinct from the other, connected only by cables. Some hang slack, others taut, depending on how the flotilla moves; even now she can see some pieces pushing together, other pieces pulling apart. When they drift away, the cables pop and hold them. When they drift together, the cables stiffen—they don't act like any wires or cables she's ever seen.

What's easy to see are the engines.

They circumnavigate the whole flotilla—a massive ring of hover-panels and turbines strung together. She can't tell how far away they are. Gwennie's close to the epicenter of the flotilla down here, which means those engines are miles away on the other side of this floating island. Which means—

Which means this isn't going to work.

To get to the Engine Layer—where she will supposedly find her father—is a journey too long and too dangerous. Her plan of slowly and steadily making her way along the underside of the Ormond Stirling Saranyu, looping the reins and stabilizing the harness a few feet at a time, will take her forever. When night creeps up, it'll swallow her whole—she won't be able to see what she's doing, and the air will grow cold. Maybe even freezing. She's already away from the sun and feels the chill crawling along her skin; once it slithers into her bones, it's all over.

Which means that she needs a new plan.

She thinks, *I'll just crawl back inside. I'll go to the Elevator Man and have him take me . . . somewhere, anywhere.* But then what? They'll catch her eventually. The peregrine lives up there. It's his roost, and she gets the distinct feeling he can see everything.

But down here she feels . . . free. Separate. As if this is hers and nobody else's. This ugly, upside-down place suddenly feels more like home than any part of the flotilla has yet.

Think. Look. Pretend you have Cael's eagle eye.

Hell, she *does* have Cael's eagle eye. He saw a lot, but he missed some things, too. And who was the one to see them when he did? Gwennie.

She squints and scans the underside of the flotilla. She could maybe—*no, that won't work.* Or maybe it would work if—*too dangerous, too dangerous. Wait. What's that?*

Ducts. Everywhere. She spies a vent a ways off, the vent tilted outward toward the sky. No hissing steam. No dripping water. It's about a hundred yards away—which is a long way given how she's going to have to get there, but it's a helluva lot closer than those engines are. If she can crawl up in there and use the duct system, she can go anywhere without having to rely on the elevators. Nobody will be looking for her there.

She begins to undo one strap of her harness.

And as she does, she hears the voice coming down from the hatch just behind her. "Gwennie? Gwendolyn?"

It's Balastair.

• • •

Down in the stables he finds a few harnesses gone and the hatch open. Whistling wind keening through. At first he thinks, *She jumped. She couldn't take it anymore, and she threw open the hatch to end it.*

But that doesn't make sense, does it? She wouldn't steal tack—or his visidex—and then jump to her demise.

Which means . . .

No. Could it be?

Could she have really climbed out there?

He feels his knees buckle just thinking about it. He's not used to the sensation—vertigo is not a common problem for those who live on the flotillas or on outlying vessels. But thinking about Gwennie alone, with nothing separating her from the wide-open nowhere, is . . .

He shudders.

He kneels by the open hatch.

Balastair cups his hands around his mouth and calls to her: "Gwennie? Gwendolyn?"

His words, snatched by the wind. Taken to her? Or thrown to the void? He doesn't know.

Erasmus reiterates the call: "Gwen-do-lyn! Gwen-do-lyn!"

"I can help you," Balastair calls. "You don't have to do this alone. I'll help you find your family. I'm already . . ." *I'm already trying.* He's been working to find out where her family has been located all this time. He also thinks to tell her that he's already a young man in trouble, a man whose mistakes may yet hang him, but he's not sure it matters. Does she hear him? Is she even alive? She may not have jumped, but who's to say she didn't fall?

Clinging to the underside of the flotilla like a flea on a cat's belly is not the safest of plans.

He waits for a while, and then he gets up to go.

Words on the wind reach her.

Balastair's words.

I can help you.

You don't have to do this alone.

She wants to trust him.

But she can't.

He knew. All this time, he *knew.* Those papers of his showed the locations of her father, her mother, her brother—and he kept that from her.

Gwennie wants to trust him, but she can't. What's to say he won't snatch her up out of the hatch and drop her right in the peregrine's lap? Or worse, march her out to the end of a gangplank himself? The decision is made.

She stays. And slowly begins to cross the space between her and the vent—one agonizing foot at a time.

23

THE ATTACK

PIECES OF THE SCOWBARGE rain down on him, and Cael rolls to his side and covers his head with his arms. Massive metal shrapnel crashes down against a stack of drums. The drums tumble and roll, a hell-born clamor. Crates smash. The bulk of the barge catapults to the earth soon after, the air growing hot as fire belches from the wreckage.

Hands grab under Cael's armpits and drag him backward: back up onto the loading bay platform, onto the concrete, and into the depot. He looks up, sees Lane's face there, gazing out in shock at the flaming hunk of barge sitting in the middle of the storage yard.

"Lord and Lady," Cael says, coughing into the crook of his arm. Lane helps him stand. "I don't . . . I don't understand—"

"I think we're under attack," Lane says.

"The Empyrean?"

But Lane doesn't have time to tell him what he already

knows—that the Empyrean wouldn't attack its own—because out in the yard, a rusty canister hits the ground and rolls a few feet. Followed by another. A third clatters to the concrete behind them, tossed through the door-gate from which they'd originally entered.

The canisters click and *hiss*, one after the other.

Red smoke—blood colored like what might belch from King Hell's sulfurous chimneys—begins geysering out.

Behind them, Peterson drops to the ground and hides his head. Eggbaum and Swiggins both hightail it through a door marked DEPOT EMPLOYEES ONLY. The door slams. Cael and Lane hurry over and try to open it—but the door won't budge.

"Locked," Cael says.

Lane utters a frustrated grunt. "We gotta get out of here."

The red smoke begins to fill the depot. Drifting toward the rafters. Visibility goes south as the smoke swallows the doors, the crates, even Peterson kneeling over there as if he's praying for rain. It's like standing in the middle of a piss-blizzard.

The smoke burns Cael's eyes—he takes a breath of it, and suddenly he starts coughing as if he just inhaled a lungful of sawdust. Lane's feeling it, too, covering his mouth and squinting.

Then Cael hears the sounds of boots falling heavy on cement.

At the front and the back.

Man-sized shapes begin to emerge through whorls of red smoke—Cael's eyes are watering, and already it's hard to make out who it is, but he sees one, then another, then a half-dozen coming in from both sides, striding as if they already own the place.

Dark cloaks part the smoke.

It's then Cael thinks: *These aren't men.*

They're monsters.

They have long, lean faces—impossibly inhuman skulls, muzzles like wolves, eyes like black pits. Long braids that are less like hair and more like manes. Hooves at the ends of their legs. Claws at the end of their arms.

He hears Lane gasp next to him. He sees it, too.

The monsters begin to close in.

Lane turns toward Cael and stares with smoke-stung eyes.

Lane whispers, "Run."

Cael needs no further encouragement.

He runs.

"Gods*damnit*," Boyland growls, looking through his long, brass spyglass toward the depot. "Who are these sons-a-bitches?"

Boyland had them set down the yacht in the corn. Eben wanted them just to charge right in and "step on those little mice," and it was then that Wanda saw the hate flashing like fire in his eyes and decided that this man was not entirely together— or as her mother used to say, *His quilt is comin' apart at the squares.*

Wanda felt a kind of impatience, too—the thought of Cael being *right there*, only a hundred yards off in this Empyrean bunker in the middle of nowhere—made her feel giggly and sad and mad and twitchy all in equal measure.

Together they stood and watched as a scowbarge came and settled in low over the corn, south of the depot, drifting in like a brick thrown in the slow motion of a strange dream, and Boyland started saying how the plan was for them to wait

until they came out, but Eben argued that the boys were likely planning on hitching a ride on that barge and—

That's when the scowbarge exploded.

Something streaked through the air like a rogue firework on Saint Independent's Day and struck the side of the barge. There came a big burst of fire from the other side, and the whole thing went crashing down, a flaming skeleton of metal and melting plastic.

Then—

From the far side of the depot came a series of ships borne on a cloud of dust: a fleet of cat-marans and pinnace-racers moving fast, and behind them a bigger, slower trawler that Wanda's never seen before—its bow carved into the long face and lean neck of a wolf, its sides lined with sweeping steel blades that catch the bright white of the noon-day sun.

"Raiders," Eben says.

Boyland curses.

One of the monsters swings for Cael—a swipe of claws swishing through the air, cleaving the red smoke and pulling it with them. Cael ducks and pumps a knee up into the creature's gut—but what he finds there isn't the soft paunch of a human stomach but a hard and dull plate. *A thick hide?* he thinks. *Or armor?*

The creature shoves him and draws something from behind—

An ax. Short handle, its blade like an animal's fang, the thing spinning in the monster's hand, slicing the air into crimson ribbons, *swish swish swish*—and Cael thinks, *Why the hell does a monster need an ax?* Then: *Why the hell am I not using my rifle?*

But by then it's too late; the beast is upon him.

The monster brings the ax down—

In the space where Cael once was but is no longer.

He dances to the side and smashes the butt of the rifle forward. He hears the wood crackle and splinter even further, a fact he's none too thrilled about, but survival means saving himself, not some old, antique weapon of his father's. He drives the rifle butt forward a second time.

And a curious thing happens.

The monster's face tumbles off its head.

A mask, Cael realizes. *They're wearing masks.*

The smoke parts for a moment, and he sees the haggard face of a man with a dark, patchy beard. The man blinks, looks after his lost mask, then returns his gaze to Cael with a snarl and a sneer.

Cael smashes him in the nose with the rifle butt.

The man's nose pops like an egg, squirting blood instead of yolk.

Once again Cael's plan resumes: *Run.*

The pain is hot, intense, a carpet of fire ants crawling all over Rigo as rough hands drag him by his arms through the corn— the socket of his arms burn, and every butt-bounce on the hard earth sends one more miserable pulse of pain to the margins of his ruined leg and back.

He tries to cry out, but his voice is weak, a gassy wheeze. And as soon as he makes even that small sound, the faces of those trailing after turn toward him—monstrous faces that he

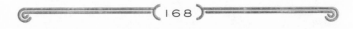

realizes too late are masks, some rusted, rough-welded metal, some crudely carved wood, all meant to mimic the faces of dogs or wolves. (*Rovers*, comes the absurd thought. *Rovers are real, and they're men in masks.*)

One of them mutters from behind the Rover-face: "Shut up."

Rigo doesn't shut up. He cries out again.

The back of someone's hand cracks him across the mouth.

Cael darts out through the smoke—the sun seems bright, too bright, washing out the corn in a wave of white. The tip of his boot catches something—a stone—and he pitches forward. His hands stop his head from hitting him. His palms sting. His chest itches, the skin tugging.

He gets his legs up under him. Sees Lane standing there in front of him, his friend's eyes gone bloodshot, wet with tears.

Lane's eyes go wide.

Cael follows his gaze.

There. To the far side of the corn. Boats. Ships. A fleet—hell, a whole armada of them. More boats than Cael's ever seen in one place, hovering over the corn. Black-bottomed pinnaces and cat-marans the color of calves' blood. And one massive trawler with a wooden wolf's head at its prow, jaws big enough for both of them to step into and stand in.

The sun almost washes out the flags flapping on long poles.

Red flags with white paint.

The paint shows the eyes, muzzle, and jaws of a beast much like the one at the front of that trawler. The beast is drawn in the middle of a red circle. And it's then Cael realizes.

Lane speaks it aloud: "The Sleeping Dogs."

"Raiders."

Then Lane says something that surprises Cael, even though maybe it shouldn't.

"They can help us."

"Don't. You saw them in there."

"That wasn't about us. They know the Heartland; they know—"

"They *know* how to raid. And rape. And kill. We have to go."

As if on cue, the red smoke parts at the front gate, and men in dog and wolf masks begin stepping out in square-toed, thick-soled boots. Their gloves are tipped with pinched metal—made to look, and maybe *act*, like claws.

"Go!" Cael twists, turns, sprints for the corn.

Lane follows after—

Doesn't he?

It's him.

Boyland doesn't even need the spyglass to see it: the mussed-up blond hair, the pauper's shirt, those bright-blue eyes catching light.

Cael McAvoy.

They say it was probably Arthur McAvoy who murdered his father. But he figures that's just the Empyrean trying to pin the crime on the old man so they have something to use against him. Boyland knows the real score. He knows that Cael killed Daddy.

As if to prove it, the sonofabitch has the rifle with him.

I'm gonna kill him with his own gun. That thought, it's stark and surprising to Boyland. He's not sure he ever wanted to kill somebody—really *kill* them, not just beat the booger-paste out of them or choke 'em till they're gasping and apple cheeked— but there it is. A shining thought, as clear as a sail standing tall above the corn.

I'm gonna kill Cael McAvoy.

Then I'm gonna get Gwennie back.

Another glimmering thought: *I love her. I love her more than I love anything. More than this boat. More than Momma. More than me.*

Love and hate.

Two strong tastes that sit bright and bitter on the back of his tongue, and next thing he knows he's ditching the spyglass and reaching behind him to grab a corn sickle, the blade gleaming along its moon-silver curve. Felicity's knife, once upon a time.

Before he even knows what's happening, he's running.

Hate carrying him headlong into the corn.

Eben watches the thick-necked bull of a boy go charging off into the corn. Then, to his surprise, the girl goes after him—the way she runs calls to mind the galloping of a sick and skinny goat.

Still, some guts there he did not expect from the girl.

Eben feels rage mingled in with his admiration.

He needs to hurt the McAvoy boy. The sins of the father must be paid by the son. But descending into the nest below?

Eben knows, if he goes down there now, he might get lost. Or killed by the raiders.

But the fire burns inside him. His hands tingle; his fingers stretch and flex. A hunger tightens his throat. He wants to kill. He *needs* to kill.

"You hear that?" the drunk asks him. Cozido.

Eben says nothing. He just stares.

"I swore I just heard my boy," Jorge says, staring off into space, tilting his head. "I swore it."

"Could be you did."

"I have to go to him."

"So you can beat him?"

Jorge gives him a cold, surprised look.

"I heard what the others said. It's okay. I ain't gonna judge."

"I need to bring him home. Make things right."

"Course you do. So go ahead. I'll tell the others."

Jorge nods. He turns to grab his flask sitting on the edge of the boat.

Eben draws his pigsticker knife.

One minute Lane's behind him and the next—

Cael whirls. Corn on all sides. "Lane?"

Shit!

Did they get him? Did he go back on his own?

Then—Cael hears the crackle of corn and breathes a sigh of relief as he wheels on what he think is Lane coming up but is really—

"Boyland," Cael says.

There he stands. Not a ghost. Or a projection from one of those hologram theaters. But really here.

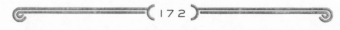

"You killed my daddy," Boyland says, spitting the words like venom.

"What? I didn't—"

A sickle swings fast. Cael leans back—the blade whistles through the air only inches from his nose, and it lops off the top of a cornstalk at the end of its arc. Boyland lurches forward and slams into Cael as if he's nothing but one big, giant fist—

Boom.

They lift up and slam down into the dirt, the corn shuddering all around as if excited by the blood sport.

Cael's hands paw at Boyland, trying to push him off, but the mayor's son is strong, even stronger than he remembered, big hands pressing down on Cael's cheek and pushing his head into the hard ground. Boyland grabs the rifle out of Cael's hand and tosses it to the ground.

Cael twists his body and manages to lift Boyland. The two start to get up, Cael reaching for his gun, but Boyland brings them both back down again, this time side to side among the stalks.

Boyland's thumb hooks in Cael's mouth. Cael bites the thumb. He tastes blood as Boyland howls. A knee slams into Cael's gut. One hand finds his throat. Closes tight. His vision begins to bruise at the edges—the panic of lost air strikes him in the pit of his belly. Cael thrashes like a cat what just lost his tail to the swipe of a knife—

Cael claws at Boyland's face. He can't see. Can only feel. Hair. Forehead. *Eyes.* He digs in—feels the soft eyes start to give—

Boyland roars, shoves Cael backward.

Air rushes in where it had been denied. Cael gasps—

Boyland staggers to stand, knife held high—

A corncob thwacks against the side of Boyland's head.

He turns. Blinking. A second cob flings through the stalks and pops him dead center in the forehead.

Cael thinks, *Here comes Lane*—

But he's wrong.

Wanda. Wanda?

Wanda!

Is that even possible?

He thinks: *Doesn't matter. Don't think about it.*

All that matters is the rifle.

. . . which Wanda now has.

She fumbles with it and points it at Boyland.

Boyland's eyes dart between Cael and her. Like a feral animal watching a pair of trappers coming for it.

"We've got him, Wanda," Boyland says. "He's right here. You're pointing that gun at the wrong fella. There's your Obligated!"

"Go back to the boat, Boyland," she says, hands shaking, tongue nervously licking her lips.

"Don't do this. He's mine, godsdamnit!"

"No. He's *mine*." Her chin sticks out. "I got this."

Boyland reaches for the gun, but she jams the barrel forward, jabbing him hard in the palm with it.

"You little—" Boyland promises: "You'll pay for this."

Cael gives the mayor's son a hard shove. "Watch your gods-damn mouth, you big bully," he says. The crazy thought strikes him: *Because she's my Obligated.*

Boyland sneers and retreats into the corn.

When he's gone, Wanda points the gun at Cael.

"Wanda—whoa, hey."

"You left me," she says. He can't tell if she's mad or sad or both.

"I had to."

"You should've brought me."

"C'mon, you can see why that was a bad idea—"

"We're Obligated!" she cries out, eyes filling with tears. But she doesn't drop that rifle—instead she seems to point it at him with greater intent. "Cael McAvoy, we are set to be married in less than a year's time. I will be your wife and you will be my husband, and that is Heartland law."

"Wanda—"

"And you better be nice to me when we are married. I understand you're a teenage boy in a bad fix, but you could stand to be *nicer* to me." Again she gestures with the gun. Her finger hovers nearer to the trigger.

"Wanda, c'mon—"

"We got a posse together. You're wanted! There's a bounty on you, Cael! Me, Boyland, Rigo's daddy—we're here to take you back. You're coming with me. Right now."

Her hands shake.

He takes a step toward her. "I can't do that. I won't do that."

"I'll shoot."

"No, you won't. You ain't gonna kill your Obligated."

She points the rifle at his leg. "I'll . . . shoot you in the leg."

"No medical attention out here. I'll die." He reaches gingerly for the gun, a hesitant hand moving slowly, slowly—

Just then, from behind them, back toward the depot—

Lane's voice. Crying out in pain.

Shit!

Cael sees her gaze flit away from him—

He snatches the rifle from her and takes a few steps back.

As he flips the weapon around, the sights catch on his shirt. The fabric lifts, exposing his stomach, then his chest—

Wanda's eyes go wide.

He looks down. Sees the fresh green stem poking out from the skin of his breastbone. Two leaves, this time, are slowly unfurling.

"Cael," Wanda says quietly. "You . . . you . . ."

He tugs down the shirt, suddenly exposed and ashamed.

"Go home," he says. "You don't want to be Obligated to this."

"The Blight. Cael, please—"

"I'm sorry, Wanda. I'm sorry for everything."

Then Cael turns and rushes back toward the depot, jacking the rifle lever and putting a bullet in the chamber as he runs.

THE DESCENT

BALASTAIR HURRIES UP the steep white cobblestones of Palace Hill, Erasmus nestled tight in the crook of his neck as the wind kicks up. All around him are the houses of not only the wealthiest among the flotilla's citizens but also the earliest. Whenever an architect ascends to a Grand Architect and the Empyrean commissions a new flotilla for one to build, the newly minted Grand Architect receives an entire tract of real estate all of one's own on Palace Hill. Anyone the Grand Architect chooses to bring along is allowed to live here without cost, without care, for as long as the Grand Architect chooses. The people who call the Hill home are the birds on the tallest perch, the bubbles topping a gin fizz.

Though, frankly, Palace Hill makes Balastair uncomfortable. A sour septic layer pickles his gut as he walks. The discomfort is not because of the wealth; oh, Balastair has plenty of that. More than he could ever want or understand. Most flotilla denizens do, except those who toil in the Undermost or, worse, the Engine Layer.

No, it's all the concentrated power. Thick like a sauce reduced for too long, till it's just a salty syrup. Power held tight in the hands of a few dozen men and women—many of whom are demented by the bends of age. Some are young, more vital, but also turned mad by the power they did nothing to deserve.

Lord and Lady, the *praetor* doesn't even live here—and she is the foremost authority, at least on paper, on the Ormond Stirling Saranyu. She and her administrators, including the peregrine, live on an entirely different hill: the Hill of Spears (*Blessedly all the way on the other side of the flotilla*, Balastair thinks as he looks over his shoulder to make sure none are watching him from behind parted curtains).

These houses are the finest homes on all the flotilla. Marble from the quarries at the foot of the Crowsblood Mountains. Granite from the peaks of the Workman's Spine. Red khaya and black kohekohe woods from the River Glades. The addition of polished chrome and frosted glass give the homes a motley hodge-podge feel—almost comical in the way they don't match—but wealth and prestige do not necessarily partner with good taste. And besides, what these old, shriveled walnuts think looks good ends up transmitting like a virus of grotesque discrimination.

Bad taste all around.

Everyone here is a known personage. There, the sun-bleached white home of the sculptress Janus Janus, with her husband, Caidan, and her wife, Juno. Across the way, the massive oaken door, and above it a bas-relief of winged horses and mighty angels doing battle with mer-creatures leaping up out of the sea—all hand carved by the shipbuilder F. E. Quercus (who is quite fond of correcting others as to the type of woods they are seeing: "That is mahogany!" is a famous refrain). Farther up the hill: the gold-leaf-on-red-lacquer door of Grand Engineer Domin Arravore. Next to that, the great, arching windows of Fenton Franklin the Eighth, administrator of the Wine-Makers' Cooperative. He's more than a century old. And quite the alcoholic, having had at least three livers brined to fatty lumps before they had to be replaced.

Finally, beyond all that, a house Balastair recognizes intimately.

And perhaps the true source of the ill feeling in his stomach.

There, a house of beige brick, the color of cashews. Once that bland, soft neutral was counterbalanced by a wealth of botanical accents: two urns of sprouted lilacs, windows framed by fingers of angel's ivy, a climbing trellis of wandering eye with flowers as purple as fingers stained by blueberries. Green leaves and dark vines, petals of every color.

His heart jumps in his chest—a curtain moves, and for a moment he sees her there, hair the color of sunlit wheat, eyes of sea foam, the curve of her collarbones casting shadows, the angles of her shoulders, arms long and lithe like the delicate legs of a glassqueen butterfly.

Then the curtain flutters again, and he sees it's not her—not his mother—but rather a small child. A young boy. Different from him—dark hair, olive skin—but still, that could have been him once upon a time.

"That was my bedroom," he says.

"Bedroom," Erasmus echoes.

"I lived here, you know. With my mother."

"Anastasia!"

"Yes. Yes, that was her."

"Gangplank!"

Balastair represses a shudder. "Let's go."

It isn't far from his old home. The alley. A crooked sign hanging from an old nail reading BLACK SLIVER ALLEY—a sign of notched wood, the words in faded, chipped paint—the alley itself grown up with weeds. All quite out of the ordinary for the otherwise pristine Palace Hill.

Every flotilla has a Palace Hill.

And every Palace Hill has a Black Sliver Alley.

And at the end of every Black Sliver Alley is a portal—a hatch, a set of double doors, maybe a trapdoor. That portal takes one down into the Wolf's Lair, sometimes called by its old name, the Lupercal.

It's one of the worst-kept secrets. Even children know of it.

Balastair darts down the alley before anyone sees him.

It's early yet. The moon is still up. Few will be going this way now.

He steps over broken stones. Weeds whisper and rustle at his thighs.

There. The trapdoor. Ill concealed beneath an overgrown brush.

He opens it and descends, Erasmus the grackle flying down with him.

• • •

Bang. Bang. BANG.

The now-dented vent drops off its screws and hits the floor. Gwennie's foot throbs from the effort, but she's been in these vents for a long time. Too long. Six hours? Seven?

She crawls on her belly and peers out the vent.

A hallway goes left and right. Everything is flaking rust and grimy, once-white plastic—pipes and bundles of wire are clamped to the wall and run the length of the hallway. The floor is grated; beneath it is darkness.

Here the smell is strong: burning fuel. The air is damp, too—warm and wet like a heavy breath. And everything vibrates with the deep thrum of hover-panels and booster turbines. That's how she found the place in the maze of ductwork: when the smell and sound grew stronger, she kept going. If it started to fade, she turned around.

Gwennie pulls herself out of the vent. She marvels at how filthy she's gotten just by crawling through the ducts—her hands are streaked with black, her sleeves tattered and smudged.

She drops headfirst—bracing herself with her hands.

With a groan she sits upright, then stands.

This, then, is the Engine Layer.

Gwennie takes a deep breath and heads right.

The hollow space beneath Palace Hill is lit with flickering sodium lights—they buzz and hum, casting everything in a yellow glow that calls to mind that child's game of holding a buttercup flower up against your chin and letting it color your skin with the hue of the petals.

It's mazelike. Men have gotten lost in the Lupercal. Lost coming down in search of distant, discrete pleasures. Or lost on their return instead—too drunk on wormwood or goggled on poppy-smoke. Or perhaps led astray by some brothel doxy or boy-toy looking for a few ducats to buy the next fix or passage to another flotilla.

Balastair knows that had he not taken her as his ward, Gwennie could have been sent down here. She's a strong girl; she would have survived.

But it would have changed her.

She could *still* end up here, if the peregrine catches her in his talons. They might just toss her over the side, but they might send her here. To work in a way none should be made to work.

But Balastair can stop that from happening.

Not because you like her. Not in that way, he tells himself. A simple Heartland girl? Scant years younger than he, yes, but worlds apart. They don't understand each other. They'd never work together.

She's his ward. So it falls to him to help her.

Which is why he's here.

He follows the signs that hang along the wall, signs that are utterly blank until you run a penlight with a black bulb over them—then the messages are revealed. This way lies Madam Treachery's House of Joy; the next tunnel leads to Madam Joy's House of Treachery; a third path reveals The Black House Distillery; and around the bend is what Balastair seeks:

The Slap-Me-Dead Speakeasy.

The brick tunnel becomes a narrow hallway of shattered concrete, and there he passes by a droopy-headed lad rubbing his back against the wall like a cat stropping up against a lamp-post. The boy—fourteen years of age, maybe—says nothing as Balastair passes but is like a hound smelling the apron strings of a passing butcher. The blood is in his nose, and suddenly he's up and following Balastair.

"Hey, fella," the boy calls.

"No," Balastair says. It's all he says.

"I could use a few chits. Maybe a ducat if you can spare it."

"Here, yes, fine." Balastair stops fast, fishes in his pocket for a few chit-coins minted with the face of the sky-goddess, Saranyu, buoyed by a pair of clouds—currency minted specific to this flotilla, though good across all of them—and pitches them onto the ground with a tinny clatter.

The boy scoops them up, and now Balastair sees for sure that he's dealing with an addict—the hollow-set eyes, the bony wrists, the lips chapped with peeling, ash-white skin.

Balastair keeps walking.

He hears footsteps behind him. Shuffling. Hurrying.

Trying to be quiet.

"Fella," the boy says again.

Balastair quickens his step.

"Fella."

A hand reaches, grabs Balastair's elbow—

He turns, thinks, *He just wants more money; I'll give him more money.* But when he pivots, he sees the flash of something—a knife. No. Not a knife. A sliver of broken glass, a swaddling of dirty cloth forming a safe grip.

The boy shows his teeth. Like an animal.

"I need a fix," the boy says, the words a desperate moan, a

forbidding plea. "Give it to me." He rears back with the shard of glass—

A flutter of bruise-purple feathers—

Erasmus the grackle launches himself at the boy's face. Clawing and pecking. The boy screams. The glass knife drops, and Balastair hastily steps on it the way one might anxiously stomp a roach. He feels it break beneath his feet as the boy backpedals, his face a mask of little scratches—

He mewls and scurries away.

Erasmus lands back on Balastair's shoulder as if nothing happened.

"Thank you, Erasmus."

"Need a fix!" the bird chirps.

An ant in a maze.

She's already lost.

Every ten steps sits another junction, another choice of left, right, or straight—another intersection of vibrating pipes and rattling floor-grate, of heavy hot air and eye-watering engine stink.

When she was a little kid, she and Scooter used to sit on the dirt mounds outside their driveways and make these elaborate—well, elaborate for little kids anyway—labyrinths out of flat rocks, wood chips, and cornstalk stubs. They'd take these fat black wood-borer ants and drop them into the maze one at a time. They'd have perils set up along the way (for all mazes in all stories have perils along the way) such as deep pits or puddles of water. A couple times they even caught barn-spinner spiders and let them wander the maze: monsters hunting the intrepid heroes.

It never worked. The ants weren't smart, but they were made right by the hands of the Lord and Lady and would just climb up over those walls and disappear. The spider caught one once. Just once. Rest of the time the ants just escaped.

She wishes she could escape now. But there is no up-and-out for her.

She misses Cael.

She misses the Heartland.

She misses Boyland and stealing chicha beer from Busser's, and she misses flying over the corn in *Betty* the cat-maran and scavenging junk from dead towns and boat wrecks and old motorvators and—

She misses her family, and suddenly they feel farther away than ever.

Gwennie presses her back against the wall and slides down until she's sitting. A break. She just needs a break. Her muscles are sore. Back kinked up. Neck, too. Her head thunks dully against a pipe. It's hard. Uncomfortable. But still, her head seems to rest right against it. . . .

She gasps, suddenly awake.

Was she asleep?

She was totally asleep.

What woke her?

Footsteps.

Shaking the floor beneath her. Closer and closer.

She scrambles to stand, hoists her bag—time to pick a direction. Back the way she came? Onward left? Right? Straight? Back into the vents? Indecision paralyzes her feet—she doesn't know who's coming, or where they're coming from, or—

"Hello," calls a voice from behind her. Gruff. Male. Wet, too. As if his words first have to gargle past strings of phlegm.

She wheels.

It's not one man but two.

The one is thick and lumpy—a body built like a broken toe. His arms are bare, muscle and flab in equal measure. The skin, greasy with oil, smeared over crooked, clumsy tattoos. He's older—older than her own father, old enough to be her granddad.

The other one is about her height. Her age, too. The boy's hair is shorn to the scalp—the stubble thicker across half.

The older man speaks—it was he who spoke the first time.

"You lost, girl?"

"Lost," the boy echoes. A smile creeping across his face.

The older man takes a step forward. The boy's eyes dart toward the older one, and he shuffles forward, too, as if to mirror the steps.

"I'm . . ." She hesitates. "Looking for someone."

"Oh?" the older man says. The look on his face—is it sympathy? Mock sympathy? Something meaner, something worse? "Tell me who, now. I know this place pretty well, I do. Let me help you, girl."

Another step closer. She matches it with one back.

"My father," she says. "I need my father. Richard Shawcatch."

"Shawcatch," the boy echoes, and suddenly she wonders if he's a little bit mule kicked.

The lumpy one grins—half his teeth are jagged spurs jutting up from puckered, wine-stained gums. "My name isn't Richard, but I'm happy to be your daddy for a little while. Would you like that?" Another step closer. "I could take you over my knee. Pull your little leathers down. Spank that naughty behind of yours until it's good and *red*. And warm. Oh so warm." A foamy, pale tongue licks his lips, and he chuckles.

The boy laughs, too, a half second after.

The older man lunges—

She shoves him back into the boy and turns tail and runs, her sore muscles screaming. Behind her, she hears the fat one yell, "Go after her, boy! Go, you dull turd, go!"

Balastair steps into a small antechamber off a curving tunnel; the walls are lined with books. Old books, the kind that give off the smell of dust and decay, an odor Balastair associates with the scent of pure knowledge. Knowledge of new things. Knowledge of new places. Every book a doorway—a cabinet of curiosities opening to a new land. His childhood was given over to books. Nose deep. Eyes crossed from reading too long. This room calls all that to mind in a sudden nostalgic wave, and there in the back of his mind is his mother again, telling him to come out and play: the sun is up, the day is warm, the flowers are calling to him. . . .

A man clears his throat.

Ah. Yes.

Behind the desk sits a thick-chested, barrel-bellied man. Skin the color of dark, loamy earth. The man peers out from behind a curtain of tangled dreadlocks.

"You need something?" the man asks. He crosses his arms in front of him; he's got salt-stung brands lacing up his arms, pink and puffy. Symbols of anchors and ocean currents, of biter-fish and the barbed hooks that catch them. He's a Brineborn. One of the men and women who know the Shattered Coast and the slate-gray water beyond.

"Salutations, Mr. Redjohn," Balastair says with a small flourish. He hopes he's not still shaking. The encounter with the addict has him rattled. So much so that he has to take a moment to remember the password. "The books are in alphabetical order, I see."

Redjohn stares at him. Waiting.

Oh. Right.

He completes the password by stepping forward and knocking on the bookshelf three times—two quick knocks, a pause, then a third knock.

Redjohn nods and stands.

At his hip, a sonic scattergun hangs.

He points a small black box toward the wall and depresses the red button on it—

The bookshelf clicks.

Hums as the magnetic lock disengages.

Then the shelf drifts open.

Music. The din of the crowd. The smell of smoke and booze and sweat. Balastair gives Redjohn a small nod, and he disappears into the bowels of the Slap-Me-Dead Speakeasy in search of a friend.

It all blurs. Same passageways. Same conduits, same pipes, same cables and wires, same rust and steam. Her feet pound on the metal grates. Footsteps aren't far behind her. The boy. She sees

him over her shoulder. Coming at her, arms stiff, hands reaching. His face is a leering mask, empty of anything but lust and hunger. Animal mad. As if he's been twisted into something by this place. Maybe by that fat man. The boy makes these sounds as he runs: giggly squeaks and desperate grunts.

She thinks: *I could take him. I can fight.* Hell, she was the one who taught Cael to throw a punch.

No. Don't stop. Not now. She doesn't know this place. Doesn't know these people. She's tired. Achy. Lost. This is not the time to—

A bellowing laugh.

The fat man steps in front of her. Clapping his sweat-damp hands.

But how—

She's been running in circles.

Damnit. *Damnit.*

She skids to a halt. The boy almost slams into her, but she shoves him back even as he tries to paw at her. The flabby arms of the old man wrap around her from behind and pull her tight against him—the boy comes at her again, and she lashes out with a foot, catches him between the legs.

The boy brays like a willow-lashed donkey and drops, clutching his pearls as his head thunks dully against the wall.

"Feisty," the old man says. "Daddy will have to teach you a lesson." A rough hand slides under her shirt, hot and clammy at the same time, his middle finger thrusting into her belly button and pushing so hard it hurts—

She slams her head back. The man turns his head just in time and catches it on his cheek—he snarls in response, but he doesn't let her go. He only renews his vigor by pulling her tighter. His one hand clamps over her throat, thick fingers pinching the sides of her neck, cutting off blood flow. His other hand searches the hem of her pants, begins to slide under—

Her own hand darts to the bag even as darkness pushes in at the edges of her vision, even as her heartbeat is dull, booming cannon fire, deafening her to all other sounds—

His hand slides farther down—

Her own hand wraps around something.

She brings it up against his head.

Crash.

The bottle of Klee-Ko Club Soda smashes against his head. He staggers backward as she stumbles forward, over the boy's moaning body. Her attacker roars, soda foaming over the glass shards stuck in his flesh and mingling with the bright-red blood.

His face a mask of crimson froth, he rushes toward her.

A warbling shriek fills the air—

Then the old monster pitches forward onto his hands and knees.

His vest is ripped at the back, the leather torn open like petals of a flower. The skin, too, is torn open: muscles exposed, looking like raw steak.

Behind him stand a man and a woman. They're wreathed in dark leathers, their faces barely visible behind blast-shields.

The woman holds a sonic pistol in her hand.

Gwennie tries to say something, tries to find words for what just happened, but none seem eager to leap from her lips into the air—and then the feral boy on the floor scrambles for a pipe and hoists himself to his feet, suddenly panicked.

The man steps forward.

His wrist flicks—a telescoping baton descends with three quick clicks. He cracks it down on the boy's head. Once. Twice. A third and final time before the boy drops, shuddering once, then remaining still.

Then the woman comes for her, the sonic pistol pointed.

Gwennie screams.

The speakeasy offers a dim brown half darkness punctuated by oil lamps on tables. The crowd here is thin at this time of the day, though down in the Wolf's Lair it's always night. The patrons are ill-seen in the dark, just shapes blending with muddy shadows, flickering light playing off their moon faces.

Balastair passes through a haze of perfumed smoke. He feels the capillaries in his face and eyes go flush. A dizzy rush sweeps over him, and it takes a moment to once more find his balance.

Bodies shift. He sees a flash of skin. A head bobbing in a lap, hands gripping the sides of the recipient's knees. In the other direction, two young men, almost boys, twine their arms, tipping back fluted glasses of something that looks silver, like liquid mercury. They laugh and begin to kiss.

Discordant music from a string quartet fills the air—the ribald pull of clashing notes does little to ease Balastair's nerves as he winds his way through the tables toward the bar.

The bar. Long, flat, slate-top. Itself a bookshelf: at knee level are more old books stacked next to and upon one another. Balastair lets his fingers drift along their dry, papery spines. It centers him.

He sits on a high-back stool, an oil lamp flickering right in front of him. He taps the rim. *Ting, ting, tinnnnng.* The fire jumps with every tap.

From the far end of the bar comes a small man. Ink-black hair in a midnight topknot.

His mouth breaks into a wicked boomerang grin, and he laughs and reaches across the bar. Balastair meets his reach, and they engage in a clumsy yet earnest embrace.

"Kin," Balastair says, "It's good to see you, friend."

"Balastair," Kin Sage says, clucking his tongue. "It's been too damn long."

"Has it?"

"At least a year."

"Then it has." He shakes his head. "Time escapes me."

"You sound like an old man."

"I feel that way sometimes."

Kin shrugs. "They don't let us be young anymore, do they? Always expecting us to make something of ourselves the moment we pull free of our mother's tit." They both laugh; nobody breastfeeds anymore. "I hear that you're on the Pegasus Project. That's an honor, right?"

"If you say so."

"Uh-oh. Trouble in paradise."

"It's not what I want to be doing. Plus: politics. Which I'm not very good at. I'd rather be down here with you."

"You'd never make it down here." Kin's eyes flash. A bit of that old competitiveness flaring there like match-tips. Balastair's not really sure who's winning so far in the game of life.

Kin lifts a finger and holds it out: a perch. Erasmus instantly hops from Balastair's shoulder and flies over to the finger. A bit of sleight of hand, and Kin conjures a palmful of sunflower seeds out of thin air.

The grackle eats greedily.

Peck peck peck.

"I see Erasmus is doing well."

Balastair nods. "He's quite the charmer. And the eater, as you can see. Shen is still everyone's bird girl, I presume."

"She is. Just hatched a few new eggs. They don't all talk like Erasmus here."

Erasmus stops pecking seeds for a moment and, as if in defiance of his gift, merely chirps instead of mimicking words. "If ever the day comes that you don't want him anymore, my sister'll gladly have him back."

"Never. He's my constant companion. Don't know what I'd do without him, honestly. Come, Erasmus, stop bothering the nice man." He taps his shoulder twice with a finger, and the bird returns, cheeping and peeping.

Kin continues: "Why *are* you down here? This isn't your scene, Bal."

He's not yet ready to go there yet. "A drink, to start?"

"Micky Finn's?"

"And Klee-Klo, yes."

The leering, toothy shark from the Micky Finn's bottle greets Balastair as Kin flips it, pours some into a glass shaker. A squeeze of lime, a few marbles of ice. But then Balastair sees Kin's eyes dart, casting his gaze toward the back of the speakeasy.

"What is it?" Balastair asks. He starts to turn around, but Kin issues a short, sharp hiss that gives him pause.

"I think it's time to cut the fog and tell me why you're here." Deep breath.

"I need passageway off the flotilla."

Kin pauses in making the drink. "For you."

"For me and the girl."

"The Heartlander."

"Mm. Yes. She's . . ." *In trouble.* "She's gone to the Engine Layer. I think. Someone will need to . . . to find her there and get her off the Saranyu. Somehow. Some way. As for me—"

"I can't do anything for you."

"What?"

"You've got a tail. One of the peregrine's people."

"He . . . he might not be here for me. You don't know—"

"He's Frumentarii." Kin slides a fizzing glass toward him, plops a slice of lime down over the rim. Juice drips to the bartop. "If they're watching you, I can't risk it."

"But that's *why* I need you," Balastair says between clenched teeth, suddenly angry. "If everything were acey-deucey, I wouldn't require your help, would I? For Crow's sake, Kin, we're old friends; we were kids together playing on Palace Hill; my mother treated you as if—"

"Your mother's gone. The fix is in. Things are happening, Balastair. Big things. We can't jeopardize our plans and turn the peregrine's eye toward us. Not now. Maybe soon. Get safe. Hide if you have to. Contact me again—maybe then we can do something for you."

"Damnit, Kin." He holds the drink with white knuckles but does not take a sip. "The girl, then. The Heartlander."

"We'll find her."

"What's the price?"

A puckish smile twists his face. "I'll add it to your tab."

Balastair lowers his gaze to his drink. He takes a long, slow sip. The bubbles tickle his tongue, but he barely feels them. The horse kick of the herbal gin is warm. He tries to relax. Forces out the breath he's holding.

"I need to get out of here, then."

Kin nods. "You do. I can help with that." He lifts a finger, makes a small gesture toward the back, mouths a few silent words. Now Balastair risks a glance, sees a tall, fire-haired waitress with legs as long as the sky heading toward a gruff, silver-haired thug in the back. She swoops over him, pouncing like a cat, pinning him to the back wall.

"Now?" Balastair asks.

"Now."

He hops up. Heart beating.

Erasmus shifts nervously from foot to foot.

Balastair winds his way through the tables.

The thug pushes the girl aside.

He turns, looks in Balastair's direction—

But she's on him again. Like ants on honey.

The man shoves her—

Into a table. A glass breaks. The noise reverberates.

The distraction is just enough.

Balastair winces and ducks through the doorway back toward

the antechamber of books. The shelf opens and then closes behind him. Guilt and fear chase his steps like a nipping hound.

Gwennie drools blood.

She makes a small, panicked sound in the back of her throat as her tongue finds a molar toward the back—the tooth wiggles in the socket.

Tears run hot through the dirt on her cheeks.

Her hands are bound tight behind her. Legs tied to the chair legs beneath her. Her head throbs. Her arms, too. Her hip.

Everywhere they hit her.

The man and woman she thought were her saviors were anything but. They beat her. They dragged her here—to a small room in the Engine Layer. A storage room by the looks of it: crates of provisions, tools bracketed to the walls with chains fixed by padlocks.

The man comes back into the room. His face shield is raised. He's handsome. Young, like Balastair. Face like a fox.

"I am Adrian," he says. He removes the face shield entirely, sets it on the ground. Then he pulls from his pocket a couple of small green leaves, which he begins to chew. "The woman was— well, *is*—my sister, Adriana. We're twins, if you're wondering."

He holds up a visidex. Her picture is on it.

Gwennie tries not to whimper. Tries to turn it into a snarl.

"This is you?" He tilts the visidex, peers at it. "Gwendolyn Shawcatch. You went off your leash, poor puppy." He clucks his tongue in faux disappointment. "Oh, my manners—I still haven't told you exactly who I am. I am a member of the Frumentarii.

The Peregrine Guard. Curious point, there: in the Old Words, *Frumentarii* means 'corn,' or 'corn farmer.' Now obviously"— here he does a small spin—"I'm no corn farmer. But just as corn, or what we derive from it, helps keep this city flying, so too do we keep it flying by protecting it from the threats above, below, and beyond it. So, you'll see, the metaphor is quite apt."

He takes a few steps closer. He sets the visidex on the ground by his feet and then draws from his back pocket a pearlescent handle from which emerges the square blade of a straight razor.

He flashes it in front of her eyes—not a threat, not yet, but to show off. "Whalebone. So I'm told. You don't know what a whale is, do you? Big creatures. Apparently bigger than most boats. They're dead now. Have been for years when the seas changed after the coast . . . broke."

Adrian moves fast. Pain burns across her cheek. Her jawline feels suddenly wet. Her collar. All she can see is white. She cries out.

Balastair hurries back through the tunnels, a thousand worries clustering in his heart like an orgy of snakes—he expects that the addict boy will emerge from the shadows with another knife of glass. Or maybe the peregrine's man will know a shortcut— the Wolf's Lair pretends to be uncharted territory away from the prying eyes of the Empyrean administration, but everyone knows that the Lupercal exists only because it is *allowed* to exist. Will they find the girl in the Engine Layer? Is she already dead? Could she have fallen?

Will she escape?

Will *he?*

Erasmus senses the energy. Chirping and squawking.

"Go go go!" Erasmus clucks.

"I *am* going," Balastair snaps at the bird, though he doesn't mean to.

There. The way out and up. Back to Palace Hill. Crooked stone steps lead to a rusted metal ladder bolted into the wall. And above it, the trapdoor to the outside. He hurries up and up and up—hand on the door.

The sunlight of the afternoon is no longer above. Evening is coming on, casting longer, leaner shadows. He hurries back down Black Sliver Alley toward the street—

He emerges, heart pounding. Looks left, looks right. Sees an older couple out walking their ocelot, a few teenage girls standing on a porch behind some columns, passing around a visidex and laughing, pointing, sneering. He hears the wind. The distant creaking of the flotilla.

No agents. No Frumentarii. *We're safe.*

Back to the elevator then. Then onward to . . .

Well, he doesn't know where. Somewhere. To hide.

He knows a number of crannies, crypts, and cubicles. He's had to hide before. As a child. When his mother—

A black shape out of bright sky.

Headed right for him.

He cries out—

Sees the shape of a hooked beak, the curve of talons thrusting forward, the sweep of wings out, then back—

A white-and-gray falcon flies over his shoulder.

Erasmus squawks—

Purple feathers fly. Dots of something wet fleck Balastair's cheek.

"No!" he screams, spinning as the falcon—a peregrine falcon, he sees that now, small yellow beak, empty black eyes—pins Erasmus to the ground. The falcon begins to peck at the smaller bird as it thrashes—Balastair sees the splash of blood, and already the falcon is yanking its head back, bird guts in its beak like so much red yarn—

He roars and tries to kick at the falcon—

The shrill sound cuts the air.

Something like a giant fist hits him at the base of his spine. His hips go cockeyed, and one foot goes out from under him. His body crashes to the white cobblestones. Shoulder and head hit hard—*crack*. His vision goes double, but then he sees two Erasmuses pull away from two peregrines, four dark little wings flapping, his friend starting to catch flight.

The world goes from two to three and swims back to one.

Go, Erasmus. Fly!

The falcon hops. Talons catch the smaller bird.

Again pinning the caviling grackle to the earth.

One talon plunges through Erasmus's eye.

The little bird lies suddenly still.

Balastair cries out, but his scream is lost in his throat, swallowed by a surge of vomit. He rolls over on his belly and pukes—the hot acid of herbal gin leaving his throat a seared channel. In the back of his mind he knows he's been hit by a sonic blast, but in the front of his mind the world is lit up with memories of the little bird—eyedropping little vitamin mixes into the baby bird's beak, Erasmus's first word ("'Rasmus!"), the

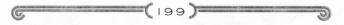

time the grackle spilled all that seed in the kitchen and rolled around in it like a child playing.

Balastair crawls over his own spew, swiping at the falcon that's now ripping the body of the little bird to bits and swallowing gobbets of grackle meat. The falcon grabs Erasmus's carcass and takes flight.

Balastair weeps.

Then—across the street:

The peregrine himself.

A sonic rifle slung over his back. Descending from the roof of a dark house on a rope. He lands and takes long strides toward Balastair.

Balastair tries to stand, but his limbs go rubbery. He can't manage.

"Hello, Balastair," Percy says. "You know, it was really very rude to leave me there in your home like that. Here I thought we were friends."

"I'll kill you," Balastair says with a gasp, the words coming out soggy and mush mouthed, containing little of the venom he intended.

"Yes, yes, I'm sure you will." He looks up to a lamppost where the falcon now feeds. *Erasmus . . .* "I see Horus has found a meal. Ugly little birds, grackles. You did know we raised falcons in the Peregrine Guard?"

"Kill. You."

"So you've said." The peregrine kneels down next to Balastair. "I'm going to take you away now. Somewhere we can get to know each other for a good long while—away from all the distractions this place has to offer. The Lupercal, for instance. I never pegged

you as the type. Oh, but you used to live here, didn't you?" He suddenly snaps his fingers. "Right, right, I knew there was something I wanted to tell you. It relates to our *last* discussion—the girl. Remember her? The one you were left to monitor and control? Turns out she escaped. She found her way to the Engine Layer, of all places, which is really quite an impressive feat. I'm not sure anyone's ever tried that one before. Just the same, I want you to find comfort in the fact that she has indeed been found. I have my best men keeping her safe."

The peregrine stands.

Balastair gags. Pushes himself up on his wobbly arms.

"I swear," he gurgles. "I will *kill*—"

Percy smashes him in the back of the head with the sonic rifle.

His last sight before darkness is a lone purple feather blowing across the cobblestones. Painting in bird's blood.

Adrian speaks over her mewls and whimpers.

"Just marking you," he says, grunting a little as he carves into Gwennie's cheek with the straight razor. "The symbol of the peregrine. To show the world to whom you belong. That you are a *kept* girl."

She wrenches her head back, tries to pull away from the blade—

He grabs the back of her head and pulls her forward.

"Please," she cries out. "Don't do this—"

But she sees something.

Above his head. Between two long, looping pipes.

A grate. A metal grate. Slowly sliding backward.

The pain brightens again—more blood flows.

"And so, since we have you here, we can do whatever we wish to you. Adriana and myself; we could share you. There's a room down here for that sort of thing. We can go there next as long as—"

Again she pulls her head back and cries out.

The metal grating has moved all the way back.

Something is descending. Something thin.

With a loop on the end of it.

The Peregrine Guard sneers and rolls his eyes before once more wrenching her head forward.

His face brightens in glee.

"Ah-ha-ha! Finished." He wipes her wounded cheek with the back of his hand and beholds his handiwork. "I am a failed artist, or so I thought. Perhaps I should reconsider my vocation—"

The looped cord from above suddenly drops over his head.

A look of surprise flashes across his face.

Then the cord tightens. *Vvvviiiiip.*

His eyes bulge.

He tries to cry out, but the only sound that comes is a whispery gurgle. His neck darkens. His cheeks redden.

And suddenly he's yanked upward.

Just high enough so that his feet are off the ground.

They kick. Furiously. One foot catches Gwennie in the chest, and the chair suddenly lurches backward, falling. *Boom.* The air blasts out of her lungs as Adrian thrashes in midair, hands desperately fumbling at the cord around his throat—but his fingers can find no purchase.

His arms drape by his sides.

His legs quit kicking.

Capillaries burst and bloom behind his freckled cheeks.

Blood runs from where the cord bites into his neck.

Then the cord goes slack, and his body drops.

Fwuddump.

From the darkness between those two pipes, Gwennie sees two faces peering down. One is the face of a girl, younger than Gwennie by at least five years, her cheeks greasy with oil, white-blond hair matted with filth. She grins and drops through the hole as easily as a drop of water plopping from a leaky faucet.

The other is a man's face. Long, crooked, beak-like nose. Dark eyes beneath shaded brows. The stubble on his face matching the stubble on his head almost perfectly. He drops down, too.

He rubs the little girl's head, tousling her hair.

"Good work, Squirrel," he says.

"Thank you, Papa." The girl beams.

Together they both step over the body and toward Gwennie. She thrashes in her bonds. "Get away from me. Please."

The man offers a lean, callused finger pressed against his lips, and then hers. "Shhhh. Don't get the wrong idea. We're not here to hurt you. We're here to rescue you, dummy."

The little girl giggles.

CIRCLE OF DOGS

CAEL BOLTS THROUGH the corn, the stalks recoiling from him.

Even Hiram's Golden Prolific fears what he is. Or worse, what he is *becoming*.

It's enough to distract him from forming any proper plan, so that when he finally emerges back into the open ground at the fore of the depot, he does nothing to prepare himself for what might be waiting.

And what's waiting are the Sleeping Dogs.

A dozen of them, easy. Behind them, red smoke dissipates from the open mouth of the front depot gate like demon's breath.

All the men wear canine masks. Some metal, others wood. A few have manes like the one he saw on the raider inside. The bearded one whose nose he broke is here, too, holding a ratty handkerchief to his busted face.

They have Lane and Rigo.

Lane kneels, black tape across his mouth and a long-barreled sonic shooter pressed to his temple by a man Cael thinks isn't much older than the three of them—the young man's mask is pulled up over his head, revealing dark eyes, a cheeky grin, a few wisps of facial hair on his chin and cheeks.

Rigo sits slumped against the depot wall. Chin to his chest. He's breathing. But he's not conscious.

Cael lifts the rifle and aims it at the man with the pistol against Lane's head. He stares down the iron sights and places the raider between them.

"Ahoy," the man calls, giving a little wave with his free hand. "Nice of you to join the party." His eyes widen, and he whistles. "Looks like quite the shooter you've got there."

"So do you."

"This? It's all right. Sonic. I've got it dialed up so if I pull the trigger—"

"You'll kill my friend."

"I'll empty his pretty head like I'm gutting a pumpkin."

"You kill him, then I kill you."

"Yeah, see, that'd be just awful, wouldn't it? Thing is, friend—"

"I'm not your friend."

"*Thing is*, you kill me, I've got men all around me here and men on the boats beyond. One of them will kill you. And your friend with the bum leg—who, if I'm being perfectly honest? *Does not look good.*"

Cael's weapon wavers. Just slightly.

"So, what, then?" Cael asks. "I put down my gun, you put down yours, and we all go our separate ways?"

"Can't have that. You've seen us. Don't want you running to your skybastard masters and giving us up."

"I figure they pretty much know who you are by now, wouldn't you say?"

The raider captain shrugs. "Eh. What's the verse? 'You shall not suffer a traitor to live.'"

Cael takes a tender step forward, gun still up. "That ain't the verse. It's 'You shall not suffer a witch to live.'"

The raider shrugs. "I'm not much of a reader these days."

"And we're not traitors. We're no Empyrean fools. We're Heartlanders. Like you."

The raider grins and winks. "Hardly like *me*."

"Let my friends go or I'm throwin' a bullet right between your eyes."

The other raiders prickle at that. They begin to move in toward him. One slow step at a time, the circle closes, the corn at his back.

"I think instead I'd prefer you to come with us."

"To what aim? We're no good to you raiders."

"We'll find a use for you. If only to find out what you know."

"We don't know shit."

"Everybody knows something. Put down the gun."

Cael hugs the rifle tight against his shoulder. Bracing for the recoil. "Let. My friend. *Go*."

The raider, with his pistol still against Lane's temple, pulls another pistol from the back of his pants. He—slowly, cautiously, no fast moves—levels the gun at Cael. Cael thinks: *Shoot him, godsdamnit, shoot this cocky prick right godsdamn now*, and his finger

hovers over the trigger, feeling the cold steel underneath, one squeeze, one pull. . . .

Lane looks up. Eyes wide. Full of fear.

Rigo isn't moving.

The realization hits him like a gale-wind of hissing pollen: *There's no way out of this.* The raider's right. Cael pulls that trigger, everyone dies.

He curses and lowers the barrel.

The raiders sweep over him.

26

THE CHOICE
AND THE OFFER

THEY SAY TO HER, *We're the Sleeping Dogs.*

She's dizzy. Beaten up. Confused. She doesn't believe them. The Sleeping Dogs can't be on the flotillas. That doesn't make sense. But they say it doesn't matter if she believes them because belief doesn't change truth, and this, dear girl, is truth.

They say, *We're getting you out of this place.*

Out of the sky. Off this floating island.

Back down to the Heartland.

She's elated. At first. They say it's time to hurry. They have a small dragonboat waiting. She can imagine the ground beneath her feet already. Hard dirt broken between pressing knuckles. She can hear the wind whistling a tune between the corn.

But then she says no. *I can't go.*

You're going, they tell her. They'll tie her back up and chuck her into the boat if they have to. She tells them they can try. But she'll kick. And bite. And scream herself raw and then scream

some more. And if they manage to get her off the flotilla, she'll just find a way right back.

Because she has family here. Mother, father, and her little brother.

They sigh. They look at each other. As if they're not sure. As if maybe she's a burden, a heavy bag of stones around their hips, a bloody anchor dragging behind them—

But there's that other look, too. The one that says maybe there's something here. They watch her.

As if they're looking for the fire in her eyes.

She tries to show it to them. The fire. The anger. That desperate, flinty spark in the darkness. She bares her teeth, too. Let them see. Let them imagine their skin between her teeth. Let them picture her hands around the Empyrean's neck.

Fine, they say.

You can stay.

But there's a cost.

You stay, they tell her, *then you're one of us.*

She nods. *I'm one of you*, she says. Spoken with some finality. One of the Sleeping Dogs.

PART THREE

WOLVES AT
THE DOOR

27

RETRIBUTION
AND RECOMPENSE

PERCY GASPS AND SHUDDERS and lays the flat of his hand on the naked expanse of Merelda's back, the fingers splaying out and holding her firmly. She pants gently, delicately like a little bird, into the white cotton pillows.

She feels the peregrine bend down and forge a trail of small kisses from between her shoulder blades to her neck. Then he cups her chin and lifts—one final kiss on her cheek before he gets up.

Merelda turns over and straightens herself out. She pulls sheets up over her hips, sheets so airy they might as well be sewn from strands of passing clouds. She smiles. Overwhelmed by the luxury of it all.

Percy whistles a tune, heads to the washroom. She hears him pump water into the sink. Hears his hands splashing.

She feels sore. And warm. This was a nice moment. A break.

A break that ends with the short, sharp shock of a single question:

"You haven't seen her, have you?" he asks, poking his head around the bend of the restroom. Water drips off his chin. Cleaning himself of her.

"Her?" she asks.

He senses her little deception; she can see it on his face. "You know who I mean, Mer."

"Gwendolyn." *Gwennie.*

"Yes. The Heartland girl."

"No. I told you, Percy, I—"

"—Didn't know her well, yes. I understand. I just thought—" He steps out of the bath now, a fluffy white towel around his midsection, still showing the clean handles of his hips, the sharp V above his . . . "If she would come to see anybody, it might be you."

Gwennie has been gone nearly two weeks at this point. She escaped right out from under Percy's nose. Merelda knows no other details except that this girl has crawled up under his skin. He's been intractable all week. Cruel little jabs and jibes. Not just to her. But to his wife, Yasmin, too. As for his young son, Jace, well, Percy has barely acknowledged the boy.

Since Gwennie slipped the noose, it's as if he's been stomping around on dark clouds, flinging thunderbolts.

Today, then, felt like a nice respite from that—a break in the storm, a soft ray of sunlight through all that rain.

And now this. Back to Gwennie.

A grim thought slithers its way into her brain: *I wish they'd just find Gwendolyn Shawcatch and make her go away.*

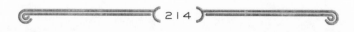

The starkness of that thought—the coldness of it—horrifies her. She doesn't mean it. Not really. But she's not lying to Percy when she says how little she knew the Shawcatch girl. Gwennie was Cael's age and came for dinner now and again (and of course the two were rutting around together like a pair of Ryukyu rabbits). They talked. They were friendly enough, and everyone in town knew everyone else. But they weren't *friends*.

Still. Gwennie had to come *here*. Had to *complicate* things. Though Mer reminds herself that it wasn't Gwennie's fault. The Lottery—not as prime a prize as they'd long figured, a fact that disturbs her still, at least until she feels the softness of the sheets on her skin, smooth like milk. . . .

"So, you haven't seen her."

"I haven't seen the dang girl," she says, hearing the sudden pluck of a banjo string in her voice—as the saying goes, 'The twang in your dang.'

Percy catches it, too. He hurries over to the foot of the bed and tilts his head the way he does when he's about to impart a lesson.

"Careful," he says, voice low. "You don't want to sound like a Heartlander—"

Her turn to interrupt him: "I am not a Heartlander."

"Yes." He bristles. "And don't interrupt me. I don't care for it."

"Sorry." She tries to smile. "I am. Sorry." This train needs to switch tracks. "Where do you think she went? The Shawcatch girl, I mean."

But he's not budging, not yet. "If anyone finds out you're from the Heartland, you know I'll have to disown you, yes?

I'll have to put you out. Or worse, administer some kind of . . . justice. We don't embrace refugees from the dirt." He runs a small towel along his jawline. "They'll have me drop you in some dark hole inside the Engine Layer, make you turn a crank for the rest of your life. Or worse, they'd make you serve in the Lupercal, working a whole different kind of crank, believe me."

"I . . . understand. I don't want to leave here."

It's true. She doesn't.

She loves this place. Loves its comforts. Loves sneaking little luxuries back to the Heartland for her family.

And she loves Percy Lemaire-Laurent, the peregrine of this flotilla.

"I love you," she says, struck by the need to confirm that to him—it feels desperate, blurted out like that. It's not the first time she's said it.

"We don't know where the girl's gone," he says, choosing *now* to switch the tracks of the conversation. (It's also not the first time he's avoided her overtures of love.) "She was in the room. Then she wasn't. One of my men—my best men, at least down that far—is dead. We suspect she'll try to find her family. And when she does, we'll have her. It won't be long. She can't stay hidden forever. Eventually the rat will come for its cheese."

"Shuck rats don't eat cheese," Merelda says, pushing off those small but significant thoughts that threaten to darken her mood just as they're darkening his. "They eat corn."

"It's a saying," he says, irritated. "We don't have rats on the flotilla. There hasn't been a rat seen on this ship in the last ten years."

"No rats. But you do have corn. A lot of corn."

He narrows his eyes. "What does that mean?"

"We grow the corn. A lot of it. And it all ends up here. It's why the Heartland life is a hard one. My father—"

He flings the smaller towel at her. It hits her in the face, and she bats it away. By the time it hits the floor he's grabbing her chin once more—no gentle touch. His fingers and thumb are like pincers. She tries to pull away, but he's holding her fast.

"You. Are not. A *Heartlander*. You don't know anything about corn. Or rats." His voice takes on a tone of forced whimsy, his free hand gesturing like a butterfly taking flight. "You are an *Empyrean* girl. A *house-mistress* to one of the most *powerful men* on this flotilla. So sit back. Enjoy it. Stop asking questions. Stop pretending like whatever happened on that pollen-choked dirt-farm you once called home is anything but a distant memory—or better yet, a total illusion."

He lets her face go.

Then rips open a drawer by the bedside.

He flings a package down onto her breasts. A small box of chocolates—little truffles dusted with ingredients she'd once never seen before. Tongue-tickling spices. Smoky salts. Powdered flowers—violet, rose, dragons-ear. And none of that compares to the chocolate, which is so good, any Heartlander would slit his mother's throat for a taste.

But right now it feels like a box of kiln ash.

"There," he says. "Eat your treats. Stay in bed in this fine suite I allow you to have. And get shut of any notions of being anything but my curious, mysterious little *Empyrean* house-mistress."

"You're being mean," she says. "I don't like it."

"So make me happy and do as I ask."

She knows ways of making him happy. Her hand moves toward the inside of his knee. Her thumb draws circles. His gaze flits down.

"What are you—"

She lets her hand drift farther. Wider circles with her stroking thumb.

"I don't have time," he says, but the wind is out of his sails.

Her hand crawls up, up, up until it can grip him and pull him back to bed. He falls onto her. His mouth on hers. The chocolates swept aside.

KNIVES OUT

HER ARM IS SORE, but she doesn't care—the anger Gwennie feels hasn't diminished; it's a fire that keeps burning, keeps feeding on whatever she gives it, and so she grabs at her belt and flicks her arm three times in quick successions—*fwip fwip fwip.*

Three knives flung toward her victim.

Each clatters against the rusted metal wall behind it. Each drops to the ground. She curses. And spits. And kicks at the ground.

Her victim—a head and a torso made of sandbags and swaddled together in an extra layer of burlap—remains standing.

But then she sees a tiny whisper-stream of sand trickling from her target's "shoulder."

She whoops and pumps her fist.

Davies scowls. His brow furrows like a freshly dug ditch. "I'm not impressed. You want me to be impressed, but do I look

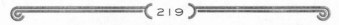

impressed?" He calls to the back of the room, "Squirrel, am I impressed?"

"No, Papa."

"But I hit the dummy," Gwennie says.

"I don't think our burlap friend over there enjoys being called a dummy by such a dummy."

"Hah, dummy!" the little urchin girl yells from the back.

Gwennie shoots her a look. The girl gives her the middle finger.

She turns back to Davies. "I'm no dummy, and you watch your mouth."

"*You* watch where you're throwing those knives."

"I'm getting good."

"You're getting one degree less awful."

"That's something."

He rolls his eyes. "You want to see what *something* is? Squirrel!"

The girl skips and traipses over, la-la-la. "Papa?"

"Knives, my darling little girl, the knives."

The girl pirouettes as if she doesn't have a care in the world, as if she's a sweet little princess playing with dolls instead of a motherless, smudgy-cheeked rebel girl in the bowels of a flying city. She picks up the knives, dainty as anything, as if she's picking up crumbs of bread, then dances back over to her father and Gwennie.

"Papa," she says, offering him the knives.

"Show the dummy how we throw knives, Squirrel."

The first two knives fly in two blinks of Gwennie's eyes— one minute the girl is standing there giggling, the next she spins

around and her arm is outstretched and the two sides of the target's neck are torn open. Sand pours out. One knife remains.

Squirrel turns back around, facing away from the dummy.

She cranes way back and flings the knife backward and upside down. The blade finds the center of the dummy's sand-filled head and sticks there like the prong of a hat rack.

Squirrel giggles again and twirls.

"*That's* how you throw knives," Davies says. "My ten-year-old throws knives better than you. *Way* better. She makes *you* look like the child. A child with a dirty nappy hanging off her bottom, sticky jam-hands fumbling with some cat turd she found in a nearby sand pit, cheeks wet with tears and—"

"I get it," Gwennie barks. "So, what's the secret?"

Davies kneels by his daughter. "What's your secret, Squirrel?"

"I just don't think about it!" She holds up her hands, like, *I don't know!*

"See?" Davies says, standing. "She just doesn't think about it."

"Is that how you throw knives?"

"Bah. I don't throw knives. I like a gun at my hip."

"I want to try again."

"Nuh-uh-uh," he says. "It's time."

"Time?"

"Time to meet with Salton."

Mary Salton is a hard-looking woman. Her face is dark leather marked by the tines of a fork. Her hair, short: little curls of dark hair tight to the scalp. Gwennie met her when she was first offered the deal to stay. And she hasn't seen her since.

Salton sits at a table made from a few corn-fuel drums with a plywood board laid over the top.

Gwennie enters the room.

Davies closes the door behind her, leaving her alone.

"Sit," Salton says. An empty half drum waits, serving as a stool.

Gwennie sits. Hesitant.

Salton slides a visidex across the table. The screen is dark. "Tap the screen."

Gwennie's not sure why this feels like some kind of trap, like she's going to touch the screen and the floor will open up and she'll be tossed into open air, down through the clouds, down toward the unforgiving earth.

Still, what can she do? She taps it.

A half-blurry image appears on the screen.

Two figures sitting in a café.

One of them, a man she recognizes as the peregrine.

The other, a girl a half inch away from shoving a cupcake in her mouth. A cupcake with frosting so tall it's like the Babble Tower men once tried to build to be closer to the glorious manse of the Lord and Lady—a tower the Lord and Lady struck down with world-drowning storms.

Gwennie knows that girl.

Merelda McAvoy. *La Mer.*

"You know her," Salton says.

"I . . ."

"You do. We know you do."

"Yeah. Yes. I know her."

"We want you to go to her."

Gwennie almost laughs. "*What?* Go to her?"

"Sorry, do I have shit in my mouth?"

"I . . . wh . . ." She makes an incredulous little snort. "Merelda McAvoy is with the peregrine."

"Clearly."

"The peregrine who probably won't be very nice to me if he catches me visiting with his little . . . house whore."

"She's not a whore; she's a house-mistress."

"I don't get the difference."

"She is his mistress. She chooses to be with him. The look in her eyes is one of love. Or, at least, fascination." Salton sniffs and scowls. "It is *because* she is with the peregrine that you will go to her."

Gwennie stands. "Whoa, no, I'm not doing that. I have one job here, and it's to find my family—"

Salton scowls.

"You *do* have one job," Salton says, "and it's to help us. You are to support the cause before you support yourself. Let me remind you of the deal you made. You're with us or you're against us. The ship you'd use to hop off the flotilla and float back down to the Heartland like a little feather has *literally* sailed. You either commit to our goals or we dump you over the edge like so much wind-frozen waste."

Gwennie gapes. She doesn't know what to say.

"You'll go to her. You will solicit her help one way or another."

"Help? Help with what?"

"Help with destroying the Empyrean, Miss Shawcatch."

29

SHINING THE HORSE APPLE

THE FLOTILLA is a black beast passing across the sun.
The flying city casts a long, dark shadow over the town of
Boxelder.

Proctor Simone Agrasanto stops and stands in the middle of
the street, staring up, shielding her eyes from the ragged fingernail of white sunlight creeping around the edge of the flotilla.

She wonders which flotilla that is. It's either the Ormond
Stirling Saranyu or her own home city, the Keppert Shinehart
Anshar. No others would be floating this close at this time of
the year.

Squinting, she returns her gaze to the town around her.
The bubbled-up plasto-sheen "main street." The tavern, the
Tallyman's office, the doctor's, the general store—and, beyond
that, not much else but the swaying corn. Her skin feels greasy.
Her fingertips as dry as the inside of an old bone. And the pollen

has swollen her sinuses, made it feel as if she's trying to push a chicken's egg from the corner of her one good eye.

Since the other is just a dead pucker and all. Just thinking about it makes it itch. Folks watch her from the windows of their businesses and from between buildings, and so she has to resist the urge to flip up the eyepatch and go crazy scratching the skin around the ruined socket.

Nearly two weeks ago she thought her purgatory in this bowl of dust was swiftly fading: Boyland's crew had done what she felt was impossible. They'd found Cael and the two other boys.

Of course, they'd found them at the same time the Sleeping Dogs swept in over the Provisional Depot.

Boyland had been both apologetic and apoplectic.

Simone had told him to calm down. She'd said, *This is a good thing, not a bad thing.* Getting a bead on both Cael McAvoy and the raider army that's been a splinter under the Empyrean fingernail for decades?

She had told Boyland to follow closely.

Then she'd ordered a small strike-fleet of well-armed swift-boats to attack the raider contingent.

And, finally, she had the Anshar lob a torpedo at the Provisional Depot. Now it, like the town of Martha's Bend, is a smoldering crater.

A good way to send a message to these Heartlanders, she thinks. And, more important, to the raiders. *Anything you touch, you corrupt—and anything you corrupt, we destroy.*

But now . . .

She stomps into Busser's Tavern. As is her wont this time

every day. Devon, her attaché (his arm still hanging in a sling like a pigeon's broken wing), stands by the table. *Her* table. And there on the table is a bowl of chicha beer, a sour, fermented drink. After her first taste she'd called it a bowl of horse urine—it was acidic and made her cheeks pucker. But then the next day she had an unusual desire to taste it again.

And so began her daily ritual.

There, across the room, stands the barkeep. Tom Busser. Arms folded. Eyes staring out from under the dark slashes that are his brows.

She puts down the visidex. Has a sip of beer. She shudders the way she does every time, then taps the screen and initiates contact.

The face of the mayor's son appears.

He looks nervous.

He *should*.

"You have botched things," she says, taking another sip.

"We'll pick up the trail again. It won't be long."

"It's not just that, boy. It's that you pointed my swiftboats south. You know what they found in that direction?"

"The raiders?"

She almost laughs. "The raiders? Are you really that daft?" He starts to say something, but she shushes him with a short, sharp shake of her head. "They did *not* find raiders. They found corn. Wide-open tracts of empty corn. They were not where you said they would be."

"Hold on, I said they were *going* in that direction. I can't help it if they changed or decided to go east or west or disappear down a godsdamn rabbit hole—"

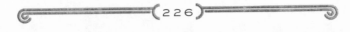

"Find them," she growls. "I don't want excuses. You know what excuses are? Lamentations to justify our own failures and weaknesses. You failed. Own your mistake. Fix what you broke. We'll talk again this time tomorrow."

Boyland nods. She can see the fear in his eyes even across the great distance connected by two visidexes.

She closes the connection and darkens the screen.

Outside, she is serenity. A sip of beer. A tight smile at Devon.

Inside, she's a swarm of starving locusts.

Boyland looks up and flings the visidex down on the floor of the yacht. On all sides, the corncobs thud against the boat. Stalks cracking as they push on. He keeps the boat down in the corn. All an effort to stay low. To stay *hidden.* The sails stick up over the tops of the stalks, but nothing there should catch the light, reflect back to those who might be looking from above.

"Why'd you lie?" Wanda asks, hands tucked into her pockets.

He says, "Because I don't like her. Or trust her."

"But we have a deal with her. You piss her off—"

"*I* have a deal with her. You have a deal with me."

She scowls. "That's not how I remember it."

He steps closer to her, chin up and out. "Then you remember it wrong." He smiles as he sees her looking left and right. "You're thinking your drunken angel with broken wings is going to protect you, aren't you? In case you hadn't noticed, Mr. Cozido bailed on us, Wanda."

"Maybe you ran him off."

He laughs that high-pitched pig laugh of his, a laugh that

arrives fast and dies quick. "Yeah. Maybe I did. Just like I ran those swiftboats south."

"Why did you tell her that anyway?"

"Because, *Wanda*, I don't want to get in the middle of a shooting war with the Empyrean. And I want to be the one to do it—to scoop up that piece of shit you're Obligated to."

"To which I am *Obligated*," she corrects him. "Though it could be *to whom*, but you said *piece of ess*, so I thought—"

"Whatever, priss."

"You didn't tell her about Mr. Cozido, either."

"No, I did not. That's not her problem; it's ours. And far as problems go, it's a pretty good one to have."

"You really hate him, don't you?"

"I don't bend much either way for that old drunk. But I am glad he's gone, because he was stinking up the boat with his whiskey farts."

She makes a face. "Not Rigo's dad. Cael."

Boyland doesn't need to answer given the way his cheeks redden and a fat vein stands out on the large, plains-like expanse of his forehead. But he answers anyway: "It's his fault all this happened. Him and his gimp father. Now my daddy's gone. And my daddy was no prize bull, but he was my daddy just the same. And my girl is gone, too, and she *was* a prize, a real peach, maybe the best thing that happened to me."

"That wasn't Cael's fault."

"But what *is* his fault is that he was sticking it to her before she ever got Obligated—"

"What, like she's ruined now?"

"Maybe not ruined but, but—*tarnished*. Like a mushy spot on a perfectly good apple."

"Some of us aren't the children of mayors who get to eat apples all that regularly, and I might add that it sounds more like you're mad at Gwennie than you are at Cael. You ought to be nicer to the women in your life. I seen the way you talk to your momma. No respect."

"Way I talk is my business, and I'm not mad at Gwennie, because it wasn't her fault. You hear me? She was . . . she was *made* to do it. Coerced! That's the word. *Coerced.* You talk to me about being nice to women, but Cael's no gentleman. He was the captain of that crew, and he could make her do whatever he wanted—"

"You're the captain of this boat. You think you can make *me* do whatever you want?" She stiffens and sticks out her chin, defiant.

"Clearly not, what with the way you ran off after Cael and pointed a damn *gun* at my head. Same gun that punk used to kill my father. I still haven't figured out what I oughta do to you for that." Boyland growls and steps forward, his finger thrusting up under her chin, his lips twisting into an angry sneer—

Thwack!

He yelps and jerks his arm back, and a small rock rolls by his feet.

Boyland's eyes cast skyward.

Up there, in the crow's nest, is Mole. He yells down, "You be nice to her, now!" And then he looks at Wanda. His tone changes. "Hey, Wanda. Hey, look what I'm learning!" He

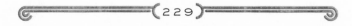

waggles a crudely made slingshot in the air. "You like the sling-shot, right?"

She smiles awkwardly and wiggles her fingers. "Hi, Mole."

Boyland yells, "You come down here so I can kick your ass!"

Mole spits a loogey that spatters against the yacht deck—Boyland has to dance out of the way so it doesn't hit him.

"Looks like you have another protector," Boyland says just to her. "Though for the life of me, looking at you and listening to that voice, I can't imagine why anyone would want to protect you. Hell, even Cael doesn't want you. Probably why he's running—just to get away from you."

She tries not to show her tears. Tries to keep her chin up as if she doesn't care. But she's not good at hiding that sort of thing.

Boyland's pleased with himself. She can tell that just by looking at him. He chuckles and says, "Now get to the back of the boat. Go make eyes at the hobo; maybe he'll give you some love."

A JORUM OF SKEE

CAEL'S BEEN IN this room for . . . weeks, maybe, he doesn't even know, what with the way the rats are squeaking and chattering in their cages—little feet digging into thatch nests, teeth tapping against the metal ends of water bottles jury-rigged and hung outside the wires.

He's been pacing. Doing push-ups. Sit-ups. Occasionally he visits with the little shuck rats since they're the only interaction he gets most hours of the day. It amazes him how different each of them looks from the others. Some are all black. Others gray or brown. The one in the cage in the top-right corner is all white, with eyes the color of blood blisters.

Cael calls that one Old Scratch, and it's either odd or utterly appropriate that the little albino rat seems the friendliest of the bunch. Squeaking and dancing around, trying to lick at his finger instead of nibble at it. He tells the rat, "If I saw you in the corn, I'd kill you and eat you."

The critter eeks and clicks its teeth and dances in circles.

"Don't worry, I'm not eating you today."

He sits back down on the floor. Doing nothing makes his body ache. And his mind, too. His body can't wander, so that's all his mind does: drift, wind, double back on thoughts he's trying to avoid.

Sometimes his fingers feel the top of his shirt, touching the small bump underneath. He doesn't want to think about it, but how can he not? He hasn't looked. He *refuses* to look. But he's let his hand wander under the fabric. Felt the margins of the three—not two anymore but *three*—leaves. Bigger than they were yesterday. And next to the stem is another small lump. Like a sprout pushing up a bulge of dirt before it breaks through.

He fails to suppress a shudder.

The Blight will be the end of him. Assuming he *doesn't* go the way of Earl Poltroon—taken over by vines and leaves, driven all the way mad by what must've been runners and shoots burying into the meat of his brain—everything is still ruined. The world will shun him. His friends will fear him. Gwennie won't ever want to touch him.

But Wanda . . .

The look on her face—shock and dismay.

But something else, too. Sympathy. As if she still cared about him.

He thinks about her a lot. Which surprises him. She seemed different, somehow. Less . . . well, less like the Wanda Mecklin he remembers. She had a toughness to her. Way she stuck out her chin. Way she held that rifle.

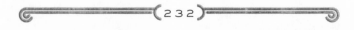

Cael imagines Wanda walking to him through the corn, this time without a stitch of clothes on her—he tries to think about what she'd look like. A lot of freckles, maybe. Gwennie has a birthmark on the inside of her thigh, just a little thumbprint like a smear of chocolate, but even when he tries to think about Gwennie, he thinks about Wanda instead. His hands on her hips, his lips against hers. And as he thinks it he can feel his own body responding, his heartbeat quickening, his pants growing tighter as—

Suddenly his chest starts itching as if he just rubbed the skin with nettles, and he can feel the stem-and-leaves twitching, curling, *straining*—

The door to the rat-room opens.

Cael gasps. Stops scratching his chest even though it's driving him batty not to.

There stands the raider who had the gun to Lane's head.

The one Cael has come to understand is their leader.

The raider has a bottle in one hand, two tin cups in the other. He walks over to the corner, hooks a chair with the toe of his boot and pulls it closer, then sits down on it, leaning forward.

"Jorum of skee?" the raider asks.

Cael eyes the raider as the man holds out the two cups. He rattles them: *cluh-clink cluh-clink.*

Cael reaches out, takes a cup.

The raider uncorks the bottle, which has no label.

He pours a draft in Cael's cup, then his own.

"You first," Cael says.

The raider shrugs, slugs it back. Sucks air through his teeth.

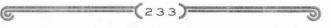

Cael bites his lip and then drinks deeply.

The whiskey is smooth. Burned sugar and charred wood. Lights him up like a hobo's barrel fire but doesn't sear him—there's just a spreading warmth like a puddle of hot caramel.

"That ain't no cheap fixy," Cael says.

"Nah, it's real deal skee," the raider says. "We make it ourselves. We call it Hair of the Dog That Bit You."

Cael drains the last drops of the whiskey and tilts the cup forward. "Might as well put some more in there."

The raider hesitates. "First, introductions. My name's Killian Kelly."

"All right."

"And you are?"

"Bored. Pissed off. You give me some sweet-tasting whiskey after leaving me here for Lord and Lady know how many days—"

"Two weeks. Or thereabouts."

"And now we're expected to be all chummy. But last I remember you had a gun to my friend's head and a bunch of you dog-headed bastards blew up our one chance to get on board the flotilla, so you'll excuse me if I don't feel like being chatty to some raider scum."

"Scum. Okay, Cael McAvoy, don't tell me your name."

"How the—"

"Your other friend. Lane."

Godsdamnit, Lane. Cael snorts. "I bet he's all moon-eyed over being held hostage by you raiders."

"He seems sympathetic to our cause. And I thought you might be. Especially given that rifle you were carrying."

"My rifle ain't got anything to do with your cause."

"Doesn't it?"

"Where I'm from we don't dance around the things we want to say; we just say the dang thing and get it over with. Like pulling stitches: just make it quick."

Killian's grin wavers a little before bouncing back. "One sec," he says, holding up a finger.

Then he steps back out of the room—Cael thinks, *When he comes back in, I'll rush him; I'll knock his ass to the ground and—* but when Killian steps back in, he has Pop's lever-action rifle in hand.

"This rifle," he says, pulling a small tool from his pocket. Screwdriver, by the look of it. "Is really quite interesting." He flips it around, starts unscrewing the butt-plate at the far end of the rifle. Cael's about to protest, but then he sees that someone has done a repair job on the splintered stock. Screws through metal plates do a hasty but effective job of bolting the wood back together. Finally, Killian says, "Here we go."

He turns the gun around so that the stock is facing Cael.

With the butt-plate gone, Cael sees a symbol in the wood. In black char, as if carved there and then burned, too.

A wolf's head inside a circle.

"That's our sigil," Killian says.

"I . . . I see that."

"This rifle belonged to a raider."

"That rifle belonged to my *father*."

Killian gives him a look like, *Well.*

"Oh, hell no," Cael says. "My pop was no dang raider. He hated you Sleeping Dogs same as any of us did."

"Then he must've stolen it from one."

"Must have."

"Though with as few bang-sticks like this one out there, I can promise that no raider gave up a shooter like this easy."

Cael shrugs, sticks out his chin. "Then Pop must've killed someone for it."

"That who your daddy is? A killer?"

"Say that again, I'll grab that rifle and stick it so far up your ass you'll taste gun oil for weeks."

Killian grins. "Maybe you're a killer, too."

That's it. No more of this.

Cael launches himself up, grabbing for the rifle.

But damn if that raider isn't fast, and Cael is slow. Killian darts aside, leaving only an empty chair for Cael to crash into. He cautions Cael—"Stay down, Cael"—but Cael doesn't listen. Instead, he grabs the chair, plans on throwing it from the ground up into Killian's dumb, smiling face.

Then Killian's boot connects with his side.

Pain throbs up and down his body, and he finds it suddenly hard to draw a breath. He rolls back over and makes a bridge out of his body and just . . . stays like that. Panting. Wincing.

"I hope I didn't crack a rib," Killian says.

"Go to hell," Cael groans.

"Yeah. Well. Here's the deal, Cael. You want me to spit it straight, I'll spit it straight. The Dogs are a shit-or-get-out-of-the-outhouse group. So I'm making you a choice: you either reel it in and decide to don the dog-mask with us, or you keep on clawing and hissing like a licked kitty and I dump your ass off into the corn. Though, to be clear, not before we slice off your tongue and slap you about the head and neck with it." He

grins and winks. "Just to make sure you don't blabber to any Empyrean about us."

"My friends won't stand for that," Cael says with a groan.

"Lane's already on board. He's an eager boy. Hungry for a little rebellion. He's got a real rage-face for the Empyrean—just the thought of him kicking their ass gets him a little stiff, I think. We can use that."

Godsdamnit, Lane!

"And Rigo?"

"Rigo, yeah." And it's here Cael sees the raider's smile give way to a grim mask and he starts to speak but no words come out. Finally, he says, "Time we had a real talk about your friend, Cael. I'm sorry, but . . . but Rigo didn't make it."

OBLIGATED

WANDA PACES THE back of the boat. Anxiety is like a wave of pins and needles washing over her. She doesn't trust Boyland. The hobo just keeps staring at her as if she's a shuck rat dancing back and forth. She hasn't been home in weeks, hasn't seen her mutt, Hazlenut, or her parents or Boxelder, and even though it's silly and hasn't really been *that* long, it's almost as if she can't remember what it all looks like: Was the window on Busser's tavern door a porthole or an octagon? Did Doc Leonard have chairs out on his front porch or was that the general store? Will she soon start forgetting things about her family and her dog?

But all that's a distraction. Pulling her away from what she's really trying oh so very hard not to think about—but that keeps haunting her like a ghost from the mouth of the Maize Witch—

Cael has the Blight.

She tells herself maybe it's not true. Maybe what she saw wasn't what she saw. They were all fighting in the corn. Maybe a bit of plant fell off, hooked on the underside of his shirt, stuck to his chest with a little . . . stem sap or whatever and . . . dangit, is stem sap even a real thing?

It was the Blight.

She could see it. Not just stuck *to* skin but growing up out of it, the way a plant grows out of the dirt. Pushing the skin up. Leaves uncurling.

The Blight is a sickness. A plague put here by Old Scratch and his daughter, the Maize Witch. That's what folks say. Though when her father was in his cups sometimes, he'd let slip a different idea: that the Empyrean did it to us. "To keep us afraid," he'd said one time. "Keep us scared so we don't notice how they're ruining us all."

But then her mother would step in, laughing as if it were just a joke or she was just covering up Daddy's drunkenness—a rare event at the Mecklin house, honestly—and then Daddy would realize it, and he'd laugh, too, and they'd change the subject faster than the grackle flies.

Whatever its origin, the Blight is a disease of the flesh and eventually of the mind. Men are not meant to be a seed-bed for plants. It just isn't right.

Cael having the Blight means he'll be exiled. (Though he already is, isn't he?) A hobo. (He's one of those, too, right?) And she as his Obligated and eventually his wife . . . she'll be exiled, too.

She'll be a hobo.

Her parents will never want to talk to her.

The townsfolk will say, "There goes that Blighted bride again."

They'll think she could have it.

And their kids . . .

She reaches out with both hands and grabs the railing of the boat to steady herself, forgetting that they're not floating *above* the corn but rather *within* it. Corn leaves reach for her and slice paper-thin cuts along the tops of her fingers and her knuckles, and she pulls back—

And bursts out sobbing.

The hobo comes up behind her.

"Don't cry, Little Mouse," he says. "It'll all be over soon."

Then he whistles a strange, discordant tune and wanders back toward the front of the boat. For some reason it only makes her sob all the harder.

TO LIE DOWN WITH DOGS

THEY LEAVE THE RIFLE and the whiskey behind, and Killian leads Cael down into the depths of the trawler, out from the rat-room and down another ladder to the belly of the beast.

Cael's hands are shaking.

Rigo . . .

He doesn't want to see the body. And yet he feels as if he has to.

He no longer thinks about anything else: not about Gwennie or Wanda, not about Pop or Mom or Lane or the dead men back at the farm. Not about the Blight, either. All he thinks about is Rigo.

And it's then it hits him: *This is my fault.*

He pushed and pushed. Rigo didn't need to come along on this adventure. But he was too good a friend, and Cael didn't have the sense the Lord and Lady gave a corn-weevil to see that his friend wasn't up to the task. And then when Rigo got hurt from Eben's jaw trap . . . again they kept pushing and pushing. Just a hundred more feet. Just another hour. Just another day. All while his leg was messed up something fierce.

They waited too long.

The guilt hits Cael like an auto-train.

Killian pauses before a door. He gives Cael a sympathetic look, a slight tightening of the mouth, a faint downward cast of the eyes.

Then he opens the door.

Rigo sits across the room in a rocking chair, blanket over his lap.

"Cael!" Rigo says, voice hoarse and raggedy. He gives a little wave.

"Sonofabitch," Cael says. *He's alive.* "You're alive."

He's about to turn around and haul off on Killian, maybe pop him in the cheek with a hard punch or just slam his head with Cael's own—but then the fire is sucked out of Cael's engine as Rigo stands.

Tries to stand.

He grabs first for a wooden crutch padded at the top with a swaddling of dirty rags, then uses it to pull himself up—

Cael rushes across the room, around a lumpy cot to help—

But it's too late. The blanket falls off, and when Cael rounds the edge of the bed he sees: Rigo's wounded leg isn't healed.

It's gone.

He's still got the knee, but the foot and most of the shin are . . .

"I think I lost something," Rigo says, followed by a weak *heh-heh-heh*. His eyes shine with tears that fail to fall.

"Jeezum Crow, Rigo, I'm so sorry." Cael helps him get the crutch under his armpit. Then Rigo hugs him. A lingering hug.

Into Cael's shoulder, Rigo says, "Not your fault, Captain."

"We'll get you home soon as we can."

"Naw, I'm still here. I'm still with you."

"Rigo—"

"Cael, I lost my leg, but I still have you guys. Losing a limb that's . . . that's just life in the Heartland."

"I . . ."

Killian snaps his fingers, gives a little whistle. "We gave him some Annie pills to keep the infection down. Why don't we let him recuperate a little, huh, Cael? Give the boy some room."

Cael stares darkly at the raider but then nods.

"I'll see you later," Cael says to Rigo.

Rigo smiles softly—unconvincingly—and sits back down in the rocker. Cael helps him with the blanket and then leans the crutch between the chair and the cot.

Back out in the hallway, Cael grabs hold of the high collar on Killian's coat and jacks him up against the wall.

"Why'd you cut his damn leg off? And why the hell'd you tell me he was dead?"

The raider just laughs. "Second question first: because I thought it'd be funny, Cael. No sense of humor on you? You do seem awfully serious. Shame—a good laugh can make even the most dire situation passable." Cael slams him against the wall again. "As for the *leg*, what would you have us do? The infection had taken hold. Like the roots of a tree crawling up under his skin. Like the Blight, but better because we could solve this problem with the chirurgeon's saw. Can't fix the Blight with anything but a bullet and some fire."

Cael's grip softens. *The Blight. Rigo. Raiders.* It all seems as if it's falling away from him—tumbling down, down, down, like falling out of the sky or worse, up into it—out of reach, into the clouds.

He lets go.

Killian dusts himself off, straightens the angles of his long collar. "And here I thought you would've been grateful, what with us saving your friend's life and all."

"I . . . I am."

"He says in a small, unconvincing little voice. Let's try that again with a heaping helping of crow at the end of this fork. Say *Thank you, Killian, for your hospitality and for saving my friend's life.*"

"You kept me in a room for what felt like forever."

"We fed and watered you like a good little plant—" *Does he know? Could he possibly know?* "And that *still* doesn't sound like a thank-you."

Reluctantly and regrettably he says, "Thank you."

"Those two words did not *drip* with the gratitude I expected, but for now it'll do. Let's go up top, see your other friend—who is not dead, nor is he missing any particularly critical *parts.*"

• • •

The sunlight washes out everything: a white wave bleaching his eyesight. Cael holds his hand over his face as he emerges onto the trawler's deck. And it's only then that he gets a real sense of the scope of the Sleeping Dogs. The trawler is big, he knew that much, but looking out over the boat he sees dozens of men and women working as part of the crew. A short little ember-spark of a girl spars with a fat man, two oar-poles cracking together. Nearby, a young lad scrubs the deck, showing off an ear that looks less like an ear and more like a little hillock of unformed skin—as if his creator gave up right before finishing the boy. Across the way, the bearded bear with the busted nose—the nose Cael busted—polishes a massive steel gun, an Empyrean sigil gleaming on its side in the noon-day light.

But it goes beyond the borders of this one ship, for all around them fly the boats of this armada: lean-nose pinnace-racers and fat-sailed cat-marans that call to mind Cael's own boat, *Betty*.

And they fly along like that. As if nobody gives a damn. As if the Empyrean couldn't stomp down with a big foot at any time, crushing them into the clay and gravel.

Cael's just about to ask how that's even possible before he sees someone striding over to him, arms out—

Lane.

The two crash together in a hug. Lane laughs, claps Cael on the shoulder, sticks his ditchweed cigarette back into his mouth, and lets it hang over the ledge of his lip.

"Good to see you, Captain."

"Captain?" Killian says, standing next to Lane. "They keep calling you that, Cael. You captained a boat?"

"I do." He clears his throat. "I did."

"Good to know. Maybe if your friend Mr. Moreau can convince you to stay, we'll get you piloting a ship before too long."

Lane gives Cael a look, and it's then that he notices. Lane looks . . . a little bit like Killian. A few wisps of hair on the sides of his cheeks. No long, red coat but a billowy button-down white shirt with half the buttons undone.

"I'll leave you to catch up," Killian says. "I've got business with one of my captains. If you'll excuse me."

Then, like that, he marches over and grabs a fat-barreled pistol off a peg and jams into it a three-pronged grappling hook. He lifts it without even looking, giving both Cael and Lane a wink and a smirk before—

Foomp!

The grappling hook fires off the side of the trawler.

It catches something on one of the cat-marans—winding around the top of the mast, as far as Cael can tell—and then Killian runs and takes a leap off the edge. Then comes the sound of the wire retreating into the pistol—*vvvvvviiiip!*—and the raider is flung onto the other boat some thirty feet away. It's all pretty damn crafty, but what's interesting, Cael thinks, is not what just happened *there*, but what's happening on Lane's face.

Lane's staring off. Smiling. *Admiring.*

"You've really bought the buck on this Sleeping Dogs thing," Cael says.

Lane is jostled out of his reverie; it's as if he forgot Cael was there. Or that he had a cigarette in his mouth. He takes a long pull and blows two streams from his nostrils like plumes of

steam from a bull's nose, then laughs. "What can I say? I'm in. You can't be surprised."

Cael grunts, starts walking toward the back of the boat. There the corn recedes from them, and somewhere out there, far, far away, is the town of Boxelder. And it's receding from them, too.

"I guess I'm not," Cael says. "Can't say I like it, though."

"They didn't need to keep us around. They didn't even need to let us live, Cael. C'mon."

"Is that what they did to those other workers at the depot? Kill 'em?"

Lane doesn't say anything.

"Those people were Heartlanders, Lane. They weren't Empyrean bootlickers. Just folks trying to do a job."

"The hell do you stand for?" Lane asks.

"What?"

"You heard me. What. Do you. *Stand for?* Because I just don't get it. Your pop was running a secret grow operation with a hobo army. He stood for something. He stood against the Empyrean. And now when you're asked to do the same, you don't seem to give a rat's tail."

Cael barks a mirthless laugh. "Don't gimme that happy horseshit, Lane, for Crow's sake. Just because my balls aren't tickled being among these raider scum-nuggets doesn't mean I'm sucking on the Empyrean teat, either, okay? I stand for . . . I stand for you, and me, and Rigo. I stand for Pop and Mom and Boxelder and everybody I know and love."

Lane sneers, flicks his cigarette out into the corn. "You know what I think? I think you stand for *yourself.*"

"Are you drunk? Right now? Like, did you drink a whole bottle of Killian's skee that set those coals up your ass a-burning?"

"I'm not drunk. I just think—you're out here because you want to find your girlfriend. That's really it, isn't it?"

"Oh, go to hell, Lane. Two weeks with these guys, and you're already dressing like them. Already got your little"—he reaches up and tugs at the tiny wisps of hair growing on Lane's cheeks—"your little Killian beard coming in. If I didn't know you better I'd say you were in love with *him* as much as you were with the raiders in general."

Lane bristles. "I just admire him."

"I see that."

"I don't know if they killed those people back at the depot. Maybe they did, maybe they didn't. But if you work for the Empyrean, you know the drill. You buy the buck from the sky-bastards, you best accept the consequences."

"Your mother's in the Empyrean employ, isn't she? Is that what you'd tell your mother if you saw her? *Sorry, Mother o' mine, you best accept the consequences.* Just before you let the raiders take a crack at her? Or would you slit her throat yourself?"

It's like knocking the chair out from underneath a man about to hang—the fight goes out of Lane. He looks gutshot.

"I'm sorry," Cael says.

"No, no, it's . . ." Lane rubs his eyes. "It's fine."

"I didn't mean to bring your momma into this—"

"She's one of them, not one of us. She made her choice just as I've made mine." The fire is gone from his voice, replaced with a quiet, steely determination. "Cael, if you don't want to be here, I'm not going to make you stay. I *do* want to be here. But if you

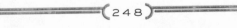

say we go, I'll . . . I'll trust you, and we'll find a way off this boat."
He pauses. "There's something else. Something I'm supposed to
tell you."

"What's that?"

"If we join up, all of us, then Killian says he can get us onto
the flotilla. Long as we help him with his problems, he can help
us with ours."

Cael shifts from foot to foot. Part of him feels as if this is Old
Scratch offering Jeezum Crow that famous deal, the one that
forced him to be trapped in the Heartland, never again to see the
sky-manse of the Lord and Lady. But the other part of him says,
here it is. *Here's* the way forward. He's been gnawing over that
problem, turning it around in his mouth again and again—*How
will we ever get onto a flotilla now? Another depot? Get captured and
brought there as criminals?* Now this: an opportunity.

He says the words before he realizes he's saying them.

"I'm in," Cael says. "You can tell your friend I'm in."

33

THE CAPTIVE SEA

ON THE COUNTER, a music box plays. It's a small brass platform that opens like a flower. From inside, a little auto-mate emerges: a man with a swan's long neck and lean head, dressed to the nines in a sharkskin suit and playing a little violin. Merelda tells it what song to play: "The Doggy Went A-Courtin'." A song her mother used to sing to her when . . .

Mom used to be so pretty back then. So alive.

Merelda feels as if her mother's spirit is in her as she dances around the kitchen of her small apartment—what they call a "ballet flat," an apartment meant only for a mistress, many of whom were once plucked from the roving ballet troupes on the flotilla.

She whirls and twirls, pretending she was just such a dancer. She pops the top of the small, shimmering gift box and places within its depths several small gifts: a lush wine mango, a trio

of chocolate bars in their wrapping (sky-salt and marshmallow crème), a small bottle of Bentley's Bitter Amari for her father, a bottle of Moon-Kiss Cola for Cael. And then the final component: a beautiful ostrich egg. Merelda holds it and stares at it for a while—a wondrous thing, this egg. Heavy enough that it must be held with two hands. She doesn't know what the bird looks like that lays such a massive thing, but it must be a *tremendous* creature.

Percy assured her the birds are really quite dull. He said he knew someone who raises a small flock of them on the Utrecht Carlotta Jumala. For racing, he said. She laughed at the thought of someone racing birds.

Now she bites her lower lip and has the little swan-man play "Madam, I Have a Very Fine Farm" as she puts the music box into the package and ties the whole thing up with a shiny silver bow. The music is now muffled, but still she sings and still she dances.

Living in the sky is the most wondrous thing.

Big eggs. Sweet fruits. Strange birds.

And chocolates.

"*Cannot send,*" the Parcel-Mate says, metal jaw rattling as its speaker intones the words. Whenever it finishes speaking, it ends with a little *ding!*

Merelda looks down at the box on the counter scale, the brass gears and counterweights shining in the bright overhead lights of the Parcelman's Office. Maybe the mechanical man did not

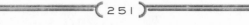

hear her. "I want to send this to"—and here she speaks loudly and clearly and very, very slowly—"the McAvoy Farm, that's in *Boxelder*, down below in the *Heartland*."

"*Cannot send*," the Parcel-Mate says again, round egg head and big, painted glass eyes turning toward Merelda anew, as if regarding her with a moment of robotic curiosity. *Ding!*

"But . . . I've sent packages before."

"*Cannot send. Please reclaim package. Thank you!*"

"Wh . . . why? Why can't I send it?"

"*Provisional Depot for Boxelder has been closed. Access to Boxelder has been closed. Closed by the Empyrean Department of Zoning under order of the Initiative, authorization signed by Project Leader Parl Juniper and flotilla Praetor Ashland Garriott. Thank you.*"

Ding!

The little bell makes her heart jump.

Why would Boxelder be closed?

"This must be a mistake," she says.

"*Parcel-Mates are not privy to mistakes.*"

Ding!

She hurries out, flustered, and suddenly afraid.

She's back at the apartment, which sits at the top of a set of side stairs, entirely separate from the peregrine's house. She'd only met his wife and son once. The wife had been nothing but warm hugs and handshakes and the kind of sincerity Merelda knew was as fake as the white on the woman's teeth, but it still had been better than the reception the boy'd given her.

He'd just stared at her. As if his eyes were little knives.

Sometimes she sees him still. Peering out of his third-floor bedroom porthole at her—the chubby, squirrel cheeks doing little to diminish his hateful stare. (A sudden thought strikes her: sometimes she sees Percy give that same look. Not to her. Of course never to her.)

Right now the porthole is empty—no boy staring.

A fact for which she's quite thankful.

She stands for a moment at the platform outside the red door that marks her apartment. They're near to the top of the Hill of Spears. She can see farther up the massive white manse that belongs to the praetor. Farther down she sees the white homes (always white here in the Hill of Spears) of the administrators of education, of currency, of mercantile society—all men with soft hands. (Blessedly her own hands are soft, too, for her lot down below was to handle a darning needle.)

Beyond those white houses sit the other hills and skyscrapers of the flotilla, swaying, bobbing, drifting apart and easing slowly together. Everything clean. Cloud-swept. Beautiful.

Nothing like the Heartland.

She thinks about that from time to time.

How much these people have. How much *she* now has.

But the Heartland suffers. . . .

No! She won't think that way. Just won't do it. What good does that get her? Nothing. The Heartland is a cruel place, its people hard and unpleasant. It's no place to dream. Those people don't give two whits about a girl's dreams.

Besides, the Heartland treats the hobos the same as the

Empyrean treats the Heartland. There's always an order to things. Someone's always on the top. Someone's always on the bottom.

She'd rather be on the top, thank you very much.

She nods as if answering a question she asked herself. Then she opens the door to her apartment and steps inside.

She nearly screams.

Gwendolyn Shawcatch sits there at her nook table.

And she has a knife. Facing down, the heel of the hilt in her palm, the knife-tip digging into the white lacquer-top table, the blade spinning lazily as she turns it. She's got bruises on her cheek that have started to yellow and some cuts that look to be healing up, but sometime between now and the last time they saw each other, someone worked Gwennie over good.

Merelda drops the package, startled.

Something inside the package goes *pop*. Goopy yolk begins to bleed out.

"Oops," Gwennie says. "You, ah, dropped something."

The egg. She tries not to cry.

"I'll scream."

"That's no way to greet an old friend."

"I'll do it. I'll really scream."

Gwennie rolls her eyes. *Such a dismissive, crass girl.* Always was. She never understood what Cael saw in her. "You go ahead and scream. Nobody's home over there, and I think you know that. The peregrine is off doing whatever it is he does. Looking for me, probably. His family is shopping. For the festival tomorrow."

"Festival . . ."

"The Tidings of Saranyu," Gwennie says. "Or that's what I'm to understand. I'm told they have a lot of festivals up here."

Merelda gives a small nod. "They . . . they do." So many it's hard to keep track of them. At her feet, the yolk slowly spreads, a gift her father will never have now. "What do you want, Gwennie?"

"I want your help."

"You can't have it. Get out."

"Ugh, what an attitude. Look at you. Barely recognizable as a Heartlander girl anymore. You're so rude."

"*You're* rude. I always said you were rude."

"Me? You were the one always up and running off. Leaving your family in the lurch." Gwennie shakes her head. "It's because of you that everything went to hell anyway."

"What do you mean?" Merelda feels a sudden tightness in the chest.

"Oh. You don't know. Do you?"

"Dangit, Gwennie, know what?"

"Jeezum, Mer. They got your pop. Maybe Cael, too. Proctor and the Babysitters went to the farmhouse . . . there was a shoot-out. I don't know what happened after that. It's been a while. Maybe they're okay. I hope they are."

"You're lying." But something itches at the back of her mind, and she hears the Parcel-Mate's voice: *Access to Boxelder has been closed.* . . .

"Believe what you want."

"I hate you."

"If that helps you sleep at night."

Merelda stiffens. "I can't help you. Even if I wanted to."

"You can and you will. Because here's what's going to happen if you don't—we're gonna tell everybody who you really are. Merelda McAvoy. Cornpone cracker girl born from the cradle of dirt. Smell her fingernails; you can still smell the clay caught under them."

"It won't matter. Percy loves me."

"Maybe he does. But it won't change what he'll do to you. Mistresses aren't permanent. Did anyone tell you that? What happens when your shift is over? When the work is done, huh?"

"I'm not a whore," Merelda says. Arms crossed.

"I don't know what you are, Mer, or even who you are. But if you want this ride to end now, refuse to help me. Then you can be whatever it is they decide, because they own you. But if you want to keep on living your pretty little life of . . . shiny boxes and shinier ribbons, then help me."

Panic races through her. A part of her knows that Gwennie is right. If she's compromised, Percy would stand by her, she's sure of it—but others may come for her. The praetor might see it differently. Might swoop her up and drop her down in the Lupercal, where she hears girls and boys have to do horrible things just to get by . . .

That's like the Heartland, too, in a way. A place below, where folks gotta whittle themselves down to nothing just to feed their families. That's why she had to get away from there. Why she had to try to help feed her own family with the spoils of the Empyrean.

But now, Pop, Mom, Cael . . .

"What do you need?"

"The peregrine's visidex."

"That's absurd."

"Be that as it may, I still need it."

"I can't . . . I can't help you with that."

"Sure, you can. He comes here most nights. To see you."

"So?"

"He brings his visidex. He's never without it."

Merelda looks left, looks right, as if she's going to see a door she can escape through, a door that will take her— Where? Somewhere. Anywhere. But there's no door. No escape.

Gwennie says, "When he comes in tonight, I'm going to be here. And you're going to distract him long enough for me to get that visidex."

"You're crazy. He'll kill you."

"And maybe you, too. So let's play this real cool, huh?"

CHOKING LAUREL

CAEL SLEEPS. If one can call it that. He rolls. Restless. Left to right. Leg over the edge of the cot. Back on the cot. The moth-eaten sheets make him too hot one minute, but as soon as he tosses them off: too cold, too cold.

He flits in and out of dreams, a stitching needle threading fabric.

In one dream Pop lies dead in the driveway outside a house that's supposed to be their farmhouse but is somehow bigger, emptier, and more decrepit. He's got one eye. His throat's been cut.

In another dream he's with Gwennie at the bow of his old cat-maran. Their clothes sit in a pile. Her hands sweep over him. The sun moves to stars above, light to dark, blue to black. He feels under the small of her back, fingers tracing down to the round tops of her buttocks, and he lifts her up—but he feels something there at the base of her spine, a nub of something that ends in a soft, velvety leaf. It fills him with horror, but his body betrays him, every part of him suddenly stiffening with excitement—

Gwennie turns toward him. And now it's Wanda's face. Peering from behind a webbing of vines that tighten against her straining skin, her mouth forming an "oh" of pleasure as vines emerge past her lips—

That dream melts away into a dozen smaller dreams, like a mirror broken, each shard reflecting a piece of an image: men in dog-masks, a horse flying, Rigo limping, the corn turning dark and dying, hands reaching for him through the blackening stalks.

He gasps awake.

His chest, itching so bad it hurts.

A voice whispers in his ear: *Soon, Cael, soon.*

Come to me. . . .

He tries not to whimper, but he feels under his shirt—

Oh no. Oh no oh no oh no.

The stem has grown. It's long now. Longer than his forearm. A vine. A damned *vine*. Not two leaves. Not three. But a dozen of them. Twitching and tugging under his fingertips.

Suddenly, it moves: fast as a snake. It shoots out from under his collar, coils around his neck—

And tightens.

He gurgles.

Across the room in the half darkness he sees Lane sleeping, head craned back, mouth open. He tries to call out to him.

Tries to reach for him—only a few feet away, fingers stretching, tendons burning—

The vine tightens. A deeper blackness threatens.

The voice again: *Do not try to fight it.*

Hell with that. He fights. He rolls out of bed. Claws at the vine around his neck. Feels the vine start to break apart under his fingernails—the stems splitting, spilling juice, then blood. Leaves pop off and fall into shadow.

Cael takes a swipe for Lane's hand—and just misses.

Fine. He'll have to do this himself.

He gets his fingers under the tightening collar—

He *rips.*

The vine splits. He hears it scream, and he doesn't know if everyone can hear him or if it's a scream only inside his head, but it's loud and it's terrible and it chills every inch of his marrow.

But it's done.

He lies on the floor. On his back. Panting. Palms slick with blood and sap. Lane moans. Rolls onto his side. Eyes still closed. Mouth still open.

Cael almost laughs. All that and his secret is still kept.

But then—

His shirt ripples. His breastbone feels as if it's cracking apart, splitting as if by a hatchet's blade—

A massive vine, this one as thick as his wrist, tears through the fabric of his shirt and launches forward—not toward Cael but toward Lane, where it plunges into his mouth, his throat bulging, his eyes opening wide and popping out beyond his eyelids, the whites flooded fast with blood. Then the eyes pop out and two more vines emerge from Lane's sockets—

Cael wakes up.

Clothes and sheets soaked through with sweat.

Lane sleeps soundly.

He pats at his chest—first over the shirt, then under it—and there he finds the same stem with three leaves he had before he went to bed.

Just a dream.

Just a damn dream.

He stands up, stumbles out of the room, and heads to the deck.

He needs some air.

The back of the boat—a few men sleep out here under the white stars and slivered moon. The darklight catches across the sheen of corn leaves, little curls of puddled moon—white as far as the eye can see. In the distance, the winking red lights from the underside of the flotillas. Others might not see those lights, but his eyes are better than most, and when he turns his gaze back to the horizon line—

He sees something out there.

Behind the fleet.

A small light in the corn. Different from everything else. It moves, juddering just a little before it's gone again.

"Hey, Captain" comes a voice behind him, and it startles Cael enough that he about pisses his britches. He says so, too, and Lane smirks, strikes a match to light a crooked cigarette. "You look like you peed your whole body. You're wet, head to toe."

"It's just sweat," Cael says. "Couple nightmares. I'm fine."

"You don't look fine."

"Is it hard for you?" Cael asks, changing the subject from anything that has to do with the Blight. "Being away from home, I mean."

"Nah. You and Rigo are my home. My father's dead. My mother's a dang Babysitter somewhere out there in the wide-open nowhere. I'm good out here long as you guys are with me."

A small voice of worry dogs Cael. *What happens when the Sleeping Dogs become his family instead of us?*

Still, he says, "You think Pop's okay?"

Lane shrugs. "I guess if anybody is, he is."

"I'm worried. About him, and Mom. About us. Shoot, about Rigo. He lost his leg, Lane. And it was my fault. Dragging him out here with us—he was never up to salt for this kind of adventure."

"Rigo'll be all right. He's tougher than you think."

"I hope so."

"Besides, it isn't your fault. You want to blame somebody, blame the skybastards. The Empyrean are the ones keeping us down. If we had access to real food, medical care, even one-tenth of what they have, none of this would've ever happened. Rigo would damn sure have his leg."

"I guess."

Lane claps him on the shoulder. "It's all right, Boss. Don't bust yourself up over it."

"I gotta tell you something," Cael says, and for a half second he thinks, *I could tell him about the Blight; I could just say it right now. Lane says we're family. He'll understand. He saw the Blighters at Martha's Bend, the ones working for Pop.* But instead, he says, "Back there at the depot, I saw . . . Boyland. And Wanda."

Lane snorts. "Were they k-i-s-s-i-n-g? Or f-u-c—"

"Ew, no, no, like, I wasn't hallucinating. They were really there." He tells Lane the whole story. Minus the part where Wanda saw the Blight.

When he's done telling the story, Lane goggles. "What? Are you shitting me?"

"I would not dare shit you about this."

"King Hell."

"Yeah. There's more."

"Uh-oh."

Cael points out over the moonlit corn. "I saw something out there. A . . . light or something. Moving around just above the stalk tops."

"You think it's them."

"I do."

"That is not good news."

"Not precisely. If Wanda's with him . . . who else?"

"That's a question I almost don't want answered."

Cael says, "Don't tell anyone."

"Cael, if we're being followed—"

"Let's see if we can find out more information first. Maybe

we can handle this instead of making it a thing. I don't give a sack of rats if Boyland gets blown to greasy bits, but . . . I don't want to see Wanda hurt."

"Okay," Lane says. He pitches the cigarette. "I'm gonna head back to the bunk. You coming?"

"Nah. I'm still worked up. Don't suspect sleep is really in the cards tonight. Go on; I'm good."

THE TIDINGS OF SARANYU

THE FESTIVAL BEGINS at dawn, which is when it
always begins, for that is when the goddess Saranyu—one of the
old goddesses, and the patron goddess of this flotilla—was born.
The whole flotilla wakes early. Children run around in black and
white masks: those in white are the avatars of Saranyu; those in
black are the agents of Chaya, the dark god born of Saranyu's
shadow. Chaya chases Saranyu. Saranyu chases Chaya. Children
chase children, laughing, roughhousing.

Adult women wear long, colorful dresses. Men wear colorful
trousers and baggy shirts: turquoise blue, coral pink, orange the
color of fire's heart, red the color of pig's blood. They chase each
other, too—not as enemies but as men trying to find and seduce
the women, much as the god Vivasat chased and seduced the
flotilla's patron in the sky.

Cloud cannons belch forth big puffs of white and gray on
days when the sky is clear, for it is said that Saranyu dwelled in

the clouds, until her husband found her hiding as—of course—a winged mare. The day gets later and the clouds are given color—until soon everything is wreathed in a rainbow haze.

All day: drinking and laughing and chasing. Men on rooftops, throwing flowers. Women on propeller-bikes, trying to catch them. Auto-mates on stages, acting out scenes from the Saranyu mythologies.

Percy tells Merelda all this as they lie together in bed. As he speaks, his fingers walk forceful little steps up her shirt, toward the buttons around her collar, while his other hand holds her hip.

She can see the visidex behind him. On the bedside table.

She keeps asking him things to distract him. And maybe, though she's hard-pressed to admit it, to distract herself.

"I'm done answering your questions," he says, pressing hard, cold kisses along her jawline. "The festival is tomorrow morning. My family is asleep. We are awake. Let's make the most of it."

She swallows hard, trying not to sound nervous. "Why didn't you get me one of those . . . pretty, colorful dresses?"

He pulls back from the kissing and levels a look at her—the look a parent gives to a child when he's about to administer a lesson. Or, rather, the look *Pop* used to give *her* in that situation. A greasy layer of discomfort settles over her at the thought.

"La Mer," he says with a sigh. "The Tidings of Saranyu is about men and women, yes, but Saranyu was married. Vivasat was her husband. And so it is a day to celebrate that—and many husbands and wives, or wives and wives, or husbands and husbands, choose to consummate their marriages again on the day. That is why they call the night of the festival the Night of Reconciliation, for once the children are in bed . . ."

She bristles. "Is that what you'll be doing?"

"Of course."

"You'll be with *her.*"

"*Her* name is Mercy."

Percy and Mercy. Ugh. "I hate that name."

"Oh, *tsk-tsk.* I told you in the beginning; jealousy will not suit this arrangement we have. You are the mistress. She is the wife. These are the roles we play." He smiles and lets his hand drift downward until it's cupping the inside of her knee. Finger tickling the back of her leg. She fails to repress a small giggle. "Besides, it's you I truly love. And when I make love to her, as is my husbandly duty, she will lie there like a bird that struck a window and fell prone in the street. But you're not like that." He stops tickling, and she stops squirming. His hand drifts farther north. Across the expanse of her thigh. "Besides, tomorrow is just . . . nonsense. The old gods are a joke. They do not exist. Nor did the Lord and Lady come and usurp them. Nor was there ever a Jeezum Crow, or an Old Scratch, or the Saintangels or Sea Devils. We are the gods of our kingdom, the keepers of our domain."

Fingers now just at the inside of her thigh. Tracing small circles.

"And you," he says, "are my domain."

They own you. Gwennie's words echo in her head.

He reaches in to kiss her.

She pulls away.

He gives her a look. Conflicted. Confused. Almost angry.

Gwennie's gotten under her skin. Forced a little splinter of doubt into her mind. Doubt and shame and guilt.

That angers her. She shouldn't have to feel angry. Percy is good to her. A spike of jealousy rises in her against his wife, and she thinks, *I need to get on his good side; I need to show him that I'm loyal, and Gwennie can go to hell and—*

Before she even realizes it, she whispers: "I saw Gwendolyn Shawcatch."

The peregrine's hand recoils from her. Her flesh aches to have it replaced, but the mood is dead; the alarm is plain in his eyes—dancing like ball lightning. "*What?*"

Tears line the bottoms of her eyelids. "She came to me. Earlier today. She . . ." Her eyes press shut. *Stop crying, stop crying, you can do this; you can make this all go away.* Her voice becomes the tiniest, breathiest whisper. "She's here, Percy. In the closet. Behind you."

The look of love and warmth and lust that lingered on his face is now well and truly gone.

He gives her a stare—she can't tell if it's a caution against danger or a warning that he *is* the danger. Either way, he slides out of bed, pants still on, shirt off, the half-light from the corner lamp drawing lines across the etched contours of his broad shoulders.

He reaches down. Pulls up his ankle holster—which was pooled on the floor in a puddle of black straps—and draws his long, sleek sonic pistol before standing and creeping toward the closet.

Merelda pulls the sheets closer. Then pushes them away. Then backs up off the bed and stands, all the while thinking, *I'm so sorry; I just couldn't do it.*

Percy turns toward her. Presses a long finger against those pretty lips of hers.

Then he flings open the closet.

Gwennie lunges for him.

The realization lands in her gut like a swallowed cannonball: *Merelda McAvoy betrayed me.*

She shouldn't be surprised. But she's furious just the same. This stupid, selfish girl may have cost her everything. Her freedom. Her family. Her home.

All of that, knocked off the table with a sweeping arm.

When he throws open the door, she leaps out with one of the three unsheathed knives, the blades spun around so that she can stab instead of slash—

But he dismantles her. *Dissects* her attack. He catches her knife-arm, slams it backward so the wrist hits the jamb of the closet. The knife clatters. She swings a fist—he leans back as if it's nothing. His knee pumps into her gut. The bulbous back end of his pistol cracks against the side of her head.

She remains standing, but the whole flotilla tilts suddenly, spinning like the blades of a windmill. Then her cheek hits the carpet, and she realizes, *I'm not standing at all.*

He grabs her. Sits her up. Slams her against the end table. She's having trouble breathing. She knows her arms are there, but they feel like scarecrow arms stuffed with hay and corn—no muscle, just twin sacks hanging off her body like so much useless meat.

In the background is Merelda, watching in glassy-eyed horror. Standing by the lamp. One hand over her mouth.

The peregrine thrusts the needle-like barrel of his sonic shooter in between Gwennie's lips. The metal clacks against her teeth. She tastes the tinny tang of the weapon.

"You should have left the city when you had the chance," the peregrine says. "You could have fled, little sparrow. Over time we would have forgotten. But here you are. Why? *Why* are you here? To see your old friend? To hurt her? To hurt me?" He rattles the gun in her mouth. She tries to cry out and struggle, but he grabs her throat. "Truth is, I don't care. I told you if you crossed me, I'd hurt everything around you. I'll recall your family. I'll kill your father in front of your mother, and your mother in front of your brother. And that little brother of yours, I'll break him apart like a sugar cookie."

I'm going to die, she thinks.

Defiance roars through her like a lightning strike.

"Uck oo," Gwennie snarls around the barrel of the gun.

He sneers, his nostrils flaring. "Take good fortune, because *you* won't be around to see them suffer. Bye-bye, Miss Shaw—"

The lamp crashes down on his head.

The peregrine slumps suddenly to the side. Shards of porcelain sticking out of his hairline. The gun out of his hand and her mouth.

He moans. Eyelids flutter like a corn leaf in a sudden wind.

But he doesn't wake. He just lies there. On his side.

Blood pooling.

Merelda stands there. The broken base of the lamp still in her hand.

Gwennie gasps. Reaches down, picks up the pistol.

She points it at the peregrine's head.

Merelda grabs her wrist. "Don't! Please."

So Gwennie points the pistol at Merelda instead.

"You betrayed me," Gwennie says.

"I know. But . . ." She looks at the peregrine as if to say, *I fixed it.*

Gwennie hisses: "I almost died."

"I'm sorry. He's been . . . good to me."

"Well, he's been *really godsdamn bad* to me."

"I'm sorry. You don't understand—"

Gwennie cries out in rage. Her hand is shaking. Her knees wobbling. The walls feel as if they're closing in. As if her whole world is threatening to crush her to bone dust and red paste. She grabs the visidex off the nightstand and shoves Merelda onto the bed, storming past.

By the time she's at the front door, Merelda's calling after her. Sobbing. "Please! Take me with you."

"Eat dust," Gwennie says, reaching for the door. Merelda grabs her wrist and holds it. Her face is a twisted mask of sorrow, tears pouring, mouth open in a grief-struck hole—strands of saliva connecting her lips.

"He'll kill me. Don't you understand? *He'll kill me.*"

"Good."

"My brother!" she cries in a wretched, weeping stutter. "Don't tell him. Don't tell him what I did or who I was. Please. Please."

Cael.

What will she tell Cael?

She betrayed me but then saved me, and I left her behind. To whatever horrible fate awaits her. He'd never be able to look at her again.

"Damnit!" she says. She tucks the pistol into the back of her pants and pulls her shirt over it. Then she pokes Merelda in the chest. "Stop crying. You can come. You can come! But I swear, Merelda McAvoy, you ever think to betray me again like that, I'll shove you in a box and wrap it with a pretty bow and deliver you to the peregrine personally. Let's go."

THE OPEN DOOR

LANE FEELS THE HESITATION all over—in the back of his throat, in the hinges of his joints, in the well of his belly, as if his body is resisting what he's about to do, as if all parts of him are straining to turn away from Killian's door and march back to the bunk room and—

And it's too late. Because he sees the light framing the edge of the door, and here he is, knocking. Wincing. Cursing under his breath.

The door opens.

Killian. Framed by the light from a pair of electric lamps. A glass of whiskey—his so-called 'jorum of skee'—in his hand.

"Howdy now, Lane," Killian says. The side of his cheek bulges out with the thrust of his tongue. "It's late."

"I like late better than I like early."

Killian smirks. "In this we have an accord. Come on in."

He's never been in the captain's chambers before. Maps on

the walls. Shelves of old books and sheaves of withered, weathered papers. In the corner stands a small, ornate cabinet—metal etching in the glass doors—showcasing bottles of various liquors. Lane recognizes the toothy shark of Micky Finn's Botanical Gin staring out front and center, as if ready to leap and bite. Killian pulls over a chair, plants it in the middle of the room.

"Go on. Sit. I'm just here figuring out the fleet's next move." That wicked smile of his flashes. "You look tense, Lane Moreau. Lean back. Let the Saintangels carry your worries in their teeth to the bountiful garden of the Lord and Lady."

Lane laughs nervously. "Glass of that gin would help."

"Oh ho ho, you a gin drinker? I shoulda pinned you to the board as a gin drinker. It's not my style, not really—too many things happening on my tongue, and, if I'm being honest, it tickles my nose a little. The skee, though, the skee is always my friend. Gotten me through many a troubling night."

"I'll take some skee then."

Killian laughs. "Lane, don't change yourself to suit the tastes of other people. You're the one who has to live the life; they just have to watch. Might as well enjoy it, and if they don't like it, stick up a pair of middle fingers and ask them very kindly to screw off and die alone. You, my friend, are drinking some gin tonight."

Into the cabinet. Cap off the bottle of Micky Finn's.

He hands a glass of gin to Lane.

Lane sips it. Licorice and evergreen and—sure enough, he feels a little tickle in his nose.

"What can I do you for, Lane Moreau?"

"Something I have to tell you."

Killian doesn't sit. He just paces around Lane in a circle—like the orbit of a buzzard flying over its kill. "Confession time," Killian says. "Confessions are always so intriguing, and thus I am intrigued."

"Cael saw something."

"Saw something? Saw what? Shooting star? Skunk ape? One of the Saintangels come down on a chariot made of moonlight and starshine?"

Lane thinks, *Don't do this; don't tell him; divert, change the subject, make something up—Cael is your captain, not Killian Kelly.*

"Cael saw a boat. Following us."

There it is. Out in the open. It feels better. Doesn't it? Suddenly he's not so sure.

"A boat." Killian sucks air through his teeth, takes a noisy sip of whiskey. "That is curious. Can't be Empyrean—those sonsabitches are like termites; once you see one they're already all up in your walls. Someone else then."

"Cael thinks it's . . . people from our town. From Boxelder."

"That where you're from? Boxelder? I never thought to ask." Killian stops right behind Lane. He sets the glass on the floor. Then his hands drop to Lane's shoulders. Give them a squeeze. "So you're being tracked by a posse from home, huh?"

"We—" And now Killian starts massaging Lane's shoulders. Thumbs pressing hard circles. Fingertips pushing skin and muscle toward his collarbones. Warmth radiates. His whole neck tingles. Lane clears his throat. "We got into a bit of a row back home. Cael's father was growing a garden. Had some . . . ah, hobos helping him out."

"Hobos. We're friend to hobos, that's for sure. If you're a

raider, you're an exile, and if you're an exile, you're a hobo." Killian draws a deep breath through his nose, and Lane finds himself doing the same. "I do appreciate you bringing this to my attention. You're loyal. That's good."

One hand leaves Lane's shoulder.

Moves to his cheek. Starts caressing that cheek with the backs of Killian's knuckles.

"Uhhh," Lane says, mouth suddenly mealy and unable to form proper words. His heart kicks up like a tornado. He stands. Spins around. Hands out. "I should go."

"Whoa, whoa, settle down, horsey; you're working yourself into a froth." Killian reaches out and clasps both of Lane's wrists together. He uses them like a rope to pull himself forward. Grinning, tongue snaking across the flat whites of his teeth. He leans in for what is unmistakably a kiss, and again Lane gasps and pulls away—

His mind is going crazy. *This is what you want. This is who you are. What the hell are you doing?*

Killian echoes the question. "What the hell, fella? Have my eyes been duplicitous traitors all along, seeing things that weren't really there? Because here, Lane Moreau, I thought you'd been giving me a certain look since the moment I took that gun away from your head."

"I . . . I don't—"

"You sure?"

Killian's hand moves to Lane's stomach. Slides under the shirt. Dips downward, begins to fiddle with the buttons on Lane's pants. He doesn't pop the button. Not yet. But Lane can feel him toying with the clasp.

"You tell me no, I'll stop right now. And though it will be a sad and lonely night for me—in which I will surely soak my pillows through with a couple-few tears and a whole lot of sweat thinking about you—I am obliged to respect your wishes." Killian clacks his teeth together. "You don't want this, just walk away. No harm, no foul, friend."

Lane doesn't pull away.

"Last chance. Pull away or stand right there."

Lane stands perfectly still. Trembling a little, maybe.

"Thought so," Killian says, and kisses Lane hard on the mouth.

Cael leans out over the back of the trawler, the faint lights of the other boats drifting alongside in the darkness. Sometimes he thinks he sees the shifting of shadows way out over the corn—the bright sails, he imagines, of Boyland's land-yacht. The bucket-headed bastard at the prow of the boat. And silly Wanda at the back, worrying over him even still. She's trying to figure out who he is, maybe, who she got herself Obligated to. If she's smart—and he thinks she is—she's starting to worry about that.

All told, Cael feels damn unsettled. That question of Lane's from earlier—*What do you stand for?*—haunts him now. And it feels bound up with the Blight popping out of his chest, one vine twisted around another, as if he's been caring about the wrong things—or at least not all the right things—this whole time.

He's now a hobo. And a raider. And a Blighter. Three things that a few months ago he at best dismissed, at worst hated. And being those three things, he thinks, should give him some perspective, same way that seeing Pop work with those hobos and those Blighted folk gave him some, because now it's all the more personal. Now it's *him*.

And yet inside he's got that twisting, turning feeling—a bundle of starving rats that make up that revulsion he feels, a revulsion that seems a part of him now. Like even though he is those things, he still *hates* those things. Like maybe he ought to hate himself.

But then it swings back the other way: *I should stand for something greater than myself. I should try to look past my own damn skin.*

Of course, right now his own damn skin is betraying him. And he thinks, where else is the Blight going in his body? Earl Poltroon's whole arm was gone, replaced by root and stalk, vine and leaf. Is it in his marrow? Sending wormy runners into the meat of his brain?

How long does he have?

Behind him, a drag-*thump*, drag-*thump*. He turns, startled, and sees Rigo limping up on his crutch. "Hey, Captain," he says, grunting with each syllable. "Couldn't sleep?"

Cael shakes his head. "Naw."

"You're bugged by all this."

"All this?"

"Being with the raiders."

"I feel like I'm in bed with Old Scratch on this one."

"Yeah, I know. But they seem all right. They fixed me up when they could've just left me there in the corn." Rigo leans forward with a groan, watching the moonlit corn disappear from the back of the boat. "Though damn if my leg doesn't itch something fierce."

"Rigo, I—" The words catch in Cael's throat, and he wants to tell Rigo all kinds of things. He wants to say he's sorry for dragging him along. He wants to say it's his fault that Rigo lost his leg. He wants to tell his friend that Mister Cozido is out there right now with Wanda and Boyland searching for his son.

But he doesn't know where to start. He doesn't get the time to decide, either, because behind them, a clamor—

A door opens, and Killian strides out, whistling. Chest bare, covered in a faint sheen of sweat, his hair a-muss. A man with a smashed-flat nose and a long, rat-tail braid of blond hair follows after: his first mate, Billy Cross.

"Something's up," Rigo mutters darkly.

Cael steps away from the back of the trawler and starts to drift toward the small commotion. Rigo hobbles after. The other raiders sleeping on deck wake up, snorting and grumbling and winding their way toward the noise.

Killian continues to whistle.

The watchwoman, Hezzie Orden, calls down from the crow's nest: "Something going on, Cap?"

He grins up at her, face captured in the starlights of the midnight sky. "Oh, just something your elevated gaze missed, Hezzie."

He roots through a wooden box, tosses a telescoping spyglass to Billy. The first mate and he walk up to a platform on which sits one of the trawler's big sonic cannons—

Cael's hands twist into fists. *It can't be.*

Could Lane have . . .

Killian sits in the chair mounted to the cannon.

Billy stands next to him.

The first mate cranks a lever, and the gun extends out over the edge of the ship on a set of toothy tracks—as the tracks drift outward, the gun moves across them to meet their end.

Now the gun sits ten feet over the edge of the boat.

Giving them a clear shot for—

Boyland's yacht.

The first mate pops the glass to his eye and pulls it out with three quick clicks. The glass lens at the end shines green. Cael calls out, yells for Killian to stop, stepping forward as Billy angles his gaze well beyond the aft of the ship and starts calling out numbers. Killian begins to adjust a smaller crank right above a pair of big triggers. As he does so, the gun barrel drifts a few inches left, a few inches up. . . .

"Killian, no, wait!" Cael takes another bold step forward—

The raider captain leans back, still smiling. He wiggles a finger toward Cael. "Someone want to grab that gentleman? Careful, now; I suspect he's a slippery little squealer."

Rigo calls after, panicked: "Cael! What's going on? Watch out—!"

Suddenly arms wrap around Cael's midsection. Big arms. He looks back, sees the bearded sonofabitch whose nose he broke back at the depot.

Cael yells out again—the man clamps his hand over Cael's mouth.

The man's forearm presses tight against Cael's chest. Mashing the stem-and-leaves of Blight. *Please don't notice it under there. . . .*

"Pair of sails lined up," Billy says.

Killian answers, "Ready to fire at your request, Mr. Billy Cross."

The first mate offers a thumbs-up.

Killian gives him one right back.

Then he whoops and cackles and squeezes both triggers.

The sound coming off the sonic cannon is like a shrieking wind born of a real bad piss-blizzard. Like any sonic weapon, it fires no projectiles—all Cael sees is a distorting lance of air hurling forward like a nearly invisible spear.

Killian whoops again, and some of the raiders gathered applaud, though they surely don't know what they're applauding.

Cael stomps on Beard-o's foot and breaks away from the bear-crushing grip in time to meet Killian face-to-face as he backs off the gun.

The first mate steps in between them, brandishing something that looks like a pick you'd use to chip shavings off an ice block.

But Killian puts his hand on the man's chest, eases him back. "It's all right, Billy. Cael was just coming up here to say he was sorry."

"Bullshit," Cael spits as much as he says. "Why the hell'd you do that?"

"My question is, why didn't *you* tell *me* we were being followed?"

"Because I figure you'd do something like that!"

Killian shrugs and smiles. "I guess that's fair."

"You don't even know who that was."

"No, I do not. But I can't have unknowns following behind us in the dark." Loudly now, so that everyone can hear it, the raider captain says, "We're on a mission of justice, Mr. Cael. Surely you understand that?"

More applause.

"I don't," Cael says quietly. "What *is* the mission? Travel from depot to depot? Robbing them blind? Killing their workers?"

The smile doesn't fade, but Killian's stare hardens. "Tell you what, Cael. Even though you failed to *illuminate* me as to the presence of our little shadow out there in the corn, you still proved yourself a damn fine watchman. Unlike Hezzie, who obviously couldn't spot a moth even as it landed on the *tip* of her godsdamn nose. You want the job?"

"I . . ."

From up above, Hezzie protests, and Killian gives her his middle finger, which, surprisingly, shuts her up.

"Good. It's yours. Then soon as we can get you your own boat, we'll get you on it. Meantime, starting tomorrow, the crow's nest is your home at night." A reward, or a punishment? Cael doesn't know. Killian starts to walk away but then turns around. "Oh, and you want to know what our mission is? Well, noonday tomorrow I'll clue you in. How'd that be?"

Cael says nothing. He can find no words. He can only think of Wanda out there in the corn. And Gwennie up there in the sky. Rigo without his leg. And betrayer Lane, somewhere in the belly of this boat.

Cael sees Rigo staring, and he doesn't have words.

Lane feels like he should be sleepy, but he's anything but. Feels like instead of having had a glass of gin he's had about two pots of Busser's famous black-tar coffee—which as Lane understands it isn't really coffee at all; it apparently comes from little seeds or black beans or something.

He lies there on Killian's bed. Behind him, the windows of the stern compartment look out over the midnight corn seemingly receding, as if it's the land that's moving, not the massive boat.

He knows he just screwed over Cael.

He knows Cael's gonna be mad.

Mad as a goat who had his feed taken away.

But right now he doesn't care.

He *can't* care, even though he knows he should.

The sick feeling inside is gone. All that's there is a kind of giddy elation—as if every part of him is hooked to a fleet of kites flying high.

He's wanted this for a long time.

He's liked boys since he liked anybody. But in the Heartland, you don't get to like boys if you're a boy. Or girls if you're a girl. Because there's a way of doing things and that way is Obligation and marriage, and the wife squeezes out a litter of children, and, if you live long enough (many don't), those children squeeze out their own squealing litters and on and on.

Funny thing is, the Heartland folk have been roped into that rodeo for so long they think it's their idea. They all seem to forget that the Obligations are something the Empyrean wants. Something the Empyrean *enforces*.

That made Lane feel very alone for a very long time.

He always suspected there were others like him, though. Kids talked. Hell, adults talked, too. Some folks said the old

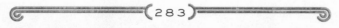

Tallyman, Murrill Franklin, was into men. Or into boys. Then came the day Franklin was gone and the Tallywoman, Frieda Wessel, was setting up in his office. Wasn't long before the rumors were bouncing around like a pebble down a hill: somebody found Franklin in one of the corn silos outside of town with a boy named Tyrell Polcyn (older brother to Alia, who is Lane's age). The stories people told. That Tyrell was seduced. That Franklin had him tied up and was doing things to him. Others said maybe Tyrell wanted it, maybe invited him out there on the idea that Murrill was into that sort of thing.

Whatever happened, one day Murrill was just gone.

And it wasn't long before Tyrell killed himself.

Cut his wrists the long way on the tines of a thresher bar, bled out in a barn while a pair of sick cows looked on.

And *that* for Lane was life in the Heartland.

So, to be here, in the bed of a raider captain—a damn fine raider captain with a wicked hook of a smile and eyes that dance like fireflies—is just about the nicest place Lane can imagine himself.

Though there in the back of his mind, the whispered threat: *This can't last. Don't get comfortable. They all leave you in the end. . . .*

From somewhere up above: the sonic blast. Like a flock of blackbirds screeching all at once.

It's enough to jar him from his thoughts. Particularly the poisonous ones. But only for a moment. He closes his eyes for a time and wakes up again with Killian rubbing his chest with the flat of his hand. Killian tells him it's all fine: Cael is good; the situation is handled. They kiss. Lane feels his body stirring anew.

BLOOD CHOKE
AND BROKEN STICKS

IT COMES OUT OF NOWHERE, screaming like
a banshee—and by the time Wanda's pulling herself from within
the twisting corridors of failed sleep, everything's already gone
to King Hell. An explosion—then a rain of splinters down upon
her. Then something's got her in its grip, some foul, twisting
thing darker than the night itself and redder than blood. She
grabs at her face and tries to pull it off—realizes she's got a handful of torn and tattered sail.

That's when she hears Mole screaming.

She's up. In the dark. Stumbling forward. Boyland's there,
too, a light in his hand shining over the wreckage of mast and
sail. Mast into matchsticks. Sail into swatches of fabric caught on
the wind and blowing out over the corn. All he says is "We're hit;
we're hit," and then he's pulling away sail and netting and yelling
for help, and Wanda runs and tries to help him lift the shattered
mast off Mole—

At first she thinks it's just the sail pooled beneath him, but the red catches the light, trapping it in its liquid surface, and she realizes too late that what's beneath Mole is what's spilling out of him.

Then she really sees: it's his arm. Thank the Lord and Lady, it's just his arm. But when Boyland lifts Mole and Mole screams, there's the white bone sticking out, the limb bent the wrong way, his face draining of blood just as the shattered deck darkens with it.

Mole's screams are living things, full of electric pain and snapping, sparking panic. In the band of light across his face, his eyes rotate in their sockets until they fall on her, pupils as fat and twitchy as horseflies, and in the middle of his screams he gasps words. No—not words. Her name. *Wanda, Wanda, help, help.* More screams.

She doesn't know what to do. A wave of realizations crash against her like buffeting winds: *I am unprepared for everything. I don't know how to do anything. I can't help. I can only hurt.* And then she's mad at herself for making this about her, for being selfish enough to think about *her* problems, *her* woes while a young boy is screaming at her feet.

Suddenly, there's a shape behind Mole.

The hobo. Eben. He's lifting Mole up. He's got the boy's neck in the crook of his bent arm, his other arm pressed like a hard bar against the back of Mole's neck. Mole begins to make a choking noise, thrashing about—

Wanda screams. Steps over the wreckage of the mast and begins clubbing at the wild-eyed hobo, clawing at his head, dragging the swaddling off his face and revealing the still-glistening wounds there—

He gives her a hard boot to the stomach and knocks her down.

Boyland's yelling now. She sees him standing there, the sickle knife in his hands, but all she can do is try to rock forward and catch her breath—

Mole slumps. Slides down the hobo's legs to the floor.

Boyland rushes at Eben.

The hobo doesn't have time to react—he tries to step out of the way, but Boyland's there, knife raised, dropping the vagrant to the deck—

"He's asleep!" the hobo yells.

"What?" Boyland asks.

"I put—" The hobo shoves Boyland off him. "I put the little mouse to sleep. Him thrashing about like that was just going to break the arm further. No time to do anything else but knock him out. Now get the hell off me before I cut off parts of you and feed them to the corn."

Eben knows he's overstepped, threatening the thick-necked bull when the boy's got his back up. But to his surprise the lunk is more concerned over the boy with the broken arm. The now-*sleeping* boy, thanks to Eben's blood-choke—press in on both sides of someone's neck and it cuts off blood flow, and then they sleep the sleep of the Saintangels.

Later, when they've put the boy on a pallet of sacks toward

the aft of the land-yacht, they discuss what to do next—the boat crawls forward, buoyed by hover-panels and pushed on by a pair of small, cage-bound fans, but already it's clear that the raider fleet will outpace them quickly.

"They spotted us," Boyland says, marching back and forth. He growls and kicks a coil of rope, nearly trips on it. "Godsdamn raiders. *Godsdamn thieving-magpie raiders.*"

Wanda asks, "Wh—what are we gonna do?"

Boyland fishes around, holds up the visidex. "I'm gonna call it in. Gonna call the proctor. The raiders are getting away, but if she brings her ketch-boats to us now, they'll pick us up, and maybe we can catch up—"

Eben stands. Growls a hard, fast "No." They come here, they'll find out who he is. They'll throw him in another dark hole somewhere—he can't go back. *Won't* go back.

"No other way," Boyland says, throwing up his hands in a gesture of *That's it, end of discussion.* But it isn't the end of the discussion. Eben's face feels hot under the fresh layer of cloth wrapped round his burned, weeping skin. The knife hangs suddenly heavy inside his coat. It occurs to him then: he's going to have to kill again.

The girl will fight more than anyone would expect, but in the end she'll meet the knife just the same.

The big boy will be hard. He'll fight. He'll hurt Eben because he's large and fast and strong. He's thick, too. That body is layered in muscle and fat. One stick of the knife won't do.

But the boy, Mole. Eben doesn't know. Something reminds him of what his own son might've been like. Maybe not in the face but in the child's demeanor. The kid doesn't take any shit, and he gives a lot of it.

Eben thinks that's the right attitude.

So he's not sure about that one. Maybe Mole—if he survives the break in his arm and the bone poking through—gets to live.

The others, well.

To Eben's surprise, Wanda speaks up. "No, we can't call Agrasanto." She seems suddenly panicked, too. Eben can hear it in her voice. She's afraid of the Empyrean. Was that fear there before? He didn't recognize it. Why now? What's changed? "We do this ourselves. Somewhere along the way we'll find a town. We'll mend the sails. We have Annie pills for Mole. We know what direction the raiders are heading."

"Unless they change direction," Boyland says.

Eben feels in his coat. Hands tightening around the hilt of the blade.

"They can't hide forever," Wanda says. "We're not the Empyrean. We can ask around. Someone will know where the raiders are. Someone . . . sympathetic to them. The Empyrean will just swoop in. Probably ship us back home. They'll take this away from us. That's what they do. Take things."

Their lives hang in this moment.

The knife, cold in his hand.

The corn rasping against the boat.

A caviling grackle squawking somewhere not so far away.

It's like watching a building collapse. One moment Boyland is granite faced and resolute. But then the next it all falls away. He rolls over. Gives in. Gives *up*. The big boy nods.

"No calling the proctor. For now."

And that's it.

Wanda doesn't know it, but she just saved their lives.

Of course they still have to die in the end. She, and Boyland, and anyone else who stands in his way.

38

THE GILDED CAGE

BALASTAIR IS STARVING AGAIN. They feed him. He's not dying. But the food is just trays of nutritional paste. A yellow pile here. Green there. Something meat-like that is most certainly not meat. He's seen the packets. It's the same faux-food they send down as provisions below. Scraps for the Heartlanders.

And for those who betray the Seventh Heaven, the Empyrean.

The "food" is nutritive enough to keep one from dying. And a little sweet from the corn mash. Most of it is corn, really. The green stuff. The brown stuff. All corn. He knows what goes into it. He helped *design* what goes into it.

Balastair mills about his birdcage, his wispy gray robe—just a gauzy swath of fabric with a hole for his head and two for his arms—dragging on the floor. He tries to roll it up to no avail; the fabric has no tension, no grip, and it just unrolls with the next three steps he takes.

They call these the birdcages because that's what they look

like: each an ornamental dome—brass and iron. No simple deco-
ration, either, but gilded with leaves and birds and berries made
of metal. The leaves are sharp. So too are the beaks of the deco-
rative birds. He thinks sometimes, *I could kill myself. Drag a wrist
across the razor-tip of a bronzed leaf, bleed out here in my prison.* It's
happened before and will happen again, and nobody will complain. But suicide is not his way.

Even though every time he runs his fingers across one of the
little metal birds he thinks of Erasmus.

It occurs to him that Erasmus was one of his only true
friends. A young man whose only companion was a little chatty
bird. It makes him sad.

No, that's not sad. That's just pathetic.

He's pathetic. This whole place is pathetic.

He presses his head against the cool bars.

No gawkers today. He hears the sounds outside. Ah. Yes.
The Tidings of Saranyu. Cloud cannons going *boom.* Fireworks
somewhere crackling, hissing, popping. Distant laughter way
down below that sometimes drifts up to his tower like snippets
of music far away—the tune familiar but hard to grasp when
broken into so many little pieces.

All around him: benches, chairs, a small snack machine by
the Elevator Man—a cruel twist of the knife since he knows
what treats come out of that machine, and he knows how badly
he'd whine and cry and kick and kill for a taste of a Flix Bar, or a
Caramel Gobbler, or a trio of Pemberton's Cloud Crèmes.

As he stares, imagining those little, creamy, vanilla puffs
melting in his mouth like sugar-lacquered snowflakes, the elevator dings.

The Elevator Man announces, *"Visitor to Birdcage #17 incoming!"*

More gawkers. Kids lining up to throw stones. Teenagers to mock. Men and women who just want to see what it is to fall so far—and, ironically, be kept up so high. (Some come for the view, after all.)

As if on cue, the wind sweeps through the open air.

A flutter of plump-bellied pigeons gathers above his head. Shitting on his bed, as they are wont to do.

The elevator opens.

The peregrine emerges.

A hot flush of hate courses through Balastair—it burns up his fatigue, makes him feel woefully, painfully alive.

Percy approaches. Slow steps. Shoes clicking on the marble floor, hands clasped behind his back.

"Come to poke me with a stick?" Balastair asks. "Come to gloat? To mock? To behold your prize, to have your precious falcon come and tear the eyes out of my traitorous head? Ugh." He thunks his head against the bars. The peregrine just stares. "You have to let me out of here eventually. What I did is a crime, yes, but others have done worse and served lesser sentences—the girl got away from me, and I secured her escape. Not exactly treason."

"You didn't secure her escape," the peregrine says.

"You can't just *say* something and have it be the reality, you know. You actually have to have *evidence* for things. It's called science." He snorts, happy with the jab.

"Evidence," the peregrine says. "Fine." He tilts his head forward. He pulls back his hair as if he were parting grass to show

the dirt beneath. There, a ragged red scar held fast with gleaming staples. "See that?"

"Someone finally had enough of you," Balastair says.

"Yes. Gwendolyn Shawcatch. Working in concert with my now former house-mistress, La Mer. Or, rather, Merelda McAvoy."

Gwennie.

And that name—McAvoy.

A cold wave ripples over Balastair's flesh. He tells himself it's the wind, but . . .

"Wait, when was this? She did this before she escaped?"

"This was yesterday. That's what I'm telling you, Balastair. She never escaped. She's still here. She killed one of my men. She conspired with my girl. Stole my visidex. The likelihood is high that she's working with the Sleeping Dogs."

Given how much of this is truly shocking, it's not hard to sell what is ultimately *feigned* surprise. "Sleeping Dogs? Here? On the flotilla?"

The peregrine rolls his eyes. "You're going to be executed, you know."

Balastair's hands grip the bars so hard the blood drains from them. "Wh—what? On what grounds?"

"Conspiracy. Treason. Being a pompous ass. While I was at the auto-docs receiving my lovely new *head-staples*, I had some time to do some research—on a new visidex, of course."

"Research." Balastair swallows a hard lump.

"On you. Mostly, in the records, you come across exactly as you are. A somewhat high-strung, socially liberal geneticist with a rather famous mother and a legacy you never could quite live

up to—coupled with a small fall from grace as you continued to pursue inadvisable courses of research that led to you being . . . reassigned to the Pegasus Project."

"That *is* me—"

"Ah, sidenote, you have lost that competition. Eldon Planck did it. He created an automated Pegasus that's really, truly a work of art. The wings are ornamental, but they apparently help steer the thing—something about hover-panels and a rocket booster bolted into its hindquarters. I don't particularly care how it works, but I *do* care that it stings you. Lemon juice on a paper cut. Planck stole your project, and then your glory."

"I didn't do it for the glory." It's true. The glory wasn't why he committed himself to the project. But then comes the lie: "I did it for the science." *No, you fool, you did it because of jealousy.*

He did it because of Cleo.

"Your reasons are your reasons. Back to the point, which is, in digging beneath the surface of your elegant and seemingly infallible masquerade, I found a curious point of data. Three parcels. Small packages, by the bills of lading. They went down below. To the Heartland. To a town called Boxelder. To a man named—and here is the fascinating part—Arthur McAvoy. McAvoy, McAvoy—now where have I heard that name before? *Oh*, right."

Balastair listens as the peregrine picks it all apart. Like watching the falcon tear Erasmus into stringy red bits and floating feathers.

"So then I looked at Merelda's records, and, don't you know it, the Parcel-Mate system records *her* sending items to Arthur McAvoy, too. Layers and layers, peeled back. Like an onion.

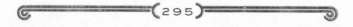

Isn't that your thing? Fruits and vegetables? The legacy of your mother?"

"My mother's legacy is none of your business."

The peregrine snaps, "*Everything* is my business, as you are fast discovering, Harrington. Turns out, Arthor McAvoy has caused quite a bit of trouble down below. Do you know what kind of trouble? He was growing a garden. A forbidden garden of forbidden fruits and vegetables, all of which seemed designed to thrive in the hard, unforgiving soil—"

Balastair begins babbling as the threads pull apart. "We've destroyed the ground. The corn, Hiram's, it's greedy, a sponge; it drinks up everything; the soil is nutrient-weak, and we've made sure it never rains—"

"Certainly none of us believes that a worm-bellied Heartlander like Arthur McAvoy managed to genetically engineer these seeds himself. And yet, who in the Empyrean might be capable of doing such a thing?"

"I . . . it could be . . . There are other scientists, many others—"

"Yes, but I believe it was you. I *know* it was you. I don't even need the evidence. I don't need your fingerprints or the genetic code of the seeds. I don't need to know what was in those packages. Because the conspiracy is laid bare before me, unfurled like an ugly, bloody tapestry." He holds up a finger and smiles. "Ah. Oh. But here you may yet say, *But that's not enough for treason.* And it isn't. You're quite right about that. Helping some poor, dreck Heartlanders shows weakness—a soft heart but not a cutting treachery. Except—"

Balastair closes his eyes.

"Arthur McAvoy is not just Arthur McAvoy. He's also one of the Sawtooth Seven. Or so we believe. And the Sawtooth Seven—"

"Helped to originate the Sleeping Dogs. Yes. I'm aware of my history, Peregrine." Doomed chills dance up his arms, bolstered by a cold breeze. Balastair feels suddenly distant from his body, as if his mind is floating free. He hopes when they execute him, he can replicate that feeling of being separate from the flesh. "How do you know? That McAvoy was one of the Sawtooth Seven? Seems . . . tenuous."

"It does. They didn't go by their given names. They went by ciphers. Swift Fox. Black Horse. Corpse Lily. But we have McAvoy's photo now. I ran it through an image search, and I found an old still from a CCTV capture on one of the early raids—when we still had our own presence down there in the hardscrabble. Fort Blackmoore. It matched. McAvoy now and this blurry, muddy glimpse of one of the Sawtooth Seven."

"Ah."

"You don't sound impressed."

"Forgive my lack of enthusiasm. We were discussing my execution."

"Yes. That. Since McAvoy appears not only to be a recent terrorist but also one of the scions of the Sleeping Dogs, *that* means you were aiding a very dangerous, very bad man. And if Gwendolyn Shawcatch becomes a terrorist, too—well. They'll just cinch the noose tighter. Did the two of you have a thing? No matter, I don't care."

Balastair thinks to remind the peregrine that *he* is the one who invited Arthur McAvoy's daughter into his bed. But that

would earn Balastair nothing except a far earlier death than scheduled. A "botched escape attempt" is how the peregrine would surely spin it.

For now Balastair keeps quiet.

Of course he knew who Arthur was. Though that the man's own daughter was here on the flotilla—that, admittedly, slipped by him.

"The conspiracy's margins have been darkened," the peregrine says. "Arthur. You. Merelda. Gwendolyn Shawcatch, too, is part of the conspiracy and has been from the beginning—it seems one of her lovers is *Cael* McAvoy. And so"—he clears his throat—"we mean to execute you. Publicly, as is the way with those who threaten the sanctity and safety of the Empyrean as a whole."

Balastair says nothing. He merely nods.

"What? No bluster? No threats to kill me now?"

"Would they do any good?"

"No."

"You'll not hang me today. The festival and all. But soon, yes?"

"The praetor wishes to wait. Until we have at least another traitor in hand. Give the whole event a little more . . ." He appears to search the air for the word.

Balastair gives it to him. "Spectacle."

"Yes. There you go. Spectacle."

At the base of the birdcage tower, the praetor waits for him. Surrounded as usual by a small swarm of worker bees striving to

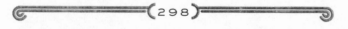

get their every wish on paper, executed properly, lest they be chastised in front of the others. Attachés and assistants, flashing visidexes, obsequious gestures and pleading faces.

It's easy to see why. Praetor Garriott cuts an imposing figure. She's not particularly tall. But her shoulders are broad. Her jaw firm and tight. That nose sharp and pointed, her gaze always seeming to look down it at you—like a hunter staring over a nocked arrow.

As the peregrine approaches, she makes a hand-swipe gesture, and the small crowd of assistants and administrators backs away.

"Percy," she says.

"He more or less admitted everything," the peregrine says. "The fear was plain to see. He knows his foot's in the trap."

"You think he'll try to gnaw it off?"

Percy draws a deep breath. "I don't. He's not the type. Too scared. Where's he going to go? To whom will he speak? No, he'll stand there and tremble and break down inch by inch, a flinty rock chipped away by the hammer of his own copious anxiety. We should put a watch on him. He'll tear his hair out. Fingernails. Maybe try to kill himself."

"Let's walk. I have a meeting with the engineers that I'm already late for. The architect wants a new art district, the engineers say they can't accommodate a bigger ship, and I'm in the middle." They continue down one of the the narrow, redbrick walkways of the Birdcage District—the white prison towers rising high around them like, well, Percy always thought they looked a bit like polished finger bones. As they walk, the praetor says, "Regarding Harrington: a breakdown is fine. But suicide, that leaves us with nothing in terms of a public example."

Example. Yes. That's a better word than *spectacle*, isn't it?

"Let's carry the example further," she says.

"What do you have in mind?"

"In going over your notes, it's plain to see that all this orbits a particular hornet's nest down in the Heartland—"

"Yes. One town. Boxelder, I believe."

"Mm. Inform the proctor there— Who is it again?"

"Simone Agrasanto."

"Right. Inform her that we're looking at Boxelder for the Initiative."

"She's likely unaware of what that means."

"Feel her out then. Bring her into the fold on it if she seems solid. If not, then quietly reassign her to some other dustbin."

He nods. "Boxelder. The Initiative. Of course." He only hopes the good proctor hasn't "gone native." Her field notes suggest she would not be the type.

He begins to break away down a sidepath, heading toward the east elevator.

"And Percy?"

The praetor's voice stops him short. "Yes, Praetor?"

"You failed me. My tolerance is a very small cup, and it fills up fast."

The assistants and administrators shuffle about, suddenly nervous. They're all trying not to look at him.

A very public dressing-down among the gossips and natters of the lower echelons. It gets across a very clear message:

You, Percy Lemaire-Laurent, are on notice.

TOGETHER, AT A DISTANCE

"IT'S HAPPENING," Lane says, pulling Cael up out of the cot. Cael was finally able to fall asleep come early morning, and no dreams or nightmares waited for him—just an uncomfortable nothing.

Lane wasn't in the room when he fell asleep.

But here he is now. Grabbing Cael by the hand, yanking him upward.

Doesn't take long for the fog of interrupted sleep to part.

Doesn't take long for Cael to pop Lane in the gut with a fist.

Lane doubles over. Coughing.

Cael hops off the cot. He sniffs. Wipes sleep crust from his eyes with the back of his hand. Rolls his head on his neck, hears his vertebrae pop. Then he puts up both fists.

"Come on, Moreau; let's dance this out."

"This is about . . . what I told Killian," Lane says, looking up while still bent over, clutching his breadbasket.

"This is about *you betraying me*."

"I had to tell them."

"You had to do no such thing. You still got stars and moons in your eyes over this whole Sleeping Dogs thing. Like you've been a raider in your heart all your life. Like I wasn't the one who saved your scrawny ass from Boyland's fists back in school—"

"Well," Lane says, straightening. "Technically you got in the way of his fists more than anything, but I suppose, yeah, that saved me a few blows."

Cael shoves Lane. Grabs his collar with one hand and rears back with his fist. "We're supposed to be friends, Lane. What was that bullshit from earlier? *Oh, Cael, you and Rigo are my true home.* I made a call, and it was to keep this secret. Wanda might've been on that boat. Blast like that—"

"They just took out the sails."

"You don't know that." The fist trembles. Like a beast held at bay. Hungry. Angry.

"I trust Killian. I trust he's a good shot."

"I don't trust anybody here except Rigo and— Well, now, just Rigo, I guess. Because you've thrown your gear in with another crew. Friends or not, I always figured you still had me pegged as your captain." Cael scowls. "But I'm not your captain anymore. Your trust lies with someone else."

Lane doesn't deny it. All he does is look at the fist and ask, "Are you gonna hit me?"

Cael thinks about it.

Lane is his friend. His family. His crew. But Lane lying to him like that? Betraying him to a raider? He should bust Lane's pretty-boy face.

But all the hot air goes out of him. Suddenly he just feels tired. Worry fills the space. Worry over all the things and people that have been plaguing him. Worry with teeth, like dogs biting at a fell-deer until they bring it down.

He lets go of Lane and steps back. "What in King Hell did you wake me for?"

"Killian. He said you could sit in on the parley."

"Parley? What parley?"

"They're planning their next move. He said he told you—"

"That I could come. Yeah. Fine. Lead the way, raider boy."

In the hall, Rigo sees Cael and Lane. And they see Rigo, who brightens as they approach—poor Rigo tries to wave but almost falls and instead just lifts his chin and looks a little embarrassed.

"Hey, guys," Rigo says. "I was told I could sit in on the meet."

Cael almost claps Rigo hard on the back but then softens his camaraderie at the last moment to a gentle tap. "Hey, buddy. Yeah, I guess we're allowed to sit at the big boys' table for today. Though I'm sure some of us will get better chairs than others." He shoots Lane a look.

Lane rolls his eyes.

"What's going on?" Rigo asks.

"Nothing," Lane says.

"Everything," Cael says. "This long-legged shuck rat over here betrayed me, *as rats are wont to do.*"

"What?" Rigo asks. "Is this about what happened last night?"

"It's *nothing*," Lane says. "We're late for the thing—"

Already they can hear people murmuring down the hall

through a closed door somewhere. The smooth twang of Killian. The gruff mumble of some other raider. No words made out, just the sounds of voices.

"It ain't nothing," Cael says. "Rigo, there's a lot you don't know." And so he starts telling him the story.

"Lane," Rigo says. "Whoa. Man. Hey. Not cool."

"You remember Boyland Barnes Junior?" Lane asks him. "Was he our buddy? Our pal? Seems to me that him following us should be a red flare in the sky, not something to keep under our hats. His father was all tucked away with the Empyrean. No reason to believe he isn't, too."

"That's a good point," Rigo says.

Cael cocks an eyebrow. "A good point my ass. The point is that I asked Lane to keep it quiet, and he said he would and then he didn't. It's the . . . the principle of the thing we're talking about here. The only point Lane has is the one at the end of the knife he stuck in my back."

Rigo nods. "Lane, you shouldn't have told Cael you'd do something if you weren't planning on doing it—"

"Who's side are you on?" Lane asks.

"I'm on both of your sides," Rigo says, always the diplomat, the negotiator, and it occurs suddenly to Cael why that probably is: two parents, one who'd take the back of his hand to his wife and children, and there's Rigo in the middle of it, trying to talk everybody down, trying to keep everything okay and make sure nobody's upset.

So that's when Cael decides to drop the bomb:

"Rigo, your dad was on that boat."

Rigo's face goes slack. "Wh . . . wait, what?"

Lane winces. "Shit."

Cael nods. "Boyland, Wanda, and your father formed some kind of . . . posse, I guess it was. He was on that boat when it got hit. No idea what happened to him."

Rigo stands there. Looking like he's a motorvator on short circuit—his mouth forms words he doesn't speak. His eyes pinch, then go wide, then his hands flex into fists. Finally he stiffens up and gives both of the other boys a long, hard look.

"He deserves what he got," Rigo says with some finality. "He should've been smart and just let me go. To King Hell with him."

Lane looks at Cael and shrugs.

Cael's about to say something, about to protest—

But then something catches Cael's ear. A sound. No. A *voice*. From behind closed doors.

He turns. Starts to wander toward it.

The other boys call after him, but he feels almost hypnotized by it. Like the sound is an invisible rope wound around his neck and he's just a goat being led to the water bucket or the feed bin or, worse, to slaughter.

Because he knows that voice.

It can't be.

He reaches out.

Opens the door.

Inside, a room of raiders. All around a big wooden table sitting on proper chairs. Killian's at the head of it, not sitting but standing, looking not at the projection on the wall but rather facing a visidex that sits propped up behind a stack of books. It's the visidex that projects the image on the wall—shaky, staticky, flickering like the light from a loose bulb.

That image is a face.

And that face is Gwennie's.

For a moment Cael can't speak.

He hears gasps behind him as Rigo and Lane come into the room.

Killian's in the middle of saying "You did just fine, Miss Shawcatch, no worries about them wiping the visidex. We anticipated such a maneuver, and we have very talented people in place who know how to crack that particular nut. Now, if you'll excuse me—"

He reaches out, taps the visidex.

Gwennie's face is gone. Another woman's face appears. Older. Square head. Leather wrapped around a couple of bricks.

"Gwennie!" Cael cries out. He hurries into the room. "No, no, c'mon, put the girl's face back up." Everyone just stares at him as if he's got a pig's nose and dog ears. He raises his voice louder. "I said, put the girl back on the godsdamn screen, Killian."

There—a little look between Killian and Lane. Killian's look is a question. Lane's short nod is an answer. Cael files that away for later, but for now it does the trick. Killian says, "Hold on, Mary Salton; I have a curious development here in my war room."

And with another tap of the button, Gwennie's face appears anew.

She's not looking at them. She's half turned around, talking to someone unseen. Cael says her name once, then louder the second time, and he sees someone on-screen—the same woman

he just saw, with the deep, furrowed lines in the tanned leather of her face—whisper in Gwennie's ear, and suddenly she's turning.

"Who?" she asks. Eyes searching. As if she's blind. *She can't see me.* But then Killian takes the visidex on the table and plunks it around the other way, on the other side of the book stack.

And suddenly Gwennie's face is frozen in slack-jawed shock.

"Cael," she says, breathless and bewildered.

"Gwennie!" he says, laughing now, unable to find any other words but her name. And though he knows that these tough, scabbed-over, scarred-up raiders are staring at him as if he's a lamebrained fool, he just can't find reason to care. "Gwennie."

"You two know each other?" Killian asks. "How fortuitous for you. Looks like the Lord and Lady have hitched your stars together and—"

Cael shushes him—earning dark looks from the other raiders, looks he chooses to ignore right now—and reaches across the table to snatch up the visidex. He turns it toward him, and the winking light from the projector suddenly spears him in the eye, and he blinks away hazy white spots.

Killian clears his throat, tells Cael to tap a little button in the corner. The one that looks like a wide-open eye.

He does.

And there, as the spots fade, is Gwennie.

In his hands.

Staring up at him as he stares down.

"I want to talk to her," Cael says. "Alone."

The bearded bear of a raider snarls, "Like he's never seen a woman before. Careful, Killian; you'll get the screen back sticky."

Cael's about to threaten to rebreak the bastard's nose when Killian offers, "Normally I'd take this as a bit of an insult, what with you interrupting the proceedings of this captains' council. And yet I am a dyed-in-the-wool romantic, and I can't help but see the look in your eyes and melt like an ice cube held in a hot hand. So, go, Cael McAvoy, talk to your lady friend. We'll be here when you're done."

Cael sits on his cot, the visidex propped up in his lap. Her hair is bound up behind her in a pair of tails, her cheeks are smudged, her face shows the ghosts of bruises and cuts, but he doesn't care because she's the prettiest thing he's ever seen.

For a while it's as if the two don't even know what to say. It hasn't been that long since they've seen each other, not really, but it feels like each day apart has been a year—and now they have to talk to each other across a pair of screens, with her in the sky and him on the ground.

But eventually they tell each other everything. He tells her about what happened after she left, how Pop set him and the other boys to riding the rails. About how they got lost out there, about the vagrant, about the depot. And about how they're now with the Sleeping Dogs—a fact that still stuns them both into fits of awkward laughing and head shaking.

She tells him about how winning the Lottery was no such thing. About how her family is gone, and about the man who took her in, and about how the Sleeping Dogs saved her, and how—

Here she takes the visidex and turns it—

—how she found Merelda.

And now Cael feels giddy and light, but the happiness doesn't last long as the balloon pops and fills the vaccum with a hot flash of anger. "Damnit, Mer, you caused us a lot of trouble and Pop's on the hook now and I'm supposed to be coming up there and finding you and *damnit*, Mer—"

"I'm sorry" is all she says. "I just wanted to get away from all that dirt. From the corn and the work and the . . ." She sighs. It hits him then: she's not happy to see him. Or maybe she's sad about something else. Her face is a porcelain mask that's about to crack, the tears behind it poised to come spilling out. "I'm sorry" is all she says again.

"The Heartland is your home, Mer."

"I know."

"So come home."

But she doesn't say anything else. She just hands off the screen, and there, once more, is Gwennie.

"I can't believe you found Merelda," he says.

"It's been a strange ride," she says, and laughs a little.

"I guess we're both raiders now."

"I guess maybe we are."

"Your face— I'm sorry."

It's as if she just remembers. She touches it. Winces. "I look like hell."

"You look pretty as a flower." *What a stupid thing to say*, he thinks.

"They have flowers up here. Lots of them. They have everything up here, Cael. They have everything where we have

nothing. Whatever we get are just . . . drips from a leaky pipe. They have so much, and I'm not even sure they really appreciate it at all."

"The Empyrean sucks."

She echoes it. "The Empyrean *sucks*."

He thinks, *Tell her. Tell her about the Blight. You have to tell someone. She'll understand. If anyone will.*

Instead, he says, "I miss you."

"I miss you, too."

"I love you."

Then that moment. Of hesitation. When her mouth opens and no words come out—and a half second later someone's pulling her away from the screen and she turns and says, "I have to go."

"Wait—"

"I'll see you soon, Cael."

The feed goes dark.

The meeting goes long, and the raiders talk, and eventually Billy Cross pulls out a map and pins it to the wall, and the raiders gather around. Rigo stands in the corner like a broken lamp, looking more than a little confused. Lane knows he should be listening intently to the whole thing given that one of his dreams has been to sit among a cabal of raiders and see what they're planning, but all he can do is throw moon-eyes toward Killian Kelly as he circles some location toward the edge of the map.

Eventually the meeting ends, and Cael doesn't return. Killian heads out into the hall to find him while the rest of the raiders mill about, breaking out bottles of skee and passing around tin cups.

Lane ducks out the door.

He follows after Killian. Catches his elbow, turns him around, plants a hard kiss on the raider captain's lips.

Killian's face twists up, and he pushes Lane aside, looks over both their shoulders front and back. "Not here," the raider says.

"I can't hold it back. It's like a spark jumping out of a campfire."

A small but wicked grin forms on the raider captain's face. "I know. I feel it, too. But work calls."

Another quick kiss.

Killian shoves him back. Not hard. Not mean. Playful. That's what Lane tells himself. Then the raider captain is gone, disappearing into one of the bunk rooms to look for Cael.

"You've been gone awhile," Killian says.

Cael looks up from staring at the now-dark screen of the visidex. "Huh? Oh."

"Thought you really might be getting the visidex sticky."

Cael gives him a look.

The raider captain holds up his hands. "My apologies. That was perhaps in low taste."

"Yeah. Well. Your taste matches my mood, so."

"Thought you'd be happy after seeing your— Well, she's your Obligated, I must presume?"

"No. Old crew member. We had a . . ." His voice trails off. "No, my Obligated was in that ship you shot last night."

The raider captain offers a gloomy whistle. "Oh-ho. I see now why you were . . . agitated about that."

"I want on that flotilla."

"Pardon?"

"The flotilla, godsdamnit. With Gwennie and my sister and the other Sleeping Dogs. I want to go up there."

Killian sits down next to Cael. Puts his hand on Cael's knee. "Tell you what, Cael. Like I promised Lane, I can make that happen. We've got a location. A town way out on the fringes. Near the Hedge, not far from the base of the Workman's Spine. Out there is a weapon—I'm not obligated to say what yet, and if I'm being honest, we don't even know exactly what it is. But that's where we're headed. Be a couple weeks' journey. If you're with us—and I mean truly with us in your head and in your heart, brother—then I do promise that we'll get you on that ship."

"I'm in."

"You're in?"

"I'm all the way in."

"See, this time I believe it. Before, I wasn't sure, but now— now I see it. The lightning in your eyes. Crackling and snapping. That's good. You're gonna need that. Because this is a fight we cannot win if we're not willing to be angry. If we're not willing to put everything we have and everything we love on the table to pay back those Empyrean monsters for thinking themselves our gods. We're gonna have to pass through some dark territory to get there, my brother, but once we do, it'll be a glorious, cleansing light on the other side. The light of rebellion. The light of freedom."

He puts out his hand.

Cael takes it, shakes it.

"The heavens will tremble for waking these sleeping dogs," Killian says, and Cael nods, wondering suddenly what the future holds.

PART FOUR

THROUGH DARK TERRITORY

THUNDERPISSER

THE CROW'S NEST is not where Cael wants to be. The pollen streams down in great, golden ribbons, hissing against the wood of the bucket that contains him, whispering against the sails, stinging his cheeks and eyes whenever the wind lashes like a herder's whip.

Thunder cracks. Lightning splits the curtain of pollen—a spear of white light dividing the sky, casting the darkness aside and making everything for a moment eye-blisteringly yellow. And then it's done, and Cael's eyes are left seeing the impression of the lightning's rootlike capillary forks burned as a negative into the backs of his eyes.

The piss-blizzard has been blowing for the last two days. Tonight's been the worst so far. He wants to climb down and find shelter—but they need him up there. Just in case the Empyrean use the storm as an opportunity to attack, Killian said. Wouldn't be the first time, he explained. They have jamming technology, apparently, antennas built into the ship masts that cloak their presence and make them hard to see from above—but should a ship spot them with their eyes, then the signal coming off those so-called "jammer-rods" doesn't matter one hill of horse apples.

The wind kicks up, vicious—the fangs of a beast, biting hard. Cold, too. Cael's not allergic to pollen like Rigo is (he's been staying belowdecks for the duration of this clinging tick of a storm), but even still, Cael's eyes are puffy and watery; his lips are dry and caked with yellow.

The wind is really howling now—but there's something else, some other sound, a vibration that hums in the wood of the crow's nest, that Cael can feel in his teeth and his fingertips. It's the sound of an auto-train, he realizes, the loud thrum of the hover-panels churning the silver bullet down the tracks. But that's absurd. No tracks out here, which means no auto-train, which means—

His eyes make a shape out of the darkness:

A twisting, living shape.

Big. Bigger than any of these boats. Bigger than anything Cael's seen.

No, no, no.

Thunder: *boom*. Lightning: *crash*.

It lights up everything for one spectacular, horrible moment, revealing:

A twister. A serpentine funnel of muddy yellow pollen writhing out there in the corn, ripping up stalks and turning them to dark shrapnel in the golden coil. Then the light from the lightning is gone, and Cael can only see the impression of the twister out there—

It's coming right for them.

He reaches up. Grabs the rope under the bell. Screams and rings it, *clang-clang-clang*, already his voice going hoarse as he tries not to choke as pollen fills his mouth—

I have to get down from here, or I'm going to die.

The crow's nest is just a half barrel banded with black iron and bolted to the cross of the mast. To get down one has to hop over the side, hang the way a corn-beetle dangles from a stalk tassel, then swing one's legs toward the ladder. Cael's nimble enough. Though he understands why someone like Mole is far better suited for this job, being so light and limber. Still, Cael can do it. Even in a panicked situation like this one.

So he tells himself.

He hops over the edge, swings down, kicks out a foot—

But it doesn't catch the rung of a ladder.

It catches a rope along the mast, a rope with a little slack that shouldn't have any slack, which means that someone (*Lane!*) screwed up—

Cael falls. The rope tightens around his ankle.

He swings, upside down.

A voice, indistinct, over the wind. He can't make it out.

Pollen cascading. Down below, the sounds of raiders yelling, scrambling, battening down gear and heading belowdecks.

The voice again. This time he can hear what it's saying.

It's calling his name.

"*Caaaaeel . . . Caaaaaaaaeeeeel . . .*"

Lightning strikes.

The twister. Close now. Right up on them. Big as a house. Tall as a barn silo—no, *taller.* Like the finger of one of the gods pointing down and pressing into the earth, drawing a cruel and unforgiving line through the corn and right toward the fleet.

Then the light is gone.

Everything is noise. Everything is vibration. It's in his bones. His stomach. Turning Cael's bowels to ice water.

The twister is just a brown shape writhing in the black.

And it misses the trawler.

Just.

But it keeps going. Cael sees it push alongside them by a few dozen yards, a wall of wind and pollen and corn that swallows all the boats off to the starboard side, breaking them apart the way a swing of a boot shatters a half-rotten box. Screams are lost in the wind. The twister dismantles the cat-marans and pinnace-racers, turning them to so many splinters—the spectral whirl of sails swallowed by the wind, spinning up and up and up.

And then the twister is gone. Moving away. Taking pieces of boats—and the raiders who worked them—off into the corn, into the storm, into the great, big, wide-open nowhere.

41

ASUNDER

SUNLIGHT. BLUE SKY. A SCANT FEW CLOUDS.

The Sleeping Dogs fleet sits in the mashed-flat corn as day comes and pushes the piss-blizzard away. Motes of pollen still swirl about in little dust devils reminiscent of the twister, but the greater beast has long fled.

Raider men and women rove the corn, looking for survivors. They've already found a few, bloodied and bedraggled, out in the fields. One had a spear of wood sticking out of his leg. Another had a corn leaf neatly, almost surgically, cut through the meat of his cheek, opening his mouth on that side another several inches. The other few were just cut up, bruised, beaten, the corn reaching for a taste of blood.

They also found bodies.

A dozen so far. Broken like stepped-on toys. Some of them barely recognizable. Corn roots already winding around them, pinning them to the dirt.

Cael sweats. He's back from a shift out there in the stalks. He found one of the bodies. A woman. Head pulped. Face a red, mushy mask. He threw up afterward. The tingling Blight-stem on his chest seemed revolted, too, tightening and twisting there beneath his shirt. So much so he had to clamp his hand down over it so nobody else could see.

The corn still avoids him. As if he is repellent to Hiram's Golden Prolific. He hopes nobody notices.

Now he's back. Drinking some water. Eating some rice and beans and green vegetable paste that in the back of his mind he knows are provisions stolen from a depot—maybe the depot where they missed their ride. These are provisions meant for Heartlanders. Other Heartlanders. But Cael's come around to accepting that the raiders are doing good. They have to be. Anybody who opposes the Empyrean has to be on the side of good.

And so he scoops rice and beans into his mouth. And dreams of plucking lush vegetables from a secret garden. He misses the days when things were perhaps not better, but they were, at least, simpler.

Raiders mill about. Crewmen from all the boats, trawler included: Sully, the cook, who's reminiscent of a goat; the bosun, Shiree, who, for an old woman, is as strong as a pair of oxen; the sailmaker, Gerhard, who even now is using a knife to cut squares of fabric to patch sails for the fleet. They stand around, jawing about twisters they've seen that were bigger, none of them talking about the wounded or the dead because . . . Well, Cael doesn't know why, but he figures because it's easier not to.

A hand falls on his shoulder. He spins, sees Striker Mayhew

standing behind him. Big fella. Skin as black as fire-licked iron. Shoulders as wide as the plow on the front of a motorvator. Arms like bundles of rope and chain twisted together.

Cael hasn't spoken to him much. He hasn't spoken to many of the men, not even after these weeks out here in the corn. He knows he isn't one of them. Not really. Not yet.

Mayhew says, "Been meaning to talk to you."

"Oh, uh. Well. Here I am."

"Your rifle."

"Uh-huh."

"Helluva weapon. Like the old raiders used to carry," he says. "My father had one. Not a lever-action like yours but a scatter-gun, with a pump on the front—" Here he mimes the motion of pumping the action on the weapon, and he even makes the noise: *Chuh-chack!* "He lost it, though. Had it taken from him by the August Guard bastards in a fight not far from Blanchard's Hill."

He says all this as if it's supposed to make sense to Cael, so Cael just puts another forkful of food in his mouth and nods.

"You ever do much hunting?" Mayhew asks.

"Used to. Back at the farm. Not with the, ah, rifle, though." Here Cael pulls out his slingshot, tucked neatly away in his back pocket. "This served me pretty well. Rats and rabbits and such."

"I'm the hunter for the fleet."

"I know." That's what a striker does. Hunts off the ship most times, and when they stop like this, goes into the corn and scares up food. "Hear you're pretty good at it, too. You got a fell-deer a couple days ago."

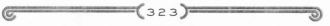

Cael hasn't had any of it. Whatever meat came off that thing went to the main-deck crewmen. Didn't trickle down to the likes of him.

"Eh," Mayhew says, waving him off. "It wasn't a healthy animal."

"Tumors," Sully chimes in. "Black sacks hanging off the outside, but what's worse is the inside—the damn tumors have got *roots* that reach out through muscle looking for blood to sustain themselves. Like the Blight. That's how the tumors survive." Some of the others give him a look. "Hey, what? I used to be a doctor, not a cook. Kinda the same thing, mostly. Turns out I'm better deboning a rat than I am fixing a broken arm."

"You and me," Mayhew says to Cael, "we can do some real damage out here. We should hunt together."

"Well." Cael looks around, "I think we're supposed to be . . . looking for survivors." He doesn't say *bodies*.

"Captain wants me to hunt," Mayhew says. "And I want you with me."

"The Dead Zone is comin' up," the bosun says. Like Cael's supposed to know what that means.

Sully must see the look on Cael's face, because he says, "You don't know the Dead Zone? Corn starts to die off. *Everything* dies off. Just cracked, dry earth with a forest of dead stalks, the hard soil beneath covered in a rime of white powder. I figure it's a fungus." He snorts. "Probably something the Empyrean cooked up. Just to mess with us."

It's now that Gerhard lifts his head from the sails, a needle clamped between his teeth, a red thread connecting it and the

patch of cloth in his lap. Around the needle he says, "They're not telling you everything, boy."

"Oh, here we go," Sully says, shaking his head.

"It's the Maize Witch," Gerhard says, taking the needle out of his mouth and using it to punctuate his words. "It is. She's out there. In the dead corn. With her army of Blighted."

At that the leaves-and-stem underneath Cael's shirt convulses, and he suddenly has to cover it with a hand. Sully gives him a look, eyes narrowing, and he thinks, *I'm busted; he sees it; he knows something's up—*

But then Sully looks back at Gerhard.

"Maize Witch. She's just a damn legend."

"She's no legend. I haven't seen her, but I know others who have. She walks the stalks. Starts whispering to you. And you can't not hear her. If she gets close, she can . . . make you do things. She'll give you the Blight. Turn you into one of her mindless, diseased slaves."

Mayhew laughs, big and booming. "I like a woman who can put me in my place. Maybe I should meet this Maize Witch."

"No, no," Shiree the bosun says. "Something to it. Maybe the Maize Witch isn't real, but we all know the Blight is. And sometimes out there in the Dead Zone, men go mad. They think they hear whispers. Men have been known to jump overboard. Run off into the maze of dry, dead stalks and never return."

Wham. Mayhew claps Cael on the back, almost knocks the bowl out of his hands. "Forget all that bullshit. You and me. Hunting. I've already got my bow. You've already got your slingshot. Unless you care to bring the rifle . . ." He grins big and broad.

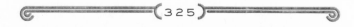

"Not sure I'm good enough with the rifle to even make it count. Let's see how I do with the slingshot."

Mayhew, twenty feet off. The corn here is jungle-thick, and normally it'd be nearly impossible to move through the field without making a stalk-cracking racket. But the corn isn't cutting him. It parts, just slightly, to let him past. A cheat, but it allows Cael to remain quiet.

Mayhew isn't making any noise at all, either. The big sonofabitch is easing through the stalks like a piece of paper sliding under a door. Once in a while Cael spies a flash of the man's dark, sweat-slick skin.

Out here Cael feels centered. Hunting? This is his speed. Feels good to get away from the raiders and the boats, and put the twister and the Blight and even the Maize Witch out of his mind.

A shape, dead ahead. *Mayhew*, he thinks.

But Mayhew couldn't be there—not that fast.

A person. Obfuscated by the corn. Standing there in the stalks, as still as a dead tree in a bleak orchard. Cael eases forward, starts to make out the shape of the body beyond the stalks: narrow shoulders, a curve to the hips, a flash of long, flaxen hair—

A voice, whispered.

Come to me, Cael.

A woman's voice. Both spoken aloud and in his mind. His throat catches his breath. His guts ratchet tight.

He tries to say something, tries to answer, but can't. The

Blight-vine under his shirt twists and coils like a knot tying and untying itself.

My home is your home.

I am inside you.

Soon we will meet.

Come to me, Cael. . . .

A hand grabs his arm.

He wheels, slingshot up, a hard stone already dropped into the weapon's pocket—

Mayhew catches his wrist with a firm but gentle grip. It's a hand big enough to break Cael's wrist into kindling.

"You okay?" Mayhew asks.

"I . . . I'm just tired, I guess" is what he tells the striker.

"Hey, we're far enough from the trawler. I wanted to talk to you."

"Uh. All right."

"I knew your father."

"Pop?"

Mayhew nods. "Mm. I was just a boy. My father was a young man. He was one of the Sawtooth Seven. With your father."

"Sawtooth who?"

"The Seven! The men and women who helped found the Sleeping Dogs. Your father was a great man! I knew as soon as I saw the rifle who it belonged to, and I thought, *I have seen this weapon before.* He is one of our founders. And now I see why you did not tell anyone."

Cael laughs. "No, I think you got that wrong. I don't know how my father came to hold the rifle, but he was no raider."

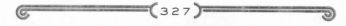

"Oh, but I think he was. McAvoy. Arthur McAvoy. I remember that name. Not from when I was so young but from later. When my father would talk. Before that day on Blanchard's Hill."

The warm day suddenly grows cold. First a sighting of that woman in the corn (*The Maize Witch*, a voice inside his head answers), and now this? Mayhew must be mistaken. His memories fuzzled.

But the questions. *Where did Pop get the rifle? Why did the Empyrean want him so bad?* Pop seemed so meek, so mild, but then of course Cael and his friends discovered his father's secret garden—and the hobos who had flocked to him as followers.

"I think I need to go back," Cael mutters.

"Your father was a great man."

A great raider.

"Thanks," Cael says, though that seems a strange response.

Mayhew calls after him as he leaves: "Later we take that rifle out. You need practice! And I want the chance to fire the gun of the great Arthut McAvoy. . . ."

Cael feels sick as he heads back up to the trawler. As if every part of him is breaking away, like bits of a hardtack biscuit yielding to the pressure from a pushing thumb. Gwennie. Wanda. Raiders. The Blight.

And now this. Pop. A raider.

No, hell, not just a raider. But one of the *founders* of the Sleeping Dogs? Jeezum Crow on a jackrabbit!

Everything he thought he knew, a lie.

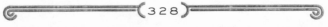

Everything he had planned for his future, gone.

He heads down belowdecks. Head in a fog.

He's about to turn left, toward his bunk, but in the other direction—

Lane's voice. Mumbled. A laugh? A laugh. *What the hell could Lane be laughing at? After last night? Why isn't he outside helping?*

Cael scowls. It was Lane's fault that the rigging was wrong, that he found himself hanging there like a mouse mere inches from the cat's mouth.

He grumbles, turns toward Lane's voice, and heads down the hall.

Lane's voice comes from behind Captain Killian's door.

Another laugh.

He tilts his head to listen.

"We should not be in here, Lane Moreau," Killian says, lip curled into a grin, tongue flicking one of his canine teeth. "In case you haven't noticed, the day is pregnant with work to be done."

Lane wraps his arms around Killian's waist, weaving his fingers together in the small of the raider captain's back.

"There's time," he says, a blush rising to his own cheeks. He can't believe he's this bold. But he's hungry for this, having been denied it so long. It feels good. He moves in for a kiss.

Killian ducks away from the kiss—playful, coy, not a refusal. Still that smile. Still the tongue on teeth.

"You know you want it," Lane says, and laughs.

"Maybe you should illustrate just how badly *you* want it." A wicked flash in Killian's eyes—like sunlight on a sword blade.

Lane nuzzles underneath Killian's neck. Takes little nibbles, runs his tongue up under the captain's jawline. Killian moans, chuckles between clenched teeth.

Then Lane feels the captain's hands on his shoulders.

Easing him downward. To his knees.

Lane smiles and begins unlacing the captain's pants.

A meaty paw falls on Cael's shoulder. Then shoves him away from the door. It's the big, bearded raider. The one he scuffled with way back at the depot. What the hell's his name? Brent? Brant?

Brank.

Brank growls. "Oh, you're dead, you little corn bug." The big sonofabitch throws open the captain's door, starts to say, "Cap, you got yourself an eavesdrop—"

But then the bearded man's mouth goes slack.

Cael sees Lane kneeling in front of Killian Kelly. Undoing the man's pants. He knew what it sounded like, but he didn't think that it could really be, that Lane and the captain were really . . .

Killian kicks Lane backward with a boot to the boy's chest.

"I *told* you," Killian says, his face contorting into a mask of rage. "I have no time for your wicked designs, Mr. Moreau."

That's all Brank needs. He grabs Lane from behind, pressing his forearm against Lane's neck. Lane kicks and thrashes as he's lifted up—

Cael doesn't know what's going on, but he won't abide what's being done to his friend. He darts in, roaring, pistoning two

punches into the bearded man's kidneys. Brank arches his back, howling.

He lets Lane go and hauls back and swings at Cael. It's a slow punch—a Boyland Barnes Jr. special, by the looks of it—and Cael's able to sidestep the swing.

Brank misses but then tucks his arm in and cracks his elbow right into the side of Cael's head—*wham*. Stars. Fireworks. Embers and sparks. Cael staggers backward; hands grab him and haul him up—

Cael feels it then. The patch of Blight. His stem-and-leaves. Starting to twitch. The skin there grows hot. Something stretches. As if it's growing. Yearning. With it burns a terrible thought, one branded across his mind as if with a hot iron: *You have the power, so why not use it?*

The thought isn't his voice. But also, it is?

The stem-and-leaves twitches.

But then—

Killian calls for it to stop.

Lane shoves past them, bolts out the door.

And since nobody stops him, Cael follows after.

Lane feels ripped open. As if someone stuck a knife somewhere above his balls and drew the blade upward, a jagged, complicated line all the way to the base of his throat.

He stumbles into the bunk room. He doesn't sit. Or lie down. He goes to the wall and slams a fist into it—once, twice—already his knuckles open and bleeding. *Why not a third time then?* But a hand catches his arm.

Cael.

Lane spins around, shoves him. "You ruined this for me."

"What? What the hell . . . Lane . . . are you . . ."

"I'm not talking about this with you, McAvoy." He feels tears running down his cheeks, and suddenly that shames him, as if he's giving Cael and all the others the satisfaction of seeing him act like a *girl* in all this.

"I heard things," Cael says. "I'm not— I mean, the captain was, you know, he didn't deny you—"

"You don't know shit about shit, Cael."

"I know what I heard."

"I'm not talking about this with you."

"Lane, if you're . . . if you're—"

"If I'm what? A faggot?"

"Jeezum Crow, I didn't say that—"

"Oh, so you're too shamed to even say it."

"No, Lane, shit, I just wasn't gonna use that word—"

"But you wanted to use it."

Suddenly Cael yells, "I'm on your damn side! You damn fool! I don't give a care what you like or . . . or who you do." He tilts his head. "Hell, actually, it kinda explains a lot. If you think there's some fence separating you from everybody else, fine, but just know I'm on the same side as *you*. Not *them*. All right?"

Lane hesitates. Then nods. All the fight goes out of him—a twister that falls apart, its vigor and rage gutted. He plunks down on the cot. Buries his face in his hands. "I thought he liked me."

Cael mills about. "Maybe he did. Or still does."

"Maybe he was just using me."

"Maybe that, too." Cael sighs. "This been going on a while?"

"The thing with the captain? Long enough."

"So there's no way he got confused about what was going on in there."

"Not unless a mule kicked him, knocked the memories out of his head. Lord and Lady, he's the one who *started* this."

"Shit."

"Yeah. Shit."

"You don't like girls."

"Nope. I mean, not that way."

"Huh."

"Yeah."

"Guess that's why you weren't too hot on being Obligated to Francine Goggins." Cael sits down on the cot across from him.

"Being Obligated in general wasn't exactly high on my list of things I was looking forward to. Being forced into a marriage is one thing, but being forced to marry someone who isn't even in the same category as what you could ever want. . . ." He lets out a held breath. "Like being told you'd have to marry a man. Or hell, a lamppost. Or a shuck rat. It just doesn't configure."

"And you're sure. That you're . . ."

Lane gives him a steely look. "Really? You're gonna ask that?"

"Shit, I dunno how this works." He holds up the flats of his hands. "Sorry. Sorry." Cael rubs his head where Brank's elbow got him. Already Lane sees a lump growing there.

"Your head all right?"

"No worse than usual. I'm dumb as a horse anyway."

"Sometimes." Lane grins.

Cael sniffs. "You could've told me."

"I told Rigo."

"That makes me feel so much better."

"It's just—you had everything hanging on that Obligation Day, thinking you'd somehow be fated to marry Gwennie and . . . you know, at the end of the day I knew you'd still at least get to marry a *girl*, and I guess that made me mad. I figured you'd be mad, too, if you knew about me. Like maybe you wouldn't trust me anymore. Or like me."

"You ever have a, uhh . . ." Cael clears his throat. "Crush on me?"

"Don't flatter yourself, McAvoy." But Lane finds a small smile and puts it on display.

"I think I'm a good-looking fella. A real smooth gent. *Dapper* even."

"Yeah, for a dirty-ass Heartlander."

"Yeah, for one of those."

They sit like that for a while. Just staring at each other's margins.

"You coulda told me is all," Cael finally says.

"No more secrets," Lane says.

"Yeah."

Lane watches his friend bite his lip. Like he's turning something over and around in his mouth. Or his mind. Cael stands up suddenly, as if he's got somewhere to be. But instead, he closes the door.

Cael turns around and starts to lift his shirt.

Lane gesticulates wildly. "I told you, Cap, I don't have a crush on—"

"I got a secret, too."

Holy hell.

A green stem, as thick as a pencil, a trio of leaves unfurling like little flags. Growing up out of Cael's breastbone, right above his heart. The stem roves. As if it's searching for something.

"The Blight," Lane says, his voice a hoarse whisper.

Game's over. Secret's out. Cael holds up his shirt. The Blight revealed. The stem is longer than when last he looked. By an inch or more.

It's moving. Like a finger drawing lines in the air.

Lane stares, transfixed. Half fascinated, half in sheer horror.

"The Blight," he says again.

Cael licks his lips. Finds his hands trembling. "I noticed it . . . back before the depot. I tried . . . I tried to cut the damn thing off, but it just came back stronger, so I haven't done it again."

"Lord and Lady."

"I need help."

"It's . . . it's maybe not as bad as it seems."

"You forgotten Earl Poltroon already?" Lane almost died by the man's terrible, twisting vine-tentacles.

"You forgotten your pop and those Blighters?"

"I don't have Pop anymore. I don't even know where Pop *is*."

"You have me. And you have Rigo. Those Blighted folk tending that garden . . . Your pop said the Blight had been stalled in them. That they were going to be okay. That it was under control, like any disease."

"I don't know how to 'stall' it."

"We'll figure out how," Lane says.

Lane stands. Offers his hand to Cael.

Cael slaps it away and grabs Lane and gives him a big hug.

Then pulls back and says, "This isn't the part where we kiss, is it?"

Lane rolls his eyes and gives Cael's shoulder a numbing punch.

They laugh for a little while, and it feels good.

"Shit, Lane. Everything's different now."

"Yeah, it is." The look on Lane's face mirrors how he feels. *It's not only different, it's worse.*

Maybe this is what it means to grow up.

42

THE TIES THAT BIND

"I WANT TO FIND MY FAMILY," Gwennie snarls, then flicks the knives. They fly free, straight and true. One in the heart of the dummy. One in the throat. One in the balls, or where the dummy's balls would be.

Davies chuffs a laugh. "You went and learned how to castrate a man. You must be great fun at parties and dances. All the men lining up to get with Little Miss Ballcutter."

His daughter, Squirrel, giggles and falls onto her back, rolling around like an overturned turtle. "Ballcutter! *Ballcutter.* Cutterball! So funny!"

Gwennie cocks an eyebrow at the crazy little girl, then turns back to Davies and talks as she walks forward and starts grabbing knives. "I'll say it again: I want to find my family. I'm frustrated, okay? I've been with you guys, doing what you want, and I'm no closer to them now than I was."

Davies sighs. Runs his hands along his scalp. It sounds as if he's rubbing a strip of sandpaper. "That's risky. You could put them in danger; you know it, and I know it, and even Squirrel knows it and she's nine years old—"

"Ten, Papa."

"It doesn't support the"—he gesticulates an invisible rainbow over his head—"*larger* goals of the Sleeping Dogs."

"They're Heartlanders. Like me. And they're *already* in danger."

"Yeah, sure, yes, but do the math, dummy. Saving three people jeopardizes our ability to save a lot more. We put ourselves out there—"

"*I'll* put myself out there. I don't need help."

"Listen, Little Miss Ballc—"

"Gwennie. Call me Gwennie, or I'll cut *your* balls."

"Gwennie. They like you here. *I* like you here. As part of us. Which means you have to play the way Salton and Killian Kelly and the other members of the Circle of Dogs want you to—"

"Imagine it," Gwennie says, jaw thrust out. "Imagine that your own daughter was out there instead of here with us. Imagine that some other family had her. That there were threats against her." She strides up to him and pokes him in the chest with the tip of a knife. "Now, what would you do about that?"

"I'd burn down the whole flotilla to get her back."

He says it without hesitation. Without blinking.

Then he sighs. "I'll talk to Salton."

"Soon."

"Yes. Soon."

"Today."

"Fine. *Fine.*" Another sigh, the exasperated sigh of a parent to a troublesome child. Curiously, a sigh she never hears him make toward his own daughter—who, right now, is still rolling around on her back. "Today."

"Good."

Then, past the door, she sees Merelda walk by.

She darts around Davies to catch up.

"Hey," she calls after.

Merelda turns. Her face is downcast. "Hey."

"You've been keeping to your room."

Merelda shrugs.

"You look . . ." *Like you're pouting.* "Sad."

"I'm good."

"Merelda, if you don't want to talk to any of these people—"

"Raiders. You mean, talk to these *raiders.*"

"Mer—"

"Raiders who are keeping me captive."

Gwennie rolls her eyes. "They're not keeping you captive."

"Can I leave?"

"What?"

"Can I leave? Like, can I walk past you, find a way . . . out, and just leave? Go do as I please?"

"That wouldn't be safe."

"See? *Captive.*" Merelda's pouty look is suddenly acidic. Her lips curl into a sneer. "Where *are* we anyway?"

"The back channels of the Engine Layer. It's why everything kind of . . . vibrates."

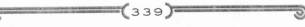

"It smells like a busted motorvator."

Jeezum Crow, Merelda. Complain much?

Gwennie throws up her hands. "Like I said, Engine Layer."

"These are—" Merelda lowers her voice. "These are *raiders*. What are they doing for us, Gwennie? We gotta think of ourselves here."

"Thinking of yourself is what got you into trouble."

"No, I don't mean— I'm just saying, they're all up in their own business. They don't care about us. I want to see my family again, and I bet you want to see yours. I want to put all this behind us."

Gwennie looks around, makes sure nobody is listening. "I'm making efforts in that direction. Okay? I'm working on it."

"It doesn't look like you're working on it."

"Damnit, Mer, I told you—"

Mer's eyes flick over her shoulder, and Gwennie hears footsteps. She turns to meet Davies. And Salton. Mary's wearing a dire, dour face. As if the cavernous wrinkles are all the deeper, like the black coals of her eyes are pushed farther back in her head.

"Gwennie," Davies starts to say, but Salton interrupts him.

"We need you to come with us."

Great, Gwennie thinks. *Davies told her what I want, and now she's going to ream me out for it.*

She looks to Merelda. "We'll talk more later."

Salton puts a hand on her back, turns her gently around, and eases her forward. A tiny part of her understands Merelda right there in that moment: the need to be free of someone pushing you

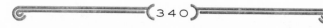

in one direction, the urge to do something different from what everyone says. She feels the desire to rebel against the rebellion.

A silly idea, she thinks. *Isn't it?*

Gwennie doesn't get it.

Mer always thought Gwendolyn Shawcatch was tough and all, but how smart was she, really? Getting wrapped up with Cael wasn't a winning move. Being a girl on a scavenging crew didn't seem too keen, either.

If Mer keeps relying on her, they'll never get out of here.

Mer thinks: *I can fix this.*

Not only can she make things right, but she can get them off this flotilla lickety-quick. And back down to home where—

Well, she doesn't want to think about that, either. The dirt and corn. Scrabbling for ace notes. She starts thinking about the Heartland, and her own heart starts getting other ideas.

She's going to fix this.

But to do that, she first needs to escape.

And Merelda McAvoy, well, she's good at escaping.

They don't say anything. Mary and Davies just lead Gwennie into Salton's spartan chamber. As they enter, other Sleeping Dogs stand by, watching from down the hall under dark brows— Gwennie suddenly understands. They know she's about to get her ass chewed out. Maybe they're worried about her. Or celebrating her comeuppance. Or just plain commiserating, since Mary

Salton seems like a hard-ass who throws her grump around like a slop bucket: everyone gets a little on them.

"I'm not going to apologize—" Gwennie starts to say, but then Davies gives her this look, and she doesn't know how to read it but it damn sure shuts her trap.

Salton says nothing, just pulls up a Marconi box—dusty, dinged, like the ones you'd see in a Heartland home—and sets it on the plywood table.

Motes of dust swirl in the artificial light.

"This came in over the Marconi about a half hour ago," Salton says. "They played it here. And on other flotillas. And down below."

She turns the knob. The screen crackles. Zigzagging black bars unkink to straight lines and then give way to an image.

Three people with red sacks over their heads.

A man. A woman. A young child—a boy maybe.

Gwennie realizes who they are even before the peregrine walks up behind them and snatches the hoods off their heads one by one.

Her family. Mother. Father. Scooter.

Wind whipping past. Wisps of clouds zipping by. The peregrine lets the hoods go on the wind—they flutter away like scarlet birds.

They're on some kind of metal platform. A catwalk just a grate beneath their feet. With the hoods off, their faces become masks of terror. They huddle together, though their hands are bound behind their backs.

A pair of men appears behind the peregrine, and the camera

pans left to a gleaming silver crank attached to a pair of inter-laced gears. The men each grab a side of the crank.

They turn.

The camera focuses on a gangplank extending out. Like the tongue of an auto-mate's mouth, mocking and cruel.

Gwennie hears herself gasp. She wants to turn it off. Wants to grab the screen and throw it. But she can't. She has to see. She has to know.

The peregrine hovers behind each member of her family. Flitting from one to the next with the delicate whimsy of a hummingbird choosing which flower to feed from.

His hand falls on the young boy's head.

Gwennie feels tears wet her cheeks. "No, no, no."

But then the peregrine smiles and shakes his head.

He steps away from Scooter.

And instead moves behind her father, Richard.

She can barely see through the tears. She can barely speak through her runny nose and closing throat. But still she can see how the peregrine shoves her father forward onto the gangplank. The sound turns on—everything had been silent, but now she can hear her mother telling her brother not to look, can hear her brother wailing in a way she's never heard before, all of it beyond the rush of blood in her own ears.

Her father tries to turn around, tries to run back.

The gangplank does not retract.

Rather, it begins to tilt downward.

Her father seizes the opportunity. He bolts forward, wobbly, hands behind his back, losing balance, about to fall—

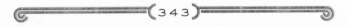

But he doesn't fall.

The peregrine draws his sleek coward's pistol.

He fires a sonic round into Richard Shawcatch.

Enough to stun. Not to kill.

Her father drops. Onto his side. Then onto his knees. He's gagging at the same time he's trying to crawl forward, all while the gangplank is tilting down, down, down—

And like that, her father slides off the edge.

The camera follows him for a moment—he's a fetal shape tumbling through sky and cloud and then—

Gone. Nothing.

Gwennie can't contain it. She loses everything she was holding on to. She screams. Grabs the Marconi box and hurls it off the table. Grabs for Salton, thinks, *This is your fault, you bitch; you kept me from rescuing them, and now they're all dead*—

And as Davies is behind her, wrestling her arms backward, she hears the peregrine make a proclamation from the sparking Marconi.

"If the Sleeping Dogs give themselves up, then we can stop the senseless killing of this family whose only crime is to have a terrorist for a daughter. Gwendolyn Shawcatch, if you're listening, heed this offer well. If you and your raider friends turn yourselves in before this time tomorrow, your family will live and live well. If you don't, then at this time tomorrow, your mother will be next on the plank, and we'll have this conversation again, when you'll have only your little brother to save."

She swings for Salton. Her fist connects. The woman's head rocks back just as Davies presses something against Gwennie's mouth.

A cloth. A stink fills her nose. An acrid chemical burn and—

Everything drifts. Her head separate from her body. Her skull a cage, her brain a panicked bird—Erasmus the grackle cackling *dead, dead, dead* again and again until she feels the floor melt beneath her. Darkness rushes up to greet her.

Merelda doesn't know what all the hullaballoo is about.

A bunch of raiders gather around. Mumbling. Talking.

Watching something on a Marconi box. Or on visidexes.

She doesn't care what. Probably more bullshit raider propaganda. Pop used to say that propaganda was just a lump of coal wrapped in an apple skin: made you think one thing when it was really another.

Doesn't matter.

What matters is, they're distracted.

And that means she has a way out.

Nobody's guarding one of the side-hatches. She grunts, spins the wheel, and exits into freedom.

It's time to go see Percy.

LAST RITES

BALASTAIR OPENS HIS ARMS wide and cackles, "I don't believe in your gods!" Then he does a mad dance, stomping his feet and spinning around, possessed by the ecstasy not of divine breath but of unadulterated atheism.

The two figures who have come to see him look on. The votary of the Lord and Lady stands by in his black cassock and looks equal parts embarrassed and frustrated. The old man straightens his prodigious white beard and looks away from the spectacle.

The priestess of Saranyu stares, as placid as a cup of water. She with her purple sari and orange sash, with her hair in a pair of dueling braids and her arms inked with the dark filigree of dyed scripture up to her bare shoulders. Her smile is as small and still as a mouse.

"You're being executed in a matter of days," the votary says. Votary Rimfin is his name. Balastair knows him—or did, once.

Old, shriveled bastard. Likes the wine. Likes the smoke. Likes all the indulgences he is allowed by the laws of catechism. "We should pray. And not to some old goddess whose presence here is purely cursory."

The old man's eyes flit toward the priestess.

For her part, she maintains a hold on serenity and says, "Saranyu only wishes to bless you on this, your journey into the life beyond."

Balastair grunts. "Life *beyond*. Beyond what? You don't get a life after a life, old woman! Oh, in the scientific sense one supposes there is something there—my body will decay; bacteria will feast while it can, but then the bacteria will all scream out in a chorus of pain as their world—which is me—burns in an oven. Then they'll cast the ash out of the ship—unless they choose instead to use the gangplank for me, but I'm told it'll be a hanging—and I will fall down below. Like the snow that the Heartland will never see because we've ruined the clouds and stripped the sky of its moisture just as we've done to the dirt and the plants and the men and the beasts. My ash will merge with the hungry, possessive corn. *That's* my life beyond."

The priestess nods. "Even in a divine sense that is true. But your mind and soul will be on the wind. In Saranyu's bosom—"

"Bosoms," Votary Rimfin harrumphs. "Such profane talk. Now let's talk truth, young Balastair. Your *mother* was a devotee of the Lord and Lady—"

"My mother made the corn," Balastair hisses. "Named it Hiram! After her own father. She created the only life I'll join after death, votary. You think I don't remember you? I do. You'd come to our house. And you'd drink and eat our food and look

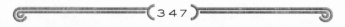

through our bookshelves, and you'd fill my mother's head with these fool notions of consequence and castigation, of justice meted out by invisible gods and how humanity must know its place beneath the eyes of the Lord and the Lady—"

"Balastair, your mother—"

"Just because you got to her doesn't mean you'll get to me! I remember you as a drunk. I'd be surprised if your breath doesn't stink a little *even now* of brandy or rye. And why wouldn't you be? Drunk, I mean. The people of the Empyrean have surpassed your gods. The breath of life, the wave of death, the kingdom of the sky with great, floating palaces, the lordship over the earth— these are things that once belonged to the Lord and Lady, but now they belong to us. Because we took them. Because we saw the gods as models and made ourselves after them. And now we are them. We're *better* than them. And you're nothing. And when it all falls apart, they'll send you below. Planted in the soil like another bad seed. More poison for the poor fool Heartlanders."

"You utter blasphemies."

"Well, *you* utter bullshit."

"I'm leaving," the votary says. Though for a moment he stands there, probably thinking that Balastair will realize his mistake and beg for forgiveness, *pray* for last rites. "I won't return."

"So, go! Go on. Scoot. Skedaddle. *Flee* my birdcage, foul crow."

Rimfin harrumphs again and hurries out, almost tripping on the hem of his dress. The priestess remains. Watching it all with curiosity.

"That was dramatic," she says finally.

"I don't believe it. That we're gods. I don't believe anything anymore." He *hrm*s and rolls his eyes. "Go on, shoo. Your devo-tion is fine and nice for you, but for the rest of us it's an excuse to have festivals and put up pretty sculptures and friezes of your fake deity—"

"Balastair, please shut up."

"What? What did you just say?"

"I have something for you." She reaches into her sari and pulls her hand back out. Before she opens it, she says, "I see they clipped the wings."

At first he doesn't understand, but then he sees she's looking at the bars of the cage. "Yes. The wings and the leaves. A man came in with tin snips. Cut them all off. Said I wasn't to be kill-ing myself anytime soon. That the public was owed my demise, and I was not to rob them of it."

She extends her hand out. Not through the bars. Not yet.

Her fingers open like the petals of a flower.

There, in her palm, a small pink pill. Pink like roses with the red half drained from them.

"I'm sorry," he says, "but what am I looking at?"

"It's a pill."

"I see that."

"Then you didn't have to ask and yet you did."

He frowns. "What does the pill *do*?"

"I'll say only that this bird's wings are not yet clipped."

A suicide pill.

"I won't take this."

"Then you'll die by their hand."

"I don't— It's not—"

Here she eases her hand through the bars. "If you have no

faith in any god or goddess, then granting yourself this mercy has no spiritual ramifications." He makes no move to take the pill from her hand. She changes the subject. "Your ward. The girl."

"Gwendolyn. Yes. Do they have her? Do you know? They said they wouldn't execute me until they had her in hand—"

"I do not believe they have her. But they seem confident that their move will work."

"Move. What move?"

She tells him. How today the peregrine executed the girl's father and then offered her a very public deal over the Empyrean signal. An *impossible* public offer to bring in not only herself, but her raider cohorts.

Balastair feels the color drain from his face.

He cannot imagine what this news will take from the girl.

"You can punish them before they punish you."

"What do you mean?"

"You can rob them of the satisfaction they get from killing you."

"I don't . . . I can't."

The priestess takes his hand, presses the pill into the palm.

"Just in case you decide to reclaim your power."

"I've never had any power."

"History suggests otherwise." A sly smile. Then she retreats from the bars of the cage. "May Saranyu bless you and carry you on the winds to the places your soul must see."

And then she's gone.

• • •

An hour later the priestess—Amrita is her name—returns to the birdcage room. There, in the center of the cage, the scientist lies on his back. Hair splayed out behind him. Arms wide in a gesture of openness to things behind this curtain, to things beyond this veil.

His chest rises and falls. Then stops for ten, fifteen seconds and rises and falls again. Little lifts. Little drops. Like the slowing heartbeat of a small animal: a hummingbird, a toad, a baby fell-deer.

And then it stops rising and falling altogether.

She withdraws her visidex. Taps the screen to record a message:

"It is done," she says. She sends the message into the ether.

GUNBREAKER

THE RAIDER FLEET—what's left of it—hurtles out over the blasted Heartland, the Dead Zone where all that's left is dry, lifeless stalks sticking up out of the split skin of dry earth. Cael sits toward the back of the trawler. The stalks look like bones to him. Arm bones. The desiccated tassels like skeletal hands, frozen and arthritic.

He also thinks, *I'm really drunk.*

Everybody's drinking. It's a funeral of sorts for those they've lost. Though nobody's talking about that. It's just a lot of drinking and yelling. Boasting and belting songs. Play fighting that sometimes turns into real fighting. All of them forming one big pressure valve that needs release.

As the wind sweeps over him, so too do whispers.

Come to me, Cael.

It's almost time.

It's as if they're coming from inside his own head.

Or worse, inside his own heart.

But at the same time, he thinks he can hear them out there over the corn, just as he did when the twister ripped through—

Whatever. He takes another long pull of skee.

Ohhh. Warm. Hot. Cool. Everything foggy. All a little numb. The finger-stem scratches at the fabric of his shirt, and he smacks it the way you'd slap at a fly. He's come to hate this thing just as he's come to accept it as a part of him.

Lane approaches with Rigo—it's slow going because that's how it is with Rigo now, hobble-*thump*, hobble-*thump*. Lane holds a couple of tin cups. "A little something different," he says with a slur. "White-fire moonshine. Guaram—" He blinks, laughs. "*Guaran*-damn-teed to strip the thoughts right out of your fool head. Which is about what I need right now."

He doesn't sit next to Cael so much as *drops* himself there, his long body slumped with the weight of the day's events.

Nobody's talking to them. Or looking at them.

They're outcasts. Again. Anew.

Word spread fast, it turns out.

Cael's been hunting with Mayhew. He learned to use the rifle a little better—how to use the sights. How to hug the butt of the rifle to his shoulder. How not to jerk the trigger but to squeeze it oh so gently—so that the shot is almost as much of a surprise to the hunter as it is to the hunted.

Cael didn't kill anything. But Mayhew got a couple of Ryukyu rabbits out there in their dens—skinny things, patchy fur, but not sick in any way, so they're part of the funeral feast going on.

But Cael's not very hungry. Thirsty, yeah. Hungry, no.

When they got back inside, Mayhew helped Cael take the

rifle apart then. Showed him a small sigil scored into the steel: looked like a long, lean fox running.

Teeth out.

"Swift Fox," Mayhew said. That was the name his father went by.

Cael says that name now, to Lane and Rigo: "Swift Fox."

"What?" Rigo asks.

"The name of a famous raider," Cael slurs.

"Not just a famous raider," Lane says, "but one of the *most famous* raiders. One of the Sawtooth Seven. They founded the Sleeping Dogs."

Cael tells them that Pop's rifle had the Swift Fox sigil on it.

"Whoa," Rigo says. "You think Pop maybe stole it from this raider?"

"Maybe Pop *killed* that Swift Fox," Lane says.

"Maybe Pop *was* Swift Fox," Cael answers.

The other two boys stare. Rigo laughs a little.

But Lane gets it.

"Oh, shit."

Cael nods. "Yep."

"Your pop was a raider."

"I think so, yeah."

"Explains why he was such a bona fide badass."

Rigo adds: "And hiding out in Boxelder."

Cael swigs from the moonshine. It's like drinking torchfire. He winces, *urp*s, and tries not to throw up.

The whispers again:

Come to me, Cael.

Before it's too late.

Cael lurches forward and stands up.

Out behind the boat, the forest of dead corn recedes (*grave-yard arms, skeleton hands, all reaching up, trying to pull the moon and stars out of the sky so that all we're left with is darkness*). Dizzy, he dips and swoons.

Lane catches his arm.

"You all right?"

"I could just jump," Cael says. "Just . . . fall out into the corn."

"Cael, hey, c'mon now—"

"The Blight. I don't want to become Earl Poltroon. I don't want to hurt either one of you. And it could go that way."

"It won't," Rigo says. An hour ago—as soon as the sun had gone down and the revelry started up—Cael had pulled Rigo into the bunk room and played the most uncomfortable game of I'll Show You Mine in history.

Rigo, to his credit, hadn't totally freaked out. Sure, he'd made a sound in the back of his throat like a cat caught under a motorvator. And his eyes had bugged out like a pair of chicken eggs about to plop into the nest.

"Can I see it?" he asks.

Cael gives him a look. "I showed you earlier."

Rigo shakes his head. "No, I mean, the gun. I want to see the rifle. And the marking of the Swift Fox." Even now he's doing what Rigo does best: avoid, change the subject, talk about something else. Same way he never really talked about his father or mother or anything else that bothered him.

"It's all back together again," Cael says. "Though only takes a screwdriver to pop the stock off. Well. All right. Hell with it."

He steps off the edge.

"I'll go get the gun. Be back in two lambs of a shake's tail. I mean— Well, Jeezum Crow, you know what I mean."

And he trudges forward, the whiskey haze pulling him along as much as his own feet are.

Rigo's worried.

He looks to Lane and says, "You think Cael's gonna be all right?"

Lane's smile is long gone. He stares down into his cup and slams back a gulp of white lightning. He winces and exhales sharply through his nose.

"Nope," Lane says.

"The Blight's pretty bad stuff."

"And someone's gonna find out soon enough."

Rigo's quiet for a while. He, too, looks down into his cup, but the fumes coming out of it seem as if they could strip the varnish off nice wood. Hell, or dissolve the wood into a goopy paste.

Finally, he says, "I'm sorry to hear about you and the captain."

"He's a prick."

"You liked him."

Lane sighs. "I did. I do."

"Just because he was a raider?"

"At first. But something about him. Always smiling. Has his own way of saying things like he's got two words for every one of ours. I felt hooked into him, connected somehow." Lane shakes his head, looks sad. "I thought he didn't care what everyone else thought. He told me as much. Turns out he's like every other Heartlander out there: full of bad notions."

"Not every other Heartlander," Rigo says, trying to sound chipper.

"You're such a kiss ass," Lane says, smirking as he pulls out a cigarette. "Killian's shacking up with Hezzie Orden now. That big-hipped girl from the crow's nest? What a slut."

"That's mean. You don't know she's a slut."

"Not her. Him. *He's* the dang slut."

"Oh."

"You miss your leg?" Lane asks.

Rigo snorts. "That's a dumb question."

"Says the king of dumb questions."

"That's fair. Yeah, of course I miss it."

"You miss your father?"

"I dunno. Maybe. Maybe I miss the idea of him. If not so much the actual *him*. That's stupid. I dunno." Rigo wonders if the old man really had been on that boat out there. And if he'd made it. A little part of him wants to see his father again, thinking, *Well, if he was coming after me, maybe he loved me.* Maybe he was going to try to do right by Rigo and his mom.

Or maybe he woulda stomped up and cuffed him in the ear and tied him to the back of the boat and made him run after, through the corn.

Wouldn't be the first time.

Lane shrugs. "Isn't stupid. I feel the same way about mine."

"I wish things were back to normal. That we were back in Boxelder again. Harvest Home and Busser's Tavern and heading out on scavenging runs with Cael and Gwennie."

"I don't wish that. Those days were bad, too, just in a way we didn't much talk about."

"Least then I had a leg. And Cael didn't have the Blight."

Lane shrugs. "If it wasn't those things it would've been something else."

Cael reaches under his cot. Finds the rifle there. On a lark he figures he'll pocket some ammo. Take it back up there, start shooting off the back of the boat. Maybe see if they can hit a couple rotten cobs as they pass by—moon's out fat and bright; should be able to see all right.

It'll draw attention. Gun going off like that. It should. Cael feels bold all of a sudden. Bolstered by a kind of unsettled, unfixed anger. It's the whiskey, but it's also not the whiskey. *Let them come*, he thinks. He'll wave the gun around, drunk. Let them worry. Let Killian try to stop him.

"I'll shoot you dead between the eyes." Cael growls even though he doesn't mean it. Just the same, it feels mighty good to say.

He starts to head back. But before he does—

He hears footsteps in the hall.

And then voices.

Killian. And the first mate, Billy Cross.

Cael once again finds himself in the position of snoop.

Cross is in the middle of saying something. "They say it's happening tomorrow morning. The timetable's moved up."

"Well, shit, Billy, that puts us in a rather *contorted* position, wouldn't you say? We won't be at Tuttle's Church for at least another day of hard going—that twister sucked the spit right out of us."

They both head toward Killian's chambers, their backs to Cael.

He sneaks out into the hallway. Creeps up behind them.

Killian. That sonofabitch. He wants to give him what-for. Teach him a lesson for hurting his friend. Above deck, there were too many others. But down here, maybe, just maybe—

I'll shoot you dead between the eyes.

But then another voice, not his own:

Come to me, Cael. Find me. Find . . . me. . . .

"Is what it is," Billy is saying. "Seems like the horse is out of the barn on this one, Cap."

Killian says, "Reckon we just keep pushing ourselves inevitably forward then, Billy Cross. We may submit a prayer to the Lord and Lady above that—" They walk through the door and shut it behind them, but Cael can hear the conversation continued, if now muffled. "—we don't encounter too much resistance there in Tuttle's Church. But if what we're hearing is true, well."

"We're hearing the Empyrean isn't even there anymore."

"And neither are the good people of Tuttle's Church. That seem like the proper sum of all the parts to you? Doesn't to me, Billy Cross, doesn't to me. If the data bank is still there in the old mine, I'll piss in my own eyes if they aren't protecting it somehow."

Cael thinks, *Now's the time. Push open the door. Tell Killian what's what. Tell him he hurt your friend. Put your gun under his chin, your boot up his barrel bung—let the whiskey and the bullets do the talking.*

And he's about to.

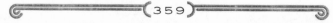

But then he hears Billy Cross say, "Lotta people gonna die when that flotilla comes down."

Comes . . . down?

"Some of our own," Billy adds.

"Like you said, Billy Cross, *Is what it is.* You ever hear the story about how one of the Sawtooth Seven got caught after the gunfight at Tarryall? Some folks say it was Iron-Red Ned, but Mayhew says he doesn't think so. Way it's been told to me, it was Bellflower. Story says they caught her, had her bound up in those whip-cord wrist-cuffs. She took her teeth, bit into the skin around her hands and wrists. So the blood could *lubricate* her flesh. That's how she was able to wriggle free, steal one of their sonic pistols, and shoot her way out. Sometimes blood lubricates the gears, Billy Cross. Revolution doesn't come with a kiss and a tickle."

A floorboard creaks just behind him.

Cael whirls.

"You again," Brank growls.

"*This* again," Cael slurs.

Brank grabs him, throws him through the door.

Cael lands hard on his shoulder in the captain's chambers.

He tries to stand, but Brank's fast like a falling tree— suddenly his shadow blankets Cael, and a hard boot catches Cael in his side.

He curls up around the rifle. Moaning. Pain radiates from his balls up to his sternum. The stem-and-leaves tightens and twitches.

Killian kneels. "How much did your little ears hear, Cael?"

"Enough," he groans.

"Time to present a very serious question then. Is this going to be a problem? We're just on the edge of this thing, and you and I had such a nice talk before, and I'd like to think you're with me on this."

"Way Lane was *with* you?" he coughs.

Killian clucks his tongue. "Your friend had designs on me that were admirable and flattering but that I was regrettably unable to return thanks to the way the Lord and Lady made me. I enjoy the company of women."

"You didn't tell me," Cael croaks.

"Tell you what?"

"About the rifle. You said it was a raider's rifle. You never said it belonged to one of the Sawtooth Seven."

"Didn't want you to get a big head about it."

"What else aren't you telling us?"

Killian just grins.

"The flotilla," Cael grunts. "You're gonna bring it down. The . . . Saranyu?"

"The very same."

"All those people on board . . ."

"As you may have heard, they will not all make it, I suspect."

"And the other raiders. My girl, Gwennie . . ."

The grin stretches tighter, like skin pulled across a tanner's horse. "She'll be safe. I'll make sure of it."

But there's a hesitation just before he says it. As if the widening smile is covering, compensating, trying to spackle over all the fear and all that doubt. It's then Cael realizes: everything

this man says is a lie. Or worse, some unsteady, unpredictable mix of lies and truth, blended so perfectly together that the distinctions have been lost.

"I think you might be selling me a story," Cael says. "*Sometimes blood lubricates the gears.*"

The raider's smile fades. His nostrils flare. "Seems you will be a problem, then. Brank?"

Cael feels another boot, this time in his kidneys. Pain blooms like a field of poppies. His head swims. He fumbles for the gun—

Killian pulls it away.

My gun— That's Pop's—

Brank drops down onto Cael, presses a meaty arm against Cael's throat to pin him to the floor. Brank stares down over that crooked, still-puffy nose.

"Whaddya want me to do?" Brank asks.

Killian pops his lips. "Shit. Kill him, I guess."

Brank lifts Cael and hurls him backward into the wall. A nearby table rattles. A bottle spins off it—doesn't shatter but rolls away.

One hand closes around his throat.

With Brank, only one hand is needed.

Cael's vision warps. One world becomes two. His head pulses. His tongue feels fat. He kicks out—driving a boot-tip into Brank's crotch, or so he hopes, but Brank turns, takes the kick on the inside of his thigh, and retaliates by slamming Cael against the wall anew.

The world pulses, *badoom badoom badoom.*

The stem-and-leaves beneath his shirt twitches and stretches.

His chest begins to burn like someone's pressing the tip of

a cigarette there. Brank makes a sound, stares down at Cael's chest. He must see something moving there because he scowls and says, "The hell's that?"

And that's when it's all over for him.

Cael's shirt splits—the fabric rips.

The Blight thrusts outward, no longer only a few inches long but now several feet of braided vine—Cael sees dozens of leaves flitting and twitching as the vine springs like a snake out of a hole, coiling suddenly around the thick, gristly arm holding Cael by the neck.

It cinches tight.

The sound of breaking bone splits the air like a thundercrack—

The arm bends opposite to how it should. Brank makes a sound like wind howling through a broken window.

Billy Cross yells, "Blight!"

The pressure is gone. Cael drops to the floor, heels skidding so that he barely remains standing.

Everything goes to King Hell.

Billy lunges, his fat-bladed Bowie already up out of its sheath. On the other side, Killian is raising the rifle—Cael's own gods-damn rifle!—and jacking the lever action to load a round into the chamber.

It's then that Cael feels it, really feels it—the Blight. Part of it is in him, but part of him is in it, too. He wills it to act.

It lashes to the right. Then coils around the rifle. Yanks the barrel to the side just as Killian pulls the trigger. *Bang!*

Billy *oofs*, staggers backward—the knife thuds to the floor. Blood flecks the wall behind the first mate. A black-red stain spreads between his heart and his belly.

Billy Cross falls, clutching his gut and gasping.

Killian calls his first mate's name—

Just as the gun is yanked out of his hand by the whipping Blight-vine.

Cael catches the rifle.

But Killian's fast.

He's already got a sonic shooter in hand—

Long, lean barrel pointed at Cael.

Killian fires.

Cael holds up his own rifle, sideways across his chest—

The sonic blast snaps the rifle in twain. Splinters spray his face. The two halves of the rifle—*Pop's gun!*—drop to the floor.

Killian raises the pistol again—

Fight turns to flight.

Run, godsdamnit, run.

The Blight-vine acts on its own—it coils around a chair leg, whips it hard into Killian's temple, knocking the raider captain onto his bed.

Outside the door: footsteps. Marching belowdecks, sounding like a herd of cattle stampeding—

Only one way out then. The window at the aft of the ship. The one that looks and hangs out over the corn. Two dozen panes of warped glass, the dead corn, and the long night waiting just outside.

Cael charges—

The vine coils around his own arm. Like a whip, a lasso.

Killian is already up, gun pointed, firing another shot—

Good fortune. The sonic blast lances through the air. Strikes the window. It shatters outward in a tumbling hailstorm of glass shards—

Cael joins the storm of glass, leaping out—

Out over nothing. Legs pinwheeling. Arms like broken wings flapping, trying to help him fly.

Suddenly he's in the corn, legs hitting hard, rolling forward.

Sonic blasts pepper the air with shrieks and warbles. Stalks and leaves pop and slice and hop like a rabbit bitten by a rattler.

But then the fleet keeps going.

Out over the corn and away.

Cael is alone. He rolls onto his back and weeps.

SCAR TISSUE

GWENNIE WAKES to the vision of her father scrabbling to stay on the gangplank, then sliding, then falling. Her mother follows him over, kicked in the gut by the peregrine, who has great gray wings thrusting up out of his back. As Gwennie's mother falls, the peregrine's wings stretch and spread, majestic and cruel with raptor-like grace. Finally, her brother: Percy grabs him. Scooter kicks and screams.

Percy tosses him over the edge. Like someone throwing a feed sack.

Their screams are loud, then soft . . . then gone.

All that's left is the wind.

And the sound of her weeping.

She's in a small cell. In the corner. On the floor.

Whatever chemical was in that cloth has her feeling muzzy headed—as if her brain is wrapped in a layer of soggy sponge.

"You're awake" comes a voice. She gasps. Startled. A hard boot of adrenaline. She squeezes some of those sponges dry.

Davies. He's sitting on her cot. Looking somber and sober, hands across his knees, hunched over. He runs a hand across his scalp, drums his fingers there. "I'm sorry I had to do that to you."

"May Old Scratch take you. May he take you and work the forges until your hands burn; may he force you into the mines of King Hell, where you work your hands bloody and down to white bone; may he rake you over the coals; may he crush your body underneath his howling steam engine!"

"You were inconsolable."

"I wonder why." She hears her own voice, like gravel rattling in a tin cup. She knows she's still young, but she suddenly feels so old.

"I can't imagine what that's like. To watch your father—"

"If you came here to relive the memory, don't bother." *Already playing again and again in my head like some flickering projection. Like a stage show for ghosts.* "Just go away."

"Mary Salton—"

"Can also go to hell."

"—has determined that now is not the time to make ourselves vulnerable by rescuing your mother and your brother."

Like a sickle blade piercing her heart. She knew that would be the answer, but it kills her to hear it aloud. It elicits from her a loud, gulping sob. She quickly quiets herself, shoves the sorrow down into a hole, blinks away any tears that want to come. She sniffs. Wipes her eyes. Stares hot coals through Davies, hoping that he can feel it: a hot poker through his heart.

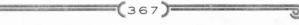

"I've decided otherwise" is all she says.

"Then I'll help you."

Wait, what? "Wait, what?"

"I . . . lost my wife just after Squirrel was born. Squirrel was born on a Tuesday, and Retta died on Wednesday. The birth . . . tore something open inside my wife. Doc Misery said wasn't much we could do; she didn't have any Annie pills or the training to sew her up. But then someone—I don't even remember who—said, *Well, they got those pills at the depot, and maybe even one of them fancy mechanical Doctor-Bots.*

"See, I lived in a town, Quarrel's Bridge—but there was no bridge and so we just called it Quarrels—and we had a depot nearby. I was just a field shepherd tending the motorvators, so I stole the Tallyman's boat—and off we went to the depot, not even a half-day's ride away."

He stares off at an unfixed point—a point that in his mind must be somewhere in the Heartland, a point found backward in time.

"I got her there, and her thighs were just . . . they were blackened with blood, her legs looking like they were covered in roofing tar, and I thought, *The people here at the depot are going to help me. They're Heartlanders even if they work for the skybastards above.*

"So I went to the door. My wife across my arms, blood . . . dripping into the dirt. And I pounded on that door. Knocking so hard I thought I might punch it off its hinges. Eventually a little voice came up over the speaker and the voice belonged to . . . well, it was a provisionist's voice, small and mousy, and he told me to go home. *Go home*, he said, *and bury your wife.*"

His jaw tenses. Gwennie can hear his teeth grind like a millstone.

"He said that because Retta was dead. In my arms, just dead. And I was mad, and I took that boat and rammed it into the depot, which broke the boat and didn't do squat to the depot. Men came out in face shields, peppered me with sonic shots. Knocked me out cold, and I woke up in a cell. Just as you did now. And I broke out of that cell with the help of some of the townsfolk who knew I had a baby girl I had to tend to, and then I took that baby girl of mine, and I named her Retta after my wife, but that was too painful to say so I just called her what I thought she looked like, which was a little squirrel. I ran. Escaped town. We lived as hobos for a couple years until I found the Sleeping Dogs—or until they found me. And here we are."

Gwennie leans back against the wall. The rusted metal is cool against her scalp and her neck. "I'm sorry" is all she can say.

"Nothing for you to apologize about. That's life in the—"

"That's life *everywhere*," she says.

"Well. It doesn't have to be. We're trying to make a difference. But Salton can be singularly focused, and she doesn't have the . . . unique perspective I have on losing our loved ones. We're scarred, you and I. But maybe we can save you a pair of scars if we do this right."

"What are you saying?"

"I'm saying, dearest Ballcutter, that we leave just before morning, when the guards shift. I've got a plan to rescue your mother and your brother. So, steady yourself for the fight ahead. I hope you truly are ready to cut some balls, because we're not going to salvage what's left of your family unless you're willing to get mean."

"I can be mean. I'll do anything." She nods. "Thanks, Davies."

He nods. "See you in about five hours, Ballcutter."

Davies steps into Salton's office. She stands by a chalkboard that's not hung but rather propped against the wall. Coordinating raiders and ship schedules. Escape vectors.

"It's done," he says. He hears the disappointment in his own voice.

"Good to hear."

"Good to hear? I could use a little more than that, you know. A clap on the back. A shot of whiskey. A freakin' parade would actually be all right for the shit-awful thing I just did to that girl."

Salton turns. He can tell she's trying to make a softer, more compassionate face, but she can't hide her eye-rolling in disdain.

She says, "This aligns perfectly. The peregrine has done precisely what he did not want to do—he wanted to anesthetize us. But we're riled up. Enraged. The saying goes to never wake a sleeping dog, and that's what he's gone and done, Davies. This is necessary. Shawcatch has the drive and the willingness to put herself out there—"

"Only if we're lying to her."

"Don't think of it as a lie. It may not be. Maybe your actions will still save her mother and brother."

"But that's not our goal," he says, realizing that he, too, isn't able to hide his disdain.

"Should it be? To save two people when we're trying to save thousands?"

"That's mercenary."

"That's reality. Do the deal. Get her to the control tower."

"We'll have support?"

"All you need."

"And we have the codes?"

"Already in hand."

But there he hears a hesitation. She's lying, isn't she?

"Good," he says. "And we're all guaranteed a way off this when the heavens start to fall?"

"Of course."

"Even the girl?"

"Even the girl."

THE DEATH AND
RESURRECTION OF
BALASTAIR HARRINGTON

BALASTAIR GASPS AND SITS UP SHARPLY.

His head cracks into the plastic molding of a bunk above him.
Wham.

He drops back down.

He looks around. Starts to shiver. Then sweat.

He rolls off the edge of the bed and pukes.

Or rather dry heaves. The most he manages to produce is a
string of thick, foamy saliva dangling from his lips and chin.

Ptoo. He spits. Crawls over the edge of the bed.

A very small bunk room. Cramped. Coffin-like. *But I'm
not dead,* he thinks. *Dead men don't shiver and sweat and spit.* Or
do they? He was dead. He took the pill. Maybe he's crossed a
threshold, some tenebrous membrane separating what is known
of life into what is unknown about death—

Below him, the ground begins to hum.

Hover-panels. He's on a ship.

He stumbles to the small door, crouches, and steps through.

A woman sits at a control panel. She presses a set of linked levers forward. The humming sound below grows.

She's pretty. Young. Almond-shaped eyes. Lips painted red: all sharp peaks and dagger-tips. She sees him. She smiles.

"You're awake," she says.

"I'm *alive*."

"Yes."

"Who are you?"

A twinge of her red lips. A smile? A scowl? "A friend."

"A friend. The Sleeping Dogs. Did Kin Sage—"

She says nothing.

But as she reaches up above her head with her other hand to flip a few switches, he sees her hand.

At first he thinks it's a glove. It's not. It's plant matter. The hand isn't even human. Those aren't fingers. They're *vines*. Leaves whispering against one another as they flick the switches and press buttons. When the task is completed, the vines braid back together and curl inward. Like a fiddlehead fern spiraling in reverse.

"My mother," he says, struck with sudden horror.

"She wants you safe. She heard tell of your plight."

"I won't go."

"You will. If only out of gratitude for us saving you from that cage and whatever grim execution was to happen next."

"I . . . you made me kill myself. I thought I . . ."

"Easiest way to get your body out. The pill simulated death."

He spots a sonic shooter sitting on the dash.

Two feet from her right hand. Her *human* hand.

She turns back toward the console. Presses a flight stick forward. The ship begins to lift.

Above Balastair's head: a hatch.

It's now or never.

He reaches in, grabs for the gun—but she sees him coming. She snatches it first, cracks him across the forehead with it.

He falls into the copilot's chair, head pounding.

She levels the pistol at him. She says, not without a hint of anger, "Just sit back and enjoy the ride."

The ship drifts upward. The thrum of the hover-panels grows louder.

Balastair looks at the viewscreen in the center of the console. Small, black and white, but a clear enough picture: this boat, maybe a Mackinaw, isn't moored like some. It's small enough to sit on a landing pad.

"You won't shoot me," he says. "My mother wouldn't like that."

"I can stun you into unconsciousness."

He shrugs. The woman has a point.

He darts his eyes once more to the viewscreen—this time feigning shock and horror at what he sees there. He lies: "We're under attack!"

Her gaze follows his.

It's the only moment he'll get. He jams his foot up and then brings his heel down on the elevator levers—

Suddenly the ship shudders and jerks downward.

He doesn't know how far up they are—twenty, thirty feet?—but it's enough. The Mackinaw pitches forward and crashes hard

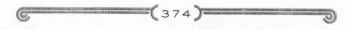

into the dock. The woman's head hammers forward into the steering column, and the gun drops out of her hand.

Balastair is thrown off the seat, slamming hard against the floor between the two chairs.

He sees the sonic shooter. Snatches it up.

The woman moans. Tries to lift her head off the console. Blood gushes from a gash above her eyebrows.

Balastair utters a small apology, drops the telescoping ladder, and clambers out of the hatch before the Blighted woman fully rouses.

THE PATH OPENS

CAEL SITS FOR A WHILE, surrounded by a forest of withered cornstalks. Above, fat, phlegmy clouds block the moon. A wind kicks up; dry leaves hiss as it sweeps over and through.

He looks down at his Blight—three vines now plaited together as one, emerging from the hole in his ripped shirt, thrust up from a crater of red, raw skin right over his heart. He can hear his heartbeat pulse through the vine and to the ends of each small, thumbprint-sized leaf. The vine now sits coiled around his arm from shoulder down to wrist.

It's quiet. As if, for now, its work is done.

He's not sure what happened back there. He was drunk. He's not now. Everything is as clear as the tolling of a bell. Crisp. Awake. Aware.

Painfully so.

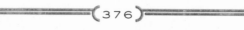

He attacked. He was attacked. The Blight reacted. Billy Cross is dead. What will happen to Rigo and Lane?

But then another thought: *They're going to bring down the flotilla.*

Not just any flotilla. The one with Gwennie on it. And his sister.

The thought sucker punches him.

He has to stop it. Somehow. But it's an absurd notion. He's alone in a dead zone of Hiram's Golden Prolific, the raider fleet fast moving toward its destination of Tuttle's Church, wherever that is. He has nothing. No way forward. No way back.

It occurs to him: *I'm going to die out here.*

Death. It haunts the Heartland. Stillborns and cancer victims and those who fall into the processing vats or get mowed down by some malfunctioning motorvator. Cael's seen it his whole life. Ghosts of it in his father and mother: Pop's bone spur hip, Mom's tumors all over her body. Corruption and ruin and *Oh hey, welcome to the Heartland.*

Just the same, he never really figured it would happen to him. He felt young and immortal. His life was always ahead of him. Obligated to Gwennie—or when reality had intervened, Wanda. Maybe some kids. Inherit the farm. He knew he couldn't be a scavenger forever, and one day he'd go and work the line or do some other job the Empyrean assigned to him, but everything *else* still seemed like forever. And now, standing here in the wide-open nowhere, forever seems as if it's been cut woefully short.

I'm dead. Dead as these cornstalks. Dead as Mayor Barnes, or Grey Franklin, or Pally Varrin. Is Pop dead? Mom? Will Gwennie

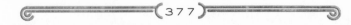

and Merelda die, too? Lane and Rigo? Is Wanda still alive, or has she gone skip-to-the-loo off this mortal coil?

All because I couldn't do what I was supposed to.

All because of that garden. Because of the choices he's made.

He stands up.

Dusts himself off.

Tries to figure out where to go.

His eyes adjust to the darkness.

And he sees something. Something impossible. Out there beyond the stalks. Hidden among them. A shape.

Like somebody standing there. Still and silent.

Just a trick of the eye, he thinks.

But then his eyes drift.

He sees another shape just like it to the left. And another to the left of that one. He lets his eyes drift, slowly spinning himself around, the dry ground cracking and complaining beneath his turning feet—

People. Standing out there. In the corn. *All around him.* Watching.

Waiting.

Can't be. Impossible. Nobody out here. Nobody.

Over the corn, a lilting, lyrical voice—

"Caaaaaaeeeel . . ."

Not a whisper. Not in his head. But real.

It's the voice he heard during that twister. As if the whirling winds had captured the voice. As if the funnel cloud was a message just for him.

The bodies all take one step forward. In unison.

Rustling corn.

Lord and Lady. He has a horrible, absurd thought: *the Maize Witch.* The devil's own daughter. With her army of demons.

Again that singsongy voice, *"Caaaaaeeel . . . Cael, we're waiting. . . ."*

He thinks, *Run.*

The shapes take another step forward. Then another. And one after that. They're coming now. Slowly. But damn surely.

He looks down at the Blight-vine coiled around his arm—he wills it to move, to lash out, to twitch or shift or something or *anything,* but it just hugs his arm tight—

Each of the dark shapes suddenly glows bright.

At first he thinks, *Some trick of the witch, some awful magic—* but then he sees the way the light dances, reflected up and out, and he realizes they're carrying lamps. Oil lamps with tall, glass chimneys.

He can smell the oil burning now.

They're coming.

"Go on!" he shouts. "Get out of here!"

He reaches for his back pocket—

His slingshot is still there.

He pulls it. Feels in his other pocket for—

Dangit, no ammo.

Cael quickly drops to a knee, feels around the ground for anything, anything—but it's just hard, broken dirt and crusty brace roots.

But then: one stone. He palms it. Pops it into the slingshot pocket—

When he stands, he sees they're upon him.

The horror of it stays his hand. His fingers slacken. The stone drops from the slingshot pocket.

Blighted.

They're all horribly, unavoidably Blighted.

Men and women. Some of them have thorns instead of teeth. Eyes yellow like pollen. Limbs of vine, stalk, and bark. Leaves thrust up out of necks and chins and cheeks. Collarbones of knotty branch. Hair like flowery filaments or green grass—Cael hasn't seen a patch of grass since he was a kid, and here it is, growing up out of a Blighter's scalp.

They open their mouths.

Their jaws creak and pop.

They collectively speak his name.

"*Cael.*"

"Get the hell away from me!" he yells. He waves the slingshot around—it bashes into the corn, shaking and rattling the dead stalks. "You leave me alone!"

Over the corn, with the wind, comes that singsongy voice—a woman's voice. The Maize Witch's voice. "*I can help you, Cael. Come to me. Come to me. . . .*"

The Blighted echo her in unison. "*Come to me.*"

"I won't. Leave me be, godsdamnit!"

"*I will help you control it. I will help you save your friends. . . .*"

"*Control it . . . ,*" the Blighted hiss. "*Save your friends . . .*"

Then the Blighted, now ten feet in front of him, step to the side, revealing a way through. The dead, dry corn shudders in the earth. Stalks contort and snap like bones breaking. Like Brank's arm.

They form a path. A path that grows longer as more and more stalks twist and break farther and farther away. He can still hear them in the distance as the path is made.

Over the corn, the voice whispers, *"Walk the path, Cael McAvoy. . . ."*

"Walk the path," the Blighted echo.

"Walk the path," Cael says himself. He draws a deep breath and wills his feet forward. It is time to meet the Maize Witch.

PART FIVE

HEAVEN'S FALL

THE INITIATIVE

IS THIS MY HOME NOW?

That question haunts Simone Agrasanto. She feels trapped by the mayor's house, by this town, by the whole of the Heartland. It's as if her boots are stuck in the mud, and the day she envisions wrenching them free is seeming more and more like a fantasy.

She tosses. She turns. The sheets on the mayor's bed are snarled around her legs like a tangle of ivy.

Eventually she kicks them off.

She's a proctor. That means administrating not just one town but many. Herding the Babysitters to do their job. Ensuring that sanctioned holidays go off without a hitch and that nonsanctioned holidays are pounded into the dust like a tenpenny nail. All in all, it's her job to inflict order and bureaucracy on these land apes, these dirt-cheeked, blister-fingered, back-broken workers.

As she heads into town, toward Busser's, she passes by towns-folk. Gives a lift of her head to Doc, who sweeps the front of his office with a ratty broom. He gives her a small smile, yells that it's going to be a nice day. She yells back her agreement, even though she knows it won't be. It'll be sunny and warm, but the breeze will be like a stillborn calf, and the smell of sweat and dust will still cling to the inside of her nose like a rime of grease.

She passes by the Tallyman's office and spies Frieda Wessel inside, working a visidex—a piece of technology she really shouldn't have, but Agrasanto felt bad for her and procured her one on the sly. Simone knocks on the window. Frieda smiles.

It's a small town, but she sees a lot of people. Little Gabby Tremayne playing with a barrel hoop. Her uncle Stanley popping kernels off a cob with the flat of a knife, setting up rat traps. The oldest Poltroon son, hammering tread onto the wheels of a Harvester-Bot with a big wrench; they still never found his father. Walking toward the provisionist's is Francine Goggins, who will be disappointed to learn that provisions still haven't come in, that Boxelder has been shut off from that. Of course, the girl has other reasons to be disappointed—her Obligated is Lane Moreau. So Simone sidles up next to her, hands her a couple of protein bars from her own stash. Francine smiles, tries not to cry, and scurries off.

Most of the folks lift their heads, say a few words of greeting.

Inside Busser's, she asks the tavern man, "Busser, I'm beginning to think people don't hate me anymore."

He shrugs, wiping off her table. "They don't. You're a better mayor than Barnes was."

"I'm not your mayor."

"Suit yourself, Proctor."

She sits. Sets up her visidex. As she does, it *ding*s.

Her breath is almost stolen by the message.

First line: *You are to leave Boxelder, effective immediately, and return to active duty after three days of holiday.*

Her laugh is bold, broad. And maybe a little hollow.

Then she keeps reading.

You will be reassigned to the hunt for Arthur McAvoy—now believed to be terrorist raider Swift Fox.

Well. Barnes was right after all. Something *was* fishy about McAvoy.

Her bosses don't know she has a posse set after Cael and his friends. They know she's handling it; they just don't know *this* is how she's handling it. She thinks suddenly that perhaps she can do both at once. Have Boyland and his ragtag lot find Cael, and she'll use Boxelder as her base to lure Arthur McAvoy into a trap.

She keeps reading.

The next sentence: *Boxelder has been chosen for the Initiative.*

And here her breath truly halts.

The Initiative.

She's . . . heard stories. They popped up on the radar a year ago, bound up with a town out at the edge of the Heartland. Something Church? Tuttle's. Tuttle's Church.

If even half the stories are right . . .

She thinks of the people out here. Francine, Earl Jr., Stanley, Frieda, Gabby, Doc. Across the room, Busser gives her a small

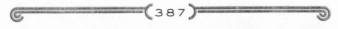

smile. She reminds herself that she hates this place and she hates these people, but suddenly those words feel like lies.

Though loathe to admit it, she was starting to think of this place as her home. But that can no longer be true. It won't be anybody's home before long. She smiles back at Busser, tries to hide the fear on her face.

OFF TO SEE A MAN
ABOUT A FLYING HORSE

THE MAN IN THE HAT pulled low knocks on the door. The door is golden—on it, a depiction of one of the Saintangels (Alice of the City of Love) with her sickle held aloft, rays of bronze light cascading from her.

As the man knocks, the Saintangel moves. Unexpectedly, though the man realizes he *should* have expected it—

The door begins to *unfold* as the Saintangel emerges. The *tink-tink-tink* of gears and flywheels come from behind her as the flat-bodied Alice of the City of Love tilts forward like a cutout. The sickle eases aside. Her head cranes toward him. Her one eye opens; a telescoping lens thrusts out like a thumb through a hole. The lens focuses on the man with the hat.

"*Who goes there?*" the Saintangel asks in a mechanized feminine warble. "*Identify yourself before Alice-Bot.*"

Alice-Bot. Hmph. If one were religious, one might take offense at seeing a Saintangel reduced to so banal a creation.

"My name is Professor Reich. I'm from the Mader-Atcha flotilla." He tries to affect Reich's curious accent. "I was called upon."

"*Scanning . . .* ," the Alice-Bot says, the lens suddenly orbited by flickering red lights.

The man presses his thumb to it, mutters, "Ah, you've got a little something, a speck . . . a smudge."

His thumb is greasy. It smears the lens.

The red lights never turn to green.

"*Confirmation impossible,*" the auto-mate hums. "*Human verification required.*"

Apparently these things can't do *everything*, can they?

The Saintangel retreats into the door with a series of clicks and whirrs. Once again the door is still and silent, as if it never moved at all.

Eventually, footsteps.

More clicks—this time as someone opens the door.

It's Cleo. Cleo *Planck*.

She gapes.

"Balastair," she says, nearly breathless. But breathless with what? Fear? Love? Disbelief? *Not love*, he thinks. Couldn't be. Not now. Not after she left him to be with this *trifling mechanic*.

Maybe it's because of the gun in his hand.

"Back into the house," Balastair says, "and I won't shoot you."

"You won't shoot me," she says. So confident. So cocky. She always was. It was part of why he loved—*loves*—her.

So he shoots her in the chest, then shoves her through the door.

• • •

He must hear her coming because he says her name as she approaches.

"La Mer," Percy says.

"Hello, Percy."

He stands there on the Balcony of Eagles. Overlooking Tailor's Point Park. The apples down below are in season. *Always* in season.

He sips from a cup of steaming coffee.

"Come closer," he finally says, still not looking at her.

She hurries up. Nervous. Her palms slick with sweat.

"This coffee is something special," he says. "Grown on the Gravenost Ernesto Oshadagea. Ground coarsely. Cold brewed. Allowed to steep in wine barrels. Drink it cold or warm, it's lovely. And it is a symbol of what we can do here as the Empyrean. We can grow coffee in the clouds. We've long escaped the gravity of the world below. We don't need the Heartland."

Merelda flinches at that. "You do need us. For the corn."

He smiles. "If you say so."

"I'm here to—"

"I don't hate you Heartlanders. I should make that clear. I respect your people utterly, and you have every right to want what we want. Your people are hard workers, which is admirable, to a point. The problem is, you work *hard* but are not particularly *smart*. You're good people in the sense that you seem noble, but 'good' is not a necessary component to success. We are smart. We are successful. And so that is why I get to drink coffee grown here in the sky."

He takes a noisy sip as if to emphasize.

"I—"

"Why have you come back to me, La Mer?"

"We have something special."

"*Had,*" he says. "Past tense. You hit me with a lamp."

"I'm sorry."

"I had to have my head stapled."

She sees the way he draws a breath through his nostrils, the way he purses his lips and closes his eyes for a moment. "You still love me."

"I do," he confesses.

"I know we can't . . . be together—"

He grunts.

"But please, Percy. Just let me and the Shawcatch girl go. I don't care what you do to the radiers. I'll take her away; you won't have to deal with us any longer—"

He reaches down and strokes her hair.

"You're not like her," he says. "The Shawcatch girl is tough as a leather belt. Hard as a stone. You're soft. And sweet. Like a little marshmallow. And so that's how I know you'll yield to me."

That last sentence, spoken so coldly.

"What?"

He grabs her face hard and squeezes. "You have their stink on you," he says after a sigh. "Raiders. Terrorists. Heartlanders. *Dogs.* I'll never be able to think of you as anything other than those things. A weak girl with a raider father and a criminal brother. A girl who betrayed me. Who ran off with that vile Shawcatch brat. A girl who threw away her trust like an old poppet doll that had come to bore her."

"But you love me; you said you did—"

"And I do."

"Please—"

He pulls out one of his Rossmoyne pistols.

She stares down the barrel. She has only a moment to wonder what it's set to. Will it stun her? Or kill her?

The peregrine fires.

Cleo writhes on the floor, dry heaving.

It kills him, what he just did to her. But she's made her alliances clear. She never would have let him in the door. Would never have let him get close to Planck. This is the easiest way. The sonic shooter on stun will leave her feeling ill, but only that. No scar other than the mental one that comes part and parcel with betrayal.

Balastair pulls her through the foyer into the parlor.

Fascinating. This is Planck's house then. Friezes on the wall that aren't paintings at all but animatric sculptures—like the door. Men crossing rivers in boats. Men with artificial wings, flying toward the sun. Great ships drifting together—the forming of the first flotilla, if Balastair is not mistaken. A proud moment. And a dark one, in many ways.

In a cage, an auto-mate bird hops on its perch in alarm. Eyes that are little brass spirals turning. Wings clicking.

Oh, Erasmus, Balastair thinks with some pain.

Everything in this place is made of metal, it seems. Brasses, bronzes, silvers, a little chrome, a dash of titanium. Gaudy and impressive at the same time. He hates it. He hates all of it.

From upstairs, the thud of footsteps.

A voice. "Cleo? Is someone here?"

Accompanied by the mechanized chirping of his little monkey.

Ahh. There we go.

The footsteps grow closer. Down the steps. Through the hall. Toward the parlor. Here.

He steps into the room. Sees Cleo first—

His face is a mask of fear and rage.

It gives Balastair pause. That Eldon Planck loves Cleo is a thought that never occurred to him before. He always assumed it was just a power play against him. The Mechanics Man thumbing his nose at the Biological Boy. Playing with his toys. Breaking them in.

"You," Eldon says.

The little mechanical monkey on his shoulder recoils, whirring and purring in a mimicry of fear.

Balastair shoots Eldon.

As the man falls, the monkey screeches, leaps to the birdcage, and clings there, shuddering. Metal limbs chattering together.

Balastair strides over. Grabs a hip-height ashtray from the corner. Then rushes the birdcage and smashes it into the little monkey.

The artificial primate breaks into pieces. Pieces that continue to chirp and twitch. Balastair bashes the ashtray down again and again. Until the auto-primate stops moving.

He drops the ashtray. Then strides over to Eldon.

Eldon gurgles. Spits. His face is the color of split pea soup. His eyes are slightly jaundiced. "You . . . bastard."

Balastair shoots him again. And a third time.

Then he kneels.

"I concede the Pegasus Project," Balastair says through the teeth of a mad smile. "Congratulations! You were the better man for that task. For many tasks, it seems: bedding my future wife, building that horse, sucking up to the loftiest among us for lucrative contracts like . . . what is it called? The Initiative? Dare I ask what that even is?" He shrugs. "You seem out of sorts. I'll slice through all this airy talk, then, and get right to the dirt of it. I want your Pegasus. I want the mechanical beast. It's mine now. I'm buying it with your life. To be clear, what I'm offering is *not to kill you* in exchange for control of the metal horse. Please nod if you accept my offer."

Eldon hesitates.

Balastair presses the gun barrel to his head. Visibly turns the dial at the back of the weapon all the way up—away from STUN, through MUSCLE FAILURE, through ORGAN DAMAGE, all the way to PUNCH A HOLE THROUGH THE BRAIN PAN AND SPILL ONE'S BLOODY MEMORIES ONTO THE FLOOR.

"*Nod* if you accept my offer, Eldon Planck."

Eldon slowly but clearly nods.

Balastair grins, pats the man on the back. "Ah. Then we have a deal. Seems I just bought myself a horse, and you just bought yourself a second chance."

LAMBS LED TO SLAUGHTER

"YOU'RE SURE this is going to work?" she asks, hands balling into fists and relaxing again and again, a nervous tic.

Gwennie and Davies stand in the mouth of the alley. Behind them, Squirrel bebops around like a rubber ball bouncing between the white stone walls. The little girl slices at the air with one of her knives.

"It'll work," he says.

"I just . . ."

"You just go over. You tell that skybastard who you are."

There, down toward the circle, standing near a fountain, is one of the *evocati augusti*, a tall guardsman milling about, looking bored. Rifle clipped to his back. Thrum-whip at his hip. Here on the flotilla they don't wear their trademark horse-head helmets.

"He won't . . . kill me?"

"Not long as you tell him you want to give up the rest of us. That'll buy you some time. Get you close to your family."

"And you'll save me?"

"You save them, and I'll save you. I'll follow you. Me and Squirrel will dog your every step."

"Doggy!" Squirrel says, giggling. She's got two knives in her hands now, doing battle with whatever invisible combatant has sprung forth from her imagination. *"Ruff ruff!"*

"This suddenly seems like an insane plan," Gwennie says.

"Don't knock insanity until you've tried it, girl."

"Just in case I die," she says, "I gotta know. Why do you call me dummy?"

"Because we're all dummies. Anybody who wants to be a part of the Sleeping Dogs is a dummy. Who just can't leave well enough alone. Can't keep tonguing the broken tooth or picking that scab every time it heals. Instead of just rolling over and enjoying the sunshine or the blue sky, we snarl and we bite and piss on what little we have in the rare and desperate hope of making a better world." He offers a grim smile. "Sounds pretty dumb to me."

It does. Dumb, and heroic, and maybe absolutely necessary.

He snorts. "Enough of this. Time ticks. Go get your family back."

And with that she leaves the safety of the alley and heads toward the guardsman near the white fountain.

Mary Salton stands at her pine-board table—the makeshift desk. A simple desk. Unadorned. Like her.

Her father made coffins. Her mother hemmed pants, darned socks, patched holes in clothes.

They were simple people who made simple things.

Things are no longer simple. Mary wishes for a day when they can again be simple—for her, for her people, for the Heartland. That day is not today. Today is complicated. Lots of moving parts. Lots of hard decisions that are already made but will be difficult to execute.

Out behind the doors of her office, the raiders ready themselves for war. Sharpening blades. Painting lines on their wolfish masks. Stringing smoke bombs to their belts. Some will have pistols. Others hammers or shovels.

Soon they will storm the control tower. As the peregrine is focused on effecting his revenge, they will take advantage of his averted gaze and move to the tower. There, they will await the code from Killian.

He'd better have that soon.

She checks her maps. Closes her eyes, goes through the plan.

Then at the end of it she opens a leather satchel at her feet.

And she withdraws a revolver. A bona fide revolver. Heavier than any of the flimsy-feeling sonic shooters. Heavy with weight, yes—blued steel and iron sights. Cylinder etched with whorls of scrollwork. The grip carved in a checkerboard pattern.

It's heavy also with power and consequence.

At the base of the grip, the symbol of the Sleeping Dogs.

Underneath the barrel, the sigil of the one who carried the pistol: a five-petaled flower allowed to oxidize with rust.

The sign of Corpse Lily.

One of the Sawtooth Seven.

And Mary Salton's own sister.

She takes the pistol. Thumbs open the cylinder, grabs a fist-ful of bullets from inside the satchel, screws them delicately into each slot.

Then, outside—

Men yelling. A sudden din. Shrieking blasts—sonic weapons.

Her hand tightens around the grip of the revolver. She jerks the weapon hard to the right, snapping the cylinder shut.

We're under attack.

Somebody gave us up.

The girl, she thinks. *Shawcatch*. Instead of abiding by the plan, she's sold them all downriver. Is that even possible this fast? She admits now that the girl was a risk: Salton chose to play on her anger and need for revenge over everything else. Judgment muddled by the fog of hot blood and spite. Her plan was always to leave the girl to the Empyrean, a lamb skidding about on the blood-slick floor of the slaughterhouse, but she didn't think that would come back and bite her so fast.

Maybe it hasn't. Maybe this is something else.

Either way—

She sets down the revolver, grabs the visidex from the far side of the table. She quickly sends a message out to Davies. The missive makes clear that this is on him now. She sends him the maps and schematics he needs.

He's a good soldier. Was once a righteous muck-up, but now he's the real deal. He'll do the right thing. He always has. And he will until it's over.

Her door is suddenly thrown open—

She sees a flash of a ponytail and a panic-stricken face. It's one of her raiders, Elsie Golden. They call her Goldie even though her hair is dark and so is her skin. Goldie yells, "The peregrine's guard—"

A screaming sonic blast pulps her head, taking her face off the front of her skull. Blood and bone bits spray, and then she falls.

Salton's chest tightens, and she points the revolver at the door, the iron sights never wavering.

It doesn't take long for the din to die down.

She hears footsteps approaching.

She fires a shot through the open door. A warning. The air suddenly stinks with spent powder. In her ears is a tinny bell caught midring.

"You're armed," calls a voice from beyond the doorway. She knows it. How could she not? Peregrine Lemaire-Laurent. "With something more than a peashooter, it would seem."

"You come through that door, I'm gonna shoot," she barks.

He laughs. "That's why I'm not planning on coming through that door. But I do plan on powering down the lights. It'll take me a little while to cut through whatever defensive programming you've done to stay hidden from the rest of the circuit, but I'll find it. And then? When it's dark? I'll send in men. You'll probably shoot one, but we have excellent health care here on the flotilla—he will live, perhaps. You'll live, too. Because we want you to live. Because we want you to tell us *everything*. Everything you know about your terrorist group. How they stay hidden from our scans. How they're organized. Who belongs. Names, faces, locations, anything and everything. And you'll tell us. Because the first thing we'll offer you is a spoonful of honey. And when

(4 0 0)

you inevitably reject our generous offer, we won't break out the knives or the pliers. We'll just give you the pharma-cocktail. The one that *makes* you tell us everything. When you first skinned your knee. When you had your first bleeding as a woman. When you smoked your first ditchweed cigarette. And you'll tell us everything there is to know about the Sleeping Dogs."

Mary holds the gun close.

Nostrils flare with panicked breath that she's desperately trying to still. She says a small prayer to anybody who will listen: Jeezum Crow, Old Scratch, any and all of the Saintangels. *Save me. Give me a plan.* She thinks, *Run out, shoot Peregrine.* But they won't kill her. They'll still save her. Even if he's dead, she'll be on the hook for all this.

And so that means one thing.

She takes the butt of her pistol, smashes the visidex. It won't stop them from finding things out, but it'll slow them down. And the Dogs have switchback programming in place; he won't learn everything.

Then she tastes the metal tang of the gun barrel.

The sights scraping the roof of her mouth.

Another small prayer.

Her finger squeezes—

It's a mess.

The peregrine wades into the room.

He can't help but feel disappointed.

Salton, collapsed backward. Half her head just . . . gone.

He really thought she'd give in. The fact that she'd rather die than give him anything else is . . . well, it shows her devotion to her cause. Which is admirable. Or would be, if her cause wasn't so misguided.

He plucks the gun from her hand.

He's never held one of these before.

To think it was here all along. On his flotilla.

Heavy. Balanced. A brutal weapon—its barrel like a perpetually screaming mouth. Contained therein is none of the elegance of the Rossmoyne at his hip. But maybe this is a time to put aside elegance. Maybe the fight is so serious, so real, that these terrorists would up and sacrifice themselves when offered a very real way out of pain and suffering.

Maybe it's time for him to become a brutal weapon.

Peregrine carries the gun out of the room. To his men who come in after, he says, "Sweep the room. Let's learn everything we can."

His visidex *dings*.

A message: *We have the Shawcatch girl.*

Well, well, well.

As he steps over the bodies of raiders in the hallway, he thinks that this has been a very good morning, indeed.

They take her away. Davies watches as they cuff her. Kick her legs out from under her so they can cuff those, too. Another *evocati augusti* shows up a minute later. By now onlookers have gathered. They gape and stare as the guards haul her off the way one might lug a rolled-up carpet.

And then they cheer. *Clap, clap, clap.*

He wants to hurt them for that.

"Will she be okay?" Squirrel asks, poking her head through his legs as if they're a pair of iron bars in a jail window.

"I think so, Squirrel. We're gonna save her and her family." Salton doesn't care if he saves her, but he's got to. His heart tells him so, whispered in the voice of his dead wife, Retta. While he saves Gwendolyn and her family, the other raiders—

The visidex Salton gave him for this mission chimes, signaling an incoming message. One hastily typed, it seems.

Been comrpomsed peregrin here killing us cotrol towr is on u do not fail repeat do not fail

He staggers backward as if gut-kicked.

The men and women he knows here . . .

The peregrine . . .

He closes his eyes and imagines bodies and blood.

The control tower is on *him*?

He's just one man. One man and one little girl.

He *had* another soldier—

But, godsdamnit, I just gave her to the enemy!

He doesn't want to do it. He just wants to get off this city. Go home. There are still a few raiders on the flotilla guarding escape boats and also a few sympathizers among the Empyrean. He could go to them. He could take his little girl and escape. But then he hears the applause of those people again. He hears the phantom sonic shots that likely took down his friends and cohorts only ten minutes ago.

Davies gets angry.

He has a shot here. To make it all count.

He could do as intended. He could save the Shawcatch girl.

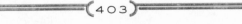

Gods, he *wants* to. But he does that, he draws attention to himself. Attention that will damage his other mission. *His other goal.*

Unless . . .

No. It's absurd. Horrible. He wouldn't dare.

"Papa, what's wrong?" Squirrel asks.

"Having a bit of a dilemma, Squirrel. Just big-people problems, is all."

"Wanna talk about it?" She beams her smile. Got a tooth missing now in the back of her mouth, and with that big, wide grin he can see the gap. It only makes her more adorable. "You said I'm old enough now to understand big-people problems."

He has said that. And he's trained her. *Trained her to kill,* a grim voice reminds him. But then he thinks, this might be the way to save those he can save. Because if he goes into that control tower, there's no guarantee he's coming back out.

"Squirrel, I think Gwennie—"

"Ballcutter!"

"I think Ballcutter needs your help."

"Okay, Papa."

"Okay? That's it? Just okay?" He barks a hollow laugh. "You're a piece of work, little girl."

"I can do it! What are you going to do?"

Everything else. "A job for Mary Salton. One last job."

"You're such a good papa," Squirrel says, and hugs his legs. He crouches and hugs her back. He holds her close for a while. He tries not to think about what happens next: letting go.

She's the one who lets go. She says, "Papa, your stubble tickles." He smiles and nods and kisses her forehead.

"Save the girl," he says. "Don't kill anybody. And then you get out of here. You find a ship and you leave this city." He shows her the visidex, points out the places where the ships dock, tells her to find a scowbarge or a small cutter, something nobody will think to check. Finally, he lies, "I'll find you. Don't worry about that. I'll find you wherever you go."

"Oh. Okay, Papa."

"Okay."

He kisses her cheek one last time.

And then like that she's gone.

TUTTLE'S CHURCH

THE SUN CRAWLS UP over the corn. Real corn, living corn—the Dead Zone is now behind them. Not far off in the distance, Lane sees the light glinting off tin rooftops and glass panes—and through the day's pollen haze a town begins to emerge. A town thrice the size of Boxelder. More like Martha's Bend. Maybe even bigger, because to the north and south he sees barns and silos and farmhouses scattered about.

But then other shapes emerge beyond the town—

Massive shapes. Shapes as big as anything he's ever seen.

"They're mountains," Rigo says, staring, mouth agape. Lane startles; he didn't even know Rigo was coming up. And it's not as if Rigo's quiet, with the shuffle-drag-*thump* he does after losing that leg.

The peaks are faded—a bleached-out purple held off by the curtain of pollen smog. Like stains from a grape that never quite wash out.

"I've heard of mountains but I never knew . . ."

"They're pretty," Rigo says. He's right. They are.

But it isn't enough to hold off the reality of his situation.

Lane thumps his head against the mast post around which his hands are shackled. He sighs. "You bring breakfast?"

"Oh." Rigo pulls his stare away from the mountains. "Yeah." He hands over a corn muffin so hard it could be used to pulverize more corn into masa for more corn muffins, an endless carousel of muffins begetting muffins begetting muffins. The absurd thought entertains Lane for a half second before he reminds himself just how bad everything has become.

He palms the corn muffin. Uses his teeth to shave off bits into his mouth. It's bland. Crunchy. Basically a hardtack biscuit.

"Remind me why I'm locked up and you're not," Lane says.

"I dunno. One of them said I'm too gimpy to do damage." Rigo chews his lip and looks down at his missing foot. "Actually, lot of them are calling me 'Gimp' now."

"Screw them," Lane says with a scowl.

The town in the distance grows closer. Now he can see light pooling on plasto-sheen and signs hanging outside of stores.

He just doesn't see any people.

Which makes him wonder if this town really *is* like Martha's Bend. Another town gutted by the Empyrean. Which makes him pissed off all over again. Lane's all piss and lightning now. He's still pissed at the raiders, too—though he wonders if it's the whole fleet he's mad at or just the one man. The one who wooed him, then threw him away like a handkerchief used only once. The one who's telling stories about Cael and his Blight. Those are just stories, right? Cael's Blight wasn't anything to

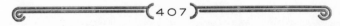

look at—just a little thumb-curl of plant matter. Cael wasn't Earl Poltroon. Not yet.

Not ever.

Still. Billy Cross is dead somehow.

Lane thunks his head against the mast post again.

Thunk. Thunk. Thunk.

"Anyway," Rigo says. "I gotta go. I got work."

"Dumping shit-buckets, I bet."

Rigo doesn't say anything, which is acknowledgment enough.

Rigo turns and hobbles away on his wobbly crutch.

Soon, the trawler and the fleet come up on the edge of the town. The broad front of the ship blocks most of it from view, but Lane can see buildings, the street, a few abandoned food carts. All empty. Windows staring back like the glassy eyes of corpses.

Raiders gather toward the fore of the boat to look. He hears murmurs that echo his own thoughts: *Where are all the people?*

Footsteps behind him.

A whiff of whiskey breath as Killian Kelly rests his chin on Lane's shoulder. "Hello, Lane Moreau."

Lane jerks his shoulder away. "Get offa me."

"Sorry. Was I flirting?"

"Maybe you were."

"I wasn't." Then, loud enough for any nearby to hear, "I do not endorse your proclivities, boy."

"Listen to you. *Boy.* You've got a few years on me, and that's it."

Killian steps around to the front. That smile is stuck to his face as if it's been nailed there—but the glimmer of puckish glee he once had has been spackled over. "Those years have provided

me with a multiplicity of wisdom. My life has been spent doing important things, while yours has been playing the role of a thieving magpie snatching scrap."

"What did you do to Cael?"

"It disappoints me that your response is that instead of *What did Cael do to you?* Seems to me you didn't seem particularly shocked by the revelation that he had the Blight. Which means it wasn't a revelation at all, was it?"

"Sorry your first mate is dead," Lane says. But then he clenches his teeth and sticks out his chin. "But I figure he must've deserved it."

There. The smile wavers. Tremble-twitch.

"I like that fire in your belly. I think we could still be allies out of all this. But you have to admit, Lane, you don't yet know rat shit from your own self-righteousness. It's all anger and spite. Bitter spunk and churning spurn."

"You talk too much."

"I may, at that. Doesn't change what I'm saying. Look around you. See that town? Something's wrong with that town, and we've known it for a while. You see any people?" His eyes flash like light caught in steel. "Me neither. Which means the Empyrean did something to them. They're doing something to all of us. They're desecrating our ground. They changed the clouds. The Blight—*Cael's* Blight—is a poison delivered unto us by the hands of our masters." He waves his arms overhead as if to say, *Behold the spectacle of the sky above.* "And yet, knowing all this, you still want to be mad at me for petty things. This is the fight, Lane. This is the time. This is when you test the heft and weight of your convictions and determine whether or not they are as hollow as the bones of a bird, or if they are as heavy as the blade of a sword, if they—"

A shrill whistle cuts the air, and the mast above Lane's head suddenly shatters.

Rigo's at the bow of the ship. Nobody looks at him. Raiders work. Before he'd at least earn a sympathetic nod—a silent *Sorry kid, tough break*. But now he's marked. He's Cael's friend. The gimp.

So he hobbles up, a sour feeling in his chest and belly about Cael, about Lane, about all this. And he stares out over the approaching town of Tuttle's Church and the ghost-shadow of the mountains behind. Mountains they call the Workman's Spine.

Rigo thought that the Heartland went on forever and ever.

But it ends. Here. At these mountains.

What waits in other directions? What happens if he goes south? North? What's on the other side of these mountains?

He'd heard tales of the coast, of course. Beyond them, a whole part of the world covered in water. But that always seemed a joke. It didn't even rain. How could there be that much water out there?

Now here he is, looking at mountains he'd heard about in a pile of old, ratty picture books he'd once bought from the Mercado with an ace note.

And then a curious thing happens.

Out in the middle of the street, he sees somebody.

This person walks all herky-jerky out from under a ratty awning into the middle of the street. It appears to be a woman,

her white-and-pink dress catching a little wind. Each step she takes seems heavy, plodding.

Sun catches and reflects brightly off the woman's face.

Which is strange.

He realizes, *That's not a person.*

Her head turns, and even from this far away he can see—the face is an artifice. Big circle eyes like mirrors. Mouth big, *too* big, one big jaw.

The head cocks with a faint whirr.

Then she raises an arm.

The hand spins, whizzing in a circle. As if unscrewing.

Rigo yells to someone nearby: a stocky raider, Olga, who stands ten feet to his left, and he points. She follows his gaze, lifts a spyglass to her eye. She grunts.

"I don't think that bitch is human," she says.

Other raiders start to gather.

Hezzie sways up and scowls. "She's doing something with her— Shit! The hand just . . . came off. Landed in the street like a—"

The handless arm flashes.

A sonic blast screams overhead. Rigo ducks. Cries out.

The ship's mast explodes.

The woman in the street, she's not alone, not anymore. Others are walking out with the same hitching, inevitable step. Metal automatons made to look like people. A man in a seer-sucker suit. A little child in a straw hat. A woman in overalls. None of them real. The day's light caught in metal flesh. Their hands begin spinning. Dropping off.

And they begin firing.

52

THE WITCH'S GARDEN

CAEL WALKS.

He walks along the path formed for him.

His Blight-vine twitches, leaves licking at the air.

The other Blighted do not follow him. But the memory of them does. He remains dogged by the fear: *That is what I will become.* He imagines a time when his teeth will fall out into his hands, when thorns will grow from the puckered gums. Fingernails of bark, skin like corn silk. His humanity, falling away like rotten fruit. Replaced by Blight. The thought terrifies him.

It keeps him moving.

Eventually, the sun comes up—morning over the Heartland—vented first through the dead corn and then up overhead. Hotter than he expected. Warm on his brow, sweat crawling across the bridge of his nose.

There comes a point where ahead, far ahead, he sees the air shimmer. And then as he walks, the shimmer begins to fade,

and in its place is a tall, white house, as white as salt, as white as bone.

Ahead, the pathway leads to a wooden archway. A trellis on which thin, curling vines grow. Vines with big, ostentatious leaves. And fat clusters of . . .

Grapes. He's seen pictures of grapes. Drawings and paintings and photos in Pop's old books. He rushes to them, suddenly aware of how hungry he is, how thirsty, and he reaches the arch and grabs at a dangling cluster. They feel cool in his hand, oddly full and satisfying, and just moving his fingers in and around the grapes feels . . . comforting somehow.

He twists one off, and the cluster springs back.

He's about to pop it into his mouth when he thinks—

No. This isn't natural. Don't.

He holds his mouth open. His tongue is wet with anticipation. He curses himself and drops the grape to the ground.

He steps on it. It gives way with a little *plop*, then soaks the dirt with purple. It kills him.

Instead, he keeps moving—

Into the garden beyond.

The garden Pop grew was nothing like this. This is an impossible place. He walks paths that are not so much ordered aisles as they are winding openings connected through a wild tangle of plants. Plump fruits hang. Wild flowers thrust up out of dense green. Scents compete almost violently for dominance: the spice of evergreen, the perfume of flowers, and a dozen other aromas Cael cannot even begin to identify.

It makes him dizzy. And giddy. And queasy. All in equal measure.

Ahead stands a black, twisting tree, the trunk warped and wound like a spring coiled by a divine hand. Sculpted almost. Red leaves shudder.

She steps out from behind that tree.

The wave of fragrance hits him almost before his eyes register what it is he's seeing—the floral scent is almost narcotic.

His Blight-vine tightens. Excited.

Or afraid.

She strides toward him, her long, diaphanous gown trailing.

She's beautiful. Young. Powerful. If this is the Maize Witch, she defies expectation. His image was of an old, haggard thing, a monster in the skin of a woman, long nails, sharp teeth, skin like the vellum pages of an old, worn catechism or maybe like dead leaves, like cracked earth.

She is none of those things. She's long and lithe, skin like milk, eyes like spoonfuls of sky—

And she's Blighted.

The undersides of her forearms are like the petals of white flowers.

Her eyebrows are small twists of pale vine.

A white rose blooms in the hollow of her neck, hanging like a brooch.

Suddenly, she stands before him. And she's changing right in front of him—through her white-gold hair grow threads of green, filaments of life that appear and retract into her scalp. She raises her arms, and drupes of red and black berries unfold and dangle from the insides of her elbows before they drop off and land against the ground—falling, dissolving, rotting. She opens her mouth to speak, and Cael sees a pink tongue, a human

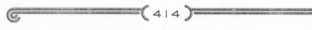

tongue, but then a tongue that splits in half and shows red pulp and sharp thorns, the halves of which braid together before becoming human once more.

"I'm glad you found me," she says. Her hand finds his—he instinctively jerks away, but his Blight-vine coils around her wrist, pulling his arm back with terrifying strength. Her fingers entwine with his own.

"I don't want to be here" is all Cael can say.

"A shame," she says. Her lips turn as red as a bell pepper as they spread into a slow smile. "Because here you are. You must be starving. Let's go inside. You may eat. I will talk."

Cael's never seen a plate of food this green before.

To get here, to this kitchen, at this table, the two of them walked through the garden, underneath other trellises—some lined with flowers, others with berries or grapes—toward the narrow, bone-white house. Up half-shattered stone steps (green shoots crawling through the cracks), through an unfinished wooden door that, even as Cael brushed past it, seemed to pulse with a kind of life.

Then through the decrepit building—where, too, the kingdom of plants reigns supreme. Thin little vines dangle from the ceiling; fat, fuzzy stems thicker than Cael's wrist climb the walls, moored there. The floorboards buckle. The branch of a tree comes in through a shattered window and shudders as they pass.

They went from a dark living area to a white kitchen. White, clean, the tile cracked, the tiny threads of verdant life poking through.

She sat him at a table and returned with the plate, a plate heaped with raw greens both flat and curly, with sliced berries and apples, with seeds as green as the flesh of new wood. All of it drizzled with oil.

It's a salad, he realizes. Sometimes Pop would try to make a salad with food that came in their provisions, but everything was always wilted. Or precooked. Or it had to be cooked just to be made safe.

Nothing like this.

The woman produces a wooden fork and hands it to him.

"I can eat this?" he asks, his stomach clenching like a fist.

"You can."

"It's weird."

"Why is that?"

"Because . . ." His Blight-vine demonstrates by tracing circles in the air.

"Because you're made of it, or it is made of you."

He swallows a hard knot and nods.

"We eat of the world and what grows in it. Or from ourselves. Everything natural is food." She smiles. "Put differently, animals are made of meat, and you're made of meat."

Permission enough. He stabs the fork down, begins eating like a starving goat. It's bright and crisp, and the oil—*the oil!*—he doesn't even know what it is, but it's fatty and full and round. The crisp. The crunch. The juice from the berries slides over his lip, down his chin.

Heaven on a plate.

"My name is Esther Harrington," she says. Her voice is sharp and clipped; it contains a refinement not present in Heartlander speech. He thinks: *Empyrean sounding is what it is.* "The people here sometimes call me Mother."

He mumbles around a mouthful of food, "You look too young to be anybody's mother."

She smiles. "Nice of you to say."

"O . . . okay."

"You *are* hungry."

"Mm-hmmph."

"I'll talk. You eat."

He nods.

"I am the one they call the Maize Witch, though I do not think the name is deserved. I despise the corn. And I am no witch. What I have is not magic. I am simply evolved. A product of our age. I am the way forward. *You* are the way forward."

Here the food sits in his mouth as he stops chewing.

She must see the befuddled look on his face.

"We have been changed for a changed world. There comes a threat to our very existence, and we are the answer."

"The Blight."

"I do not think of it as the Blight. That is a crass name given by someone who thought it a disease."

"Isn't it?"

She laughs.

The Blight-vine shudders.

"Do I look diseased?" she asks. Sprouts of green thrust up from her fingertips, coil-whips of green that search the air and then retract. The skin shows no breach, no wound, as smooth as the skin of a baby.

"No. But it doesn't look . . . normal."

"It isn't normal. It's *exceptional*. That is the very definition of *exceptional*, isn't it? To be the exception? To excel beyond the droll margins of normal? Normal is the curse. Being normal is the disease. We are special. That is to be celebrated."

"I'm afraid of it."

"Fear is good. Fear is natural."

"I can't control it."

"You can. And I'll teach you how."

"But . . . those people. In the corn. They didn't look like they . . . were controlling it."

A grief-struck look crosses her face. "Think, if you will, of our relationship with fire. It seems a living thing. If we master it, it serves us: it cooks our food, lights our way, and when necessary, burns our enemies. But those who do not master it are burned by it. Burned alive and consumed. Those poor people were taken by our gift before they learned to control it. They are together now. At least they're not alone. At least they have one another. And they still have their purpose."

Cael doesn't know what that means.

But it scares the hell out of him.

"Are you done eating?" she asks.

He looks down at an empty plate. He didn't realize he'd finished. He nods gamely.

Then he realizes they're not alone.

Standing in the doorway behind him are two more of the Blighted. A man in a ratty coat, his exposed chest a mesh of fibrous brown vines, his chin a small forest not of whiskers but of some sort of . . . hanging fungus. Next to him, a bald woman, half her face consumed by a kind of hard-leaf scale that shudders and whispers.

"That's Edvard and Siobhan."

Cael offers them a small nod. They just stare in return.

"Let's go out back," Esther says. "I'd like to show you something."

Another set of steps, crooked and crumbling.

Out back of the house is another garden of sorts.

But this one is far stranger than what's at the front.

Tall human shapes stand out over the garden. Like the little corn-husk dolls Merelda used to make, bound together with thread or dry silk-fiber. But these are huge—Cael barely comes up knee-high to these dry, dead giants. No plants grow over them, but he can see that they're hollow, and he spies flashes of green within their heads and chests and bellies.

Some of them are men. Others are women.

He knows this because they are anatomically correct.

Which causes a bloom of blush in his cheeks.

Esther pulls him by the hand into the garden.

Edvard and Siobhan follow behind. Close.

"Do you believe in the gods?" she asks him.

"The Lord and Lady? Jeezum Crow?" He shrugs. "I guess. Same as anybody. They took away the churches when I was a kid. But sometimes we'd still pray, and Pop liked to leave things for the votaries."

"Did you know there are gods older than that?"

He shrugs. He doesn't want to admit that he doesn't know anything. *She'll think I'm stupid. And she's beautiful. And she smells nice, too.* In fact, he's having a hard time thinking of anything but her.

"The Empyrean above us worship sky gods and goddesses. Deities of the clouds and air, of wind and sun. For some it's cursory. For others it's very real, part of their faith. But they only see one part of it. Other gods exist. Gods of the earth. Goddesses of vine and root. Deities of the land."

Cael could listen to her speak day and night. Something about her voice. Something about her perfume. He feels like a bee that can't quit visiting the same flower, like a drunk man who can't quit drinking.

"I thought you said you didn't believe in magic."

She smiles as they keep walking toward a pair of buildings— long buildings made of dark wood. "I don't. What we are isn't mystical but natural. And it is the oldest gods, the primordial ones, who gave it to us. I found these gods in the DNA of plants. But I found them in our DNA, too."

"Oh." He feels so stupid around her. So small. He just wants to stand here and let her tell him things. Fill him up with whatever he's missing.

"I've been watching you."

"H . . . how?"

Her hand closes around his. Tendrils creep from her fingertips and begin coiling up his forearm toward his shoulder. He feels a rush of heat and excitement—his heart starts rabbit-thumping in his chest. "I'm a part of you. I can feel you through our shared gift. One day you'll see."

"I want to see." Does he? Want to see? Could he mean that? It feels suddenly like he does. He feels drunk. But clear, too. Clearer than he's been in a long, long while. Awake and alert and . . . and *aware.*

They walk between the two buildings. She tells him this is where her people stay. Those who never could master their gift and those who came to her before it was too late. Like him, she says.

"I can help you." Her tendrils wind around his wrist again and again. "I can make you whole. And then together we can help the world and those in it."

"I want that." *I want to be whole.*

"I know you do." Her thumb gently strokes the side of his hand.

But there's something else. Something he wants to tell her. Except he can't find the thought—it's like reaching in a cloud to try to find a single drop of rain. He sees faces gauzed by the fog of memory.

"There's something," he says, "something I have to do."

"But you can't remember what it is."

"No." *I only want to be right here, right now.*

"You want to help your friends."

"My friends." *Gwennie. Lane. Rigo.* "My sister." *Merelda . . .*

"I can help with that, too," she says. They leave the space between the two buildings, feet stepping in soft grass—

There, in the lot beyond, two platforms. Landing platforms. Like the one at the end of Boxelder. One platform sits empty. On the other rests a small open-air skiff. Four people, max. But it's nicer than the corn-boats they use here in the Heartland.

It's got hover-rails propping it up and gleaming propellers on the back.

On the side of the boat is the Empyrean sigil: the Pegasus.

"You can take that skiff," she says.

"Thank you." The words come out of him with a desperate urgency—the gratitude of a starving man given food, a drowning man given a mouthful of breath. "But I don't want to leave here. I just . . . I just got here."

"You'll be back." She lets go of his hand, her tendrils recoiling—and he's suddenly filled with a ragged emptiness that he's never felt before. She lifts her fingers to his head, and the loneliness is quashed. Shoots and tendrils caress his hair and his scalp, and crawl along the top of his ear like a worm seeking ingress. "But there is something I need you to do."

"Anything." He means it. And that shocks him. A voice in the back of his mind reminds him, *This is the Maize Witch, godsdamnit! She isn't human anymore; can't you see that?*

"The flotilla. They're going to try to destroy it, aren't they?" she says.

"I think so."

"I need you to get something off the flying city for me."

"Name it."

"I need you to get my son."

He hears his own voice—surprisingly small and soft—ask her how he's supposed to find one boy (one *man*, she says) in a whole city floating up in the sky, and she tells him, *I'll help you,* and she commands him to hold still, and something slides out of her mouth and enters his—a long vine down his throat. He

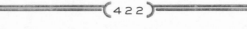

starts to gag; he tastes the copper tang of blood but then the sweet taste of crushed berries—

Then the snaking vine has left his throat, and he gasps.

"My blood calls to my blood," she says.

Suddenly she pulls away, her whole body stiffening.

She looks as if she's in pain.

Her pupils are gone. Hidden behind a milky sheen, like white sap. Then the rheumy cloud is gone and her pinprick eyes return to view, and she says, "Someone is coming. We are about to be attacked."

THE BUTCHERS

THE SICKLE IS HEAVY in Boyland's hand. He hides in the dead corn, lying flat on his belly with the spyglass held in his other hand. He stares at the narrow, white house in the distance.

For a long while they urged themselves along with oar-poles, moving ploddingly slow through the stalks, and then a heat haze seemed to part like a curtain, and in the spyglass he could see it: the tall house pushing itself out of the ground like a crooked tooth and the green growth all around it.

First they thought, *Well, here's a place to stop, ask for food, try to figure out just where in the gods-blasted Heartland they* were, but then he anchored the boat and started scouting, and lo and behold—

Godsamn Cael McAvoy. Coming out of the back of the house toward a pair of buildings, past a half-dozen giant . . . well, Wanda called them "effigies," but he's not too sure what that means and

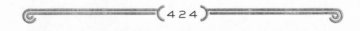

he doesn't care; they look like giant figures made of straw and stick, like sentinel scarecrows standing vigil. They creep him the hell out. What matters isn't what those are called or who lives in that house. What matters is *godsdamn Cael McAvoy.*

This is his chance.

Wanda hunkers down behind him. "You really saw Cael?"

"Oh yeah. How's Mole?"

"He's asleep again."

Boyland grunts. "Those Annie pills are potent."

"Well, we're almost out."

"We'll worry about that once we have your boyfriend."

"He's my Obligated, not my boyf—"

"I don't care, Wanda. Dang." *Stupid girl. Giving her heart to that shitbird, McAvoy.* Boyland gives the spyglass one last look-see before putting it down. "Seems pretty quiet. I figure we go, kick down the door, drag his ass out before anybody even knows what happened."

"*That's* your plan? Just storm in like you own the place?"

He rolls his eyes at her. "You got a better plan?"

"Well. No."

"There it is then. If it makes you feel any better, go ask the hobo what he thinks. Maybe we got a real *battle strategy-ologist* traveling with us, huh?"

Wanda grouses at him. But she ducks back through the stalks that separate them and the yacht. Boyland gets that fluttering inside that he usually feels before he comes up on a sweet cache of scrap or scavenge. Now he gets to drag that murderous cur into the dirt so the Empyrean can toss his ass off whatever flotilla they like. Boyland hopes he gets to watch.

But then Wanda comes back and says, "The hobo's gone."

"What? Shut up."

"Eben Henry is not on that boat."

"Well, maybe he's off takin' a squirt."

"Ew, and no, I don't think so. He took his bag."

"Well, hell. He was an asshole anyway. We don't need him. He's just a crusty old hobo with a burned-up face. What good would he have done us?"

Eben Henry knows who that house belongs to. He knows who this whole damn Dead Zone belongs to. He's met her. Many moons before. When he was a younger man. And she was an older woman. And this is not where he wants to be.

But as soon as he heard brick-headed Boyland say that Cael McAvoy was there—well, that twines all their fates together, braided like a patch of five-finger creeper.

She's got powers, though, the Maize Witch. She'll know they're here. Which means he's got to make an opportunity for himself.

He clings to the underside of the yacht like a spider. The hover-panels to the left and right of him are still humming, vibrating so loud he can barely hear anything but for the way his teeth seem to be singing.

Soon enough he sees the shuffling of feet—

Her people. Hell, they're not people at all. Not anymore. They're just . . . *the Blight*. Lost to it, taken by it, no longer human. They have *her* inside them. The Maize Witch: Old Scratch's hell-born daughter.

Her Blightborn do anything she says.

And now they attack.

It isn't long before he hears Wanda cry out. Then come Boyland's shouts of rage as he tries to fight back—that dumb turd would fight back against a motorvator if it rumbled at him too loudly.

Boyland's cries are cut short. Then he gurgles. Then nothing but the sound of her people dragging the bodies along. Through the corn and away.

Finally, they're gone. Leaving him with the boat. And the boy with the broken arm. Eben drops to the ground, arms aching, face still hot as if it's covered with ants. Part of him thinks to swing himself up onto the boat and just stick the stupid kid a few times with the knife—one across the neck then a punch of the blade through his temple—but there's still something about him. . . . He just can't do it. It might be a mercy, but again he thinks of his own son. Now dead and gone. Thanks to Arthur McAvoy.

He wants to kill so badly.

Mole will not be part of his tally.

Others deserve his knife. Cael McAvoy, most of all. Not just for his father. But now, for the face that Eben has to wear.

Won't be long before the Maize Witch realizes she didn't get them all. Her powers are imperfect, but one way or another her mojo will sort him out.

Which means it's time to move.

He hops into the yacht and revs up the hover-panels.

54

PLANKWALKERS

"I THOUGHT HE LOVED ME," Merelda says, staring off at a nowhere point. Her lips are dry. Her eyes bloodshot. "I thought I could get him to help us."

"Guess you were wrong," Gwennie says, a black mood acting as dark rider. She fidgets, standing there. Hands bound above her. Merelda's are, too. The plastic ties bind them to a long length of pipe. "You always were naive."

The wind whips. Gwennie knows where they are. She last saw her father here. Pushed down the gangplank. Tilting beneath him until he fell.

She knows what's coming soon, because the peregrine told her. He said, *I'm going to execute the both of you. Traitors to the Empyrean and all that. I'll throw your mother and your brother overboard first. Just so you can see. Like I promised.*

Gwennie told him, wait, she can help him. She can tell him

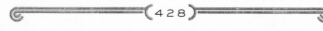

where the raiders are—a ploy, a delaying tactic, all part of the plan.

He just laughed.

Said he already knew where they were. *Thanks*, he said, *to your friend and mine, La Mer.* Then he marched out Merelda, who looked largely untouched but harrowed just the same. He sat her down and bound her, too. Told them they were both to die and that all the raiders on the flotilla were dead.

Gwennie did not weep. But it felt as if she were a rotten tooth scraped raw. All scratched enamel and exposed nerves.

Merelda. She escaped the raiders. Ran to her boyfriend.

"They used drugs," she said. "They injected me with something and then . . . I couldn't stop talking." And she wept, trembling like a dangling leaf in a sudden breeze. And now here they are.

Gwennie hates her.

Hates her.

And still a little part of her says, *Forgive her. She thought she was doing the right thing. She didn't think we'd end up here.*

But that's the key, isn't it?

She didn't think.

Now nobody will come for her. She has no leverage to save her family. Davies and Squirrel are a lifetime away.

The plan is dead. And so are they.

Unless she can do something.

"I'm sorry, I'm sorry," Merelda says. "I just . . ."

"It's *fine*," Gwennie snaps, but the venom she can't hold back comes across as clear as a snakebite. "No good worrying

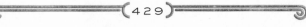

about it now." She almost thinks to tell the girl that they need to get out of here somehow—but she's afraid Cael's sister will ruin it.

"Maybe he'll have mercy on us."

Gwennie's jaw clenches. "Maybe he'll have mercy on *you*. I don't think the rest of us will be so lucky."

She sees the peregrine approaching. With three of his Frumentarii guardsman—men who are not dressed so lavishly as the *evocati augusti* but dressed instead like Adrian and his sister. And then she sees: one of them *is* Adrian's twin sister, isn't it? Through the face shield she sees Adriana's wicked smile.

This is revenge for her.

How can I fight them? I have no chance. . . . She has no gun, no knives, nothing.

She hears her mother pleading. Her brother weeping.

The guards bring them out. Her mother looks haggard. Worn down to a nub, a pencil sharpened past its usefulness. Her brother is a live spark. Screeching, thrashing, kicking. *Fight*, she thinks. *Fight!*

Gwennie cries out. They see her. Her brother tries to run to her, but Adriana catches the boy by the hair, yanks him back. Gwennie screams at the bitch. Shrieks, *You're going to kill him!*

Adriana just laughs.

The peregrine steps in front of them. Hands clasped behind his back.

"You've made quite a mess of things," he says, pursing his lips. "But today we are afforded the chance to clean up all this and go on with our lives. We do not abide terrorists. We cannot,

because what message does that send? It only emboldens those who hope to exploit our mercy. And so we do as we must; we tamp down our most merciful instincts and—"

"You're a monster," Merelda says.

If only you'd realized that sooner, Gwennie thinks.

The peregrine walks to Cael's sister. Cups his hand under her chin. Strokes her cheek. He leans in and kisses her forehead. The look on his face makes Gwennie wonder if it's sincere—did he really love her? The gesture is enough, she thinks, to soak up any of the poison Merelda has in reserve—

Or so she thinks, until Merelda spits in his eye.

He blinks. Scowls. Wipes it away with the bend of his wrist.

"Well," he says. "You can take the girl out of the Heartland, but you can't take the Heartland out of the girl."

"You'll pay for this," Gwennie seethes.

"With a good night's sleep, I think."

He snaps to the guards. "You two, take the mother to the edge." He points to the woman. "Adriana, grab this one. Cut her down, hold her over the edge. I want her to watch as her mother falls. I'll set up the camera."

Everything seems to happen slowly—bubbles caught in honey, warping, distending. Adriana comes over. Flicks a knife. Starts to cut Gwennie down, chuckling.

Gwennie's mother calls to her: "Gwendolyn! Don't look. Close your eyes. *Don't look.*"

A guard breaks away, begins extending the gangplank.

The peregrine sets up a small camera with a hover-panel beneath it. It bobs out into the air, tethered by a small, golden

chain. Its lens telescopes. Focuses. Watches. *Transmits.* Likely to everyone. Even to those below.

They push Gwennie's mother out onto the gangplank.

Gwennie struggles, tries to strike Adriana, but the woman counters with a hard sucker-punch. The air goes out of Gwennie. She doubles over.

Adriana's laugh is lost to her brother's panicked wails.

She sees his face. Scooter's. It's a mask of horror. Eyes unblinking. Mouth wide. The sound coming out of him is barely human. One of the guardsmen backhands him. Splits the boy's lip—blood drips, and the child falls silent, still weeping.

This is it, Gwennie thinks as rough hands grab her hair and start to lift her head. *This is my only chance.*

She drives a knee up into Adriana's crotch.

She *oof*s. Then coughs.

But it's not enough.

She hauls Gwennie and meets her face-to-face, wearing a feral sneer. Adriana rears back and slams her head into Gwennie's. Gwennie sees stars. The world explodes. Her nose pops. She tastes blood.

The peregrine watches. Smiling just a little.

Adriana spins Gwennie around. Turns her face toward the execution about to unfold. Her mother, now pushed the very end of the plank.

One guardsman at the plank controls. About to turn the wheel and tilt it—just like they did to her father.

But then—

The guardsman's head jerks.

A knife sticks out the side of his neck.

A knife that suddenly looks a whole lot like a key.

The peregrine shouts, and Gwennie seizes the moment of distraction. She cracks her head backward, earning revenge on her own bloodied nose by smashing her skull into Adriana's—

Then she sprints. The guardsman wobbles on a heel, pawing at the knife in the side of his neck, moaning.

Gwennie grabs it. Unsticks it. A jet of blood squirts. She shoves the man aside. He lands like sacks of cornmeal.

I'm going to save my family.

That thought, as clear as rain on glass.

Adriana has her sonic pistol out and up—

But Gwennie was trained well. Her wrist twists. The knife is gone—and then it reappears, stuck in the center of Adriana's chest. The sonic shot goes wide, and the Frumentarii guard joins her brother in the afterlife, tumbling over the edge, crying out for her twin.

Then: Scooter screams. Her mother cries out—

The last guardsman gives her mother a shove.

Right off the edge of the gangplank.

Gwennie cries for her mother and runs.

What felt inevitable no longer feels so certain.

Chaos ensues, and Merelda watches, dumbstruck.

One guardsman, suddenly dead. Gwennie, free, rescuing the knife, then burying it in the heart of the woman holding her. Percy, staring in horror, backing up, shouting, the realization that he's lost control shining in his eyes. And then Gwennie is crying out, and the last guardsman is shoving her mother off the edge of the gangplank and—

Gwennie's mother reaches out, catching the man's wrist. Hanging there as he tries to shake her free.

The older woman claws uselessly at his face guard—

He raises his free hand to strike her—

Gwennie grabs him from behind. Her forearm around his neck. Peeling off his helmet with one hand. Hitting him with it as he spins away, off the edge of the plank—

Mother and daughter crash together in a hug.

"No, no, *no*," Percy says, raising the revolver.

Merelda screams at him.

The pipe above her suddenly shudders. A girl perches on the pipe—the little raider girl. The tiny psychopath. The girl slashes downward with a knife—

Merelda's hands are free.

She leaps for Percy. Thinking she has the advantage. She doesn't. He's trained. Capable. He backhands her with the heavy revolver, and her world is lost in a flash of white, and before she knows it, she's staggering backward, blood in her eyes, back pressed against the flotilla bulk.

When her eyes clear and she blinks away blood, she sees him. Standing there, only ten feet away. The gun pointed at her. His face contorted in a mask of rage.

"What have you done?" he asks. "You've ruined me! The cameras are watching. *Everyone is watching!*"

He pulls the trigger. The gun roars.

Choom!

The gun kicks like a horse.

It kicks him right in the face.

He's not ready for it. Merelda knows he's used to his sonic pistol. A Rossmoyne, he always said, was an elegant weapon for men of empire—but the gun in his hand is different. He staggers back, the recoil hammering the gun into his chin as the shot goes wide—*spang!*—ricocheting off the metal near her head.

The little girl, Squirrel, flings a knife—he holds up his arm, and it catches him in the meat of his bicep. Percy cries out and then bolts as more knives just barely miss his heels.

He ducks his way through the elevator hatch, slamming it shut behind him. *Good riddance*, Merelda thinks.

And like that, it's over.

Merelda watches as Gwennie pulls her mother off the gangplank. She and Scooter—and the raider girl she knows only as Squirrel—collapse into a hug. They hold one another. Crying. Rocking back and forth. Merelda feels empty. She wants to be there. Hugging her brother. Her father. Her poor mother.

She can't. They're not here. She left them all behind.

This is all her fault. She sees that now.

When she looks up again, there's Gwennie.

"Are you going to kill me?" Merelda asks.

Gwennie's face twists into a grimace, as if what Merelda said was absurd. "What? No."

"Oh. I'd understand. I . . . I deserve whatever I have coming."

"Shut up, Mer. We have to go. We have to hide. This isn't over."

"He'll come for us," Merelda says. "He won't just let us go."

"I know."

Squirrel chimes in: "I know the way!"

Davies watches from inside the vent as the way is cleared.

All but a pair of horse-head guards leave their posts, opening the long, bowed bridge to the control tower. He waits until he knows the ones who left are really and truly gone—no false alarm, no temporary abandonment, no quick pop-out for a snack or a piss.

They're gone.

The bridge is open.

The tower guarded only by two men.

Which means his daughter did her job.

Still, the task ahead: not easy.

Once he drops to the ground from the vent, he'll be exposed. They have sonic rifles. And thrum-whips. And the talent to use them. He's a nobody. Just some old field shepherd from down in the dirt.

He's going to storm the control tower and get killed doing it.

You need to get in there. You need to be ready.

He has no plan, no means to accomplish this.

But his daughter did her job. Which means it's time to do his.

He thinks of his wife, Retta, dead in his arms. He thinks of that corn, curling and writhing and hungry for blood.

The dead earth. The empty sky. The gods in their chariots above the peasants' heads.

Davies dials up the intensity on his sonic shooter. Then he opens the vent and drops to the ground.

He tucks the pistol in the back of his pants.

He takes a deep breath. Time to improvise.

He runs, full tilt, across the arch of the white bridge. Toward the brass gate at the base of the massive tower, the tower in which all the flotilla's movements are controlled—they're automated, as he understands it, for no one truly needs to pilot the ship. It receives orders and translates those orders to the hover-panels and to the Engine Layer. It requires very little human intervention. One of the first mechanical choices the Empyrean made: a pilot would necessitate tireless hours sitting at a console, but automating the process—mechanizing everything—was elegance and simplicity.

And it would be their godsdamn downfall.

So Davies runs.

Arms waving.

He starts screaming.

"Raiders!" he shouts. "Raiders are coming! Terrorists! They're killing folks!" He continues to scream and wail, half his words not even coherent—just a steady stream of raider-borne panic.

The two guardsmen in their horse-head helmets turn to each other and then put out their hands and catch him as he skids to a halt.

The taller of the two grabs a fistful of his shirt in a hard glove.

"Calm yourself," the guardsman says. "You've got three seconds—"

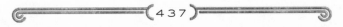

Hell with three seconds. Davies turns his head over his shoulder, makes a wretched face. "Here they come!" he says.

They each jerk their heads to look behind him.

It's a moment.

A small moment.

It'll have to be enough.

He grabs the pistol from the back of his pants, shoves it into the helmet of the taller guardsman. He pulls the trigger. The man's face is erased. The entire helmet fills with blood and hair.

The other guard shouts, steps back, reaches for his thrumwhip—he's fast, impossibly so—the whip out and lancing a crackling arc toward Davies.

Davies shoves the dead guardsman forward—

The whip catches the dead man's neck.

Davies gives the corpse one last shove. The body crashes into the other guardsman, and they both fall over the edge of the bridge.

Hundreds of feet. To the fog-shrouded mechanics beneath them.

Davies gasps. Pants. Tries not to puke. Moments later he hears their bodies bang into the next layer down. A sickening couple of thuds.

He wrenches open the brass gate and steps into the elevator.

SCREAMS AND STEEL

I'M DYING. That's what Lane thinks. He can't breathe, can't punch or kick, can barely move at all. The world went ass over teakettle, and now he's dying. He can't even see anything.

But then the grave shroud is pulled from his head, and he realizes, *It's the sail. I'm trapped under the crow's nest,* and lickety-split there's Rigo, dragging him out from under it.

All around lay the pieces of the splintered mast. Lane doesn't see the raider who was last up there—but the edge of the crow's nest sits rimmed in sticky red. *If Cael had been up there . . .*

If Cael had been up there, he'd have done his damn job.

Rigo snaps his fingers. "We have to go!"

Lane realizes suddenly that the air is filled with the shrieks of sonic blasts. The trawler shudders and rocks. Men scream, fire back their own weapons. A pinnace off to the right takes a hail of fire—the front end breaks apart like a little girl's dollhouse smashed with the swing of a sledgehammer.

The two of them duck behind a heap of metal drums secured by netting. Rigo yells, "This is our shot. Come on!"

Lane nods. But he's not sure. These people—*my people*, he once thought—are getting torn apart. He looks around—no sign of Killian Kelly at all. Where's their captain? Where's their *leader*?

Who's attacking them?

He doesn't even realize he asked the question out loud until Rigo answers, "Metal men! They're like . . . motorvators, but they look like people!"

Jeezum Crow. He'd always heard that the Empyrean had mechanical men doing menial tasks for them—but as soldiers?

This is *not* life in the Heartland. Not as he knows it or imagined it.

"What happened to the people who lived here?" Lane asks.

This time Rigo just gives Lane a sad look. Neither knows the answer, but both can make a pretty troubling guess.

"You need to man one of the cannons," Lane says.

"*What?*"

"I've got something to do."

Lane jumps up and runs.

Rigo is left for a moment, mouth agape.

You need to man one of the cannons.

Oh no. Oh no no no no. That's a fool's parade, the worst idea since that time Rigo bragged he could jump onto that one rogue Thresher-Bot without anybody's help—and as a result he ended up falling into the slashing, cutting corn. After that he knew to leave those jobs for Cael or Lane because he wasn't cut out for that kind of thing. He was a thinker. Planner. Diplomat. He liked maps and figures.

But it is what it is. His friend gave him a task, and he can protest to no one but his own— Well, he was going to say *two* feet, but that's not going to happen. A pang of grief hits him again. *I miss having two feet.* It's a strange and silly thought in the middle of a firefight with metal men, but there it is.

Rigo draws a deep breath. Tries not to piss himself. Then pulls himself to a wobbly stance by using his crutch as an impromptu ladder.

Man the cannon, he thinks. *Shit shit shit.*

Lane has a plan, and he tells anybody he can scream it to. He barks orders to every raider he encounters.

Billy Cross is dead, so the first one he tells is the helmsman, Robin Worley—she's a young woman, only a few years older than Lane, with a pair of flinty tenpenny eyes and copper hair cropped short like a boy's.

She tells *him* they need to retreat.

He tells *her* they need to swing this boat starboard so that the broadside faces the town of Tuttle's Church. Then the other, smaller boats need to get behind the trawler. Stand protected. Let the trawler take the brunt of it, use the cannons to fend off the attack as best as they can.

She says, "That might actually work."

He nods, and she goes.

Then he runs, spreading the plan to anybody listening.

Ducking a rain of splinters. Stepping over a pair of raider bodies—one of them Sully, the cook. Face a bruised mask. Body a red mess. *Can't stop. Can't grieve. Just go.*

Then he sees—

Killian. Throwing a line over the back of the boat. Standing there with Striker Mayhew, Bosun Shiree, and the craggy scarecrow of pitted, pocked flesh that is Tammar Conley, the ship's quartermaster.

They don their wolf-head helmets. Then they rappel down the back of the boat, into the corn.

The sonofabitch is leaving them behind.

He's not leading. Not telling anybody anything. He's content to let them die as he makes his getaway. The damn coward!

The trawler shifts beneath his feet, doing a counterclockwise turn—

He laughs. *They're doing it. They're using my plan!*

He hears it shouted from raider to raider, yelled over to the other boats between sonic blasts. Already those other boats begin to move, pulling away from the massacre ahead of them.

They're on point. Which means he's free for a whole other task.

Lane takes a deep breath, grabs a machete sitting on a nearby crate-top, and runs for the ropes at the back of the boat. He's gonna drag Killian's ass back to this boat and hold that sumbitch accountable for all he's done.

A dead man sits in the gunner's chair.

Rigo doesn't recognize him. That's how badly the sonic blast

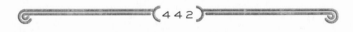

has ruined the raider's flesh. Another pang for his lost leg but also gratitude that he still has the other one. *If I man this cannon, I may not—*

The boat starts to turn. Sonic blasts pepper the side of the trawler, punching holes in the wood—*kachunk, kachunk, kachunk.*

If he mans this cannon, he may lose more than just another leg.

He reaches for it. Then hesitates.

I don't want to die.

I don't want to lose any more of myself.

I don't want to be here anymore.

He hears a bleat of fear come from his own mouth.

He withdraws from the cannon. Let someone else man it.

Rigo just can't do it.

Into the corn. Leaves search and slice the air, looking for a taste. But Lane doesn't have time for that. He clutches the machete—he's going to bring Kelly back to captain that ship or pay for the crime of abandoning his crew just when they need his leadership most.

A small voice tells him, *You're angry and you want to punish him. Angry and jealous and confused. Don't get it twisted, Lane.*

He tells himself to shut the hell up—

Then he makes a run for Tuttle's Church.

It's only once he's out in the open that he realizes what he's done.

A patch of dirt a hundred feet long separates him from the town.

A town with a main street now home to a dozen or more metal men and women with sonic arm-cannons lancing screeching blasts toward the raider fleet. This is the closest he's seen them, the mechanicals. They're crass facsimiles of people, their metal flesh caked with pollen, human clothes rippling in the wind. He realizes he's running, staring, not looking ahead—

His foot catches on a cracked lip of hardened clay, and the hard ground rushes up to meet him. The machete drops, his hands go out, his palms catch the earth, stung.

He cries out.

He doesn't mean to, but Lord and Lady, he cries out.

And when he looks up, one of the metal men is coming for him.

The mechanical is dressed in too-tight overalls. Clean except for a fine rime of pollen. The metal man comes running—a hitching step, torso rocking with each heavy footfall. Its automated features turn inward, giving the metal man a grave and sinister countenance.

The arm raises. Sonic cannon up.

Lane scrambles to get his feet under him—

The cannon fires. Lane leaps forward as the ground beneath him explodes in a cough of dust and broken clod, and again he's falling forward, slamming his knee on the ground, twisting it hard—

The mechanical man again aims his cannon-arm—

Lane closes his eyes.

The air fills with the raptor shriek of a sonic cannon.

And Lane feels his body dissolve under the blast.

Or that's how he imagines it. When he pats himself, he's still there. All there. No pain. Just a tingling wave of fear and relief.

He looks up and sees that the metal man has been knocked to the ground. Head spun the other way. Sparks hissing from its chest.

Lane sees the high wall of the trawler floating there in the distance. Rigo waves from the cannon. Lane gives him a salute—

Just as rough hands drag him forcefully away.

Rigo sits by the cannon. Finger on the trigger.

He laughs. Half mad. All scared.

"I can do it," he says. "I can do it!"

Then he cranks the cannon, levels the gun, and begins firing.

"What in all the Heartland do you think you're doing?" Killian asks. He and the others—Mayhew, Shiree, Tammar Conley— have weapons drawn and leveled at Lane's face from above. Mayhew with his bow and arrow. The other two with old, dinged-up sonic pistols. They dragged him behind the back of a general store and now here they are.

"I'm coming to bring you back to the ship," Lane snarls. "Deserter."

"Deserter?" Killian laughs, but there's no humor there. "This is the task at hand, Lane Moreau. This was always the task at hand, complicated as it has become. You seem to have forgotten that we've come to Tuttle's Church with a purpose, and that purpose is to hurt the Empyrean. Has that been lost on you? Do you now feel pity for them?"

Lane thrusts out his chin. "I feel pity for those who thought you were their leader. These are people. Flesh-and-blood people who you've *abandoned*."

Killian kneels down. Puts a hand on Lane's shoulder. Lane bats it away. "You listen. I don't cherish losing any of my raiders in this. My men and women are not meant to be pawns in a greater game. But we all put our names on the same list. We all die in service to a single cause: bringing the Empyrean low. Bringing the whip to our masters. Delivering a little *equity* to an *inequitable* world. You like that, you come along. You don't? Then piss off and run back to the boat and die there. Or go find your Blighted friend. Or do anything but be a godsdamn *anchor* around my godsdamn *ankle*."

The Heartland. The Empyrean. Tuttle's Church. A battle between metal men and raiders of flesh just on the other side of these buildings. In the main street of a town that must have once been home to people, to *human beings*, who are now just . . . gone.

"You weren't abandoning us?"

"I'm trying to *save* us," Killian says.

Fine.

"I'm coming with you," Lane says. *If only to watch your ass, make sure you don't sell us all upriver, you shifty prick.*

Killian smiles. "Now, there we go."

The others put their weapons away. Mayhew reaches out with a massive hand and helps Lane stand.

As he pulls him up, Mayhew says, "I am sorry to hear about your friend."

Before Lane can respond, Killian starts talking. "We're not talking about McAvoy, so shut it. Now. Plan is as simple as it gets—the fleet distracts the mechanicals. Our job is to take precious advantage of that distraction and duck along these buildings. Because at the far end of the town, I am assured there is a portal, a trapdoor into the ground, into an old mine, and there we will find the data bank we seek. We get to the data bank, we get the codes, and . . ." His mouth twists into a grim smile. "We show the Empyrean that we will not be worms ground into the dirt. We good?"

The raiders all nod. Lane nods, too, though it occurs to him he barely heard what Killian said. Too many thoughts are going through his head. His heartbeat is too loud in his chest. But he nods. Because he's ready to fight.

56

FLYTRAP

IT SEEMS IMPOSSIBLE. That they found him all the way out here. In the house of the Maize Witch. Cael stands in the middle of the parlor as her Blightborn drag Boyland Barnes Jr. and Wanda Mecklin through the front doorway. Wanda calls to him, her cry cut short as vines snake out from the ceiling, curling under both their armpits and around their throats and hoisting them high toward the ceiling. Legs dangle like the limbs of a doll held in the hand of a careless child.

Cael reaches for Wanda, looks to Esther. "Please. No. She's not gonna hurt anybody." But then a wave of perfumed breath sweeps over him, and his knees start to buckle. For the tiniest moment he can't even remember Wanda's name. . . .

"You have no idea how many will want to hurt you," Esther tells him. But then her gaze softens and she gently nods. The vines around Wanda's neck loosen, and the ones beneath her arms gently drop her to the ground. She gasps, clutching her

throat. No tears fall, but the sound she makes is one of a gulping sob. Cael looks to Esther—a gesture he recognizes as seeking permission, a gesture he's not used to making, and part of him bucks against it, pulling on whatever leash and collar she's looped around his neck. And yet there it is.

She grants him permission: he can hear it in his mind: an acquiescence, an *approval*.

He runs to Wanda. He throws his arms around her, helps her to stand.

"What are you doing? I told you to go home," he says.

"I . . ." She looks around, shock-struck by the room, the woman, the vines that were just around her and remain around Boyland. "I told you; we were coming to bring you . . . home. But then the raiders fired on us. . . ."

"I'm glad you're okay. I was worried."

"You should've come," she says, tears gathering in her eyes. "I'm your Obligated. You should've come to see if I was okay."

"I'm sorry, I . . ." His words die in his mouth as she regards him with some fear. She's watching the Blight-vine coiled around his arm, curling now in the space between his fingers—almost like another hand clutching his own. An inhuman hand. Yet one that also belongs to him.

"Does it hurt?" she asks.

"No."

"I'm sorry this happened to you," she says.

"I'm sorry you have to see it. You deserve better than me." It's not a pity-play. At least not *just* a pity-play. He means it. She does deserve better.

She kisses his cheek.

The Blight-vine twists and stirs.

Next to them, Boyland kicks and struggles. He's trying to say words but can't—they're coming out as angry gurgles. The tendons in his neck are like rigging ropes pulled taut. His face is as red as an apple.

Cael pulls away from Wanda and stands before Boyland.

The zombie-eyed Blightborn stand by the door, shuffling from foot to foot. Thorn-teeth clicking like fingers running along the tines of a comb.

"You should've stayed in Boxelder," Cael says. "Probably could've taken up your father's job. Lived a pretty cushy life. But you didn't. You couldn't quit fiddling, and now here you are, following after me like a wasp all pissed off 'cause I threw a rock at your nest. Caught up in a trap. You made a mistake, Boyland."

". . . killed . . . my . . . father . . ."

"I didn't kill him. My father killed him. Because *your* father was in love with my mother. I don't know why. I don't know the history there, nor do I much care at this point. But your father didn't love your mother. And I'm not sure he loved you very much, either. Your father was a sonofabitch who deserved what he got. You keep pushing, same will happen to you."

He feels a hand on his shoulder. A warm ripple shudders over his skin.

Esther. Her fingertip tendrils trace lines up his neck.

"This boy is your enemy," she says.

Cael nods. "I reckon so."

"And this girl is your Obligated."

He looks to her. He doesn't answer.

Then Esther says, "Do you love her?"

"I . . . ," Cael starts to say. He can't look at Wanda. So he looks away. And shakes his head. "I don't know."

Wanda makes a sound: another airless, desperate sob. He turns to her, sees her visibly swallow and retreat within herself.

Damnit, Cael, you're such an asshole.

Esther says, "What shall we do with them? We can do whatever we want. They're fragile people. Frail like the wing of a moth. What of your enemy? This fat-necked thug, as base and inelegant as the tire on a harvester. We could kill him. You could exert your will against him, and we could pull him apart like a poppet at the seams. All his stuffing and straw pouring out."

Cael blanches at the thought. He almost says, *Whatever it is you want to do with him,* but he bites his tongue. "Wanda, I want her safe. As for Boyland, I . . . say to just let him go."

Esther's eyebrows raise. "Truly?"

"Yeah. Let him take his boat and go home."

"An act of mercy, then."

"If you care to call it that." Cael's head is filled with the vision of Boyland returning home, tail between his legs.

Esther turns to him, her fingers still on his neck. "We think of mercy as a gift given, and sometimes it is. But know that sometimes it returns to us like the crack of a whip in an ill-trained hand. Sometimes mercy is a gift to others but an injury to ourselves."

There, again, her scent filling his nose. Flowers and sweetness. His vision goes soft at the edges. He realizes suddenly, *It's more than that, more than just her perfume—she's inside me.* He can feel her there. Pushing. Pulling. Not in any one direction, but reminding him that she can, if she wants to.

Then she's gone. The scent from his nose. Her presence from within his heart and his mind.

"Let him go," he says one last time.

And like that, the vines uncoil, and Boyland drops to the floor like an anvil tossed from a second-story window. *Whump.* He gasps. Props himself up on his elbows, rubbing his neck and panting like a thirsty goat.

Boyland looks at Cael with a feral gaze.

"Shoulda known you were a Blighter now," he growls.

"Don't push me," Cael says. "I'm letting you leave."

Boyland stands, dusting himself off. His throat is a ring of red already darkening to a wine-dark bruise. His gaze flits left and right, scanning the room, the ceiling, Wanda, Esther, her two Blighted servants behind him. He's sizing up his chances. "I oughta kill you here and now."

"Good luck with that," Cael says.

"This ain't over," Boyland says with a sneer.

"Good luck with that, too."

Esther walks to the door and stands between her two Blighted servitors. "You have been granted a reprieve on this day. And now I'd like you to leave my home."

She opens the door.

Just as a boat crashes into it.

Boyland's always thought of his yacht as a woman. It's big and bold in the front, which to him calls to mind a heaving bosom, a heavy bust of a beautiful lady.

And that lady's fist is now jamming itself through the front doorway—as if she's punching somebody right in the mouth.

The boat breaks apart the wall—walls already weak and half rotten by the looks of them—and part of the ceiling collapses, too. Seeing his boat's hull crack and rupture is like a knife stuck up between his ribs—

But it's a wound swiftly salved by seeing all of it fall atop the witch-woman and her two Blighted monsters in a big, godsdamn heap.

Because with that, everything has changed.

Boyland cracks his knuckles.

Cael stands in the middle of the room. Gaping, gawking.

"Now," Boyland says, "I'm going to make you hurt."

Cael blinks.

Boyland reaches out.

The Blight strikes. The vine uncoils from Cael's arm as fast as lightning discharging from a rain-heavy cloud, and Boyland tries to catch it as it dives for his face—

He fails. Again a thick cord of green tightens around his throat—slamming Boyland back into the half-shattered hull of his own boat. Once. Twice. It pins him. He grabs the vine. Tries to twist it. Rip it. Tear it in half. But thorns suddenly line the vine, thrusting up into his palms—blood flows, his grip grows slick, and his vision darkens as the vine constricts.

Everything goes blurry. Cael's vengeful shape is now just a hazy smear, like a smudge of oil across the lens of a spyglass.

Then, movement.

Behind Cael.

A loud *thud*.

The Cael-shape falls to the ground. The vine loosens. It uncoils and crawls back to Cael like a retreating serpent. Again Boyland is left with his skull throbbing, with air rushing fast and furious back into his blasted lungs.

Cael lies crumpled on his side, clutching his head.

Blood wets the back of his hair.

Wanda stands there with a broken board. It, too, is wet with red. Bits of hair stick to the end.

Her mouth goes slack with the horror of what she's done.

The board clatters from her grip.

"I'm sorry," she whispers. "I'm sorry, sorry, so sorry."

Boyland storms over.

He grabs Cael. Throws him over his shoulder. He says to Wanda, "C'mon, there's a skiff out back."

But she just stands there. Eyes wide. Trying to speak but failing.

"I said we gotta go!"

She's trauma-jacked. Lost to him, like a motorvator off its program.

He doesn't need her. He doesn't even want her.

"Hell with you then," he says, shoving past her.

Movement. Light filtered through closed eyelids. The world lifting and dropping, air pushed out of lungs in little puffs. Consciousness pushed out in little puffs, too—one moment awake, another moment down there in the dark, lost in the corn, falling from the sky, trapped in an old pine box as hard heaps of broken earth mound on the lid.

And then Cael awakens for real, this time as the ground beneath him begins to vibrate and hum. He sits up, sees that he's in a small open-air skiff, a six-seater with a head's-up display flickering across a dirty, cracked windshield. He tries to remember what happened—*the Maize Witch, Boyland, Wanda, the Blight-vine around Boyland's throat, then a creak of a board behind him and a white flashbulb of pain*—

A familiar shape sits two rows ahead of him in the pilot's seat—a bucket-headed silhouette, with short, square ears; broad shoulders. Boyland. *Boyland.* He looks around, sees that they're in the skiff out back of Esther's house—and that Boyland's starting it up. The skiff lifts off the ground, the hover-panels blowing clouds of dust and pollen, yellow motes captured in midair before falling again to the ground.

Cael tries to clamber over the seats—

But his right arm, his *Blight* arm, is bound to a handrail running along the edge of the skiff, tied there with a loop of rope and a constrictor knot: a hard knot to undo, a knot he knows himself how to tie (though Lane was always better at that sort of thing). He tries to wrench his arm free—a ridiculous idea, he knows, and it only causes bursts of pain to rip through his shoulder like wildfire. He tries to will his Blight-vine to do something, anything, and it does suddenly—

The vine uncoils from his hand and reaches for Boyland—

But it's too short. It whips across the air along the back of his neck like a beast's tongue looking for a taste. Useless.

Boyland looks back. Grin as big as the broad side of a barn.

He gives Cael his middle finger.

Then something hits the side of the boat like a bull—*boom!*

Cael thinks, *It's her. Esther is here.*

But someone climbs up over the edge of the boat. Someone Cael thought he'd never see again: Eben Henry.

No, no, no—no!

"Thought you were dead," Boyland says.

"Let's go," the hobo barks. Boyland launches the skiff skyward.

57

EDGE OF THE WORLD

THE ELEVATORS won't work for them. They don't have the right faces. They don't have the right voices. None of the dead guards has a visidex. Gwennie asks Squirrel how she got here, and the girl—after a couple clumsy ballet twirls, a bloody knife held in her little hand—says she came in through the ducts like they always do because nobody in the flying city ever likes to look in "dark places."

Gwennie hunkers down in front of Squirrel.

"Are you okay?" she asks her.

"Ducky," the little girl says, a manic gleam in her eyes. One that suddenly rattles Gwennie to the core.

"Thank you for saving us."

"Papa said to." Her face suddenly scrunches up as if she's trying to think about what she wants to eat for breakfast. "But he also said not to kill anybody, and I think I maybe killed some people."

Gwennie doesn't know what to say to that. She brings Scooter over. His tears have dried, but he looks like a rag that's been wrung out. "This is my little brother, Scooter."

"Hiya, Scoots!" she says. "I'm Squirrel."

"Hi," Scooter says. A fearful, uncertain voice that sounds as if it lives a thousand miles away. Gwennie thinks, *This is going to mark him. He'll either turtle into himself or he'll become like Squirrel—numb to it, maybe a killer.* Neither option is a good one.

She has to get them off this city. Now.

She has no idea how to do that.

But Squirrel chimes in: "We're near the Fabrication District! Papa says that's where they make stuff and that's where ships will be."

Ships. There we go! Gwennie asks Squirrel, "Can we get there without using the elevators? Is there a way?"

The gleeful twinkle in Squirrel's eyes again. "Yup! We just follow the edge and"—here another pirouette—"voilà!"

Gwennie stands. Gathers everyone.

"We okay with the plan? We're going to play follow the leader, and this little girl is going to take us to some ships. Once there we're going to . . ." She takes a deep breath. "Get off this floating city. We good?"

Suddenly, her mother pulls her aside.

"Your . . . your father . . ."

"I saw," Gwennie says. Her throat tightens. She pushes emotion down inside her into the rest of the churn. "Mom, we have to go."

"He loved you, and we never knew what it would be like up here."

"Mom, please—"

"Gwennie, we're so sorry. We're so, so sorry. This place is poison. If we knew what happened to Lottery winners—"

She doesn't mean to, but she shouts at her poor mother: "Mom! I can't do this right now. Later. Okay? *Later*. We have to *move*."

Her mother looks shocked—but blessedly, she's shocked into submission. The woman gives a curt nod.

"Squirrel," Gwennie says. "Lead the way."

They're coming.

And Davies still doesn't have the code.

He's in the control room. Getting up here was hard enough— he had to shoot the Elevator Man with the sonic shooter three times before he could even get into the circuitry and command the damn thing to take him up. He silently thanked the many years he, as a field shepherd, had to tend to an occasionally (more like *frequently*) grumpy motorvator. Helped him learn his way around electronics and electrical systems.

The elevator took him up.

Then he destroyed all the circuitry, ensuring it would never take him down again. He tries now not to think about what that means, about how this is a one-way trip for sure, about how all he has here in his last stand is the image of his wife and daughter living inside his head.

Don't think. Pay attention. Present, not the past. The future isn't written. All you've got is the right bloody now, dummy.

At first he thinks the control room is some kind of joke, a

prank for anybody dumb enough to try to break in. The console is brushed nickel, all curves and contours but not a single button, switch, lever, or knob. No screen, either. Just a wraparound window showing the whole of the flotilla in every direction. He laughs looking at it. Just a cruel joke, a dummy station for a dummy intruder.

But then he runs his hands along it—

And it responds to his touch.

Metal pulls away from metal; invisible seams suddenly become visible as pieces of the outer shell slide back or lift up and out of the way, like pieces of an old puzzle coming apart before his very eyes.

There, then, sit all the buttons, switches, levers, and knobs.

A black keyboard awaits.

Two antennas—the amber metal of polished brass—rise up over the sides of the console. They crackle and spark.

Between them an image is projected: a single, winking cursor.

It wants a code.

It wants *the* code.

And he still doesn't have it.

He hears them now. The shouts of men drifting up to this central tower. Soldiers. Guardsmen. Trying to hammer their way in. Maybe there's an emergency way up—certainly should be, given that the central control tower commands all aspects of the flotilla. Automated, for the most part, but for a single code override . . .

He checks his pistol's battery. It still glows green, though its color has dimmed. Another ten shots it'll be orange; another ten

beyond that, red, and then that weapon is dead until he can find another battery to screw in.

So he tries to still his heart and quiet his mind. And he looks out over the flying city. The afternoon sun caught in a hundred skyscraper windows. The many hills with their many homes. Skybridges and elevator conduits. Ships at the edges of the city, some of them flying over and through.

Beautiful. A feat of human engineering. And kept from the bulk of humanity. A privilege reserved only for those lofty enough and with the right heritage. It's a shame, really—he doesn't want to do what he has to do. But the Empyrean have to learn. They have to learn that you kick a dog long enough, eventually that dog's gonna bite.

Squirrel is fast while the rest of them are slow. She hops railings, clambers under and over metal grates, swings on chains to close gaps—frequently she disappears out of sight, which at first worried Gwennie. But over time the same events play out in sequence again and again: Squirrel dashes ahead with great nimbleness and what seems to be no fear, then disappears, leaving them all behind. But soon they catch up and she's there, waiting for them. Impatiently, arms crossed over her chest.

Then it happens again. She brightens and takes off and gets way ahead of them once more.

Gwennie's mother moves with hesitation, her legs trembling, her hands shaking as she frequently does what Gwennie advises her not to do: look down.

Scooter, for his part, seems emboldened by Squirrel. As if he wants to be her. As if her recklessness suits him. Gwennie has to time and again stop him from trying to leap too far ahead, too fast.

They walk along fat, rusted pipes.

They climb down one ladder and up another.

They cross rickety, squeaking walkways.

And as they do, the sun slowly drips down from its place above their heads, easing toward the horizon, ready to melt into it as evening calls.

Then a small but present triumph awaits.

They edge past a sharp corner and see ahead a scalloped bay carved out of the side of the flotilla: a shipping dock of massive proportions with silver cranes lifting pallets and containers into scowbarges. Everything is automated. Mechanical arms moving boxes and barrels. Human-shaped auto-mates whirring about on wheels and textured treads. No people at all.

She says as much out loud.

Merelda nods. "They don't like to work. So they make the machines do it for them."

"Then why do they need us?" Gwennie says.

It's her mother who speaks up now. "Maybe one day they won't." A sad look crosses her face, as if being needed is at least *something* to count on in this world. She lifts her chin toward the dock.

Now's not the time to worry about it.

"We have to get over there. How?"

"I think that question's about to be answered for us," Merelda says, and points. Several ships suddenly appear from the center of the flotilla, ketch-boats hovering over the docking bay. Cranes move out of their way as they slowly ease forward. One of the ships looks different from the others: the front end looks like the beak of a falcon. "Percy's ship. The *Osprey*."

Shit! He's already ahead of them.

"We have to go back," Gwennie says, but then Squirrel appears from around the corner (did anyone even realize she'd gone?) and clucks her tongue.

"Nope," Squirrel says. "Big ships thattaway, too."

Gwennie slides past the corner, leaning out and giving a quick look.

Double shit! Sure enough, another pair of ketch-boats hover a quarter mile back.

They're trapped.

The *Osprey* slides away from the other ships, easing slowly across the bay, threading the needle between a pair of scowbarges.

It's coming right for them.

58

EXPOSED

THE RAIDERS HUNKER DOWN by the overturned hull of a scrapped pinnace—the mast gone to splinters, the sail a tattered blanket falling over the gravel lot out back of the ship-man's garage.

The sail has handprints on it.

Dark brown. Rusty. Lane shudders when he realizes it's not dirt. It's blood. Old blood. *What happened to the people of Tuttle's Church?*

Over the boat they have a vantage point—

There, in the street, a rusty hatch in the asphalt, exposed by a cutout in the plasto-sheen.

A mechanical stands there, as silent and still as a scarecrow. It wears a simple farmer's shirt that ripples in the faint stirring of air. Its arm-cannon is already exposed—the other arm dead-ends in a machine hand of little pistons and pulleys and flywheels. The whole thing is plastered with a rime of corn pollen.

"One mechanical," Killian says, his voice a whisper. In the distance the sounds of the battle rage on. Sonic screams. Men yelling.

"I don't get it," Lane says, his words hushed. "Why here? Why a data bank in the middle of nowhere? What the hell is going on here?"

Shiree answers, "It's about distance."

Killian explains in a low voice. "These data banks have the codes to the control towers of all the flotillas up there in the big blue. Why do they keep them here? If I had to wager, I'd put smart money on what Shiree just said: it's all about distance. Only a few folks on the flotillas actually have the codes. Praetors, peregrines, maybe a few others. But they don't want those codes up on the flotillas where they can do harm if somebody finds them. So they shuffle them off-ship to somewhere nobody would ever think to look for them—at the edge of the Heartland in a town where no one lives. But they didn't count on us."

"We ain't got a shot," Tammar Conley growls, his voice a rotten rumble in the back of his throat. "That mechanical will tear us apart."

"It's just one," Mayhew says. "One of us distracts it. The rest open the door, head below." He pauses. "Relax. I'll do it. I'll distract."

He's afraid, though. Lane can see it. For a master hunter and big sonofabitch, Mayhew's scared. But that's telling, too—because being scared isn't stopping him. He's still willing to do it. Because he believes.

Am I really a believer? Lane asks.

Does it matter now?

The plan is the plan, and suddenly, like that, it's in action.

Mayhew slings his bow over his shoulder, then climbs quickly atop the hull of the overturned boat. Above him is a broken window leading into the garage—he hoists himself up and in, as silent as a bird in flight.

Then: nothing. For what feels like forever. Time yawns and stretches, pulled like taffy. Lane feels impatience gnawing at his gut. Fear, too. It makes him feel alive in a way he doesn't much like.

He's about to say something to Killian when an arrow launches out of nowhere and pops the machine man square in the center of his sensor eye. The eye pops, cracks, sparks.

A voice from out of sight—Mayhew's. "Come on, you metal bastard! Come hunt the hunter!"

And then the mechanical is on the move, sprinting forward with that unnatural hitch in its gait.

"Clear," Shiree says.

"Godsdamnit, here we go," Tammar growls.

Killian grins the maddest, most unhinged grin Lane's seen yet.

Then he bolts forward toward the middle of the street.

Suddenly they're out. They're *exposed*. As Killian dives to his knees, skidding to the rusted hatch in the middle of main street, Lane looks around and sees at the far end of the street the metal citizens of Tuttle's Church waging their war against the massive trawler. Already the trawler looks riddled with holes, pieces of wood hanging off, sails torn asunder, a few dead raiders draped over the edge like rugs bent for dusting. And the mechanicals are moving forward now, easing toward the fleet in what Lane suddenly fears is an act of slow-motion extermination.

Here, though, their own mechanical man is crashing through the doorway to the local saloon, where a big, crooked sign up top reads WILEY'S PLACE. *Mayhew must've run in there*, Lane thinks.

Killian, meanwhile, wipes a sheen of rust free from the hatch, revealing a small screen that lights up with a muddy, blurry image as if from a visidex. On the screen a series of concentric green circles radiates outward, as if the device is waiting for input.

The raider captain takes the visidex and presses it down against the screen.

It's like a key opening a lock.

The rusty hatch *ding*s.

Then the street rumbles. From far below, Lane hears the sound of gears turning. And something rising toward them.

For a moment that's all there is—the calm before anything else happens, the seconds ticking down.

Then: *crash*.

The mechanical tumbles out of the second floor, metal arms flailing. It lands on its back, shattering the asphalt beneath the plasto-sheen coating. Mayhew leaps out after it like a man possessed by demons, an arrow in his hand like a knife. He lands on the mechanical, straddling its chest, and he stabs the arrow into its eye again and again, turning his face away from a shower of sparks—

Below them, a *ding*.

The rusty platform springs open.

A smooth-sculpted elevator pod rises from the street—

Mayhew gasps. He rears back, staring down at the mechanical in horror. Lane calls out to him to see what's wrong, and all Mayhew can do is look at Lane with shock-struck eyes.

The machine man beneath him wrenches an arm free and fires a sonic blast up into Mayhew's gut. A spray of red. Mayhew screaming. And then he's down on his back, clutching at his guts as they threaten to spill out of him—

The elevator doors slide open.

Another mechanical awaits inside. This one is designed as a woman, with a long dress on her lean, metal body and red and blue wires for hair. Instantly the mechanical arm goes up; the hand spins off, bounces on the plastic; the gun pops out—

It begins firing.

A sonic blast tears through Shiree's chest—a splinter of white bone through red—and she spins like a top, falling to the ground. Tammar ducks another blast and raises his own pistol, firing a series of shots into the thing's face. But sonic blasts do a lot better against flesh than metal, and though the thing's skull vibrates and dents with each hit, it keeps on coming.

One more shot and Tammar's gun-arm disappears. One minute it's there—the next his face is flecked with his own blood, and his hand and forearm have been all but erased.

Killian gets low and slams into the mechanical from the side. Lane sees his chance and lunges for the thing from the other side, grabbing at the gun arm and giving it a hard yank—

Like a cow tipping, the metal figure falls hard and fast. Lane has to backpedal out of the way so as not to be caught beneath it.

Before he even knows what's happening, Killian is grabbing him by the arm and hauling him into the elevator—

Killian stabs the single black button on a faux-wood panel.

The elevator makes a *ding*—

Beneath them is the sound of gears turning.

But the doors do not yet close.

In the street, the first mechanical is standing.

And turning toward them.

Lane gets it now. He gets what Mayhew was so horrified to see. Because he feels that horror, too.

He knows suddenly where the people of Tuttle's Church went to. They didn't go anywhere.

They're still here.

Half of the mechanical's face has fallen away. A pale human face hides behind the metal carapace. The cheeks are lined with bruises. The one eye revealed stares off at nothing—wires thrust up under the lids.

They've been turned into these metal monstrosities.

The elevator doors start to close.

The mechanical raises its arm and fires.

The shot strikes Killian. Lane tastes the copper spray of blood as the elevator *ding*s one last time and the doors close.

59

THE BLACK HORSE

THE SKIFF JUMPS over the corn as Boyland punches it forward. Eben Henry kneels in the middle seat and turns toward Cael. He draws a knife, held firmly in dark, tight fingers, a white-toothed grin spreading between the folds of his pink-stained swaddling.

"Little Mouse," Eben says with a throaty chuckle. "You hurt me. Now I hurt you."

Cael launches forth with his vine. This time his prey is close enough, and the vine wraps around Eben's face, tightening against the wound gauze. The man screams in pain, the pink stains of the bandages turning red where the vine has cinched.

A flick of the knife upward cuts the vine in twain. Cael feels it—a cold rush that travels back through the Blight-vine to his arm and shoots deep into the chambers of his heart. He cries out.

Boyland yells, "Leave him be, godsadamnit! He's *mine*." He leans back and reaches for the vagrant—

Eben plunges the knife into the meat of Boyland's shoulder.

The knife raises again, wet with red—

The skiff suddenly dives toward the corn. Before Cael knows what's happening, the boat lifts, then shoulders hard into the ground, ripping through stalks of dead corn, the ass-end of the skiff tilting left—

We're gonna flip, Cael thinks.

And when that happens, he's gonna lose his arm, which remains tethered to the boat.

But then enough corn gathers at the front that the boat suddenly crawls to a stop, lifting up and then slamming back down before going still.

Evening begins to settle in around them. Crickets begin to chirp.

Ahead, two bodies lie silent, unmoving. Eben Henry is slumped forward. Boyland to the side.

Cael coughs. Rolls out of the skiff. The rope still anchors him. He feels around on the ground for something, anything— he palms a rock. He brings it down against the rope. The rock cracks, shatters—not a rock at all but a dang dirt clod. *Sonofab*—

He keeps feeling. There. *There*. A rock. A real one. Flat. Hard. A sharp edge that doesn't come apart as his thumb presses against it. He jams the rock against the rope, which doesn't do a damn thing. Panting, he takes it and turns it, sharp edges down—

And begins to saw back and forth.

The rope frays. Eventually, it cuts.

I'm free.

He turns to look back at the skiff—

Boyland's still in the front.

But Eben Henry's gone. Like a ghost turned to vapor.

Oh shit.

His Blight-vine—cut off at the tip, now weeping white fluid—suddenly writhes and begins to panic, and Cael realizes, *It's warning me. It knows something is wrong—*

He spins around just as the vagrant comes at him with a knife.

Cael launches himself to the side, the knife coming down on the edge of the skiff and tearing open one of the seats. Puffs of white stuffing float out. Cael drives a hard punch to Eben's kidneys, but the older man takes it like it's nothing—then cracks an elbow across Cael's jaw.

A bitten cheek. A loose tooth. The taste of blood. He was already woozy, but now he's slipping on a carpet of rotten corn, falling backward—air knocked out of his lungs as if with a hammer. *Oof.*

He tries to will himself to stand, tries to put all of himself into his Blight-vine, but it just flips and flops like a snake with its head cut off. Cael can't even get a proper breath into his pancaked lungs.

Eben Henry stalks over to him.

Knife in one hand.

With his free hand he unwraps the bandage around his head. It *peels* away, stickily, noisily, like pulling a dead leaf off drying paint. In the fading light of the day Cael can see that the man's skin is red and raw, the wounds popping open with every

472

miniscule muscle flex of his face. He clacks his teeth, blinks his eyes, both so white against the burn-blistered face.

"You scarred me," Eben says, dropping to his knees on Cael's chest. What little air Cael pulled in is gone again, and all he can do is make a whistling, squeaking gasp. "Your family burned mine."

"Who . . . I don't . . ." His words are bare whispers.

"You still don't know, Little Mouse. Do you know who your father was?" The vagrant spreads his legs, moves his knees so that they pin Cael's arms to the ground. Then he takes the tip of the knife, presses it against Cael's forehead.

"He was one of the Sleeping Dogs," Cael says. "One of the first."

"That's right. And so was I."

"What?"

"He was Swift Fox. Your mother was the Bride of Hatchets. The others—Iron-Red Ned, Creeping Charlie, Bellflower, Corpse Lily. And me. Black Horse. The Sawtooth Seven. I've killed two of them. Creeping Charlie died in the washtub, his throat slit. I betrayed Iron-Red on Blanchard's Hill, shot him in the back. But it was *your father* and *his family* I always wanted. Because your father killed my son."

Cael manages to draw a small breath—it enlivens him, a small whorl of embers turning into a full-bore campfire.

He won't abide these lies any longer.

He wrenches his Blight arm free—

Here's my chance—

Eben slams a fist into his nose. Everything is white light. His eyes water. The fight is sucked out of him, a puddle of water drying fast beneath the hot sun. The hobo takes his pigsticker knife, presses Cael's hand to the ground, and stabs the knife clean through the palm.

Red, hot pain. As if he's holding the lit end of a torch. Blood crawls between his fingers. Pain lances like a thrum-whip to his shoulders.

Tears creep down the sides of his face.

"There we go," Eben Henry says, "the little mouse has his tail trapped, doesn't he? Little Mouse isn't enjoying the bedtime story. Alas. For the tale continues, and you ought to listen to this accounting of his sins. Your father and I were mates. We did everything together, Arthur and I. We were a *team*. He didn't think we were the leaders of the Sawtooth Seven, but we were, *oh*, we were. We were bound together in our hatred for the Empyrean. The skyrapers were just starting to really seal the deal, taking things away from us that we'd always assumed would be there: our farms, our education, our *choice*. We'd already had to put up with them floating above us and telling us who to marry, but now we had no choice as to what we did with our lives. And the way to the sky was *shut*."

The vagrant's words reach Cael—but he retreats from the world. He pulls into his own head. Tries not to listen. Tries futilely to unstick his stuck hand from the ground. Eben slaps him.

"Come back to me, Little Mouse. Be present in this moment. As the Lord and Lady said to their son, Jeezum Crow, *Be not the rat that flees the justice of the fire—be the hawk that flies proudly toward it, for only then will you prove yourself our son.* Ah. But you're not my son. My son is dead. So is my wife. So is everything I was. Came a point in our reign as the Sawtooth Seven when your father began to have second thoughts about all the bad things we'd done in the name of the Heartland. We'd hurt people, you see. *Killed* folk. But suddenly your father grew a conscience—a soft fruit hanging on a crooked branch, that conscience. Was it your mother who breathed such weakness into his ears? Was he just a weak man coasting too long on the strength of others? I still don't know. All I think about when I think of your father is my son's face. My *young* son's beautiful face. Splattered with his mother's blood. And then his own."

"I . . . You're lying. . . ."

Another hard slap.

"Don't tell me I'm lying, you little shit." He bellows, "My son is dead! Your father betrayed me. He didn't like what I'd been doing on my own. He didn't *approve* of my tactics. I said the Empyrean were cruel, so we needed to be *crueler.* I said the Empyrean would kill one-tenth of us, so we needed to kill *nine-*tenths of them. Your father told them where I was living. *He sent them to me.* They came. Eager to get their hands on one of the Seven. But I wasn't there! My wife was there. My *son*—a boy I named after your godsdamn monster of a father!—was there. I buried them both under the rising moon. That was the last night of the Sawtooth Seven. Your father destroyed our fellowship. Everyone went their separate ways. But the movement continued on. Those who followed us were inspired by what we'd done. They became the Sleeping Dogs. But I didn't care. I still don't care. All I care about is *this.*" He waves his hands above him, as if to behold the bruise-dark sky, his arms circling back around to Cael. "I care about having Arthur McAvoy's son in front of me. A sacrifice to the gods. A just killing in the name of all that's sacred and true. Son for son, sin for sin. Are you ready to die now, Little Mouse?"

"Go . . . to . . . *hell*."

Another hard punch to the nose. Cael's head slams into the unforgiving earth. Eben laughs. Loud. Bold. Brash. The burns around his lips splitting like the ground with lava beneath, his face a mask of scarlet skin and weeping pus—

Crack.

An oar-pole slams the vagrant's reared head.

Eben Henry topples to the side, clutching his skull.

Boyland stands. His right side and arm soaked with blood. Hair mussed. Face pale. He drops the oar-pole.

Cael tries not to whimper as he moves—even now he cannot abide the thought of Boyland thinking he's weak—but he fails to stifle the cry as he reaches over and wrenches the knife from his palm.

Fresh pain blooms like fire in the darkness.

New blood flows. Spattering into the dirt.

He stands. Face throbbing. Woozy.

"Kill you," Eben growls, getting up on all fours and staring at them with a blood-slick face. "Kill you both. *Kill you all*."

"What—" Cael has to cough past what feels like a dry bird's nest in his throat. "What do we do with him?"

Boyland shrugs. "You kill him."

"I don't know if I can."

"Weak," Eben says, chuckling. "Weak like Arthur. Faggot. *Faggot*."

"Kill him, Cael. Just get it over with."

"I'm not a—"

The vagrant launches himself up—

—grabs Cael hard—

And then freezes. His body stiffens. The knife in his gut is sunk all the way to the hilt. A hilt held in Cael's hand.

Eben Henry peels away from the blade. Then falls backward. Eyelids fluttering. Lips forming words that are not spoken. Spit froth. Black blood.

And his eyes go unfocused.

His body goes still.

Cael looks at the bloody knife in his hand. "I didn't . . ."

"You did," Boyland grunts.

Cael turns to face Boyland. They're both bloodied. He sees now that one of Boyland's eyes is swelling shut—an injury from the crash, maybe. Cael sticks a finger up toward Boyland's right shoulder, pulls at the hole in the fabric right below his collarbone. Where the knife got him.

"That hurt?" Cael asks.

Boyland nods. "Your hand?"

"Like a sonofabitch."

The two of them stare at each other for a while. Each listing a little like a boat sailed by a drunken captain. Each bleeding. Eben Henry's dead eyes stare up at the darkening sky.

"Now what?" Cael asks.

Boyland sniffs. "Now we get in that boat, and I drag your ass back to the proctor."

"That ain't gonna happen."

Boyland's hands form into mallet fists. "Gonna have to."

"You love her."

"What?"

"Gwennie. You love her. Isn't a question, so you don't need to answer it. I know you do. I could see it back in Boxelder. I saw it on your face the day of the Obligation. You love her."

"That's right. And you're in the way of all that."

Cael nods. "Be that as it may, Barnes, she's in danger."

"What?"

"She's on a flotilla, and the raiders are aiming to bring that city crashing into the Heartland. I bet you'd like to save her."

"You're lying to me. To save your own hide. No way raiders can bring down a flotilla. Never been done."

"Not a lie. And maybe they can't do it, but they sure mean to. Something about some code. Planning on using that to crash it. And she's on the flotilla they plan to crash. Hell, she's helping them *get the code*. She doesn't know she's in danger."

Boyland's cagey now. Cael can see he's alert, aware, as if the thought of Gwennie in danger has pushed the pain aside. "I need to help her."

"*We* need to help her, dumbass. I know how to find someone on the flotilla. Esther . . . the . . . woman back there, she told me how to find her son. We can use *him* to find her. But we have to go. Now."

Boyland looks at the skiff. "I think she'll still fly."

"She'd damn well better, Barnes, or Gwennie's going to die."

PREDATOR AND PREY

THE *OSPREY* EASES TOWARD THEM. No fast lurch, no burst of its engines or pulse from its hover-rails. Just a slow, steady drift.

Because time, Gwennie realizes, is on the peregrine's side.

From the *Osprey*, little floating cameras release—they pop out and hover, lens-eyes staring and pointing.

Her mother says something truly startling. "We can jump."

Gwennie wheels on her. "What?"

"They're going to kill us. They're going to *humiliate* us. We can jump. We can be with your father and rejoin the Heartland. The Lord and Lady will see us through—"

"The Lord and the Lady are bullshit!" Gwennie shouts. She doesn't even mean to say that—is that what she believes? She knows suddenly that yes, it *is* what she believes. The gods aren't real. They're just characters, like in a book. Except people put everything onto these characters. Hopes and dreams. Fears and

failures. Reasons to dismiss, hurt, even destroy. "We're not doing that. He wants to kill us, let him kill us. Let the world see."

Her mother begins to cry. "But we still have power here—"

Gwennie points a finger toward the others. "You shush. You're scaring them."

It's true. Even Squirrel looks scared.

Her mother says, "We're all scared." She stares at her feet.

Merelda steps next to Gwennie. "He will kill us, I think," she says.

"Maybe he'll save you," Gwennie answers.

"Not this time. When these people are done with you, they're done. I see that now."

"A little late to learn that lesson." Gwennie can't help it. She smirks, just a little.

"At least I learned it."

"Open the hatch," Percy says. A pair of Frumentarii pop the two latches, and the hatch above opens with a squeak and a hiss. A red metal ladder descends. He climbs up into the fading light of day and steps out onto the upper deck of the ketch-boat. Wind in his hair. Sleeves of his suit billowing. He feels powerful here.

The winds are shifting. As day turns to night, so does Percy Lemaire-Laurent reclaim his power. The praetor will have nothing to say to him about this . . . hiccup. All she will do is heap garlands of laurels on his brow. He'll get a parade for the extermination of the terrorist cells on the Saranyu. He thinks he'll even push for the creation of a new position: a Peregrine of

Peregrines, someone to oversee security across *all* the flotillas. It is time for each flotilla to stop being so damn *independent.*

He steps to the golden railing. Mary Salton's gun hangs in his hand, heavy, pendulous, *consequential.*

There. Trapped on an access walkway like little grackles with their wings clipped. They all stare up at him, huddling together like orphans, hate in their eyes. He wonders then: Will he spare any of them? He looks to Merelda. La Mer. Such a beauty. Ravensblack hair. Skin like pooled milk. Young and fresh and able to compete with him in bed. He could save her. He thinks then that maybe he will. He'll save her. He'll send her to the Lupercal. And once a year he'll visit with her. He'll take her away from that place. He'll wine her and dine her and bed her. It will be his mercy.

For the peregrine is a merciful creature.

"You have been judged," he calls down to them. "There is no escape from this. Know that this justice is essential in the eyes of the Lord and the Lady and all the Saintangels and the sky gods and goddesses that came before them. Take comfort that your mistakes will serve as a lesson for all, for your failure is an instructional manual written in scar tissue." He raises the revolver. "You have been judged by the peregrine, by the praetor, by the whole of the Empyrean. May your cradle be your grave."

He holds up the weapon. They huddle tighter together now, and he thinks, *Maybe I'll kill more than one with a single bullet.* There's that phrase, two birds, one stone; he likes the poetry of it. And though that may mean he'll kill La Mer, too, he braces his one arm with his other and then—

He pulls the trigger.

The gun spits its bullet, bucking like a bull—

All clamor and smoke.

A pipe above the Heartlanders' heads busts free and spirals off into oblivion. Steam hisses.

He missed.

I missed.

Impossible!

Now his hand is shaking. Anger and embarrassment threaten him. He grits his teeth. Ignores the sound of the hatch behind him opening. Ignores the footsteps behind him. But he cannot ignore the hands that reach for him, begin to drag him backward—his own guards! Betraying him!

"Get off me!" he cries. "Let me take my shot!"

"Sir," one of the guardsman says. "Sir! *Something's happening.*"

He pulls away and wheels.

Is he in danger?

One of his agents points off the starboard. Out toward the horizon.

He almost laughs at the absurdity of it.

"I can handle this," he says.

And he raises the revolver once more.

Gwennie peers out over her mother's embracing arms.

The peregrine and his men are arguing. Pointing off at something away from the flotilla—

Her gaze follows the gesture.

What she sees seems impossible. In fact, it seems *insane.*

The last light of the sinking sun glints orange off a flying horse. A Pegasus. Eldon Planck's *automated* Pegasus.

She can hear the thrum of its hover-panels.

Close. Closer. Close enough now to see its animatronic head rearing back. To hear the mechanized snorting. Metal wings of a hundred brass feathers extend out and collapse inward in some rough semblance of flying, though it's not the wings that hold it up but a series of hover-panels.

Legs gallop on invisible ground.

It's heading right for the skiff.

The peregrine fires. *Boom.* The gun jerks in his hand.

The horse keeps coming.

He fires again—

Boom!

This time the horse's head clangs with the shot and spins around on its axis, suddenly hanging limp and useless. The peregrine fires another three times—*boom, boom, boom*—and sparks leap off the Pegasus. One brass feather spins away into nothing. One hoof suddenly hangs loose by a mooring of red wires. The final shot finishes the job of the first—the head leaps off the neck, but it's held fast by a series of cables. And the Pegasus is still coming, heading toward the *Osprey.*

The men rush the peregrine back into the belly of the ship.

In the moments before collision, Gwennie sees something strapped to the bottom of the Pegasus's belly. A bag taped there.

She doesn't know what it is, but she can suddenly guess.

She hugs everyone together and shields them quickly—

The Pegasus strikes the *Osprey.*

The explosion is deafening.

THE CAPTAIN CONFESSES

THE ELEVATOR DOOR OPENS, and for a moment Lane thinks, *It looks like stars*. The data bank consists of black boxes almost twice as tall as Lane. Each stacked against the other, each winking blue and green in the half-lit dark of the room.

Then Killian collapses forward, his left shoulder a ragged mess from where the blast struck him. He's got his hand against the wound, blood pumping through his fingers. Already the color has drained from his face.

He turns toward the elevator and fires a sonic round into it, finishing the job the mechanical started.

Sparks shower.

"That should slow the metal bastards down," he says, wetting his lips with his tongue. His voice is weak. He almost falls. Lane catches him.

"Careful," Lane says.

"I wager we're about a hundred miles past careful," Killian says.

"You're going to be all right."

"I wasn't going to be all right the day I came kicking out of my mother. She died that day. My father killed himself two weeks later. I was never going to be okay, Lane Moreau, not ever."

He sniffs and sits down in the middle of the floor.

Lane crouches next to him.

"We . . . need to get the codes."

"We will," Killian says. "First I need to say some things."

"This is one of those bullshit deathbed confessions, isn't it? You're not going to die here."

"Maybe not from this . . ." He peels his hand away, and the palm is thick with crimson. "But we're trapped in a bunker below a town where the people have been . . . *transformed* into mechanicals. Or half-mechanicals. I did see that, right? I'm not hallucinating? I hope I'm hallucinating."

Lane doesn't say anything. He can't muster the words.

"So consider this not just my deathbed confession but yours, too, because I cannot be assured we will both be alive at the end of this. Maybe we'll be made into metal men. Wouldn't that be a thing?" He suddenly winces. "Point is, you have my apologies, Lane. My dearest, deepest, stupidest-ass apologies. I made a terrible error—"

"We don't have to do this."

"Godsdamn, yes, we do!" Killian yells, pounding the floor. "I do. I need this. I messed up. There I went spinning some glittery spider's web about how we all should be who we are and rebel against what people think of us, and then the hard wind of real life came in and swept that away. I didn't want people to know." He presses his thumb into the space between his eyes, rubbing it in hard circles. "Because I'm a liar and a fool and a damn, candy-baby coward."

"I get it," Lane says. That's all he really has to say. "I get it, I do."

"Sorry, too, about your friend." Killian sniffs. "He attacked my mate, it's true. But we didn't give him much choice, either."

"Cael's good people. He stands up for what's right even when he doesn't know what right really is."

"What's right and righteous is truly a mystery for the ages." Killian props himself up against a blinking bank of black boxes. "Let's get on with this, then." He takes the visidex, slides it across the floor to Lane. "Should be a station on the far side. Just plug in the visidex and hit Transfer."

Lane holds the screen in his hand. These things really are keys. The Empyrean never should have allowed a single one of them to fall into the hands of a Heartlander. He feels his heartbeat pulsing in his fingers. He nods to Killian, sees the station—a blank screen tilted upward, no keyboard, just a space like a podium. He slots the visidex against the black glass.

A new icon shows on the screen: **Transfer.**

Gingerly, he taps it.

A little black progress bar begins to fill up with alarming swiftness.

The visidex chimes when the bar is full.

Transfer Complete.

"Holy hell," Lane says. He withdraws the visidex. It feels

heavier somehow. It isn't. Not really. Data can't weigh anything, can it? But he imagines it, just the same.

Killian looks up at him as he approaches. His face is a gray sheet, the color leeched out of it. The blinking lights of the room reflected in the blood slicking his shoulder. "Is it . . . done?"

"I . . . think so."

Killian reaches up. Fingers wiggling. "Take my hand."

Lane eases forward. He takes the raider captain's hand.

Killian squeezes it. Not hard. Not a lot of strength there. Then he lets go.

The captain says, "Tap the screen. Should be a handful of new icons. One of them should be called something like—"

"Codes. I see it. Codes."

"Tap it."

Lane does. The screen is filled with a series of numbers, letters, symbols. "It's gibberish."

"It's not. Icon in the corner. Looks like the wings of a Pegasus. Tap that. It'll give you the option to send it to another . . ." He coughs into his hand. "To another visidex user."

Lane sees the little icon that looks like a pair of wings—and sure enough, the option to send it along appears. Killian recites a code. "That's the code for our people in the control tower. Go on."

Slowly, Lane types it in.

"Send it."

Lane's finger hovers.

"What will happen?" Lane asks.

"Huh?"

"When I do this. When I send this. What will happen?"

"They'll have the code. They'll use the code."

"But what will the code do?"

Killian's nostrils flare as he pulls a long, slow breath into his chest. "It'll bring the flotilla down."

"That'll kill a lot of people."

"Thousands."

"It's murder. Isn't it?"

Killian closes his eyes. "Maybe. Let me tell you how I see it, Lane. I think that ending the lives of bad men is not murder. It may be vengeance. And it is most certainly justice. They've poisoned our earth. Taken the sky for themselves. They feed us shit like we're pigs. They work us to the bloody bones. All our lives are blisters and cancers and stillborn children, and all their lives are parties and fancy drinks and pretty sunsets. Maybe if they die we rebalance the scales. Maybe they have to die to even up the odds and show Heartlanders that the time to change is now. A symbol."

"It's a damn serious symbol."

"That's life in the Heartland."

Lane nods.

And he hits the button to transmit the code.

CONTROL

THEY'RE COMING FOR HIM.

They have ships. Hovering outside. They don't know what to do yet, Davies figures—they can't just open fire on their own control tower. But they're starting to gather cables and breach charges.

They'll be in before long.

It's all over. No code. No nothing. He wonders what it'll feel like, eating his own sonic shooter. Sticking it in his mouth and pulling the trigger. Will he hear the sound? The sonic bird-scream as he tears the top of his head off? Or will it just be silent? There one minute, gone the next?

The visidex chimes.

Incoming Packet.

"Holy gods," he says.

It's the code.

He hurries over to the console.

Pulls up the codes. He scans for the Saranyu's code—

The three letters, *OSS*, are buried in the middle—Ormond Stirling Saranyu. Followed by a sixteen-digit code of numbers and symbols.

With shaking fingers he begins to hunt-and-peck the code on the keyboard. *Tap, tap, tap.* Mistype. "Damnit." Delete. *Tap, tap, tap.*

Four more digits.

Then two.

Then just one.

His hand is shaking.

His daughter. He doesn't really know if she made it off okay. He has to believe she did. By now. Has to have *faith*.

Kathunk!

Cables. Firing from the ships. Suctioning to the outside of the tower.

Here they come, he thinks.

"I love you, Retta," he says. The name of his wife. The true name of his daughter. *I have faith.*

He taps the final number into the code.

And everything begins to flash.

THE IMPROBABLE DYAD

THE SKIFF CUTS THE AIR. Boyland pilots. Cael sits back in the seat, cold air rushing over the windshield and rifling through his hair. He closes his eyes once more and reaches out—

At first Cael couldn't do it. They got the skiff flying again, but out there in the great expanse he found nothing. Worry plagued him. Would Wanda be okay with the Maize Witch? He had to believe that she would. She loved him. Did he love her? He didn't know. Would Gwennie be okay? Lane? Rigo? Were Pop and Mom dead? He couldn't do it. Couldn't focus. No sense of where Esther's son was. He pushed and tensed and bit the inside of his cheek so hard he drew blood, but then—in the moment just as he relaxed, started to give up—there it was.

The Maize Witch's son. Balastair. A tiny seed buried not in the earth but among the clouds. He pointed the way, and Boyland aimed them toward a distant flotilla. A flotilla now closer and

closer, a dark shape starting to take form—from a shapeless blob to a thing with towers and bridges and the craggy bottom of hover-panels and burning engines.

The Ormond Stirling Saranyu.

"There she is," Boyland says.

"Don't personify her," Cael says. "It's not a woman. It's just a thing."

"Jeezum, so touchy." Boyland looks rough. They tore a strip off the bottom of his pants and tied it around his collarbone. Cael did the same for his hand. Each looks like an old leather belt swallowed by a goat and squeezed out the other end. "You didn't kill my father, then."

"No. My father did."

"And mine really had a thing for your mom, didn't he?"

"Ayup."

"That's twisted. I kinda knew it. When he'd get drunk once in a while, he'd call my mama by your mama's name."

"Pretty twisted, yeah."

"He was a sonofabitch."

"He was your father."

A grim nod shared between them.

"Gwennie's mine," Boyland says. "I need you to know that."

"I know she's yours by right."

"Good."

"But soon enough rights might not matter like you think. And when the day comes, the choice is going to fall to the person it should've fallen to the whole damn time—Gwennie. She'll get to make her choice. And we both have to be ready for whatever choice she makes, whether that's you, me, or some fancy Empyrean lad she met up here on the flotilla. This is on her."

"She'll choose me." But Cael can't help but hear the doubt in Boyland's voice. "She *will*, McAvoy."

"If you say so, buckethead."

The shape looms ahead. Up here they can see lights—lights of a thousand tiny windows, winking ships orbiting the city, running lights along the side. The lights shine like spears from the city in the dark. Cael could never have imagined what it would look like from up here.

No Heartlander was meant to be this high.

Suddenly, the city shudders.

"Did you—"

But Boyland doesn't have to finish the question. No mistaking the way the silhouettes of the buildings now lean toward and away from each other, pieces breaking off. The red glow of the engines is gone, and the blue glow of the massive hover-panels beneath the city flickers and goes dark.

Which means they're too late.

"It's happening," Cael says.

Gwennie.

But then he hears a series of bangs, like distant cannonfire. Massive balloons begin to inflate, dark shapes against the wine-spilled sky. Some parts of the city remain buoyed by these huge inflatables, but other portions of the flotilla are offered no such protection.

And those pieces begin to drop out of the sky.

It seems slow at this distance—as if they don't so much fall as *drift gently downward*, pieces of bridges and pipes and mortar crumbling to the earth below. Trees. Balconies.

People.

They can see people falling.

"Jeezum Crow," Boyland says.

Cael growls, "Faster. *Go faster.*"

Balastair is still there, still up in the sky.

Cael can only hope that Gwennie is, too.

MY FAIR LADY

THAT, HE THINKS, *WAS FOR ERASMUS.*

Balastair leans back. Contented. This, *this* feels great. Watching from the camera buried in the steel Pegasus's eyes as the peregrine fires his little cannon—*plink, plink, plink.* As they rush him inside. As the metal beast plunges into the deck of the *Osprey,* as his fertilizer bomb—made before his visit to Planck, created from his own forgotten supply in his now-derelict greenhouses—goes off in a great, gulping fireball.

He looks over to Eldon Planck, who sits bound up with Cleo. Their mouths taped shut. Balastair chuckles. He feels raw. Abraded. *Alive.*

"You idiots," Balastair says, popping his knuckles. "So proud of your little accomplishment there, eh? 'Oh! I created a flying metal horse!' Well, I *stole* your flying metal horse and turned it into a torpedo. Hah! And now that damnable Peregrine is gone. Dead. Likely burned to a foul-smelling cinder."

He stands. Pulls a small nail file from Cleo's makeup table. "Curious, though, that you had the control station right here in your own home. You truly are a narcissist. And it suggests to me that you work too hard. Cleo didn't like that *I* worked too hard, and yet here she is, falling in with a man all too similar. She would have left you before too long." He spies a guilty look cross Eldon's face. "Oh ho ho, she was already on her way out, wasn't she? You caught wind of it. Yes. Well."

He steps over to Eldon.

He uses the nail file to pop the tape and rag in the man's mouth.

"Tell me something," Balastair says.

"I don't have to tell you anything."

"And yet you will because, as previously discussed, you're a classless narcissist who will jump at the chance to talk about himself the way a cat jumps at a sprig of nip. Was the Pegasus part of it? Part of the Initiative?"

Eldon chuffs a humorless laugh. "That was no part of the Initiative."

"What is it, then? What did they hire you to do?"

"You really want to know?"

"I do."

Eldon grins. It's almost feral, so pleased is he with himself. "We're planning on . . . changing how we deal with the Heartlanders."

"Oh? Because they're not obedient enough? Not worked enough?"

"Not hardly. Not by a *long* shot. It's already begun. Tuttle's Church, and next up, Boxelder. Take the people captive. House them inside auto-mate bodies. Turn them into mechanicals to do the work. Tireless workers. Utterly obedient. A hundred times more productive. Smarter, too, because it uses their brains—no longer the dumb programs of any old auto-mate."

Balastair's blood goes cold.

"You're not serious."

"Oh, but I am, Harrington. And you missed out on that contract. They did consider talking to you about a *variant* approach. Genetically modifying the Heartlanders. Dulling them. Cutting out their free will but making them physically more capable. It would have been interesting, but flesh, as it turns out, remains so very weak."

Balastair backhands Eldon.

"You're right," Balastair says, noting a line of blood now snaking down from the man's split bottom lip. He smears it with a thumb, and Eldon flinches. "Flesh *is* weak. But why? Why merge them with machines? Just make your damn metal men and be done with it."

"Because the brain is still the most powerful computer we have. Plug into it, and it can power the machines, give them capacities and problem-solving algorithms like we'd never before seen. The personality is largely gone. But the brain is active. And the flesh remains, too, feeding the robot. Each cell destroyed is a small boost of battery life."

"You're sick."

"I'm ambitious." Eldon smirks. "That's why your lady left you for me. You weren't *ambitious* enough, Harrington. You were—"

Balastair backhands him again.

And with the hit, the entire room shakes.

That's not right.

He's about to say that very phrase—*that's not right*—but suddenly, what was once a small tremor becomes a massive one as the entire room, *the entire building*, dips downward, leaning left. Furniture moving. Lamps shattering. Balastair falls—

And then, above their heads: *boom*.

The building drops farther. The floor splits in half—the makeup table disgorging its contents and lipstick tubes and mascara tins rolling toward the fissure, dropping into the rooms below—

It stops.

Everything seems still. Though the room has a . . . *sway* to it. Back and forth. A gentle pendulum.

"Oh gods," Eldon bleats. "We're under attack."

Balastair suddenly realizes what's happened. The engines stopped. The hover-panels, too. The city is on the verge of collapse. Outside he hears the crash of buildings, screams drifting downward from above.

Because parts of it are still falling.

65

THE FALLEN CITY

THE CITY FALLS DOWN around them. Buildings tilt. Break apart. People tumble out of windows. Cael tries not to look. He likes flying. Likes going fast. But he doesn't like this. This is a hell-ride through the mouth of Old Scratch himself. Broken teeth. Lashing tongue. Purgatory.

All this time, he thinks, *I never gave Boyland enough credit*. Because while the buckethead may not be able to spell his own name, shit if he can't fly like a sparrow. Ducking, dipping, sharp cuts to the left, the right. He flies like a man possessed—who is one with the skiff he pilots.

"There!" Cael points—ahead, a massive columnar building, square and severe, its windows arched, the lights within flickering and sparking. Inside he can feel Balastair Harrington, Esther's son, the Maize Witch's *seed*. His vine twinges and tightens. "Take her down. Down! He's toward the bottom—"

Boyland pulls up on the stick, and the skiff plunges.

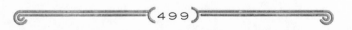

Cael's guts feel about thirty feet above his head right now. But it's then he understands. Boyland isn't possessed by any demons or devils. He isn't one with the skiff.

He just wants to save Gwennie.

Cael admires him for that. And hates him all the more.

Balastair makes the mistake of looking out the window.

Fires bloom in the coming night. Gas catching fire. The city collapses against itself. Some buildings and districts remain buoyed by giant plastic balloons; other parts are left unprotected and unsaved, plunging out of the sky—black blurs, lights smearing, people screaming.

Oh gods, people are dying. So many people.

Clouds of dust and ash begin to roll in.

And then—a skiff! It drops out of the sky like a stone, dips past the window, and then floats back up. He can't make out who they are, but he sees two people in the boat, young men both—

The one in the passenger side clambers over and reaches out with his arm.

A vine extends outward, shattering the window. Balastair shields himself, staggering backward as the young man pulls himself through the open space.

Balastair falls on his ass. He points a finger and seethes.

"Mother sent you, didn't she? Did she do this? Is this *her* doing?"

"She did," the young man says. "But first, you need to help us find some people. Because if you don't, I'm throwing you to the birds."

"I can't . . . I can't help you. Who are you looking for?"

"Gwendolyn Shawcatch. And my sister, Merelda."

Gwennie?

"Her? I . . . who are you? Are you . . . Cael?"

"My name's— Wait, yeah, I'm Cael. How the hell did you know?"

Balastair almost laughs. "Cael . . . I know your sister, and I damn sure know Gwendolyn Shawcatch." He stands, dusts himself off. "You're fortunate, because I even know where she is in the midst of all this. Let's just hope she's alive."

"We need to go now."

"Wait. If you want my help, I'm bringing somebody."

Balastair doesn't wait for an answer. He storms over to the bed and cuts Cleo free. He pulls her gag off.

"Thank you," she says.

"Don't" is all he can say in response.

But she leans forward and gives Eldon a chaste kiss on the cheek.

Then she heads to the shattered window.

Eldon screams. Red cheeked. Froth lipped.

Balastair gives him a wave. "Toodles, Planck. Hope your Pegasus comes to save you."

Through the window and to the skiff beyond they go.

The parts of the flotilla that have collapsed are now gone, leaving great rents and fissures in the city. What once seemed like a whole piece is now broken into sticks and crumbs, pieces floating away from one another—and into one another, too. They see

people stranded on balconies. They see Empyrean vessels fleeing in the distance—few, if any, seem to be bent on rescuing their own people.

Balastair comments from the back. "We're a self-interested people. Isn't that right, Cleo?"

The woman he saved says nothing. She stares ahead, lips pursed.

Cael can't care. He bites at his nails as Balastair directs them. The Empyrean man—only a few years older than Cael, really—tells him he last saw Gwennie and Merelda in the Fabrication District—they had been pinned down by someone called the peregrine, but with some pride he says he "took care of that."

"The Fabrication District should be protected by the emergency inflatables," Balastair says.

"Better be right about that."

"How long?" Balastair asks.

"How the hell should I know?" Cael snaps. "You know this place better than I do—"

"No, I mean"—and here the man lays a gentle hand on Cael's shoulder—"how long have you been afflicted?"

Boyland gives Cael a dark, sidelong look.

"Not . . . not long. Couple-few weeks. Maybe longer and I didn't know it."

"I'm sorry."

"Yeah. Well."

"If my mother sent you, she can truly help you."

He thinks but does not say, *I damn well hope so.*

Balastair says, "Ahead, there—up over this ridge of warehouses." The skiff flies low along gleaming corrugated rooftops—now buckling and breaking apart. Shattered solar panels catch puddles of moonlight as they pass overhead.

Then, suddenly, up over the rise is the shipping bay—a scalloped, cutout harbor of open air. It lays cracked, shattered, but it's still here—two balloons, not one, hold it up, each moored by massive braided cables as thick as a man's leg.

"Here, here, here!" Balastair cries, reaching up and pulling the wheel of the skiff. Boyland protests, but the skiff swings around and—

Cael sees the look of horror on the man's face.

They're staring down at nothing. This is where a part of the flotilla must have sheared off. It's now just a jagged wall of torn ducts, shredded pipes, sparking bundles of colorful wire.

"They . . . they were right here," Balastair says. "They were there on a platform. A walkway . . . and then . . ."

Boyland roars. He slams his fist against the side of the skiff. Cael can see tears in his eyes.

He doesn't have tears. Not yet.

They have to be alive.

Have to be.

He scans the horizon. Looks toward the shipping docks with its collapsed cranes and scattered heaps of fallen crates. A few scowbarges sit anchored, bobbing there, moored by long lengths of chain and buoyed by their own hover mechanisms.

Nothing. Nobody living or dead.

Except—

Cael squints.

"There!" he says.

He sees Merelda! And then Gwennie. They're coming out

from behind one of the scowbarges. *They're trying to find a way off the city. Thank the gods. Thank the Lord and the Lady and all the Saintangels—*

But then—

One of the still-standing cranes groans as the ground shifts.

The metal buckles. They can hear it from here.

It begins to fall.

Right toward them.

They're going to steal this scowbarge. It's their only chance, Gwennie thinks. When the peregrine's ketch-boat exploded, they figured that was it—everything was light and fire and metal raining down around them.

But they lived. The ship fell. The other ships, certain an attack was imminent, began to retreat.

And that gave them the chance. Squirrel led the way. Up over the warehouse rooftops. Down into the shipping bay outside the Fabrication District. *Home is beneath our feet,* Gwennie thought at the time. And she thinks it now, too, even after the entire flotilla begins to break apart, even after what must *surely* be the raiders' attack.

Is this what they were planning all along?

She can't think about that now.

All she can think about is home. *The Heartland. Sea of corn and shit-biscuits and the growl of motorvators and the stink of Queenie's Quietdown, and all that better than anything up here in the sky.*

Just get on a ship and go.

Their option is a scowbarge.

They have three barges, but only one is operable—the others
are damaged beyond repair. One has a cockpit smashed by a massive crate. The other slammed into the side of the dock, tearing
it open and spilling its goods like the guts of a knife-struck deer.

So, from three barges to one.

They stand there in its shadow, trying to figure out how to
get *in* the damn thing. Gwennie's piloted corn-boats before, but
these are *sky*-ships. They fly; they don't just float.

But then, just as she's about to climb over and try to find her
way in—a shadow falls on her. Squirrel shrieks, grabs her elbow,
pulls her sharply backward—

Just as a crane smashes down on the scowbarge.

When Gwennie looks up, the massive yellow crane-arm has
crushed the barge right down the middle. The hover-panels
beneath it spark.

Then they go dark.

The barge drops like a stone, taking the crane with it.

Gwennie's heart pounds like a hundred horses in her chest.

But it's nothing compared to the heart attack she feels when
a skiff drops down out of the sky and lands across the shattered
concrete of the shipping dock, skidding and sparking.

This is the moment Cael has wanted.

This is it. Since the day he'd found out about the Lottery,
since he'd seen them take her away in that ship, since he'd left
home on this journey, *this* is the moment he's been waiting for.

To be reunited with Gwendolyn Shawcatch.

Boyland skips the skiff across the docking bay ground like a stone across choppy water. Even before the skiff stops skidding Cael is up and out of the boat, nearly falling as he runs toward his sister and Gwennie. They see him, and their faces light up— genuine happiness, excitement—and an absurd thought crosses his mind. *I get to save them; I get to be here and save them and now Gwennie will love me forever.*

They crash into him.

Arms wrapped around him.

He pulls Gwendolyn toward him.

He kisses her. It's so fast and so strange he barely registers what it feels like, but everything inside him flutters just the same—

And then it goes cold. Because Gwennie bats at something on the back of her neck, and suddenly she pulls away. And Merelda does, too. They're both staring at him. And at first he doesn't even realize—

"The Blight," Merelda says.

"Cael," Gwennie says, shocked. "Cael, no. What's— Oh no."

He holds out his arm. The vine—already growing where Eben Henry had sliced it—is squirming and twisting into and out of a corkscrew. Leaves tickling the air. It touched her. He realizes that now. The Blight-vine touched her. Climbed up her neck. Oh gods.

"Gwennie, it's okay," he says, "I'm going to be . . ."

But his voice trails off.

At the edge of the docking platform stands Scooter Shawcatch. Staring out over the horizon, not watching them at all, just looking. Shell-shocked. And the platform he's on is a kind of peninsula jutting out over open air—and then the entire ground shudders

and one last piece of the crane comes down, a yellow hunk of bent metal preceded by a shower of orange embers—

It lands ten feet away from the boy.

And it breaks the platform as if it's nothing more than hard toffee.

Cael runs.

The platform falls and, with it, the boy.

He hears screams behind him. Gwennie. Merelda.

He leaps to the edge of the shattered concrete—

Skids forward on his belly. Half his body hangs over the edge, looking down across the darkened Heartland—

His arm shoots out—

The Blight-vine lashes.

There.

He knows he has the boy. He can *feel* it through the vine—the feel of human flesh against plant matter, the texture of the boy's wrist against the soft leaves of the Blight—and for a moment he doesn't know what to do. The concrete beneath him starts to crack and crumble. Those little tectonic shifts in his gut—

He does the only thing he can do. He pulls the Blight-vine toward him, wrenching his arm, rolling his body back and to the side—

The boy is dragged through the air. Scooter's arm snaps with a gut-churning crunch, the bone broken, the child crying out—

But he lands—and Cael exerts every last bit of will and energy he has to make the landing a soft one. The boy rolls over. Cries, sobbing. Gwennie scoops him up. Cael starts to stand, starts to move, already apologizing for the boy's arm—

The ground shifts again beneath him.

What once was there is there no more.

He falls. Catches the edge with his chest. The air again punched out of his lungs. His arms grab smooth concrete. He tries to drag himself forward. He can see other cracks forming along the concrete. *This place is coming apart.* Merelda is screaming. Gwennie's mother is screaming for her daughter as Gwennie hard-charges toward him. Boyland catches her, big arms around her middle, dragging her backward. She struggles. Strikes him. Gets free again, sprinting toward Cael—

Someone is yelling, *We have to go; it's all falling down*—

His vine lashes uselessly against the concrete.

Gwennie dives. Grabs for the Blight-vine.

Their eyes meet. She's saying something—but the noises of the crumbling city swallow her words.

His body sings with panic.

Then he realizes what she's saying—

"I can save you."

But I was supposed to save you, he thinks.

A dark shadow swoops over them. The skiff. Boyland piloting. He tilts the skiff—one of his big arms reaches out, catches Gwennie around the midsection, hauls her up—

She's still got the vine in her hand, but it begins sliding through her grip—Cael calls for help. *No, no, don't leave me*—

The skiff lifts higher and higher.

Gwennie screams for him again and again.

The vine slides all the way through her hands.

The skiff takes off.

The platform breaks.

Cael falls.

TITAN FALL

"YOU'LL NEED TO HIT ME HARD," Agrasanto says.

Busser looks nervous. "I don't know about this." He's got his fist cocked, and he's bobbing on his hips a little as if he's ready to throw a punch, but he's hesitating.

Behind him, a few Boxelder folks sit at the bar, staring from the edges of their half-barrel stools.

"This is the way forward," she says. Then sticks out her chin.

"You're a girl."

"I'm a woman."

"I don't hit women."

"I've got bigger stones than you, hick. So throw that fist already—"

Wham.

A glitter of starburst behind her good eye. A cascade of light falling. Her head rocks with the hit, and she tries not to show

how much it hurt. Instead, she says: "Again. Nose this time. Hit me in the nose."

Busser winces, hauls back, and pops her in the nose.

She feels the dull crunch go into her head, and that does the trick. She's staggering. Trying not to cry out but she hears the *nnnngh* come up out of her. Blood crawls across her upper lip. She tastes it at the back of her throat, too, just as her eye starts to water.

The proctor dabs at it with a handkerchief. "Good. Good." She clears her throat. "Now, someone's gonna have to tie me up—"

Suddenly, the doors to the tavern open up. Devon, with his snapped-twig arm, hurries in, saying, "Proctor, you need to see—" He freezes. Eyes wide. "What's . . . what's happening here?"

Moments of silence, hesitation, uncertainty.

Then—

Agrasanto draws her sonic pistol and shoots him in the chest. Right above his broken wing. The hole in his breastbone dribbles blood, and he makes a bubbling sound in his throat before dropping.

"King Hell!" Busser says. Behind him, the other townsfolk goggle.

Guilt prickles her flesh. *I had to do that*, she tells herself. Devon was a snitch. He'd send this story up the flagpole lickety-quick. And at this point that is not an option. Plus, as she tells the men: "It furthers the illusion. I'll give you the pistol. One of you shot him, congratulations."

"I didn't shoot anybody—" Busser says.

"You did," she asserts. "You did because that's how they're going to believe you overpowered me. And took my visidex. And found out the truth about what's about to happen to your little town. This is your way out. Your way forward into life and not something very close to death. You don't want to be metal men? You want to run for your lives? Then this is the way."

They stand there in silence for a little while.

Again the tavern doors open. A field shepherd—some screwhead named Horchaw—comes in, sees the body on the floor, and almost trips over it. "Eh. Ah. Oh, Crow. You all oughta come out here and, ahhh, see this."

She gives a subtle nod, and they all head toward the doors and filter out into the street.

There, on Main Street, most of the town has gathered. And in the distance, she sees it. A flotilla. Bright against the night. Its light scattered like a crumbling mantle of stars. Which means—

Oh, by the gods, no.

"Is that a flotilla?" she hears Doc Leonard ask.

It is, she thinks, but does not say.

Somehow, one of the flotillas is falling.

"This doesn't change anything," she says to Busser. "Except we better move faster. So let's get this done. Go get the rope."

The elevator won't take them up, what with the electronics being all borked and all. Lane and the pirate captain take a while to try to get it going again, but it's a no-go, especially since Killian has gone the color of a bleached bedsheet and is leaking blood like a speared squealer.

So instead, they work to pop the top off the elevator. Killian's got a small multitool in his pocket, and it takes a long time to get the bolts off, but eventually they manage. The top comes off, and the tunnel back up to the town of Tuttle's Church shows the blue-black of darkness pinpricked with starlight. A ladder lies faintly illuminated against the shaft wall.

They climb up. Lane beneath Killian, catching clumsy boots to the head and shoulders as the wounded captain inelegantly ascends with one arm and trembling, weakened legs.

As they get closer, Lane says what he's thinking: "I don't hear anything. No more fighting. No more of anything."

Killian sniffs. And murmurs, "That's because we lost, my boy. No way we snatched victory from the jaws of the metal men of Tuttle's Church. Our fight was always down here. In the room beneath us."

Lane stops. "Wait, so why are we going up?"

"Because we're going to make our last stand. Or run like cowards, I can't be sure yet. But I do know we'll pop our heads out of the hole like a pair of bewildered whistle-pigs and—well, probably have them sliced off by a pair of whirring blades or sonic blasts posthaste."

"Then I think I'm inclined to go back down."

"Nonsense," Killian says. "Where's your sense of adventure?"

And the captain continues his wobbly ascent.

Lane curses under his breath and keeps climbing. The journey feels like half-a-mile from forever. As he ascends, the thought dogs him: *What did I do by transmitting that code?*

They emerge into silence. The smell of smoke in the air, carrying an odor like that from melted plastic, or burned electronics.

Everything is shadow. The silhouettes of the storefronts and houses line the street ahead. All around are the shattered wrecks of robot men and mechanical women. A distant sound surprises: down the way, a mechanical without legs lies on the street, bashing its face into the plasto-sheen. Again and again, *bang, bang, bang.*

Far off, they see the crumpled mound of the trawler. It doesn't float—its husk lies ruined against the earth.

Together the two walk down the street, Lane helping Killian hobble along. They head toward the trawler.

"It looks like nobody won," Lane says.

Killian says nothing. Stunned into silence? Curtailed by pain? Lane doesn't know and sees no reason to press.

Then Killian raises his one good arm, points a crooked, trembling finger. "There. The fruits of our labors."

In the sky:

Starshine and scattered line. Like a firework in slow motion.

"The flotilla," Lane says.

"It was a success."

"It doesn't feel like success. People are dying up there."

"They woke the sleeping dog. No surprise that the dog has chosen to bite." Killian offers a grim smile in the moonlight. Almost skeletal. Lane pulls away, and Killian almost falls.

"Keep your platitudes to yourself. I have to find Rigo."

"You helped me do this!" Killian calls after.

But Lane shoves that thought out of his mind. He has to. To stay sane. Now his only thought is his friend: a friend who saved him, a friend who—

Oh no.

He sees it. The sonic cannon Rigo once manned.

It's twisted into slag. A body sits slumped in the chair.

Lane curses, blinks back tears, and leaps for the trawler. He finds a rope, begins to climb it, swings over to a ladder, and then climbs *that* all the way to the deck—a deck tilted hard toward the dry earth. He grips the railing and hauls himself up, up, up, to the gun where the body sits.

Rigo.

"No, no, c'mon," Lane says, panicking. He could still be alive. He has to be. Lane reaches in, scrapes his arm across a sharpened curl of ruined metal—the sonic cannon's barrel peeled back like the leathered skin of a sun-baked rat—but he ignores the pain and the blood and reaches for Rigo's head and pulls it back—

But it's not Rigo's face.

It's— Who is that? Jeezum Crow, it's Hezzie Orden. Her hair matted against her crushed brow. A spike of guilt lances through Lane's heart—he felt jealous of her, jealous of Killian's attention. And now she's dead. Lane feels responsible, an absurd notion that offers no evidence but whose sting is keenly felt just the same.

Then: floodlights click on, find him. The pulse-whine of hover-panels. He thinks: *The mechanicals. Or the Empyrean. And that's all she wrote.*

He awaits the shower of sonic blasts. He'll be torn apart.

But then he hears Rigo's voice.

"There! There he is! Lane! *Lane!*"

Lane almost weeps.

• • •

Wanda stands outside on the front porch of the tall, white house, shivering. It's not cold. The wind is warm. But she feels it inside: a septic chill. She can't seem to stop shaking.

I hit him, she thinks.

She hit Cael. Her beloved. Her chosen. Her Obligated.

He was going to hurt Boyland. And she has no love for that thick-as-a-brick mayor's son, but at the time she couldn't just stand by and let Cael and his Blight hurt him. Or kill him.

But now she's not so sure. Everything feels all tangled up. Like the vines braided around Cael's arm.

She's scared. And confused. And worst of all, alone.

The Maize Witch—because that's who she is, Wanda realizes—freed herself from the mess made of her house looking no worse for wear. And she hurried past, saying to Wanda: *Things are in motion. I have work to do.*

Then she was gone. Down through the garden—a garden!— and storming off into the dead corn in the distance. A cabal of Blighted hurrying behind her, loping like starving dogs.

So now, Wanda stands. The wreckage of the yacht behind her, smashed into the front of the house. She misses her parents. She misses Hazelnut. And she misses Cael and hopes like heck he's still alive.

Up in the sky, then, she sees it. Lights like a shower of sparks. Shapes darker than the night breaking, falling. A flotilla. But that's not possible, is it? How could it be?

Then, behind her, a sound—

A small sound, like the squeak of a mouse. Coming from the boat.

No. Not a mouse.

Like the squeak of a Mole.

Oh gods, Mole!

She hurries to the boat, moves a buoy, lifts a tarp—

And there's the boy. Ashen face. It brightens when he sees her.

"I love you, Wanda Macklin," he says.

"Mecklin," she correct in a small voice.

And then he passes out with a smile on his face.

Behind them, it all falls.

The skiff rockets away from the Saranyu as the flotilla breaks apart. Some pieces float, buoyed by balloons drifting slowly to earth. Most of it just crumbles, leaving streaks of light or gray shadows plunging to the Heartland in the long dark.

Gwennie wants to cry, wants to weep and tear out her hair, but she can't muster anything but empty shock. All of them, crammed into this little boat, heading down toward the corn, the cold air whipping. Her mother strokes her hair as Scooter whimpers across their laps.

Balastair behind her. Boyland in front of her.

And all she feels is emptiness.

And blame.

And the conspicuous absence of her captain, Cael McAvoy.

ABOVE TO BELOW

CAEL MCAVOY DREAMS OF FLYING.

In his mind he's aloft on hot vectors of air. The night around him. The stars watching, vigilant. The moon protecting him. The wind keeping him. He has no Blight. He has no fear.

Sometimes the dream is interrupted by the reality of falling.

There the air is cold. Rushing up to meet him. Pieces of concrete around him. Wind howling. His body battered.

Something hits him—*wham*, a piece of metal across the back of his head. He sees blue, red, black, a whirl of colors, a smear of dark—

But then the dream is back. Softening his fall in the sweet embrace of illusion. Pillows of clouds against the matte-black sky. Arms outstretched. Going up, not down. Laughing. The tears in his eyes not because he knows he's going to die but because he's flying up toward the embrace of the Lord and Lady. Toward their manse in the sky. Toward their front gates, gates of bronze and silver, gates sculpted to look like winged lions sleeping underneath rays of gauzy light. Beyond those gates, Gwennie waits, and Pop, and Merelda, and Rigo, and Lane, and . . .

The dream, as it always does, turns dark.

He flies—until he is allowed to fly no more.

Tendrils of green lash out from below. Coils of thorny vine. Stalks of battering corn. The stalks knock him out of the sky, a stick hitting a bird. The tendrils curl around him. They drag him down, down, down, faster and faster, and he screams, but his screams are lost, and suddenly he's back through the clouds, and the ground rushes up to meet him, and he sees miles of dead corn and a tall, white house, and he no longer knows what's dream or what's reality; he only knows that in both, he falls.

He loses everything, and he falls.

ABOUT THE AUTHOR

Michelle Wendig

CHUCK WENDIG is the author of The Heartland Trilogy as well as numerous novels for adults. He is also a game designer and screenwriter. He cowrote the short film *Pandemic*, the feature film *HiM*, and the Emmy-nominated digital narrative *Collapsus*. Chuck lives in Pennsylvania with his family.

He blogs at www.terribleminds.com.